S0-AWE-863

3⁰⁰
4/49

BLASPHEMY!

Beshur had an aged, crumbling specimen in his lap. Having succeeded in prying it open without destroying it, he was reading aloud.

"Inscriptions are carved in stone for many uses: for Foundation Stones and Public Inscriptions, for Mottos and Texts . . ." his voice trailed off.

"But where is the commentary?" said Potatoes.

"There is no commentary," Beshur said.

"Impossible!"

"It is not impossible. This is the earliest copy of the Sacred Texts of Panas in existence. You can see how old the scroll is. It also says *Sacred Texts I* on the tag, and given what I am seeing here, I am not inclined to doubt it. I think it dates to the foundation of the Three Kingdoms."

Potatoes also looked shaken. "But the commentary! The commentary written by God himself!"

"It's not here."

Potatoes was almost angry. "Then this is . . . this is . . ."

"A treatise on stone carving," Beshur said. "It is all here. Stripped of its commentaries, the Sacred Texts are nothing more than a set of instructions to the would-be carver of inscriptions."

BRANCH
AND CROWN

GAEL BAUDINO'S *WATER!*
SERIES FROM ROC

GAEL BAUDINO

BRANCH AND CROWN

BOOK III OF *WATER!*

A ROC BOOK

ROC
Published by the Penguin Group
Penguin Books USA Inc., 375 Hudson Street,
New York, New York 10014, U.S.A.
Penguin Books Ltd, 27 Wrights Lane,
London W8 5TZ, England
Penguin Books Australia Ltd, Ringwood,
Victoria, Australia
Penguin Books Canada Ltd, 10 Alcorn Avenue,
Toronto, Ontario, Canada M4V 3B2
Penguin Books (N.Z.) Ltd, 182–190 Wairau Road,
Auckland 10, New Zealand

Penguin Books Ltd, Registered Offices:
Harmondsworth, Middlesex, England

First published by Roc, an imprint of Dutton Signet,
a division of Penguin Books USA Inc.

First Printing, August, 1996
10 9 8 7 6 5 4 3 2 1

Cover art by Tom Canty

 REGISTERED TRADEMARK—MARCA REGISTRADA

Printed in the United States of America

To my mother,
who never figured me out.
(Which isn't to say that she didn't *try*.)
This one's for you, kiddo.

Acknowledgments

Once again, my thanks to Mr. A.E.R. Gill, whose contribution to Edward Johnston's *Writing, Illuminating, and Lettering* provided the Panasian religion with its Sacred Texts. My appreciation to my beloved Mirya Rule almost goes without saying, but I really do not think that I can say it enough. Cherry Weiner, my agent, deserves a very large mention for seeing me through some hard times; but, alas, given the constraints of such pieces as this, a single sentence must suffice.

I am indebted to those among my readers who, undeterred by my sometimes caustic observations on life, have persisted in reading my works. Gratitude is also owed to the staff of the Action Games Forum on CompuServe for their support, their friendship, and, upon occasion, some very enjoyable head-to-head and cooperative play in DESCENT.

Don't say I didn't warn you.

—Anonymous

Chapter One

"Mrrk?"

Mr. Jenkins felt very tired.

The Great Library had been bad enough, for the existence not only of such incredibly lengthy flights of stairs hewn through living rock but also of the vast subterranean room and glittering pavilion that lay at the bottom of those stairs bespoke a grasp of sophisticated engineering that hinted a little too strongly for comfort that the Righteous States of America did not reign supreme in the world of technology and power. But when, at the murmured order of the captain of the priestly guards, somebody had done . . . something, and, impelled by a current of water, the pavilion had begun to move, the hint had turned into a certainty, and the certainty had engendered the kind of cold fear that had (as Jenkins well knew) ended a good many diplomatic careers . . . not to mention the diplomatic plans upon which those diplomatic careers had hung.

"Do something about that cat," Potatoes whispered harshly.

—Do something? Beshur whispered (harshly) back. Why do *I* have to do something?

"Because it is *your* cat!" (Also whispered (harshly).)

Beshur glanced at the shadowed decking above his

head, mindful that even (harsh) whispers might be enough to penetrate the wood, that such penetration might lead to discovery, and that discovery might lead to (Here. Walk like this.) unpleasant consequences.

—*My* cat! he said . . . or, rather, whispered. (Harshly.)

The cat, unimpressed by any claims or accusations regarding ownership (Cats are like that.) stuck its tail up in the air and:

"Mrkgnao!"

(*Not* whispered. Harshly or otherwise.)

And Beshur was just as mindful (as were, no doubt, Potatoes and Sari) that *mrkgnaos*, particularly not-whispered ones, might also be enough to penetrate the wood.

"Mrkgnao!"

(Here. Walk like this.)

The thought was too much for Beshur, and he sprang for the cat. The cat in turn, delighted by this obvious proposal of some recreation to while away the time during a prolonged and tedious journey (And how long had it been? It seemed like hours. And the pavilion boat was still moving.), leaped, bouncing off of Beshur's shoulders as he plunged forward and leaving him with nothing to pursue save a bulkhead. Whether he wanted to or not.

—Ow!

"Shut up, fool!"

Cat, 1. Humans, 0.

"Worthy of all!"

Jenkins stifled a grimace. It was Abnel. The Gharat had obviously oozed (Jenkins found it hard to think of the man moving in any other way.) up to his elbow while he was considering the ends of diplomatic plans and diplomatic careers. Why, given the existence of this boat and this tunnel and this mode of conveyance—

(And what exactly *was* this mode of conveyance? How was this ship moving? Where was all that water (Oh, God . . . and that meant *hydraulics,* too!) coming from? And what else did the Three Kingdoms have up its ornate, African sleeve . . .

. . .? Gunpowder? Why, he, precious fool that he was, had *seen* gunpowder in action, and had allowed himself to be lulled into believing that it had been smuggled in by revolutionaries, that the rest of the population was a study in unsophisticated, heathen primitiveness. But . . . what if . . . what if . . . what if . . .?)

—anything, absolutely *anything*, was possible.

Jenkins darted a look at Mather, but the perfumed, kohl-eyed engineer lay flopped over on his side, snoring loudly, and Jenkins admitted that there was every chance that he would not have been lucid enough to offer any kind of an explanation or an opinion even were he awake.

"Hehe!" Mather mumbled. "Man work!"

Jenkins shuddered once again at the thought of un-Puritan mechanics.

Abnel, still uncomfortably close to his elbow, was preening. "You shall see! You shall see . . . all!"

"All," said Jenkins.

"All!"

And Jenkins, with a sensation as of sinking, began to cast about in his mind for ideas as to what *all* might be. Guns? Troops? Possibly. But the sheer size and arrogance of this conveyance to . . . to wherever, was something of an indication that *all* might quite possibly turn out to be something that would make guns and troops seem paltry things indeed.

And then he remembered. Pumps. Water.

And now hydraulics, too. Could it be?

A muffled bump startled him, and he glanced over the side of the pavilion boat, wondering whether it had touched ground. But no: the water was rippling, shining in the torchlight, the soft current that carried them along continuing uninterrupted; and a cautious look up at the roof of the lofty tunnel through which they were passing showed no obstruction: the walls of natural rock were passing smoothly along, indicating by their variations in color and strata the steady progress the boat was making toward . . .

. . . toward what?

"Clumsy fool!" hissed the captain of the guards. "Careful there!"

"But—!"

The slave who had contradicted the captain was grabbed by several guards, who immediately administered the customary punishment for such insubordination. (Panasian law was very clear about things like that.)

"Mrrk."

At any moment, Potatoes was certain, the cat was going to set up enough of a yowling that those on deck would come to investigate. It was obvious, therefore, that the cat would have to be silenced.

"Potatoes," said Sari.

"What?"

She was a ghostly figure in the darkness. "Just leave the cat alone. It will take a nap in a few minutes, and then you will not hear a sound out of it for several hours."

Beshur was nursing a bump on his head. Potatoes was creeping slowly toward the cat, tensed for a spring. "And then what?"

"And then . . ."

Sari's words trailed off into silence. She was thinking, which Potatoes found utterly charming. Beshur, he was certain, would find nothing charming except his own, much-vaunted intellect. Potatoes was very glad that *he* was nothing like Beshur. After all, Beshur was but a braggart, while he himself was a *philosophe* in the great tradition of Voltaire, Hume, Diderot, Rousseau . . .

"And then," said Sari, "we might well be at our destination."

But Potatoes, though he found Sari charming when she attempted to think, did not find her to be particularly practical. So he crept a little more, tensed a little more, and then, affecting for the better part of ten seconds the attitude of one who could care less about what cats might be doing or planning to do (so as to deceive the unwary feline), threw himself directly into a bulkhead as the cat fled deeper into the hold.

"Potatoes . . ." Sari began.

"What?" said Potatoes, nursing a bump on his head.

A moment later, a dead body fell through the hatch and landed directly on top of him.

Cat, 2. Humans, 0.

(Dead body, 1.)

"Clumsy fool," shouted the captain. "Careful there!"

"But—"

Again, the guards went into action. Panasian law was still very clear about things like that.

"The wise in the heart will receive commandments: but a prating fool shall fall."

"Quiet, Wool."

But Jenkins was only half aware of his own words, for he was considering the passing walls of the tunnel . . . and his own predicament. Really, he should have been ready for just this sort of revelation, for, in addition to the gunpowder, had he not already seen the remarkable cities of the Three Kingdoms . . . cities with pinnacles of jasper and windows of amethyst and emerald? What was a length of simple tunnel to such as had built those wonders? Even though Abnel maintained fiercely that a heathen idol had constructed them, Jenkins, a minister, knew better, and he should have realized the implications.

This was terrible. What would Winthrop say? And the Synod? And—great God!—he had sent Scruffy back for the troops! Why, in light of what he had discovered, any American attempt to invade the Three Kingdoms might well turn out to be nothing less than suicide.

But, ever the experienced diplomat, Jenkins fought down the fear and the uncertainty. Just as he expected.

Yes, that was it. Everything was going just as he had expected. It was all a part of his plan. His good plan. His righteous plan. His godly plan.

Now, if he could just figure out what that plan was, he would be fine.

"Remarkable," he said to Abnel.

"And worthy!"

Worthy. And that meant (Jenkins thinking slowly and carefully, trying to figure out the intricacies of a God-given plan to which it had pleased God to add a few more intricacies than His servant was immediately able to follow) that Abnel thought that he, Jenkins, had something that he, Abnel, wanted. But what could that be?

Well, it had to be something, and that meant that, as far as Abnel was concerned, the Righteous States *still* had the upper hand.

"Of . . . of course!"

"And you will reveal . . ."

Abnel looked about as though worried that someone might overhear.

". . . all!"

"Yes . . ." said Jenkins, trying to sound sure of himself. "Yes, of course."

"Worthy!"

Potatoes had almost extricated himself from the dead body when a second fell through the hatch. Fortunately neither he nor the cat made a sound as he was flattened, but a muffled "Mmph" came from the bottom of the pile a few moments later.

(Dead body, 2.)

—Does he need help? Beshur said. I am strong. I can help him. I am knowledgeable in such things. I am, after all—

"An apostate priest," Sari found herself murmuring.

But Beshur, who had not heard her words, had broken off and was now looking at Sari (as much as he could in a pervading gloom that was unbroken save for what faint glimmers of lamplight filtered down through the open hatch) as though a thought had suddenly struck him, and she did not need light to recognize his expression.

—But then again, Beshur said, perhaps I cannot help him at all. Perhaps it would be better to—

"Help him up, Beshur," Sari said weakly. A sense of ongoing disaster was growing on her, but she clung stubbornly to the idea that, as Naia had transformed her (giving Beshur, Potatoes, and every other man she had met since she had bruised her overly perfect nose on the walls of Katha every reason to look at her with an expression that she did not need light to recognize), so Naia would provide for her even under such extreme conditions as this.

"Mrkgnao!"

But Potatoes had already shoved both corpses to the side and had struggled to his feet, his face wearing a fixed, set expression that had nothing in common with the one Sari had learned to recognize. For a moment, Sari peered through the thick twilight, bewildered and a little worried, before she realized that Potatoes' gaze was focused not on herself, but on the cat.

"Mrkgnao!"

"Beshur!" came the (harsh) whisper from the thief.

—Yes.

And Beshur turned and dived for the cat just as Potatoes launched himself. Their trajectories, however, missed the cat (which had already fled), and brought their heads into violent contact at a distance of about one foot from the deck, said distance diminishing rapidly, almost instantly, to zero . . . in accordance with the laws of acceleration due to gravity.

Cat, 3. Humans, 0.

Faintly, from above: "But—"

A minute later, a third body fell down the hatchway, landing precisely on top of Potatoes and Beshur. The cat, startled, leaped into Sari's lap, peered insolently into her face for a moment, then curled itself up and went to sleep.

(Dead body, 3.)

"And I saw a strong angel proclaiming with a loud voice, Who is worthy to open the book, and to loose the seals thereof?"

"Be quiet, Wool."

But Jenkins could not help but reflect that perhaps Wool had a point. Who indeed was worthy to open the book? Though the tunnel through which he was traveling was one of the engineering marvels of the world, Abnel and his people had apparently renounced long ago both inclination and (in Jenkins' opinion) worthiness to open any book whatsoever, whether of divine revelation or common mechanics; and a glance at the Gharat (who was nodding complacently at his side as though he were anticipating a pleasant journey, a good dinner (doubtless featuring that damnable grape curry again), or the serving up of some wisdom that he assumed was in the possession of the Americans) went some distance toward reassuring the ambassador that the Gharat's lack of comprehension regarding the origins of the cities of his country applied equally to this tunnel and this ship.

But this brought Jenkins up against yet another conundrum, for if his reassurance was not utterly unfounded, then his suspicions regarding the Gharat's ravings about the pumps and the water could not but be baseless, and *that* meant . . .

He stared down at the water, shaken by the idea. Rote work? Turn this crank because your father and his father before him and *his* father before him turned it, and this will happen? Pull this lever because your father . . . etc., and that will happen?

An entire country run by habit? A huge, hydraulic nightmare operated without the slightest comprehension of its workings?

The concept was eerie, mind-boggling, but nothing that Jenkins had seen since he had come to the Three Kingdoms argued against it. In fact, what with stalls in the market square that had remained in one place for the last several centuries, inexplicable customs that were maintained because they were ... ah ... well ... *customary,* and cities that did not change in the slightest (aside from occasional, unauthorized renovations resulting from the action of gunpowder)—all because the work and pronouncements of a heathen god could not be altered or questioned—the evidence spoke rather more forcibly for than against its reality.

"I stand in awe of the organization necessary for the creation of such a thing as this," he said, double-baiting his hook.

"For Panas (blessed be He!), all things are possible," came the singularly useless response.

Jenkins kept his eyes on the water. Rote? Habit? It was imperative that he find out for certain ... *before* Scruffy returned with the troops.

"This journey will be a long one," Abnel said after a moment. "It is very late. It would be best if you slept."

"Hmmm? Sleep?" said Jenkins. But he had received as much of an answer as he was going to get. For now. And so, diplomatically, he acquiesced. "Yes, honored Gharat. I will sleep."

"And besides," said Abnel, "you will want to be refreshed and ready ... when you finally *see.*"

For the better part of a minute, Sari did not know where she was or what she was doing there. That she had been asleep was obvious, but how long she had been asleep, she had no idea. And why, in Naia's sweet name, would she have fallen asleep in the dim, unchanging twilight of the hold of a boat—?

Oh!

The length of her slumber was still something of a ques-

tion, but however long it had been, it had obviously been
long enough, for there had been a distinct change in the
hold. Well, perhaps not a distinct change, but a change of
some sort. It was hard to tell. In fact, she spent some time
lying with unclosed eyes, thinking and listening, before
she finally reached a conclusion upon which she was willing to act. Lifting the cat off her belly, then, and setting it
aside (it immediately stalked—with some indignation—
over to Beshur's supine form and, after considering for a
moment, curled up on his face), she rose and took a few
steps toward the hatchway, listening.

No sound. No voices. Nothing. Just the dim glow of the
lamps.

And then, just as she decided that the boat was, without
a doubt, no longer moving, there came from behind her a
muffled snuffling that turned rapidly into a screech, and
then into a loud, shrieking roar; and she turned around just
in time to see Beshur, now wide awake and sitting up in
the gloom, snatch the cat off his face (by means of the
usual convenient handle) and fling it across the hold. It hit
the far bulkhead with a loud thump, fell to the deck, then
fled directly up the companion-way, spitting, hissing, and
yowling loudly.

"Now surely that is the end of it all," said Potatoes,
scrambling upright and drawing his sword. "The guards
will be on us in a moment."

—But it was lying on my *face*!

"I am sure that the guards will readily accept your excuse," said Potatoes, "just before they impale you."

—They do not impale men, Beshur said with some
pride.

"Oh, I am sure that they will be happy to make an exception for you," said Potatoes as he strode to the base of
the steps. But a thought seemed to strike him, and he
paused, rubbing his stubbly face. "That is right. They do
not. Hmmm . . ."

Sari sagged against a bulkhead, waiting for sounds, shouts, the rattle of weapons. But, surprisingly, none came.

The silence lengthened.

Beshur looked at Potatoes.

Potatoes looked at Beshur.

Beshur looked at Sari.

—Why do you not go up and see what has happened, Potatoes?

Potatoes looked at Sari.

"I think that you ought to be the one to go, Beshur," he said. "After all, you were the cause of the noise."

—I would be happy to, Beshur said, but . . .

"And a *scholar* such as yourself . . ."

But Sari, at once determined and discouraged, had already gathered up her waist cloth and was climbing the steps. Ignoring the men who, after a moment of confusion, followed her, she reached first one deck, then another, and then, with a silent prayer, she poked her head cautiously up over the gilt coping around the main hatch.

Darkness. Lamps. No people. No cat.

"There is nobody here," she said.

"Ah," said Potatoes, "just as I expected."

"It is a large room, like the first."

"Just as I expected," continued Potatoes. "Have we returned, then?"

"I do not think so."

"Just as I expected."

Sari put a hand to her head. "Yes. Of course."

In a moment, two more heads joined Sari's. Together, they peered into a room so large that its darkness was, for the most part, undispelled by the lamps with which the boat was hung.

"The same . . . but different," said Potatoes after a time.

—*I* could have told you that, Beshur said.

"Yes, perhaps. But you did not," said Potatoes.

—I would remind a certain thief, Beshur said with some

irritation, that he really ought to respect those who have more education than he.

Apostate priest, Sari recalled again. *And he gave me water. He did not have to, but he gave me water. And I was old then.*

Potatoes was growing heated. "And I would remind a certain scholar that—"

"Hush," said Sari. "Where are we?"

Potatoes answered immediately. "In . . . ah . . . in . . ."

—Just as you expected, Beshur said. Of *course.*

"Very well," said Potatoes. "Where *are* we, O scholar?"

—I will study the available texts and give you the answer in due time.

There was a definite sneer in Beshur's tone.

Potatoes glared at him. "Pah!"

—And *pah!* to you also!

"*Pah* to you both," said Sari, and she preceded them out of the hatch, across the deck, and down the gangway.

For a moment, she stood in the middle of the room, looking around. The lamplight moved faintly on the dark walls. It was indeed much the same sort of room as the one they had found far beneath the shell of what was supposed to have been the Great Library of Nuhr. Given the lengthy journey necessary to get to it, however, the question of where they were was looming ever larger.

"We will have to go up," said Potatoes, who joined her only microseconds ahead of Beshur.

—Yes, Beshur was saying. We will have to go up. I am glad that I thought of that.

Potatoes pressed his lips together. "Pumice," came the faint mutter.

But, again, Sari was already leading the way: across the smooth and polished floor, into the doorway that the darkness and the dark stone required her to find more by feel than by sight, up the stairs. It was not a question of courage, she decided as she began what she expected to be a long climb. It was more a matter of simple progress, for

since she had fled her village, since she had left her dead
husband behind, her movements had always taken her *forward,* and only when she had tarried or allowed herself to
be trapped by courtesy or despair had she sensed that
something had gone wrong. Naia had taken Sari's natural
motion, it seemed, and had turned it to some kind of divine purpose; and here, in an unknown place, Sari was determined to go forward again, trusting that, wherever
forward took her, it would be in accord with the will of the
Goddess.

After what must have been an hour or more of steady
climbing that was interrupted only when Beshur sat down
and gasped out that he was a scholar, not a goat (to which
Potatoes responded in such a way that the scholar rose and
continued on ... albeit accompanied by an audible grinding of teeth), Sari saw light ahead.

"Daylight."

"Ah," said Potatoes. "Just as I—"

"Enough," said Sari.

The last steps were, indeed, the most frightening, for
Potatoes, by his own admission, had disposed of the
guards at the beginning of their journey. Here, though,
there could not but be ...

But no: there were no guards, only a large, empty room
that was a virtual duplicate of one they had discovered in
Nuhr. But here, (wherever here was), there was an odor as
of salt in the air, and a sense of moisture.

Sari heard a soft, distant crashing.

Potatoes shouldered his way forward. "I will climb to
the window and look."

And, surprisingly, he did, without contradiction or even
comment from Beshur. Setting his fingers and toes into the
cracks between the stones of the wall, the thief (if indeed
he was a thief: Sari was not sure about much of anything
by now) ascended slowly to the high, slit window through
which daylight was pouring in slantingly. There he hung,

feet gripping the stone, hands gripping the edges of the embrasure.

—What is it? Beshur said. What do you see?

"The sea," said Potatoes. "I see rocks, gulls, sand. And the sea.

"Where are we?" said Sari.

"It is nothing like the coast of the Three Kingdoms," came the reply. "I believe we are on an island."

Sari stared up at him. "An . . . an island?"

—An island? Beshur said. Runzen?

"No. I have been to Runzen. This is not Runzen. This is something else.

—Ah! Beshur said. Jus—

"Just as I expected," Potatoes added quickly.

Chapter Two

Is this Bakbuk? In *skirts*?

Indeed it is. Simpering her way along the corridors of the palace of Nuhr, her carefully nurtured breasts now a conspicuous fullness in the front of her shoulder cloth, her face veiled, her eyes downcast, this is indeed Bakbuk, and she has surrendered.

Stupid girl!

She has surrendered because she has failed. Utterly. Without question. Having attempted to conceal her weakness by the assumption of male clothing, gesture, and prerogative, she has instead—by her inability to prevent or even know about the disappearance of a number of inhabitants of the Palace of Nuhr—exposed it more grossly and unequivocally than ever.

Is this not what you wanted?

The prince, who is not only ill but also, in Bakbuk's frantic opinion, a potentially necessary sacrifice to her need for the concealment of her infirmities, is gone. So is the Naian woman. Abnel and the Americans are nowhere to be found. Her crime—against the palace, against the king, and (O selfish, disloyal little thing!) against herself—is obvious, as is the necessity of an overt penance, and therefore she displays Bakbuk as she is, baring what has come to be her inmost being, revealing to all what she has become. She curves her body into lascivious poses,

presses her body against the men she meets, widens her
eyes to an extent that (she hopes) indicates an equivalent
openness to appropriate male brutalizations.

And, true: were a hand to reach out and grab one of her
breasts, she would submit passively. Were casual passersby
to pinch her buttocks until they bled, she would remain silent. Were she to be grabbed, stripped, and forced into ob-
scenities, she would yield, for only thus would she
sufficiently expiate her guilt. But she waits and hopes in
vain for such punishments, for as she, with her past cha-
rades (utterly convincing, but steeped in the poison of deliberate and sadistic deceit), has so conditioned the
members of the palace staff that not even the most foolhardy guard or rut-minded stable boy would now dare to
consider even for a moment the thought of attempting anything improper with the sworder as she shambles about in
her feminine garnish, she exposes her infirmities to those
least likely to recognize them; and therefore the violations
for which she so yearns do not come, will never come.
Having realized the true nature of her soul, and now word-
lessly pleading for the fulfillment of torture and mutila-
tion, she finds herself denied, perhaps (as she admits)
justifiably denied; for to be degraded, to be raped, to be
cut, burned, or half-choked by tumescence would be too
much of a pleasure for her to derive even a semblance of
penitential satisfaction from it.

Stupid, stupid girl!

"Ugh, ugh, ugh, ugh . . . ! Aaaaaaaaaack!"

And the king still writhed in his poisoned delirium.

Haddar was off . . . somewhere. Bakbuk thought that
she recalled seeing him prowling about on the roofs of the
palace. With a net.

No matter. It had been plain for some time that Haddar
had been removed from the list of individuals by whom
the king would have matters thought about. This, unfortunately, left Kuz Aswani in the position of chief minister,
and Bakbuk was somewhat inclined toward the belief that

Haddar—prowling, net, and all—might well have been better.

But then, she is a mere woman, so what do her beliefs matter? She is, after all, good for only one thing.

(And the pang strikes deeply when she recalls again that she is not even good for that.)

"Urrrrrrk!"

"Most unfortunate," said Kuz Aswani, who, as usual, had a large bowl of raisins tucked under one arm.

Look at me! Can you not see that I am ... willing?

But if Kuz Aswani was staring at anything, he was, curiously, staring not at Bakbuk's breasts (and, yes, she has doubled up her doses of herbs, looking to make her charms even larger longer) nor at her kohl-rimmed eyes, but rather at the nape of her neck. Or, rather, where the nape of her neck would have been had her head cloth not been covering it.

Very strange. Bakbuk could not understand.

Fool! Are you blind? Are you not a man?

But: "Has the Naian woman been found?"

"N't y't," said Kuz Aswani through a mouthful of raisins. "I s'plct h'r t'bu f'nd prsn'lug."

"Eeeeeeech!"

Bakbuk considered. (And her hip swings seductively out, striving, despite her aversion to the new chief counselor, for that tantalizing, inviting brush with male warmth.) The potion devised by the Naian has obviously done some good, for she herself witnessed the temporary lucidity of the king after only a single mouthful. Unfortunately, the beneficial effects of the doses dutifully administered by the trusted servants who have stood watch at the side of the king's pallet have continued to show a distressing propensity to dissipate all too soon.

Take me!

"Arrrrrrg!"

"We should continue the treatment in accordance with

the Naian's instructions," she said to Kuz Aswani, struggling with female indecision and innate loyalty.

"Panas (blessed be He!) is good!" responded the chief minister.

Bakbuk had no idea what Panas' goodness had to do with the Naian, but she shrugged it off. (It is, perhaps, best that she not bother her pretty little head about such things.) "The Naian might well have met with foul play," she continued. "She has given us no reason to doubt her skills or her intentions."

"Eeky! Eeky! Eeky! Eeky!"

"His chisel is long and hard!" stated Kuz Aswani with, if anything, even greater enthusiasm.

Again, Bakbuk could not link statement with response, but she let it go. (It is, perhaps, best that . . . etc.) "Perhaps the king will soon recover his wits."

And here the religious police, hearing something perilously close to another matter that Panasian law was very clear about, started forward; but though Bakbuk turned a pleading glance their way, they misinterpreted it utterly. Recalling the chief sworder's previously (and actively) stated opinions, they reconsidered and retired.

At which point the servant who was standing beside the king's pallet ventured to step forward. "August chief minister," he said, kneeling and kissing the floor between his hands, "it is time for the king to have his medicine."

Kuz Aswani was still staring at the nape of Bakbuk's neck (as Bakbuk tries desperately to get the chief minister to notice her breasts). "Very well," he said. "Attend to it immediately."

In the Three Kingdoms, commands were commands. The servant rose, knelt, kissed the floor between his hands, rose, scooped up a measure of the warm potion, turned to the king, bent, set the measure of potion on the floor, straightened up, knelt, kissed the floor between his hands, rose, bent, picked up the measure of potion (now considerably less warm) and dumped it into the king's mouth.

"Ooo . . . uk-uk-uk!"

Kuz Aswani paused with a fistful of raisins halfway to his mouth.

"Where am I?" mumbled the king. "Where is Aeid?"

Bakbuk, with a fetching, helpless flutter, was immediately on her knees beside him. "All Highest, the prince is missing!"

"I . . . I . . . I . . ."

"What shall we do?"

"I . . . I . . . I . . ."

"What is your command?"

"I . . . I . . . I . . ."

"We have questioned the slaves and the servants, and they know nothing!"

"I . . . I . . . I . . ."

"All Highest?"

"I . . . I . . . I . . . will have it thought about."

Bakbuk stared at the king.

"Erk!"

Failure. Again. (And is that not just like a woman?)

"Can we give him another measure?" she asked.

"The Naian was very clear about the dosage," said the servant, keeping his eyes pointedly away from Bakbuk's neck, breasts, eyes . . . and everything else, too. "Too much, she said, and the king might be harmed. It is essential that we give him no more and no less than what she prescribed."

"When is the next dose?"

"In an hour."

"Aaaaaga!"

"We will wait, then."

"Panas (blessed be He!) is good!" said Kuz Aswani.

Bakbuk, who could still find no correlation between statement and response, remained noncommittal. "Yes," she said.

"By His strength shall the king be saved!" Kuz Aswani continued, his enthusiasm mounting once more. "By His strength shall we all be saved from the wiles of sor— ... ah ..."

He looked at the religious police and appeared to reconsider his words.

"... from ... ah ... from *evil*. Yes, from evil. By his strength—"

But he suddenly whirled toward the window. "Did you see *him* ... er ... I mean ... did you see *that*?"

"Wrg."

Bakbuk ventured a glance at the window. "Outside, Chief Minister? I saw nothing."

Which is, to be sure, something that can only be expected of a helpless woman, who, by her very nature, must be more concerned with her body and her allurements and the effects that they produce on the men about her than about what might be happening outside a window.

"Oh ... well, then ..." Looking somewhat like a man who is forced to pay attention to something other than the charging bull immediately before him, Kuz Aswani turned away from the window.

Still puzzled, Bakbuk swayed invitingly to the window and stuck her head outside. She saw the city, the harbor (Where *had* those American ships gone?), and, off down the wall, Haddar climbing hand over hand up a drainpipe, his net held tightly between his teeth.

"Ookook!"

Bakbuk squinted into the afternoon glare (recalling as she does that women should not, under any circumstances, squint, for squinting spoils utterly the clearness and light of their eyes, which are their chief beauty; and what man can resist the gracious gaze of a lovely woman, the brilliance of whose glance is undimmed by creases or wrinkles or the slightest hint of introspection, undimmed, in short, by any thoughts save those of pleasing *him*, in whatever way he wishes, a woman whose soul is thereby laid before him, open and submissive, as if fitting and appropriate for one whose inmost nature compels her to conform, to support, to give, to yield, to accept, to bleed).

"Waaaark!"

. . . and thus we find that with a conversion rate of 75 per 100 Naian families, the effectiveness of the Gharat's taxation plan proves to be great indeed, thus threatening much of the research. However, it must be noted that the conversion rate includes all members of the converted Naian households (that is, the women and children as well as the men), the conversion of the men being the only one counted according to Panasian custom. This poses some difficulties in determining the true conversion rate (CR_t) of the Naian population, for no statistical value can be derived as to the willingness/unwillingness ratio (WUR) if only the actions of the men are counted. Nonetheless, even assuming a typical Naian family of four (and this figure has previously been shown to be rather low, since they breed like rabbits), the conversion only of the men would account for only 25% of the total converted population base (TCPB), thus still disturbing the research by a considerable factor, since we are now dealing with a potential CR_t of 18.75 Naians per 100, a not inconsiderable number considering the long range gross conversion estimates (LRGCE) laid down at the beginning of the project.

Mitigating these disturbances, however, are a number of factors:

1) The disturbance of the CR_t and the WUR caused by the Gharat's taxation plan, being confined to the immediate vicinity of the city of Nuhr, may well prove to be small, though whether it can be ruled statistically trivial remains to be seen. (It should be added that it is most unfortunate that a control group was not established for the experiment. Population bases and the unavailability of a suitable land mass (USLM) rendered this impossible.)

2) The disturbance in question (DIQ) was caused to be of short duration by quick action on the part of the Kathan priesthood, who blocked the Gharat's efforts to have his taxation plan declared universal, thus essentially terminating it, even in the city of Nuhr, after only a few weeks of implementation. Two factors should be borne in mind, however:

a) The frustration of the Gharat's plans is likely to cause some instability in the research (I_r), since he will now be acting at least partially out of frustration and anger.

b) Since indications are that certain recollections as to traditions based upon his memory of the Sacred Texts (ST_m) prompted the king to require the Gharat to procure approval for his tax plan from the Kathan priesthood, the stated policy of not allowing quotation from the Sacred Texts should be reconsidered, bearing in mind, however, not only that familiarity with the Texts might cause later problems with the research, but that this kind of familiarity was not included in the original model.

3) There is some indication that, given the forcible and economic nature of the conversion (FENC) of the 18.75 percent of the Naian males accounted for, as well as the recalcitrance and resentment of the individuals comprising the remainder of the TCPB, there will be a not-inconsiderable relapse rate (NIRR), and that therefore the final value for the CR_t will be much lower than originally estimated. This value might be even further diminished by a judicious failure to apply the standard punishments for apostasy (A_{sp}) as set out in Panasian law, though, once again, this factor is not included in the original model and could prove to have unfortunate side effects (SE_u). Again, the lack of a control group is to be lamented.

Recent reports, however, indicate that some indisposition on the part of the king has resulted in his temporary incapacitation, and that the Gharat has taken this as an opportunity to reinstate his taxation plan. While the execution of this plan is so far confined to the city of Nuhr, the continued illness of the king ($IOTK_c$) might allow the Gharat to attempt the extension of his plan into other parts of the Three Kingdoms, with or without the approval of the Kathan priesthood, thus doing potentially irreparable damage (ID_p) to the research, even in light of the above-mentioned mitigating factors (MF_{am}).

"Ugh, ugh, ugh, ugh ... ! Aaaaaaaaack!"

"Is it time yet?"

"Another moment, chief minister."

"Urrrrrrk!"

"Ah, now it is time."

"Eeeeeeech!"

"Hurry!"

"Arrrrrrg!"

"Almost ready."

"Eeky! Eeky! Uk-uk— ... where am I?"

"You are in your bed, All Highest."

"What am I doing here?"

"You have been ill."

"Ah ... and Aeid?"

"He is ill too. And missing."

"Ah ... and the Naian woman?"

"She is missing, too."

"She has done good things for me. I will make her my chief concubine. Have her loins perfumed immediately."

"May it be as if it has already been done, All Highest, but there is the matter of—"

"Though I must have that thought about."

"As the All Highest wishes, but—"

"Oook!"

"All Highest?"

"Erk!"

"What?"

"Aaaaaga!"

"He has relapsed again."

"Wrg."

"Another hour."

"Ookook!"

"And what of the Gharat and the Americans?"

"Waaaark!"

"There is no word."

"Ugh, ugh, ugh, ugh . . . ! Aaaaaaaaack!"

Approaching footsteps had driven them from the room
with the slit window to a shadowed doorway. More footsteps had banished them from the doorway and sent them
down a long corridor. Yet more footsteps had forced them,
against all wisdom and prudence, into choosing a branch-
ing hallway at random and plunging headlong into it, and
a sound as of a door opening had at last precipitated them
into . . .

Here. Wherever here was. It was hard to tell. The darkness was absolute. Sari had never seen (or, rather, not
seen) such darkness. She waved a hand before her face.
Nothing. She peered in all directions. Nothing. Not a glim-
mer. An odd kind of sweet odor hung in the motionless,
stagnant air. Silence . . . and a sense of both oppression
and vastness that she could not understand.

"Just as I—"

—Shutup, Beshur said from somewhere close by.

Sari shrugged. "Where are we, Potatoes?"

"Why, we are . . . ah . . ."

Sari did not have to *see* Beshur in order to know that he
was gloating.

". . . in . . . ah . . ."

Potatoes trailed off into silence for a minute. Then: "I
will have to consider in order to say exactly, but . . .
ah . . ."

But Sari was moving, carefully, her hands outstretched
before her. Within moments, she had come upon a kind of

wall. Like the darkness, though, it was like nothing that she had ever seen (or, rather, not seen) before. Parts were wood. Parts were loose, movable. Parts rustled. Parts seemed to be hollow.

"What in Naia's name is this?"

"What?"

"This!"

—Shh! said Beshur.

"Be quiet, Beshur," said Potatoes, "or you will have the guards on us."

—Oh, Beshur said, so you are certain that there are guards here.

"There are guards everywhere," said Potatoes. "The worst guards of all are in your own mind."

—My mind?

Smugly: "What there is of it."

But Sari felt Potatoes grope his way to her side. She sighed inwardly as her hand was taken and pressed for the better part of a minute as though Potatoes had no idea whatsoever what it was or who it belonged to, but then with an "Oh. Sorry," he dropped it and began probing at the strange wall.

"Hmmm."

—Just as you expected, I am sure, Beshur said from somewhere close by.

"Wait. I have flint and steel."

"You do?" Sari found herself asking in surprise.

"Thieves always have such things," said Potatoes. "But I need something for a torch." A pause, then. "I do not suppose that I can trouble you for the loan of your head cloth, can I, Beshur?"

—Certainly not!

"Just as I expected," Potatoes said, punctuating the statement with a well-placed and completely disingenuous cough. "What about your . . . hair?"

—My hair!

"Well . . . perhaps there is something else here . . ." Sari heard him fumbling along the wall. "Could it be?" he said, almost to himself.

"What?"

"I think I know where we are."

—You said you knew that already, Beshur said peevishly.

"Well ... I did. But I ... ah ... know better now."

—Of course, Beshur said. Just as you expected.

"Here. This will have to do."

Sari heard a tearing sound, heard Potatoes kneel down on the stone floor. Two clicks and a shower of sparks told her that Potatoes had found his flint and steel.

A moment later, a square of what looked like paper was flaming on the ground. Potatoes rolled it carefully into an impromptu torch, and, rising, held it up.

Suddenly, everything about the room made sense. Though windowless, it was large and vaulted, but it was also crowded with a great many sets of shelves wellstocked with a variety of what Sari recognized as books of all shapes, sizes, and kinds. Bound volumes were there, and manuscripts, and pamphlets, and loose sheets that had been crudely stitched together. One of the latter lay on the ground, obviously the source of the raw materials for Potatoes' torch.

She looked at the rapidly burning tube in his hand. The flames were just then charring down to a large word in black ink:

BATPAXOI

Potatoes looked at the tube. *"Charta lintea."*

"What?"

"Linen paper. Long lasting, but not imperishable."

The flames burnt down to his fingers and he dropped the flaming stub on the floor and ground it into darkness under his sandal.

"Particularly by fire."

—Just as you expected, Beshur said.

"Hmmm. Indeed. Just."

Sari heard Potatoes running his hand along the shelves before him, heard a rustle as something was withdrawn from them, a thump as it was replaced.

"Amazing," came his voice. "And on an island!"

Sari's confusion was such that she all but felt dizzy. "Where are we, Potatoes?"

The sound of tearing again. In a moment, Potatoes had another torch. Again Sari saw the shelves, the vaulting. Off in the distance there appeared to be an archway that led . . . perhaps into a corridor, perhaps into another room like this one.

"We are in the Great Library of Nuhr," said Potatoes. The flames burned down and devoured another word:

$$Αριστοφανης$$

Chapter Three

It was indeed the Great Library, and, as Mr. Jenkins was finding out, it was even larger and more fascinating than Sari, Potatoes, and Beshur could guess (and they were indeed guessing at that moment, being, quite literally, in the dark about it all).

Jenkins, however, was not in the dark, for the main floor of the multi-storied Library, devoted as it was to the management and upkeep of such an immense collection (which, as Abnel explained, included not only books but actual objects and even *mechanisms* of various sorts—

A muffled *boom!* drifted into the room.

—of which the sacred guns used for the defense of the holy place against the curiosity of the unworthy (leading Mr. Jenkins to wonder once again about gunpowder ... with particular emphasis upon its relationship with guns), were but one all-but-trivial example) was lit by large windows of the clearest glass.

Jenkins examined the layout of the room. Generally square and open, its simplicity was complicated by the extra rooms that bulged out from each corner and by an octagonal something-or-other in the middle—obviously some sort of well down through the center of the building, judging from the light that entered the room by means of the windows that it possessed, one per side.

Throughout the room were the usual low tables and

fluffy cushions of the Three Kingdoms, as well as a number of higher workbenches such as those Jenkins had seen in some of the shops in the marketplaces—at which one could labor standing. In fact, when he looked closer, he saw that on the workbenches lay a number of widely disparate and at times unidentifiable objects that artisans and craftsmen (Jenkins assumed they were artisans and craftsmen) were tending as solicitously as the scribes and secretaries (Jenkins assumed they were scribes and secretaries) who occupied the fluffy cushions were tending the books and manuscripts on the low tables.

Another muffled *boom!*

"They are testing the guns," Abnel explained.

"Guns . . ." Jenkins was still wondering. It was perfectly possible to worm, load, and fire a gun without possessing any particular understanding as to the chemistry of gunpowder or the mechanics of ignition, but he needed to know for certain.

"Yes, guns," said Abnel, "For the defense of the Library against—"

"—against the curiosity of the unworthy," finished Jenkins. "Yes. Quite right, my dear Gharat. Just as I thought. A very . . . ah . . . worthy endeavor."

He was already choosing his words, preparing to fish unobtrusively for information, but the irrationality of his hopes was becoming distressingly evident. All of this? By *rote*? Impossible! What a dullard he was for having entertained such a thought even for a moment! But that meant that he would have to . . . have to—

"I am not worthy of the least of all the mercies, and of all the truth, which thou hast shewed unto thy servant," came the monotone from behind him, where servants and guards—and Mather and Wool—waited on the stairs.

"Quiet, Wool."

—have to do possibly unmentionable (and, judging from Mather's present condition, potentially crippling) things in order to provide for the success (and, possibly, the simple survival) of the American troops that Scruffy would be bringing.

Jenkins shuddered at the thought of what that might mean; but he also noticed that he . . . he . . .

Oh, good God! Had anyone *noticed*?

But his fishing and his discomfiture were interrupted by the entrance of a bustling, middle-aged man wearing the polished cotton garments of an official of the Three Kingdoms.

"The venerable Yourgi," whispered Abnel. "The librarian. A priest and a wise man."

Yourgi had come out of a doorway on the far side of the room, and when he suddenly appeared to become aware of the presence of the Gharat and the Gharat's company, he headed straightway toward them, detouring around several tables that lay in his path, stepping over a pile of wood shavings that had fallen from one of the workbenches, pausing only for a moment to glance at the work being done by one of the scribes.

"Is it not amazing," the Gharat continued. "You would never know that he is blind."

"Blind?" said Jenkins.

"Absolutely blind," Abnel assured him. "For many years now. I believe he suffers as a result of excessive study of the Sacred Texts. A wise man and a pious one, too."

Jenkins was very moved. "Astounding."

The librarian arrived, examined Jenkins with piercing eyes made all the more piercing by the spectacles that perched on his narrow nose like a wireframe bird, then dropped to his knees before Abnel and kissed the marble floor between his hands. "Panas (blessed be He!) is good," he said.

"His chisel is firm," responded the Gharat.

"We of the Library are honored that you have come to visit us, O Gharat."

"I am always pleased to meet worthy men who do the will of Panas (blessed be He!)," said Abnel.

"I perceive you have brought guests with you, O blessed Gharat," said Yourgi, still on his knees.

"Is it not amazing?" whispered Abnel to Jenkins, switching back to French. "Blind, and yet he senses your presence!"

"Truly astounding."

"God is good," said Yourgi.

Abnel. "Rise, Librarian, and meet Ambassador Obadiah Jenkins of the Righteous States of America! He has come in accordance with the words of the Sacred Texts which demand that the priesthood grant dispensations to the rules which normally bar the iniquitous from the sacred precincts!"

Iniquitous? Jenkins kept his face very carefully cheerful.

"Dispensations?" Yourgi remained bent over, but the question in his voice was evident. Even the top of his shaven head looked incredulous.

"Surely you have read the Sacred Texts, Yourgi!"

"I . . ."

"Have you . . . not?"

The top of Yourgi's head looked incredulous for a moment more, and then: "Oh! Oh, yes! Of course! Dispensations! Forgive me, O Gharat! I was preoccupied with . . . ah . . . with work!"

Abnel was nodding. "Blind," he murmured to Jenkins, "and yet devoted to the work of reading, the work of the sighted."

Jenkins kept himself looking cheerful.

"Blessed *are* they that have not seen—"

"*That* is quite enough, Wool."

But Yourgi had risen and was now peering at Jenkins once more, examining him with what would have been, in the ambassador's opinion, remarkable acuity for even a sighted man. (Did *he* notice? No . . . no . . . he could not. He was blind, after all. But maybe . . . maybe amazing as he was . . .) But Jenkins' surprise was even greater when Yourgi offered his hand in the manner of Americans and Europeans. "Good day to you, Ambassador," he said in perfect French. "You see, I know the customs of your country: one of the benefits of overseeing (so to speak) the wonders of a library which contains all knowledge."

All knowledge! The implications were staggering. But Jenkins took the librarian's hand with what he hoped looked like cool assurance. "Good day, reverend sir."

"I hope the ambassador found his journey to the Isle of Kanez pleasant?"

"The Isle of Kanez?" They were on an *island*?

Abnel broke in. "This is the Isle of Kanez, Ambassador. The Library is on the island. In fact, the Library *is,* in many ways, the island, since it utilizes most of the island's resources.

"Resources . . . ?" Island? They had traveled under the sea? Oh, this was . . . this was . . .

And Scruffy would be returning with the troops! Lambs to the slaughter!

"Flocks of sheep," said Yourgi as Jenkins stifled an involuntary start, "provide us with parchment for the copying of manuscripts. Minerals and sand, the metals and glass used in the preservation and restoration of the quaint devices of faraway lands. Forests yield wood for shelves, cases, and storage chests. Quarries give us stone to improve and enlarge the Library."

Jenkins noted that the prohibition against rivaling the works of the local deity did not seem to apply here on Kanez; but listening to the words of the blind librarian, he was falling further and further into barely suppressed panic. What if he had been *wrong*?

"Panas (blessed be He!) has graced us with the isolation necessary for the work of scholars, and has given us the beauty of the natural world"—and here the librarian swept out a hand to indicate the view of ocean and forest provided by the windows of the room, leading Jenkins to marvel once again that one who had been blind for many years could still appreciate visual beauty enough to call it to the attention of the sighted—"necessary for the refreshment of those devoted to the intellect."

Yourgi's spectacles glinted as he reached up and resettled them on his nose.

"Stablish thy word unto thy servant, who *is devoted* to thy fear," came the monotone.

"Shhh, Wool," said Jenkins.

"As you can see, the island is the Library, and the Library"—and here again Yourgi swept his arm out, this time to indicate the room and all the things in it, once again astounding Jenkins with his demonstration of knowledge that was usually associated only with sight—"is the island."

"Is he not remarkable?" said Abnel.

"Remarkable, indeed."

"Ah," said Yourgi, "I see that our most holy Gharat has made you acquainted with my . . . infirmity, Ambassador." Removing his glasses, he began to polish them absently with a corner of his shoulder cloth. "Some call it a tragedy. I consider it a command from the lips of Panas (blessed be He!) Himself, for as He has taken my sight from me, so does He challenge His humble servant to better serve Him without the distractions that sight would bring. I might look at a lovely book, for example, and lose sight (so to speak) of the fact that Panas (blessed be He!) alone caused that book to be made, and is, or should be, thereby glorified by it. I might contemplate the ever-moving waters of the sea . . ."

Jenkins felt a renewed sense of urgency. Water. Pumps. But if the Library contained *everything,* then perhaps he might find what he was looking for . . . right here!

". . . and forget the ever-present and ever-moving power of God. And so have I, in my blindness, attempted to serve Him better."

A scribe bustled up with a large piece of parchment in

his hand. "O Librarian," he gasped, "are these good enough?"

Jenkins was a little astonished that a mere scribe would interrupt what was essentially a meeting of state, but then he reflected that, here in the Library, matters concerning knowledge, manuscripts, and the preservation of artifacts had, doubtless, attained something of the status of a religion, and that therefore they might well be allowed to supersede matters of state.

Heathens, he thought to himself.

But Yourgi was examining the parchment, peering at it first through his glasses, then from below them, then from above them.

"It is truly amazing how he can do these things, as completely blind as he is," Abnel murmured to Jenkins.

"Yes . . . yes . . ." But Jenkins was leaning forward to see the parchment. It appeared to be covered with writing of some kind, and when Jenkins looked more carefully, he realized that he was seeing Roman letters—Spanish, perhaps—carefully handwritten so as to duplicate the look of a printed page.

"It is the power of Panas (blessed be He!)! The wisdom of the past burns brightly within him!"

Jenkins was still staring. Yes, this was no calligraphic hand such as the old scribes of Italy used for their correspondence. This was an actual imitation of print, painstakingly set out, each letter drawn with excruciating care and accuracy.

"Strange . . ." he murmured.

"Remarkable, I should say," said Abnel, moving a little too close to Jenkins.

Yourgi peered once more at the parchment. "Very good," he said. "Your letterforms are greatly improved."

"Forgive my curiosity," said Jenkins, "but that is . . . handwritten?"

"Yes, indeed," said Yourgi. "Every descender and serif of it. All handwritten."

"But it looks like . . . like printing."

"Yes, is it not wonderful?" Yourgi held up the parchment and scrutinized the text once more. "Bodoni, as those who have not irrecoverably lost the use of their eyes can see."

"Yes," said Jenkins, "I believe it is indeed Bodoni."

"Ah!" said Yourgi, "Here is an ambassador who has not forgotten the value of letterforms! My compliments to you, sir!"

Jenkins, acutely aware of Abnel pressing up against him (and reminded thereby of what he might have to do in order to learn what he had to learn (*Had* anyone noticed?) . . .

"He-he!" Mather suddenly mumbled behind him. "Man work!"

. . . started violently at Mather's words, devoutly wishing as he did so that Mather would stop doing that. But, "Thank you, Librarian," he managed. "I am honored."

"Ah, but the honor is mine! After all, it is the God himself who has commanded the . . . ah . . ."

He looked quickly at Abnel, who was nodding.

". . . the . . . ah dispensations which brought you here, and it is always a pleasure and a sacred honor—no, a sacred duty!—to do that which is . . . ah . . ."

Another look at Abnel, who was still nodding.

". . . ah . . . commanded by the God."

Abnel was still nodding.

Jenkins felt the too-close presence of the Gharat, tried to move away, wound up too close to the blind librarian. And did he . . . ? Did anyone . . . ? It was, after all . . . "I am curious, though . . ."

"Yes?"

Jenkins looked again at the parchment. "Why have you taken such pains to reproduce a printed page? Why did you not use ordinary handwriting?"

Dead silence in the room. For the moment, no one even seemed to be breathing.

"He-he!"

Except, perhaps, for Mather.

Jenkins, feeling as though he had opened a cupboard to find one of Bonaparte's cannon staring him in the face— and, indeed, the *boom* he had heard a few minutes ago indicated that he might well have done just that—kept up a carefully nurtured diplomatic smile. Just as he expected. Really. It was all quite simple.

"Why?" stammered the scribe in halting French. "Because . . . because . . . because that is what the original looked like!"

"Ah . . ." said Jenkins, who was more bewildered than before. "Of course." He looked again at the parchment, made out a few words. "Cervantes?"

"Who?"

"The writer. *Don Quixote.*"

"Don Quixote?"

"Spanish."

"Spanish?"

Jenkins stared, perplexed. "You . . . ?"

"Panas (blessed be He!) is good!" cried the scribe.

"His chisel is long and pointed," replied Yourgi. "Thank you, Scribe. Continue with your excellent work."

And suddenly, Jenkins forgot to worry whether anyone had noticed anything about *anything,* for other matters had driven that concern from his mind.

Copying . . . printing . . . and ignorance.

"Arrrr-uk-uk-uk!"

"All Highest!"

"Who . . . who are you?"

"I am Bakbuk. Your sworder."

"Oh . . . yes . . . of course. I will make you my chief concubine. Have your loins perfumed immediately."

"All Highest, it shall be as you command, but what are we to do about Aeid, the Gharat, and the Americans?"

"Who are they?"

"Why ... they are ... they are ..."

"It is no matter. I will make them my chief concubines. Have their loins perfumed immediately."

"All Highest!"

"But I must have it thought ab—"

"May it be ..."

"Eeky! Eeky! Eeky! Eeky!"

"Panas (blessed be He!) be praised!"

"Oook!"

"What?"

"Panas (blessed be He!) be praised!"

"Erk!"

"I see nothing to praise Him about at present, Chief Minister."

"Let me hear you say *Panas (blessed be He!) be praised!*"

"I really do not think—"

"Aaaaaga!"

"Say it!"

"Wrg."

"How long until the next dose?"

"Ookook!"

"Say it!"

"Waaaark!"

Inwa Kabir, despite even intermittent fits of poison-induced delirium, was not a stupid man. He had governed the Three Kingdoms for nearly seventy years, he had patiently held to the reactionary doctrines that had stood his fathers and his grandfathers in good stead, that had, with the passing of generations, turned the government and the society of his land into monuments of inefficiency, but he was not stupid. Consider: he was alive, and he had absolute power. Absolute monarchs are judged by their survival, are they not? And Inwa Kabir (again, like his fathers and grandfathers before him) had survived splendidly. And therefore he had been successful. And, in fact, he had every expectation of continuing to be successful by surviving splendidly until he died, after which . . .

But there was the rub. After which . . . there was Aeid, and the boy had shown . . . distressing tendencies. Those books. And his disappearance. Republican sentiments . . .

Now, Inwa Kabir, as aforesaid, was not a stupid man, and while a general policy of unremitting reaction might appear to many to be short-sighted, this quality is, in fact, not at all a deficiency in such individuals as Inwa Kabir and his fathers and his grandfathers, the reason being that reaction demands, above all things, continuity, else there is nothing by which to guide one's reaction and nothing to justify its maintenance. This continuity is, however, something of a two-edged sword, for while its presence is both a foundation and *raison d'être* for reaction, its absence makes utter hay out of everything, for if there is no continuity, then there is no justification or *raison d'être* for anything at all, and therefore the *after which* that would follow Inwa Kabir's death was something much contemplated by Inwa Kabir, and as he was not a stupid man, and as he judged that to feign a constant and continuing illness even after the Naian woman's potion had reduced his initial symptoms to no more than a lingering case of severe fatigue punctuated by intermittent hallucinations—and thus to buy time—was a shrewd move indeed, he had, in his private policy of inaction (a direct corollary, it might be noticed, of his public policy of inaction), much time in which to contemplate that *after which*.

The first question, of course, was that of Aeid, for Aeid was the *after which* incarnate . . . so to speak. But Inwa Kabir sensed that Aeid was going to be something of an insoluble problem for the present; and, therefore, as Aeid was first, so he had to be last. So the next first question was that of the poison. Which brought Inwa Kabir immediately back to the first first question: Aeid.

Aeid? A poisoner? Inwa Kabir doubted it very much. Though Aeid did not know it, Inwa Kabir knew a little more about him than Aeid thought he did, and one of the things that he knew was that Aeid was decidedly not poisoner material.

At least he *thought* so, though he admitted (as he lay seemingly comatose, now and then uttering something . . .

"Eeky! Eeky! Eeky! Eeky!"

. . . appropriately delirious-sounding, and taking his medicine like a good boy), that his ability to think about things himself might have gotten a little rusty over the years, and so he could not be absolutely sure. Aeid, after all, had been seen bringing a tray of sweetmeats into the palace, and the sweetmeats on the tray that had arrived in the royal chambers a little while later might (or might not) have had a slight taste of the outdoors about them. Then, too, there was Aeid's republican bent, which possibly included a tendency toward regicide. But it could just as well have been argued that Fakik, the late head chef (Panasian law was very clear about things like that.), had possessed much more of a reason to attempt to poison the king than Aeid, for Fakik's grievances could easily have been seen as strong enough—not to mention fresh enough—to provide him with a motive for such an action. Still, though . . .

So it might well have been Aeid. Or maybe not.

"Erk!"

It was unfortunate that he could not have it thought about.

(And, just then, he heard a scramble at the window, and with half-closed eyes, he saw Haddar, wearing something that looked very much like women's clothes, tumble into the room. In a moment, though, the former chief minister had picked up the net he had dropped and had bolted out into the corridor, not even pausing long enough to return the salute of the guards, who . . .

"The soldiers of the All Highest wish the former chief minister of the Three Kingdoms a long life and a happy one."

... tried very hard to do their duty ... but, having failed, were severely punished, since Panasian law was very clear about things like that).

In any case, removing a Crown Prince was not a matter to be taken lightly. Chief ministers could come and go at the king's pleasure, but Crown Princes were in rather limited supply. There were many concubines, true, but one could not just expect them to pop out so many Crown Princes like so many hot, brown breakfast cakes. By no means! Then, too, it was not just a matter of popping them out: Crown Princes had to be educated, and entertained, and feted, and taught the value of reaction (something that Aeid had obviously not quite got the hang of) before they could be proper Crown Princes. (Not to mention the concubines themselves, who *would* show a great deal of perversity in finding ways *not* to have children, and sulking, and pouting, and fighting among themselves about who had popped out the breakf— ... ah ... that is, who had delivered the Crown Prince.)

Inwa Kabir was somewhat unwilling to repeat the whole, elaborate, time-consuming experiment, and so he decided that it would be much better if Aeid was not the poisoner. Even if he was.

And then he thought of Abnel and his irritating temple tax intruded (somewhat blasphemously, it must be admitted) into the mind of Inwa Kabir.

"Aaaaaga!"

Chapter Four

By incinerating, page by page, one of the earliest extant copies of Aristophanes' *The Frogs*, Sari, Potatoes, and Beshur managed to pick their way through the mazes of overflowing bookshelves. Blazing pieces of linen paper gave them tantalizing glimpses of codices, scrolls, bound volumes, pamphlets, maps, stacks of loose parchment, boxes of letters, envelopes, charts, and a hundred other things; and still rooms opened into rooms, hallways led to rooms, doors (cautiously opened, to be sure) revealed even more rooms ... all offering the same bounteous literary harvest.

—They must have ... *everything* here, Beshur whispered.

"More than that, I think," said Potatoes, who was just then picking a copy of Addison's *Spectator* out of what looked like a complete set. He glanced at the page, puzzling out the barbaric and rectilinear letters:

... continues to wear a coat and doublet of the same cut that were in fashion at the time of his repulse, which, in his merry humors, he tells us, has been in and out twelve times since he first wore it.

"Fascinating ..."

—What is it?

"A discourse on manners and fashion."

—Fashion? What kind of fashion?

"Clothes." But the flames were carbonizing *little bottle of oil* once again, and Potatoes had just enough time to snatch another page from the priceless manuscript and ignite it from the remains of the previous.

Beshur was looking over his shoulder.

—What does fashion have to do with clothes? he said.

"Everything. In Europe."

Beshur was still examining the magazine, though it was evident that he could not read English.

—Heathens.

Potatoes, who had often wished that he could exchange his cumbersome robes and silks for a nice, well-fitting pair of European breeches and a shirt, could only stare at him. Then: "Bumpkin," he muttered. He replaced the copy of *Spectator,* held aloft another burning page of Aristophanes, and led on.

Sari was awash: having grown up in a small village, she had heard about books only by rumor and description. Like most girls of her station and religion, she had learned to read a little, write a little, and do arithmetic. But these tomes and multi-volume sets were beyond her, and she suspected that she could not have comprehended most of them even had they been written in her own language.

The blazing pages of *The Frogs* lit up more rooms, and stairs took them to other floors and passageways. Potatoes preceded them, holding his batrachian torch aloft.

"Astounding."

—*Everything,* Beshur said.

There was a mixture of superiority and greed in his tone.

—It *is* the Great Library!

And then, suddenly, all three of them froze at a muffled *boom!* that came not so much to their ears as to their skins, for the very fabric of the library shuddered as though in response to a distant but very palpable thunderclap.

Instantly, Potatoes dropped his torch and stamped it into darkness. Silence. Long, frightening minutes of silence.

"What . . . what was that?" Sari whispered at last, her words hardly more than a breath.

—It is—

But Beshur's words were interrupted, for, as if in answer to Sari's question, another *boom!* shuddered through the room, this one louder.

—Aawp!

There was a thud, and then a crash. And then, inexplicably, a streak of what could only be . . .

. . . daylight.

But, as the *boom!* had been repeated, so was the *aawp!*, and then Sari had the strange sensation that she was seeing double, for the diffuse but very perceptible light confronted her with the sight of Beshur staring at Beshur. Which, of course, was impossible. The impossibility, however, did not appear to bother Beshur in the least . . . or at least it did not appear to bother him half so much as the actuality, for after uttering the aforementioned *aawp!* once again, he was now attempting to scramble away from his doppelgänger with efforts that were more scholarly than effective, for though they were precisely correct in intent, their execution only brought him into violent collision with one of the surrounding bookshelves . . . which prevented him from moving any farther away from the apparition that itself seemed to be equally terrified of the individual after whom it was modeled, for it, too, was attempting to scramble away from the real Beshur (Sari was pretty sure that it was the real Beshur, but, to be sure, there was some possibility of doubt about this: after all, she was hardly the real Sari . . . or, rather, was the real Sari only by a technicality, and given that Beshur was an apostate priest—or something very close—she was no longer sure whether the real Beshur was indeed the real Beshur at all . . . not to mention the odd complexities that surrounded *Potatoes*), but was having no more luck than

Beshur himself, for an inconveniently-placed bookshelf
(generously supplied with large, heavy volumes, which
tumbled off the shelves and fell on its head) was doing an
effective job of blocking its escape.

—Aawp!

"Shutup, bumpkin," hissed Potatoes. He went toward
Beshur's double with an air of authority, and though Sari
nearly cried out when a double of Potatoes appeared, her
cry forced its way to utterance when the two Potatoes met,
merged, fused, and disappeared.

"It is a mirror," said Potatoes. "And a secret panel, too."

Beshur stopped struggling with the pile of tumbled
books. So did his double.

—A mirror?

"Yes."

—Ah . . . just as I—

"Be quiet and come in here," said Potatoes.

Slowly, as though relishing the effect he produced, Potatoes swung the mirror (which Beshur's initial fall had
apparently unlatched) all the way open, simultaneously
unmelding from his reflection and regaining his individuality. For a moment, he examined himself in the glass, felt
his chin experimentally, and resettled his head cloth, then
he beckoned to Sari and Beshur to follow him through the
doorway he had revealed.

Feeling foolish for having cried out at something so
commonplace as a mirror—though, to be sure, it was a
very large mirror, much larger than any she had ever seen
before—Sari followed Potatoes, starting only a little at the
full-length view of the lithe girl she had become . . . and
doing her best to conceal her uneasiness. But what took
her mind immediately away from any question of appearances or uneasiness was the room that lay beyond the mirror, for, slanting in as it did from three high, vertical
windows, the daylight revealed a veritable museum of . . .
things . . .

The sheer density of the massed collection prevented

her from seeing anything except clusters of confused shapes. Surely there were individual entities here, identifiable objects, but individuality and identity were, for now, submerged completely in the overwhelming visual impact of the aggregate presence. Metal, glass, porcelain, wire, pottery, wood ... it was all here, and Sari, accustomed to the simplicity of her village, the relative intelligibility of the cities she had seen, and the mundane bustle of life in both, was able to do no more than register gleams, angles, piles, heaps, dust, flutterings, colors ...

Potatoes and Beshur seemed equally affected, for neither of them spoke for several minutes. Even the torchlit seas of books and papers they had glimpsed in the darkened rooms were as nothing compared to this.

Finally, Beshur struggled with words.

—It is ... sacrilege, he said.

"Sacrilege?" said Potatoes.

—Sacrilege. These things are expressly forbidden by the Sacred Texts, which say clearly that ... that ...

He fumbled, caught himself, fell silent.

—I know this, he said at last.

"A holy sacrilege, if anything," said Potatoes, "seeing as how the priests themselves have collected it."

—I am sure we ... ah ... I mean, *they* have no idea that it is here.

Sari said nothing.

Potatoes eyed Beshur. "Sacrilege! Collected knowledge a sacrilege! A fine sentiment for a scholar!"

—I am a scholar, Beshur protested, not an acquisitive heathen!

"Well, perhaps you are a scholar, but you look like a common porter, and you sound like a priest!"

Beshur went white. But:

—Oh, yes, he said, and I imagine, O thief, that this is all just as you ex—

"Stop it, both of you!" Sari cried. The thought of the two men arguing in this impossible place, with danger and death waiting to spring upon them from what seemed to her fatigued mind to be every corner, dark or light, made her angry enough, even leaving aside the reason (Oh. Oh, yes. That.) that they were arguing.

Potatoes eyed Beshur, then, accusingly, looked at the mirror panel, which was still half open. Beshur eyed Potatoes, then, pointedly, did *not* look at the mirror panel.

Sari sat down on what, in Europe or America, would have been called an overstuffed chair (European, comfortable; American, godless). The rest of the collection remained unintelligible, but at least she had found a place to sit.

Dust puffed up from the cushions. Her head, she realized, was spinning. "When did we last eat?" she asked weakly.

"Why . . . ah . . ."

—Why . . . ah . . .

"I believe we need food."

—Yes, Beshur said. I could have told you that, but . . .

A clenched fist on the part of Potatoes caused his words to trail off into a mumble.

But though the room (rooms, actually) that lay beyond the mirror panel appeared to be furnished with one of everything, that everything did not appear to include anything by way of food. Nor did the stowaways, who had not foreseen such a lengthy journey, have anything with them that might be turned into a meal.

"Well," said Potatoes, "there is nothing to do but go and get something. Those with whom we traveled to this place must eat . . . and, therefore, so shall we. I will be back shortly."

"What . . . what are you going to do?" Sari was finding it harder and harder to think. But it nonetheless occurred to her that, once again, she was compelled to look to others for aid.

And, once again, though there was probably aid to be

had, its provider was (Oh. Oh, yes. That.) obviously un-willing to leave it at that.

But, "I am a thief," said Potatoes. "I have my ways."

And, with that, he pushed the mirror panel fully open and vanished into the darkness of the rooms of books.

Bakbuk was growing increasingly frantic (something that only confirmed her opinion of herself: a stupid girl, becoming hysterical when becoming hysterical would do more harm than good ... as though becoming hysterical ever did any good at all, though she had noticed that it did occasionally do *some* good when a hysterical girl wanted something from a non-hysterical man, who, in the face of the hysteria, was more than willing to give it to her ... which caused Bakbuk to reflect that she, perhaps, *should* become hysterical, and yet her mannish pride, refusing to bend to the requirements or even the doubtful privileges of her station, persisted in stifling her tears and shrieks). The king, aside from brief periods of lucidity, made no sense at all and was obviously unfit for governing the country, while those who might have been expected to take over his duties during his illness—Aeid and Abnel—had van-ished. It was either unspeakably foul play, or ...

... or ...

... or ...

She was not at all sure what the *or* was.

"Arrrrrrg!"

But it was something unpleasant, she was sure.

And so, reluctantly, Bakbuk, silly little girl though she was, steeled herself to the task of managing a country, even though she was, of course, entirely unsuited to any-thing more intellectually strenuous than painting her toe-nails. Picking up the tools she had cast away, therefore, she forced herself to be logical, forced herself to be de-tached, turned her thoughts, for the moment, away from personal abasement and toward organization.

The first thing to do? Why, cure the king, to be sure.

But, even considering the not-inconsiderable efficacy of the Naian's herbal concoction, curing the king was turning out to be something of a lengthy proposition, and so the kingdom had to be managed in the interim. Aeid, the Gharat, and the Americans had to be searched for. The Naian woman had to be found.

All this was very clear, but Bakbuk hated herself for that clarity. Perhaps the only saving grace to the situation was that she, technically a commoner without a drop of royal or noble blood in her veins, could only operate through the commands of Kuz Aswani, and thus was very much in the position of a woman. Or, rather, would have been in such a position if a woman could have had any plans, organization, or foresight with which to operate (through the commands of someone suitably male) in the first place. Which, unfortunately, was not the case with Bakbuk.

"Eeky! Eeky! Eeky! Eeky!"

Or maybe fortunately.

"Oook!"

It was a little hard to tell.

"I think that we must intensify our search for Aeid," she said as she knelt by the side of the prostrate king.

"Indeed?" said Kuz Aswani.

"It is imperative that, until the king is better . . ."

"Erk!"

". . . some official representative of the monarchy be found in order to attend to matters of state."

Kuz Aswani considered, whiffling absently through his sharp nose. "My thoughts exactly," he said after a time. "I am very glad I thought of that."

And Bakbuk, looking up over her shoulder, noticed that Kuz Aswani was not only whiffling, but was also . . . well . . . *twitching* . . . in a way that suggested that his dignified (erect) posture and manly circumspection were fragile things indeed, that what he really wanted to do was—

But, with an effort, Kuz Aswani appeared to throw off

whatever strange mood had suddenly come upon him . . . along with the concomitant whiffling and twitching. "Yes," he said. "That is very true."

"The All Highest cannot give orders," Bakbuk reminded him coyly.

"Aaaaaga!"

"That also is true," said Kuz Aswani, who, disappointingly, did not notice Bakbuk's fluttering eyelashes. "But I am chief minister. I will give them myself."

And with only the slightest of bounces to one side and the softest (and most abbreviated) of *chuckles*, Kuz Aswani left the room and wandered off down the inlaid and polished hallway, looking for someone to whom he could give orders (there being no one close by to give them to, as the guards who normally stood at the doors were gone (Panasian law having been, as usual, very clear) and the palace was so disorganized that they had not yet been replaced).

Bakbuk knelt beside the man to whom she had, from her earliest age, given her unreserved loyalty. The servant who normally tended the kettle of herbal infusion was away . . .

"Wrg."

. . . Kuz Aswani was off looking for someone to give orders to, and so she was completely alone with Inwa Kabir. Despite her feminine frailties, Bakbuk was still the king's sworder, and a particularly deadly sworder at that. Indeed, it was well known that she had, at one time, beaten no less than the Crown Prince himself at swordplay. Inwa Kabir was, therefore, in the safest of all situations in which he could theoretically have been placed.

"Bakbuk," came a faint whisper.

She lifted her head, wondering who had entered the room. But no: she was alone with the king.

"Bakbuk."

And then she realized who had spoken. "All Highest!"

The king was looking at her, and the queer light of madness was absent from his eyes. "Tell no one of my recovery," he said. "No one!"

Bakbuk's response was without hesitation, without the slightest thought of personal convenience or inconvenience. "As the All Highest wishes, may it be as if it has already been done!"

"Good. Good. I must have that—"

But the king moved his head as though to shake away a thought.

"Listen to me," he continued. "You shall be my messenger, Bakbuk. You will convey my wishes to Kuz Aswani, and he will give orders. But Kuz Aswani is not to be told whence these wishes come. He is to think that they are his own."

"Yes, All Highest. Of course." And the thought that, by royal command, she was to play the role of an insignificant woman (who had no volition or thought or stratagem of her own, but was merely the passive conduit for the will of a man), brought a tightening to her too-smooth groin.

"You will personally conduct a search for Aeid and the others."

"As the All Highest wills." Personally? But that meant . . .

"And you will also look for Abnel and the Americans."

"All Highest, it shall be done."

. . . that she would have to take the initiative in certain matters, and that meant . . .

"Use whatever means are necessary. Convince Kuz Aswani to draw whatever is needed for your work from the palace coffers."

"May it be as if it has already been done, All Highest."

. . . that she would, once again, be but a sham female; and a double-sham female at that, for of what use was her lithe body save as temptation without fulfillment, provocation without reciprocity, lust without rut? And now she would not even be able to ape a subservient role, but must give orders, search, prowl, and infiltrate . . . all on her own.

"Find them and bring them back . . . uh . . . ah . . . oh . . . ookook!"

And a footstep at the door told Bakbuk that Kuz Aswani had returned. "The search shall begin," he said. "I have ordered it."

"It would probably be well," Bakbuk, who glanced down at the king only to be met with the fixed and glassy stare of delirium, "to have someone in charge who is experienced in such matters."

"Oh, I am sure that would be you, Bakbuk," said Kuz Aswani. "I have attended to it."

"It shall be done," said Bakbuk.

Kuz Aswani was staring at her . . . or, rather, at the nape of her neck. "You will . . . ah . . . you will need gold, of course."

Bakbuk sat back on her heels, feeling the wash of surrender. Kuz Aswani was a *man*. He did not need her wiles to be prompted to do the right thing. The king was a man, and Kuz Aswani was a man, and together they would order her to do the right thing . . .

". . . ah . . ." Kuz Aswani was continuing, ". . . ah, and so you should take what you . . . ah . . . need."

. . . without any prompting from her at all!

Kuz Aswani was still staring at the nape of her neck. "I have so authorized it."

"Yes . . . yes . . . oh . . ."

Kuz Aswani was looking earnestly at her now. "Bakbuk . . ."

Bakbuk closed her eyes, all but trembling.

"Would you mind . . . that is . . . could . . . could I . . ."

Bakbuk opened her eyes. "Yes, Chief Minister?"

"Could I . . . ah . . . that is . . ."

"Tell me what to do, Chief Minister."

"Ah . . . your neck."

"My neck?"

"Yes. Your neck. Could it . . . ah . . . that is . . . ah . . . would you mind terribly if . . . if just a little . . ."

But a spasm suddenly seemed to pass through the chief minister, and he drew himself up as though he were a puppet on the receiving end of a good jerk.

"Nothing," he said. "Nothing at all." He looked around quickly, ran to the window, peered out. "Did you see . . . him?"

"See? See who?" Bakbuk glanced around, torn between fright and genuine hope that the minister was perhaps referring to the (Oooooh! *Him!*) Blue Avenger.

"Him!" Kuz Aswani ran to the carved chest of kingly clothing, looked in; ran to the door, peered into the hallway.

"Who?"

"Ah . . . never mind. It is nothing."

"Waaaark!"

"God is great!" said Kuz Aswani.

"Yes, of course," said Bakbuk.

Kuz Aswani turned back into the room. "God is great!"

"Yes, truly."

"Let me hear you say *God is great!*"

"I do not understand."

"Say it!"

"Chief Minister, I—"

"Say it!"

"God is great."

"Louder!"

"God is great!"

"Panas (blessed be He!) is good!"

"His chisel is . . . is . . ."

And Bakbuk, ordered and compliant, found herself almost fainting.

". . . is long and . . . and . . . and . . ."

Kuz Aswani swayed, his eyes open wide, his face the sitting place of ecstasy. "And He will save us! He will save us from the evil snares of magi—"

But with another jerk, he suddenly fell silent, clamped his mouth shut, and turned away.

"Do what you need to, Bakbuk," he said.

Bakbuk found herself on her hands and knees, bent, ready for . . .

"Yes," she said. "Anything."

. . . anything.

"Aeid and the others must be found."

"Yes."

"Go and do it." But Kuz Aswani's eyes were again fixed on the nape of her neck. "But . . . before you go . . . could . . . could I . . . ?"

"Could you . . . what?"

"Oh . . . ah . . . ah . . . ah . . . never mind."

"Ugh, ugh, ugh, ugh . . . ! Aaaaaaaaack!"

Chapter Five

Dearly beloved, intelligence is a beautiful thing. Is it not? Yes, it is! For God has granted us intelligence so that we may glorify His name forever, ever devising new ways of praising the Divine Author of our beings, who is, after all the ... ah ... the ... the Divine Author of our beings. Without whose grace and love we would not be. Ah ... be *intelligent*!

Or ... well ... just be at all. Or ... or, rather, just *not* be at all.

But, stubborn children that we are, we are prone to sinfulness, and it is nothing but God's goodness and infinite mercy that allows us to continue our sinful ways, for by doing so, God shows us that he loves us. Loves us, that is, enough to ... ah ... to let us suffer the punishments of the unrighteous so as to better find our way back to His grace and His love, which we ... ah ... have despite our sinfulness and our sins, for God so loves us that ...

Well, in any case, dearly beloved brethren, I was speaking of intelligence, and of the wonderful and blessed opportunity it gives us to express our devotion to God. And to illustrate the great favor with which God holds not only us but also the intelligence He has given us out of His love and ... ah ... intelligence he has given us, we have only to turn our eyes ...

In order to see the great favor with which He holds not

only us but also the intelligence He has given us, we have only to turn our eyes to the greater world about us, which nurtures the intelligence that He has given us out of ... that He has given us, and provides us with a multiplicity of opportunities for the exercise of that intelligence, so that we may so glorify God, who lo— ... ah ...

Witness this case in point, my dear brothers in Christ: Mr. Jenkins, himself an ordained minister of God (as opposed to the not-ordained ministers of a heathen idol, even though God still loves those not-ordained ministers so much that He is willing to deliver them into the hands of Mr. Jenkins and the Righteous States of America, there to suffer because of the great love that God holds for them, a love so great that ...)—where was I? Oh, yes, Mr. Jenkins, himself an ordained ... ah ... as opposed to ... ah ...

God so loves us that ...

Ah ...

Mr. Jenkins, who, as a minister, cannot but be expected to embody those godly virtues toward which we all should strive, regardless of our degree or station in society, and whose behavior we should, of course, emulate, since his nature is that of a godly man, whose virtues ... ah ... who we should emulate ...

Mr. Jenkins exhibits, without question, virtue; and so, a virtuous man, he exhibits a godly intellect, and, questing after the food of that intellect as a Christian knight quests after the lovely maiden, seeking to ... ah ...

No ... that will not do.

Ah ... as a Christian knight quests after virtue (so we are told in the old romances, which, though they embody the snares of the devil by seeking to divert our minds from thoughts of God, who shows that He so loves us by punishing us—)

Ahem.

Mr. Jenkins demonstrates curiosity.

There.

And curiosity, in that it nourishes the intellect (which is, as I am sure I have demonstrated, a godly quality) is itself a godly quality, and as Mr. Jenkins is a . . . a . . . a minister . . . who is expected to show forth . . . to . . . to show forth godly qualities . . . he is . . . he is . . . he is . . . *justified* (That is it!) in his curiosity not only by his mere demonstration of it, but also because his curiosity is useful to the Righteous States of America, which is itself godly . . . and . . . and . . . and *curious* to find out more about the quaint customs of the land to which he has come in order to offer the sweet concord and friendship of his nation, despite the fact that those to whom that concord and friendship are offered are heathen idolators, whom, nonetheless, God so loves that He will deliver them into the hands of their enemies so that they might be punished for their idolatry and learn thereby the ways of true righteousness.

Much better.

And if, perchance, Mr. Jenkins has to cloak his investigations in the obscurity lovingly provided by the nocturnal hours, why this too is an indication of God's great mercy, for He so loves us all—and especially Mr. Jenkins, who is a minister . . . ah . . . —that . . . that . . . that he has provided not only intelligence, and not only the curiosity necessary to nurture that intelligence, but also the nocturnal hours in which to give free rein to that curiosity, unimpeded by the legal or religious obstructions set forth as inviolable law by his hosts, who are, of course, heathens and unworthy to loose the sandal of such as Mr. Jenkins, who is a—

In any case, because of God's great love and goodness and mercy, Mr. Jenkins is able, by means of the obscurity afforded by the night, that great leveler of human dreams, conceit, and ambition (for who can say that he is not affected by the night, and so does God show His great love for us by afflicting . . . ah . . . by providing us with a sign of—)

Mr. Jenkins, at night, taking a lamp, and bearing its

light with him into the darkness—a potent symbol upon which all good Christians should meditate!—searches for clues with which to appease his curiosity, thereby furthering the questing of his intellect, which will, by the grace of God, thereby further the plans of the most Righteous States of America. To this end, his steps take him down hallways and through doors, past guards who seem curiously unaware and distracted, and into the rooms that make up the Great Library itself.

And, once again, I have left her with *him*! Sandstone! But what else could I have done? And by now they will be looking for me in the palace . . . and for the others, too. What did Abnel tell them? Some excuse? I cannot know. Perhaps they will miss him, too?

Moving cautiously, Prince Aeid (Potatoes, maybe), negotiated by feel the maze of bookshelves that occupied the pitch black rooms of the Great Library, relying on his memory of their position and arrangement in order to make his way to the door that had initially let him and his companions into the labyrinth.

Odor in the air. Is that food? Possibly . . . most certainly they will have to eat. But what if they have already left the island? Pumice and rottenstone! But no . . . Abnel is up to something. He has a plan. And I suspect that there would have been indications of some kind that the pavilion boat was to be put in motion again. Sounds, perhaps. I cannot be sure, though. Yet Sari is hungry, and even if Abnel and the Americans have left, those who remain behind must still eat, and if they must eat, then there must be food. And if I bring her food . . .

He came to a door that he thought he remembered. It was about the right shape, the right size, and the right material; and after pressing his ear to it for the better part of a minute and satisfying himself that there was a reasonable chance that there was no one on the other side, he took hold of the latch and eased it open . . . only to stare dumbfounded at a room he did not remember at all, a room that seemed to be dominated by three large staircases, which themselves seemed to lie in three mutually-perpendicular planes. It made him quite dizzy to look at them, since the risers of one were, from the orientation of another, actually treads, and vice-versa. Not to mention the third, which he could either see as a stairway in its own right, or as, quite possibly, the banister of one (or both) of the other two.

He closed the door quickly.

Lost my way. Easy to do in this darkness. Lamp? I have none, and I am unwilling to risk burning anything again. Cause suspicion. Odor already in the air . . . smoke? Fire in the Library? No: there was an odor like that earlier. Stronger now, though. Where is that kitchen? Where is the *exit*?

He peeked once more into the room beyond the door. Three stairways. And he blinked when he realized that one of the stairways was being ascended (or perhaps descended . . . it was a little hard to tell.) by a rotund figure wreathed in the pink silks of a pampered concubine.

And *he* is with *her*. And I am *here*. Food. Must find food.

And the figure was being followed by someone else, equally rotund . . .

Abnel!

Aeid (Potatoes) blinked again. But who was the figure in pink? And how (now that he looked again) were they managing to climb a single staircase in two different and simultaneous directions and at the same time follow one another?

He closed the door again and leaned against the wall beside it. His brow was moist.

Lack of food. It must be lack of food. Will bring a strong man down more quickly than anything. Submit to the necessities of nature. No choice. Judge food by its weight, like stone. Topaz! And I am looking for food for

... for *her*! And she is with *him*! I will have to find food quickly. Time enough to understand this later on.

Odor ...

Light!

With a barely suppressed gasp, he ducked behind a bookcase just in time to see Jenkins pass by, a lamp in his hand. Peeping out cautiously, he noticed that the ambassador was progressing methodically, frequently pausing in front of a bookcase and examining the titles thereon while he muttered in English.

Aeid (Potatoes) strained his ears.

"Ovid? Right time ... maybe. Maybe not. Ten thousand years? Bunch of heathens. Drought for three centuries. That's a clue right there. So ... *Divine Comedy*? Good for a start. Any order here? Hmmm?"

Jenkins? Here? But, yes, he was with the Gharat. What can he be doing? Titles ... *Divine Comedy* ... yes, that was good. Tuscan a little hard, but manageable. Much prefer Tully, though. Common-sensed man of letters. Oh, yes.

Jenkins was standing on tiptoe, checking the manuscripts on the top shelf of one of the cases. "But is there an order? Might as well be in heaps." A rustle as he pulled down a volume. "Pynchon? Who? I swear (God forgive me!) that there isn't any order, that they don't know what they're doing. But someone did. Once. Waterworks. Hmm. Pumps."

The light flashed as Jenkins turned, examining the book. Aeid (Potatoes) drew away, stood with his back pressed against a case. Pumps! So Jenkins was suspicious, too!

But of what?

"And nothing to smoke?" Jenkins was muttering as he flipped through the pages. "A brain-damaged loach? What is this?"

Answer in here somewhere. Not now. Preoccupied with food, hiding ... no time to think about opportunity ... but must find one ... The door must be nearby. Jenkins got in, but I do not think he will be going out for some time. Must find it by myself.

"Rote! I swear (God forgive me!) that it's all by rote! But who ... ?"

A grotesquely painted marionette descended from a knotted cord and perched a-straddle on Aeid's shoulder, but though at a later date, Aeid would think again and again that he should have immediately perceived its presence as at least a trifle unusual (not to mention other considerations ... such as *who* was controlling the marionette), he accepted it with the greatest equanimity, even nodding familiarly at it as it bobbed its painted head at him ...

... but then he noticed that its face bore an unmistakable resemblance to that of his father.

"Where have you been getting these ideas, my son?" the marionette demanded.

Aeid, worried that Jenkins would hear, put his finger to his lips and attempted to shush the puppet. But it scowled at him and gave him *that look*.

Seen it before. Many times. Father would look like that, and then he would give the word, and then no one would see them again. It would not do to speak of it. Women impaled. Never knew what happened to the men.

"I saw those books!"

"B-books?" whispered Aeid, still dreadfully afraid that Jenkins ...

Close by, too close, Jenkins continued to mutter: "Bunch of heathens. But ... what if it's *true*? Why, they could ... well ... flood the land when the troops try to come on shore."

... would hear. But no: the ambassador continued on, poking into books and cases until the light of his lamp was extinguished by turns and by distance.

Aeid (Potatoes) wanted to think about what Jenkins could possibly mean by *troops,* but the puppet leered at him, waggling its painted eyebrows. "You are a revolutionary, sworn to destroy the basic fabric of the life of the Three Kingdoms. I have had this thought about, and you can no longer deny it, for I have proof."

"P-proof?"

Something fell from the dark ceiling and landed at Aeid's feet. It was a sweetmeat, and, in the darkness (and no fair asking what was lighting it, either) it looked faintly accusing.

"You brought those, did you not?"

"I . . ."

In a moment, the books leaped off the shelves, threw themselves at him, lapped him around in a paper and leather prison. Aeid could not move. People seemed to be milling about in the distance.

"Hunna-hunna-hunna-hin!" they screamed accusingly (but it would have been so much better had they only done it *right*).

"But I love my father!"

There was a shaking, as of an earthquake. Pale and with bloody dagger in hand, Marcus Junius Brutus appeared, garbed in Puritan gray, stalking between the shelves of books, his face uplifted as though his blank eyes were seeing something in the impenetrable darkness. (And no fair asking . . . etc.)

"I loved Caesar," said Brutus.

"It is not the same thing at all!" said Aeid.

"What is the difference?"

"Well . . . ah . . ."

"I *told* you!" hissed the marionette.

"Told me what?"

"Your duty is to sleep with the wives of the ministers, not to bed the feminine and yielding body of the state itself!"

"My duty!"

Brutus nodded. "And mine!"

But there came, of a sudden, a flicker of light in the distance. Jenkins was returning, and with the upwelling of radiance that he brought with him, Aeid's bookish prison melted away, and Brutus faded ... but not before he pressed the dagger into the hand of the Crown Prince.

"You know what to do," he said.

"I do?"

But a weight on his shoulder distracted him, and he found the body of his father, Inwa Kabir, draped over him. With a cry, he started away, the body thudding to the floor and raising a cloud of dust and ashes.

"I did not do it! Father! Father!"

"You have killed me," said the corpse.

Brutus was gone, and as Jenkins rounded a corner, the corpse vanished, too, leaving Aeid (Potatoes) with just enough time to conceal himself behind yet another case of books.

The light from Jenkins' lamp flickered, and the sounds of the man's gray shoes passed by. Aeid (Potatoes), pressed up against the shelves, found himself examining, in the faint spill of light, a set of three scrolls that were carefully labeled with a tag:

SACRED TEXTS I
Volumes 1–3

... while on the shelf below was a set of six scrolls, to which was affixed a tag on which Aeid could make out, just as the light faded completely:

SACRED TEXTS II
Volumes 1–6
* * *

Was there any suspicion on the part of the staff members in charge of the kitchen of the Great Library of Kanez (nee Nuhr) that an individual not accounted for by the passenger manifest of the pavilion boat might have been lurking outside the windows of the kitchen?

There was none.

Was there, in fact, an individual of this sort?
There was.

Describe that individual.
A well-put-together young man of about onescore and ten years; tall, strong, regular of feature, dark of complexion and of eye, but, alas, inexpertly shaved, having, as a result of this defect, a rather disreputable appearance.

How conveyed?
By the agency of a hempen rope attached by subtle means to a projection projecting from the top of the library wall and stretching in a line of approximate straightness from the projection projecting from the top of the library wall down to the hands of the well-put-together but nonetheless disreputable-looking individual mentioned above.

With what object?
The kitchen itself.

To what end?
The acquisition of various foodstuffs in quantities sufficient to provide sustenance not only for the individual outside the window, but also for two others, not present.

To what purpose?
The preservation of life long enough to ... to ...

To what?
To achieve something not yet determined.

Describe the scene which met the eyes of the individual upon his availing himself of the open window of the kitchen in order to obtain a view of the ongoing activity within.
A large room furnished with the appurtenances appro-

priate to a well-stocked kitchen of the Three Kingdoms, including (though obviously not limited to) a large staff of chefs, apprentices, serving boys, and slaves.

With what employment was the staff of the kitchen occupying itself?

With the reordering and cleansing necessary subsequent to the conclusion of a large meal.

Had there been, in fact, a large meal served that evening?

Yes.

Was this an unusual circumstance?

In that the inhabitants of the library as a whole were dependent upon the kitchen for their nutriment, and in that those inhabitants constituted a not inconsiderable number, no. In that the number of inhabitants of the library had recently been augmented by several individuals, including the Gharat of the Three Kingdoms and the Ambassador of the Righteous States of America, and in that the status of those individuals had required a more elaborate meal and a more sumptuous display of food and beverage than would normally have been provided, yes.

Given that the number of individuals living in the library had been augmented, was there, as a result, a shortage of available food?

There was not.

A surplus?

Yes.

And how was this surplus stored?

Gradually, in dribs and drabs, by increments, in measured quantities (ounces, kilograms, scruples, liquid drams, spoonfuls, cupfuls, bucketfuls, little heaps under the stairs, etc.), it was transferred from the emptying cooking pots and pans and spits and tureens and trenchers into the filling pantries, drawers, nets, boxes, jars, and (occasionally) stomachs of the kitchen staff.

Was the individual outside the window aware of this?
Yes.

Did he attempt to prevent it?
No.

Explain this lack of initiative.
Any prophylactic efforts on the part of the individual would have resulted in discovery, and discovery would have prevented the individual from achieving his above-mentioned goal.

What then was the intent of the individual?
To wait until the staff had dispersed for the night, and then to enter into the kitchen, appropriate a portion of the surplus food, and thereafter depart without discovery.

Did this intent achieve fulfillment?
Yes and no.

Why yes?
Subsequent to their labors which had been directed toward the storage of the surplus food from the banquet, the kitchen staff did indeed disperse.

Why no?
It appeared (to the individual who was still outside the window) that it was the custom in the kitchen to leave a staff member on duty all night in order to ensure that the cooking fires would remain in a state of readiness.

Did the presence of this staff member thwart the efforts of the individual outside the window?
No.

The individual was, in fact, ultimately successful?
Yes.

Describe how the individual achieved this success.
Patience, caution, cunning.

Patience?
The individual, with firm self control, waited until the staff member was asleep.

Caution?
With stealthy movements and silent tread, the individual entered through the window and crossed the room to one of the pantries, whereupon he gathered together a bundle of surplus food sufficient to feed three.

Cunning?
Upon the inopportune awakening of the staff member, the individual stood very still inside the pantry. Upon the advance of the staff member to the pantry, the individual continued to stand very still. Upon the opening of the pantry door by the staff member, the individual, having previously observed the meager rations allotted to the staff and thereby judging that the staff member in question was looking for food, handed to the staff member an entire roast chicken, which the staff member gratefully accepted and enthusiastically ate, after which he (the staff member) fell asleep once again, thus allowing the individual to depart the kitchen precincts by means of the aperture of the window and the agency of the rope, returning, in the end, and via a circuitous route, to his companions.

And the staff member?

He rested. He dreamed.

Did any thought of announcing the presence of the individual in the pantry occur to the staff member?
No.

Explain.
It having been well established over many years that intruders of any sort were not allowed on the Isle of Kanez (Panasian law being very clear about things like that), the staff member judged that the individual in the pantry could not, by definition, have been an intruder.

Was this his only consideration?
No.

Elucidate.
The staff member, even though dreaming under the influence of an entire roast chicken, could not but contemplate the precarious position of the bearer of evil news. Nor could he keep himself from the thought that, in his experience, those who saw the least lived the longest. At the same time, he could not but harbor the friendliest of feelings toward an individual who had just presented him with an entire roast chicken, thus absolving him (the staff member) of any responsibility or guilt whatsoever involving the initial theft.

Did any communication pass between the staff member and the individual in the pantry at the time of the transfer of the above referenced roast chicken?
Yes.

Of what nature?
Statement and response.

The statement?

"Panas (blessed be He!) is good!"

The response?

"His chicken is brown and cooked!"

Chapter Six

Bakbuk knew from many years of experience with the irrationalities of palace life that holding to a specified course occasionally called for wide and sometimes unusual tacks. Thus, though Inwa Kabir had specifically named Aeid, Abnel, and the Americans as objects for her searches, the sworder, knowing very well (and cursing herself, to be sure, for her decidedly un-feminine surety) that direct inquiries after the prince, the priest, and the embassy would bear no more fruit now than they had a day or two before, resolved to turn her attentions elsewhere. In this case, to Sari, the Naian herbalist.

Distressingly enough, though, Sari proved problematical ... even enigmatic. Bakbuk devoted an entire day to inquiring about her in the Naian Quarter, but, to her surprise, the Naians of Nuhr (at least, what was left of the Naians of Nuhr, seeing as how the religion of Panas had suddenly taken on a remarkable attraction for the men (And besides, it was not something that had hurt *them*, was it?) knew nothing about the attractive herbalist. Sari had apparently arrived from nowhere (though Bakbuk, having traveled in her company, knew that she had come from Katha), and had, just as apparently, left again (much to the chagrin of the fish seller whose upper room she and her companions had rented).

But even knowing that Sari had come from Katha was

no help at all, for Bakbuk, with an efficiency she found infuriating, had previously made inquiries concerning Sari among the Naians of that city. And there the story had been much the same: Sari was a stranger who had suddenly arrived in Katha, who had said only that she was returning from a pilgrimage to the Caves of Naia.

And, as though that were not enough, it appeared, too, that there had been another Sari (tagged by Bakbuk, with an annoying upsurge of masculine logic, as Sari #1), who, also a self-proclaimed pilgrim (though, in this case, *going to* rather than *coming from* the Caves of Naia), had arrived in Katha a month or so before Sari #2 (the one who was presently in Nuhr, or, at least, who was *supposed* to be in Nuhr, but who was, possibly, not in Nuhr at all . . . but you get the idea).

Sitting up in her bed in the middle of the night, sheets clutched to her breasts (she made *sure* she was clutching them to her breasts, if only to ape, in fine woman *manqué* fashion, the supposed gestures of the female she struggled to be), Bakbuk pondered. Sari was not an overly common name. And yet two Saris (#1 and #2) had come to Katha within the space of a month, both seemingly without origins, both having something to do with the Caves of Naia.

But there the connection fell apart, for Sari #1 had been old, Sari #2, young. It made no sense. Or, if it did make sense, it made the kind of elusive, illusory sense that would (Bakbuk assured herself) fascinate only the silliest of girls.

Was that not the entire point, though? In running after Sari, grasping at tenuous connections between an old woman and a young one, Bakbuk was forgetting the Crown Prince, forgetting the Gharat and the Americans. But, then, maybe she *wanted* to forget. Maybe she *wanted* (loathsome though the thought was) not just to fail her king, but to fail him hugely, immensely, catastrophically. Only then would she be able to establish herself with utter

certainty as a dithering fool of a woman, fit for nothing
but . . .

No, not even that. Fit for nothing.

The thought was an ache in her blank groin.

But . . . but . . . why (still clutching her sheets to her
breasts here, striving to feel that looseness that she could
not but associate with the habitual and unselfconscious re-
ceptiveness she craved) had she turned so quickly away
from Aeid and the others? Perhaps Aeid himself was the
reason. Was not the lengthening absence of the Crown
Prince a kind of a reprieve for her, for did she not suspect
that he was actually—?

Sari, it appeared, had indeed served a purpose: she had
been a catalyst. In a moment, Bakbuk was up, out of bed,
on her feet, the conflict driving her into her (female)
clothes, out the door, down the hall. Tonight. She had to
know tonight. Now. There was no putting it off any longer.

Quickly, even forgetting for the moment to mince properly (she had forgotten to don her ankle fetters), she made
her way down one hallway, then another, stopping, for a
moment, to peer in at the door to the king's chamber . . .

"Oook-uk-uk-uk! Who are you?"

"Does the All Highest not recognize his slave,
Mauritah?"

"Ah, yes . . . I will make you my chief concubine. Have
your loins perfumed immediately."

"All Highest, I—"

"I will have it thought . . . er . . . er . . . er . . ."

"All Highest?"

"Erk!"

. . . and then passing on, satisfied that her king was not
only adhering to his feigned illness, but was also in good
hands. (Mauritah was known for his unimaginative but
complete devotion.)

Another hallway, and another, and finally she stopped
before the chambers of the Crown Prince.

Silently, she pushed the door open. The room was dark,

but she froze when the sound of a gasp from within told her that it was not unoccupied, and a moment later she cursed herself (but only a little: after all, she was a woman) for not having brought even a dagger with her.

But, woman though she was (or, at least, yearned to be) her instincts did not fail her, and where steel was absent, fire was easily pressed into martial service. In a moment, then, she had skipped backward into the hallway and seized a torch, and with this in her hand, she leaped into the room, eliciting yet another gasp from its occupant . . . who was, it seemed, attempting to hide and get into his clothes at the same time.

Haddar?

"Panas (blessed be He!) is good," cried the former chief minister.

"Indeed," said Bakbuk, who, without the proximity of Kuz Aswani and his strenuous devotions, could afford to backslide into her usual blend of the polite and the ironic.

Haddar was arranging his clothes, squirming a bit in the process. "I was . . . ah . . . investigating."

"Indeed." Bakbuk could not but notice that a woman's face cloth lay flaccid about Haddar's neck. "The Crown Prince's bed has been thoroughly investigated, I take it?"

"Indeed . . . ah . . . it has."

But before Haddar could say anything else—intelligible, sensible, or otherwise—his head jerked in the direction of the latticed window, and, in the light of the torch, Bakbuk could see his eyes widen.

"There!" he cried, and before Bakbuk could move, the former chief minister had grabbed the net that was lying on the floor beside the Crown Prince's bed and had dashed off in the direction of the window . . . without, unfortunately, noticing the low table that lay in front of him (the very same low table, in fact, that the Crown Prince encountered when we first met him some 750 pages ago).

Bakbuk winced as the former chief minister's shins struck the table, stared as the former chief minister turned a somersault in the air, and felt appropriately helpless as the former chief minister crashed down onto the polished marble floor (the rugs that the Crown Prince encountered some 750 pages ago having been removed some 150 pages ago) and skidded into a wall.

But, as he hit the wall, she heard, *from* the wall, an audible *snick*.

Haddar was on his feet in an instant, the net in his hands and then he was swinging the lattice wide and leaning out into the darkness, flailing.

"Almost! Almost!" he cried.

"Indeed . . ." murmured Bakbuk, who, though still intrigued by Haddar's antics, was much more intrigued by the possible source of the *snick*.

"Panas (blessed be He!) is good!" came a cheery voice from the doorway.

"Indeed . . ."

"Say it!" (It was, indeed, Kuz Aswani who had arrived.)

"His chisel is strong and hard," said Bakbuk, who had, by now, realized the futility of giving Kuz Aswani anything other than exactly what he wanted.

But the acting chief minister had noticed the presence of the former chief minister, and his face immediately assumed a look of the greatest interest, albeit compounded with something akin to calculation.

"And how is it with you, my . . . dear friend?" he said as he approached Haddar. "Has Panas (blessed be He!) been merciful to you?"

Haddar was, by now, looking very much as though he wanted to be out of the room, as though, were the way to the door to remain blocked for much longer, he would in fact consider the window to be an exceedingly viable option.

"Fine, fine," he said with a noticeable squirm. "He has been merciful to His humble servant."

"God is good!"

"Yes . . . yes . . ."

"Let me hear you say *God is good!*"

"God ... ah ... is good."

"Louder!"

And Bakbuk, edging around the two men—one zealous, one squirming—saw that, at the point in the otherwise flawless wall from which the *snick* had come, a dark hole had appeared. But she saw also that, for all the interest with which Kuz Aswani was regarding Haddar in general, he was also regarding, in particular, and with greater interest, the back of Haddar's neck.

"Perhaps ... ah ..."

And she felt a wave of lingering heat pass over her as she realized that she could not address the former chief minister by title without offending the acting chief minister ... and vice versa; and so she would have to wait until one of them spoke to her so that she could reply to him. A proper woman! Now if they would just ... two of them ... it would be ... but she ...

She pulled her thoughts back to the aperture in the wall.

"Come, my friend," Kuz Aswani was saying to Haddar, "it is late, and together we can go ... go ... go ..." He seemed to pull himself away from some potential utterance only with an effort, and to substitute for it: "... pray! Yes, pray! We can go *pray!*"

Haddar squirmed. Once again, Kuz Aswani regarded the back of his neck with the greatest of interest.

Bakbuk saw an opening. "I am sure," she said with the sincerest of simpers, "that the honored counselors will find the God receptive to their entreaties."

"Yes!" cried Kuz Aswani.

"Receptive," murmured Haddar with another squirm.

Almost as though in a dream, then, the former chief minister allowed himself to be dragged out of the room (though not by the scruff of his neck) by the acting chief minister, leaving Bakbuk precisely where she had wanted to be when she had first approached the Crown Prince's chambers. Actually, she reflected (not without a wrinkled nose of distaste at the efficiency she was showing), she was in an even better position than she had intended, for Haddar's tumble had revealed something that she would otherwise have found only with difficulty ... indeed, if she had found it at all.

Sticking her torch in a nearby holder, she knelt and peered into the aperture in the wall. It was obviously some kind of private storage cabinet. That in itself was nothing unusual: the palace had many such things, and they held everything from, doubtless, the poison that had been administered to Inwa Kabir by someone (and she could not but wonder who that someone was) to, even more doubtless, the extensive cache of raisins presently kept by Kuz Aswani (about which no more need be said).

But this cabinet held neither poison (as she originally— and simultaneously—hoped and feared that it would) nor raisins, nor any one of a hundred other things that might have been contained within a secret cupboard. Instead, when Bakbuk reached into the opening, she found a mass of cloth that proved, upon extraction, to be a strange garment of some sort.

"Not well sewn," she sniffed. "It would take a woman's hand to—"

But then she caught her breath, for she suddenly realized that in her hands was a fantastic costume of tatters, and there was also a mask (Do not forget the mask!), as well as boots. And all of it, every last stitch of it, was blue.

"Panas (blessed be He!) is good!"
"His tool is of the greatest sharpness!"

What is he up to now? Is he looking for proof? Of what? Did he see ... it? Panas (blessed be He!) knows it has been almost *What is he up to now? Is he looking for an escape from the inevitable? Or, perhaps, for ... him? Panas (blessed be He!) can save him but everywhere. Or is he merely trying to frighten me into some kind of an admission? Well, he will find this chief minister to be made of sterner (though, I should say, still extremely feminine) stuff than that. I can easily withstand his wiles.*

only if he is strong and guiltless. And I no longer believe that he is entirely guiltless. Very convenient, I think: the prince missing and possibly defecating in corners, and Haddar pretending he knows nothing about it.

"Panas (blessed be He!) is merciful!"
"He protects us from evil of . . . of all kinds."

And why, might I ask (being a clever chief minister) should he be employing any wiles at all? Could it be that he has something, perhaps, to . . . hide? Eh? A little something? Such as a secret identity? A criminal background? Surely my discovery of something of the sort would count for a bit more in the estimation of the king (and truly, I wish for the king's speedy recovery, and my attentions to the bed of the Crown Prince cannot but demonstrate my . . . ah . . . devotion to that sublime young man) than a . . . ah . . . weakness on the part of his chief minister.

And why, might I ask (being a man, and not . . . not something else), should he be pretending he knows nothing about it? Could it be that he is hiding something? Eh? Surely he is criminal enough, having had dealings with sorcerers and magicians (as he surely must have, else he would not be . . . well, enough said about that), but ever since he flinched at the mention of the Blue Avenger, I cannot but surmise that something else is going on. And he was in the room of the Crown Prince. The reason? Nothing, I am sure, that has anything to do with devotion!

"Panas (blessed be He!) is our help in time of need!"
"His shield is broad and . . . and . . . and impenetrable!"

But . . . but . . . but . . . is that it? Lurking over there in the shadows? Did he bring me here so as to confront me with it? And if, at the same time, he knows about the device, then I am surely lost. But if I can get an admission from him, then I will not only be safe myself (For what is the word of a criminal and an impersonator of the chief minister against that of the chief minister himself . . . even though the chief minister is . . . well, enough said about that for now.), but I will have fame and the gratitude of the king as well!

But . . . but . . . but . . . is that him? Lurking over there in the shadows? Has he come to attempt his magics upon me again? If Haddar is helping him, then surely I am lost; but if Panas (blessed be He!) is willing to continue to be merciful (and I am brave enough to continue to be strong in my faith), then I might yet triumph against both, and any defense they might attempt will be to no avail, since they have attacked the Crown Prince. And I—a man—will not only be chief minister but will have the favor and gratitude of the king as well!

"Panas (blessed be He!) is great!"

"But . . . but you said that already."

"Say it!"

"What?"

"Say it!"

"Panas . . . (blessed be He!) . . ."

"Say it!"

". . . is great."

"Louder!"

You like Eco? Yeah, I like him, too. He's a pretty cool dude. You know, professor of semantics. Or something like that. Oh, yeah, I've read all his stuff. Everything. Even his . . . even his, like, papers and things that he does

for school. I like to find the symbolism in it all. Like the
... uh ... *The Name of the Rose*. That's it. You ever read
that one? Pretty cool, huh? The way they're trying to find
the rose all the way through the book, and it turns out to
be a copy of the Bible? Or something like that. Oh, yeah,
I've read all his stuff. On account of he's so hot. That's
what I do, you know: I read other writers to see what
they're doing. I mean, they don't have much to teach
someone like me, but you never know.

Yeah, that's right: I'm a writer. I've got scripts all over
the place, and I'm getting real close to some big contracts.
I just gotta be patient. You know, being patient is the hard-
est thing about this writing biz. Pretty soon, though, something's gonna come through, and then it's going to be the
big time for me. I'm doing OK, though, no thanks to my
ex-girlfriend. The *bitch*. Sponged off me for months, then
dumped me as soon as I needed some help from her. You
want to talk about standing in the way of progress? Typical. That's all I can say. Just typical.

Not that I'm against women or anything like that. It's
just that, like, art is a man's thing. It just stands to reason.
Women have other things to do that are a lot more important. To them, I mean. Now, I'd be the last guy to run
women down, but it's not my fault if the things they're interested in don't have a lot of staying power. I guess some
gotta win and some gotta lose, and you just can't kowtow
to everyone who wants to make you responsible for the
fact that they got problems like some of those skanky
libbers. Not that women have problems or anything. It's
just that I'd think it was a problem, too, if I bled for five
days every month and didn't die.

Hey, no offense or anything. It was just a joke. I'm that
kind of a guy, you know. The writing biz is tough, but you
gotta keep your sense of humor about it. That's why I do
a lot of reading. On account of the perspective it gives
you. You know: perspective. 'Cause that's kind of like humor. Perspective. Yeah. Something like that.

But you gotta tell me ... how long you been reading Eco? You read that pendulum thing he did? Yeah, that was really hot. Especially where they build the pendulum, and then they hide the map. Yeah ... well, something like that. It's been a while. It's kind of hard to keep track of it all when you read five or six books a night. Sure, I'm always reading. It's important for a writer, you know. But *Name of the Rose* is the big one in my book. I mean, the guy whatsisname Eco was really strutting his stuff, if you know what I mean. All that Latin stuff. It was great. No, I don't read Latin, but I understood it and all. I mean, it was obvious, wasn't it? The whole rose thing? Something like that.

Anyway, I'm kind of taking a tip from Eco and doing a lot of that stuff in this screenplay I'm writing. It's gonna be a big one, you know, and I want to really impress people, on account of impressing people is the way you get ahead in this business. I mean, you can go out there with crap like elves in the forest and woman-takes-revenge-for-getting-raped shit like some people do, but all they're gonna get out of it is a big, first-class ticket to Zeroville, 'cause it's just not interesting. And if it isn't interesting, it's not gonna fly. Not that I've got anything against women, you know. Hey, I can sympathize with that whole rape thing. I mean, if some great big queerball came and gave me the business, I'd be pretty steamed, too. I'm just talking about the concept in, like, books and films. Which is what's important here. It's like art. Guy stuff. You know.

But we were talking about Eco. Here. Look ... right here ... lemme find it. Here's the diagram of the library that the dude did. Isn't it great? I mean, they let him put a picture in his book and everything. You can tell he's really hot, too. And that library is, like, laid out in a *cross*, for crying out loud. That tells you that it's got all these mystical meanings. Something like that. Which is what you gotta expect on account of the guy's a professor of

semilonix ... sym ... uh ... something like that. I mean,
he's real bright.

So I did that, too. 'Course, the doobs will never let me
put a map in a screenplay, on account of the union's got
them all by the nuts, and if there's gonna be a map in the
thing it's, like, gotta be *their* map, with all the printers'
unions getting involved and shit like that. But that doesn't
stop me from slipping in the stuff when they're not looking. So, you see, what I did is model the library in my
stuff after the library in Eco's book. It's like an acknowl-
edgment, you see what I mean?

See, I did the thing with the library, and I have the
towers at each corner of the big square. And I've got a
well-type thing in the middle. I've even got a blind librarian! You know, that's real symbolic, too, 'cause I wanted
to show that I understand what Eco was doing.

And I'm telling you, I had to do a lot of research for
this thing. You know, there was tons of local color stuff I
had to find out about (not that the Hollywood boys know
much about that, on account of they just open a bunch of
canned sets and use those, 'cause they're all just a bunch
of fags, and what the hell do they know, anyway?), and
since I wanted to put the library in, I had to come up with
library stuff, too. But it was pretty easy. Do you come here
pretty often? Yeah, I thought I recognized you. I had you
pegged for one of those intelligent girls right off. You
know: the ones that get the grunt work out of the way so
that their men can concentrate on the important things. Not
that grunt work isn't important. I mean, if it wasn't for
grunt work, then the important stuff wouldn't get done
now, would it? So, you see? Doesn't that make you feel
good? Hey, I'm the kind of guy that's perfectly willing to
admit that someone else has to support him in order for
him to get his job done. I'm not one of those chauvinists
who think they can do it all. I mean, it's a partnership,
right?

Anyway, so there's the library, and I've got the library

stuff, and . . . oh, yeah, there's that section in *Name of the Rose* where they're all doing acid? Something like that? Well, I've got drugs in my stuff, too, but I did Eco one better by slipping it in real subtle early on. Probably no one will notice it at first, but when it finally comes up you can bet there'll be a bunch a people going *Oh, yeah, isn't he hot?* and I'm not one to brag or anything but I think it's pretty hot, too. Don't you? You're the one who reads all this Eco stuff, and you ought to know, right? Sure you do! And you understand about writers and everything, on account of that, too. Sure you do! You know, I don't meet too many women who are as intelligent as you are. Not that I've got anything against women or anything like that. It's just that most of them wouldn't understand this stuff. Like my ex-girlfriend. You know: the *bitch*. She didn't understand anything about me. She even threw me out of my own apartment. And I swear that she's still got it in for me and everything, 'cause I can't find a place that'll rent to me anymore. Yeah, I been living out of my car, and I sure could use a place to call my own. You know, so I can get this writing done and shipped off so that all that money can start coming in. And I'll tell you, there's gonna be lots of money, on account of I've got this whole screenwriter gig in the bag. You can see that it's going to go over with those film guys like gangbusters. As soon as I have a phone, they're gonna be calling me, but if I don't have a phone, they can't call, so there's no money.

Listen, you're an intelligent girl. Like I've been saying, you've got this stuff all figured out. It's like a relationship, and, let's face it, a woman just isn't complete without a man in her life, just like a man's not complete without a woman. Sure you haven't lived with a screenwriter before. I can tell that. Anyone can tell that. But how do you know you don't like it if you haven't tried it? Tell me that, huh?

So what do you say? I mean, this is your chance to get

onto easy street, on account of the bucks are going to start rolling in real soon now. I mean, how could I avoid getting rich off this stuff? And another thing—

Hey! Same to you! Bitch!

Chapter Seven

The firm cradling of the screws. The pancranial enfoldment of iron grillwork. The metallic tang of the goad in his mouth. The hobbling rustle of skirts about his legs as he went from stove to churn to needle *and could not speak.*

Enforced humility. Wilting before his master's presence. Stripped of will and power both, and naked before the law as before God. His hair and his breasts outward emblems of the inner shame of guilty thoughts, guilty actions, biological breed and lust abominably commingled in the Devil's work. Just punishment.

Straps . . .

Lash . . .

A sudden, burning fullness in his groin, and Jenkins awoke, his seed hot on his thighs. Stiffling a gasp, he sat up, rolling onto his back as consciousness sifted back to him, rolling to keep the smear of his shame from staining the linen sheets and telling . . . all.

From the darkness of the far corner of the room, a voice intoned solemnly:

"Awake for me *to* the judgment *that* thou hast commanded."

"Be quiet, Wool!"

* * *

It *was* an island, and it *was* the Great Library.

Potatoes made his report to Sari and Beshur while they ate. In searching out the kitchen, the thief had been forced into considerable exploration, and he had arrived at the conclusion that the core edifice had not been so much built as hollowed out of a mountain in the middle of the island, with subsequent masonry construction attaching walls, towers, outbuildings, and so on until the mountain was essentially lost beneath something that resembled a huge fortress.

"Four-sided," Potatoes explained between mouthfuls. "With a seven-sided tower at each corner, of which two sides are, of course, lost by their conjunction with the main structure . . ."

—*Five*-sided towers, then, Beshur interrupted.

"Well, five extant sides," Potatoes admitted. "But the proportions indicate the *intent* of seven sides."

—Intent, Beshur disagreed, is inadmissible. The reality must be argued by the fact. Therefore: *five* sides.

"It is obvious that there is an *inference* of seven sides."

—It is just as obvious from your report that the builders only *made* five.

"It is a matter of *proportion*."

—It is a matter of *fact*.

Potatoes and Beshur glared at one another, neither willing to yield the argument in the slightest. Sari, wearying of the conflict, finally spoke up: "Go on, Potatoes."

Potatoes swallowed his chicken quickly, obviously in order to head off Beshur, who would, doubtless, interrupt him with yet another completely idiotic comment about five-sided towers. "There is an eight-sided well in the middle." He glared again at Beshur. "I *counted* them."

Beshur shrugged and stuffed a piece of bread into his mouth, managing, somehow, to infuse both actions with a sense of derision. Obviously, the arithmetical abilities of someone so completely idiotic as to be unable to distinguish between a five-sided (real) tower and a seven-sided (imaginary) tower were so lacking as to preclude any kind of an accurate assessment as to the octagonality of an inner well.

Potatoes ignored him. "It is truly amazing. The edifice now covers almost a third of the island."

—Krlthrulthug, Beshur said quickly ... so quickly, in fact, that he had not quite managed to swallow his mouthful of bread and thus produced the strange aural effect just reported.

"What?"

—Kanez, Beshur repeated ... without the obstruction of the bread.

"Kanez?"

—That, Beshur said (again with a shrug that indicated his low opinion of the arithmetical abilities of certain individuals), is the name of the island.

"Oh, of course." Given the tone of Potatoes' voice, low opinions, it appeared, were extremely widespread.

—Just as you expected, I expect, Beshur said, but I do not care about that. I looked into some scrolls while you were gone, and I came upon a map. This island is called Kanez.

"Kanez ... Kanez ..." Potatoes chewed thoughtfully, looking even more disreputable than usual in the faint moonlight that filtered in through the high windows. "I believe I have heard that name before."

—Oh, Beshur sneered, of course.

Sari was drooping, but not from hunger or fatigue ... at least, not any longer. Rather, it was Potatoes' report that had wilted her. Assigned, by the Goddess Herself, the task of restoring the Caves, she was now a virtual prisoner on a virtually unknown island.

"What were you looking at manuscripts for?" Potatoes suddenly demanded. "That was very dangerous—"

—I am a *scholar*, Beshur snapped. It is my *business* to look at manuscripts.

"Oh, of course," said Potatoes. "A *scholar*. How careless of me. I must have forgotten, what with all the talk I have heard about acquisitive heathens."

And Sari's despondency deepened as she was reminded once again that she was not so much a help to the two men as an object of contention.

—I said *manuscripts*—

"And understood them all, I imagine. Just like a proper scholar."

Sari had reached her limit. "Beshur *is* a scholar, Potatoes. Please stop mocking him."

But Beshur, pale in the moonlight, now went even paler.

—How . . . how . . . how . . .

"Do not ask details, I beg you," she said. "Just accept that I know."

Beshur's pallor increased, though Sari had not thought that possible.

—How . . . how . . . how . . .

"Now, both of you stop fighting," she said. "I am here because the Goddess sent me, and I will not have you interfering."

But *that* brought her back to the same questions: What was she doing here, and how was it that the Goddess had sent her? As before, she could only conclude that, as she was young because she was supposed to be, so she was *here* because she was supposed to be, and the only thing for her to do was to go on to the next *here*.

Wherever that was.

"What else did you find out, Beshur?" she said, supposing that knowing where she was might give her some clue as to where she was supposed to be next.

—How . . . how . . . how . . .

"Beshur," said Potatoes, "you know that I am a thief. If you can be condemned for some reason, then so can I. Now what else did you find out?"

Sari lifted her head, optimistic for the first time in weeks. "Thank you, Potatoes."

A (slightly too) bright smile. Potatoes' teeth (which

looked surprisingly good for belonging to such a disreputable-looking thief) gleamed. "Of course, lovely lady! It is my *pleasure*!"

Sari dropped her head again. Oh. Oh, yes. That.

But whatever else he was, Beshur was indeed a scholar, and, to his credit, he put aside thoughts of competition for the attentions of the attractive Naian girl long enough to . . .

Well, at least he *appeared* to put aside thoughts of competition for the attentions of the attractive Naian girl.

. . . describe what he had found.

—You understand, he said, that true scholarship takes time, and I did not have much time. Nor was I working under . . .

He cleared his throat.

—. . . the most ideal conditions. But I found a map. This island is about 30 leagues southwest of Nuhr. About 15 leagues due west of the coast.

Potatoes was pondering. "I believe I have heard rumors of its existence."

Beshur glared at him.

Potatoes waved his hand. "Oh . . . somewhere. It is not important."

Beshur sniffed.

Sari sighed.

Beshur hastened to resume.

—The library was built in accordance with the dictates of the Sacred Texts.

Potatoes appeared to recollect something, and was lifting a finger to speak when Beshur forged on.

—It contains all knowledge of every sort, and is connected with the mainland only by the pavilion boat by which we arrived.

Sari looked up. "So there is no way back to Nuhr save by the boat?"

Beshur preened. Just a little.

—Well . . . yes. That is true."

"What about the sea?" she pressed.

"There are cannon," said Potatoes.

Sari felt that she must have looked completely blank at that point. Which was quite logical, since she felt that way, too. "C-cannon? But I thought—"

"For Panas," Potatoes said, "all things are possible." His voice sounded surprisingly bitter to Sari. But he went on: "It was the cannon that we heard earlier. They were being tested, I assume. So a boat coming or going would be fired upon immediately. Assuming, that is, that we could find a boat in the first place. Unless we can find out how to operate the pavilion boat, therefore, we are trapped here."

Beshur blinked.

—Trapped? he said. Amid so much wealth? You might as well speak of starving at a feast! I am a scholar, and—

"Yes, yes," said Potatoes. "We know all about acquisitive heathens. Thank you. Two of us, however, are not scholars, and urgent matters call us back to Nuhr. How does the boat operate?"

Beshur spluttered for a moment, but:

—The scrolls I found do not say. The boat and the tunnel were built many years ago, and the knowledge is secret.

"Despite the claim that the library contains all knowledge of every sort." There was an ominous tone in Potatoes' voice.

It was plain to Sari that Potatoes thought that Beshur intended to keep them on the island against their will. "I am sure it does," she said quickly. "Including knowledge that will allow us to return to the mainland."

Potatoes looked doubtful, suspicious.

"Besides," she said, "we would risk discovery were we to attempt to use the pavilion boat without knowing how it works."

Potatoes looked very much like the most recalcitrant

camel of Ehar's caravan faced with a choice between further recalcitrance and a confrontation with Oued.

But then: "It works by water, does it not?"

—Yes, Beshur said. By water.

"With pumps?"

—The text does not say.

Potatoes turned away. "Pumps. Pumps," he muttered. "Something about pumps. And the land."

Sari recalled the words the Gharat had uttered in his delirium and felt a chill that had nothing to do with the equatorial night. Why had Naia brought her here? She was beginning to sense the vague outline of a reason, and, despite her misgivings, she was suddenly almost glad that the way back to Nuhr remained, for the present, barred.

"We will have to stay, then," said Potatoes as though he had reached some resolve that extended beyond the obvious. "I will gather food and drink as we need it. I will also look for signs that the Gharat and the Americans might be departing, so that we can hide in the pavilion boat and leave as we came. And I will assist Beshur with his scholarly work."

Beshur looked offended.

—What can a common thief possibly—?

A hiss from Potatoes cut him off. "As I told you once before, it is obvious that I am an extremely good thief, and I can therefore be expected to know much more than you might think. We will work together. I have some . . . questions . . . of my own."

. . . so now I have shown him almost everything there are still the Quarries but I do not think that he would be able to understand them have to know the entire plan first and I do not wish 300 years of work to go to sandstone my plan would be much better of course but they would not let me and I hope they at least continue to collect the taxes in Nuhr cannot be there to supervise because I am here with Jenkins but I believe they will be collected and the king will die there is nothing that can save him Naian idiots with their vegetables might as well stick pumice up his ass hmmm must think about that Rosebud would look very nice and then those effeminate fools in Katha who do nothing but drink coffee all day will see just what can be done with a little imagination and Rosebud certainly has had some imagining done for him he did look fine hmmm pumice I wonder in the device and I do not think that I hurt him that badly and where was Jenkins I would like to see what kind of an imagination *he* has but he was not in his room and what was he doing well I will have to show Jenkins as much as I need to in order for him to tell me the secret and then I will return to Nuhr and continue with the tax and arrange the king's burial and I must not forget the Crown Prince I am sure a hole can be found for him somewhere I think that I can manage that much and I have obviously given the Blue Avenger the slip he has not appeared in Nuhr since I returned from Katha thinks he is so clever whoever he is but I have duped him and the priests of Katha think they are so clever too but I have proved them wrong and within a few years I will have the Three Kingdoms where I want them and where *was* Jenkins and why has he not said anything perhaps he is too awestruck what else could it be he will certainly have no more excuse for thinking ill of us and I do hope Mather recovers that was very fine I am sure that he will be ready tonight and the bruises are nothing I have been bruised much worse than that and have even lost some blood but he seems more and more reluctant and I must be careful with him until he realizes that he wants what I want and there is no doubt about it but why is Jenkins not telling me what I want . . .

The hours between midnight and dawn were long ones, and Mr. Jenkins, deserted by sleep, could only lie awake amid the linens of his Panasian bed. But, in truth, he could well have pronounced his affliction a blessing, for, with

Wool asleep and Mather . . . Mather . . . Mather . . . ah . . . somewhere else, doing . . . ah . . . *something,* it meant that he would be free of distractions, whether of the Biblical or the "squirmical" variety, and he could therefore indulge in methodical thought and deliberation with some assurance that the thoughts would be unbroken and the deliberations uninterrupted.

Of the essential ineffectuality of the technics of the Three Kingdoms, Jenkins had at last assured himself. Where the copying being done by the scribes of the island was obviously no more than pure, ignorant, imitation (Bodoni!), even his first, tentative explorations of the maze of bookshelves and rooms that constituted the actual collection had convinced him that this library, though great and comprehensive and complete almost beyond belief, was, in fact, no more than a titanic mausoleum for entombed—and unused—knowledge.

Abnel, he was sure, had sought to impress him. Well, he had indeed been impressed. In fact, if disdain and contempt counted for being impressed, then Jenkins could well say that he grew increasingly impressed with each passing hour.

But the question remained: *Why* did Abnel wish to impress him?

Already the infallible religious leader of three countries, Abnel was now, in addition, the acting king. It was an enviable position, one which President Winthrop (who, all unknown to the heathens of these lands, battled every day with schisms and heresies in the Righteous States) could well envy. Yet, still, Abnel wanted something so badly that he was willing to break the secrecy in which the library had hitherto been shrouded.

What could it be? He already *had* absolute power.

And it was in contemplating Abnel's (enviable but impious) position that the thought suddenly flashed upon Jenkins that the illness of King Inwa Kabir—the illness that, concurrent with a similar indisposition on the part of the

Crown Prince, had fixed Abnel as the supreme arbiter of
the Three Kingdoms—was, in all probability, not an illness
at all. At least, not a natural one.

    . . . but I will not be able to stay here long because
events in Nuhr the king might even be dead by now happened all the time in Abramelin's day so why not revive
the practice now Panas is supreme and the Gharat should
be supreme also who knows where the kingship came
from must be some kind of unnatural addition probably
from Katha the king has always been a mere figurehead in
any case but he was interfering and there is no doubt that
it was time for him to die but if he is dead then I had better return immediately no excuse for allowing some idiot
minister whose wife goes about without her headwrap *in
the HOUSE* to claim the kingship would just be that much
harder oh he was hard that night perhaps I should go look
in on him no he needs his rest I will leave him alone until
tonight to gather the power into my hands though what
minister would be fool enough to go against the will of the
Gharat would be a proper fool just like the fool who is
probably dead but if I leave now then Jenkins will not
have time to see what he needs to see and he will not tell
me what I must do in order to put a minister in their heads
oh it will be wonderful putting it in yes putting it deep into
their heads but I must work quickly but where was he oh
so very deep and he did look fine during the night . . .

    He had, unknowingly, witnessed a coup.
    Had Jenkins been a cursing man (which he was not;
and, in any case, Wool was lying on the other side of the
room, doubtless ready, despite being asleep, to add one of
his infuriating glosses to any ejaculation on the part of the
ambassador), he would have cursed out loud. What a fool
he had been! And it had happened right under his nose!
Abnel obviously had the subtlety of an adder, to strike so

smilingly and so self-effacingly ... neutralizing even the perspicacity of an American diplomat!

But Jenkins paused abruptly in the middle of his violent non-cursing. Why, after contriving to gain for himself ultimate power, would Abnel then *leave*? Surely the Gharat understood that creating a gaping hole at the top of a disorganized government invited the first stalwart with forethought and will to rush in and fill it!

But he had left. In an apparent attempt to impress a foreigner. (What *did* he want, anyway?) It made no sense. But, then, *nothing* made any sense. Technology cast off like an out-of-fashion shirt, manuscripts and books copied without comprehension (or desire to comprehend), knowledge hidden away from any possible use, a stagnating piss-hole of a land with a know-nothing king, a fool of a Crown Prince, bafflingly reactionary ministers, a perverted High Priest ... it was all madly contrary to the will of God, and Jenkins was growing ever more determined to bring it into conformity with righteousness.

And that made the question of Abnel's absence all the more critical, for if the Gharat allowed the government of the country to slip away from him, then all Jenkins' efforts, including his sacrifice of the prurient Mather, would prove to have been for nothing, and the American troops, when they arrived, would be faced with, at best, local authorities outside the control of Jenkins or, at worst, a belligerent government and a hostile countryside through which they would have to fight and garrison their way before they could even consider making a crossing of the mountains in order to fall upon Bonaparte's unsuspecting army.

Suddenly, Jenkins' suspicions about pumps and water seemed not quite so important. In any case, he was certain that any revelations concerning the two would prove to be, in the end, as incontrovertible a statement of backward ignorance as everything else in the country. If the Mountains of Ern held some kind of a secret (and it was more than

obvious that they *did*), then American engineers and
American soldiers would find out what it was in good time
... and would, doubtless, turn it to their advantage. But
they would be able to do nothing at all if Abnel were not
both in charge and under firm, American control; and Jenkins sensed that, Mather notwithstanding, the Gharat
would be neither if he did not get what he wanted and return as soon as possible to Nuhr.

But what *did* he want?

"I've got to get him back to Nuhr," Jenkins muttered.
"I've got to figure out what he wants, give it to him, and
get him back to Nuhr."

"For thou hast cast all my sins behind thy back," came
the mournful response out of the darkness.

... that is a question I must answer but then there is
Rosebud and I am unwilling to neglect him I am sure that
the ambassador can take care of his own sleeping arrange-
ments he could not possibly be as good but he should be
watched so that he does not get among the books it might
be dangerous but it might be good too for then he would
be all the more impressed and I must take care not to of-
fend him for he has the knowledge that I desire I wish that
he would come to his senses and tell me what I need to
know for without the king it would all be complete within
a few years and Jenkins will be even more impressed a
minister in their heads and where is Rosebud ...

"Kisses, my love!"
Mather screamed.
"His kisses are flowers!"
Mather screamed.
"Flowers for the fairest!"
Mather screamed.

Chapter Eight

"Ship ahoy! What ship's that?"

The call, piercing, unbelievably clear, came drifting across the water from what seemed an impossible distance, though Elijah Scruffy knew that the man who made it had been trained to make himself heard over gale force winds.

"*Seaflower*! What ship's that?"

"*Witch of Endor!*"

Witch of Endor was a trim little English cutter, her ten guns—six-pounders—burnished and cared for as though they had been well-scrubbed children. In fact, so small, trim, and bright did *Witch of Endor* appear as she lay hove-to a cable's length from *Seaflower* that, compared with the burly, American efficiency of the double-frigate (and, for that matter, even of *Speedwell*, which was hanging just upwind), she looked not quite so much like a ship of the British navy as an intricate little piece of clockwork.

Both ships had their gun ports open and their guns run out. Hostilities between the Righteous States and England had been over and gone for a hundred years, but in these days of French privateers, blockade runners, and a fleet on the loose from Toulon (and Scruffy wagered privately that while the president and the Synod had known from the beginning that Bonaparte was bound for Egypt, the king and Parliament had not), it was best not to take chances.

But no, *Witch of Endor* was just what she appeared to

be (an English ship, not a piece of clockwork), and, in five minutes, the crews of both ships had secured the guns, and the English captain was being pulled across in his boat.

Scruffy met him at the entry port as the pipes twittered and Lieutenant Cuttle ordered his Marines to attention. On a British ship, there would have been, in addition, a number of officers, a firing of guns, at the very least an assortment of midshipmen to doff their hats; but *Seaflower,* for all Scruffy's clandestine reading and thinking, was a Puritan ship. Admiral and commander alike received courteous but reserved ceremony, and so there were Cuttle and his Marines, and that was that.

Commander James Gallant was something of an intricate little piece of clockwork himself, his (new) uniform trim and sharp, his (new) epaulette on his left shoulder gleaming with the shine of (new) gold plating, the (new) gilt of his buttons and lace worn away only a little to show the (relatively new) brass beneath. Gallant was all efficiency, brightness, courtesy, and curiosity ... this last being with regard to the American double-frigate itself, though Scruffy thought privately (How he hated the requirements of diplomacy! Give him a good, bluff, openhearted, and frank exchange over this ask-me-no-questions-I'll-tell-you-no-lies business he was involved in at present!) that it probably extended to what, exactly, an American double-frigate was doing in these waters.

Well, though Gallant would be satisfied as to the former, Scruffy would see to it that he remained frustrated as to the latter. The Righteous States kept its own counsel. In fact, in Scruffy's opinion, the Righteous States sometimes kept its own counsel a bit too well for him to feel entirely comfortable.

"God bless me," Gallant said, striding up to Scruffy and sticking out his hand, "but I never thought I'd see the day that I'd set foot on an American frigate! My Lord! What a sight!"

Had Jenkins been aboard, Scruffy would have gladly allowed him to attend to the business, but since the ambassador had remained in Nuhr, Scruffy alone was in command. There was no getting out of it.

"Commander Gallant," he murmured as he took the Englishman's hand, "I must remind you that this is a Puritan ship. 'Thou shalt not take the name of the Lord thy God in vain.' "

Gallant colored. "Awfully decent of you to remind me, Captain Scruffy," he said. "We've been at sea for six months now"—

Six months, Scruffy noted. And much too far away from the coast of France for blockade duty. Returning to England? Dispatches?

—"and we all wind up getting a bit coarse, don't we? Thought you'd agree. Easy enough to forget that I'm on a Roundhead ship . . . ah . . ."

Gallant's voice trailed off as he glanced right and left. Somber black was everywhere, and not a wig nor even a braid or a ponytail was in sight. Turtletrout, standing nearby, put his hands into his pockets and stared at Commander Gallant in his dull, slope-headed way.

"You don't mind the term, I hope?" Gallant ventured. "It's become a fond one over the years, I assure you."

"Of course," said Scruffy, bluff and good-natured as always. "I'm sure you'll hear us talk of *degenerate idolaters*. It's the same thing. Pure affection."

Gallant blinked, but he nodded. "A century heals all wounds, I'm sure."

"Sartainly," Scruffy agreed with the greatest amiability. "Can I offer you some grub?"

"Ah . . ." Commander Gallant looked worried. "Grub?"

"Some lunch?"

Gallant looked relieved. "I look forward to it with the greatest pleasure!"

With the departure of Jenkins and his staff (and Scruffy thought once again of the secretary, Mather, and his strange penchant for figures and the heights of mountain ranges), Scruffy's cabin had been restored from its previously microscopic dimensions to its full, minuscule size. Museum cases were back in place, curiosities were carefully arranged on shelves, and all was in order ... though Scruffy could not help but glance quickly at his bed. Good: all made up, neat and clean, like a good, godly captain's bed should be.

Seaflower was a frigate, true, but she was an American frigate, and Scruffy was secretly (There it was again!) amused by Commander Gallant's reaction to the plain fare set before him at the table of what was, in British terms, nearly a full ship of the line.

"Some boiled cabbage, Commander Gallant?" Scruffy offered.

"Ah ... ah ... thank you, yes," said Commander Gallant.

"The boiled ribs are very good," Scruffy continued as the ship's cook, playing the part of steward, chiseled off a piece of meat and set it on his plate. "Crayley will be glad to give you some."

"You're ever so kind, Captain Scruffy."

"Some boiled salt pork? It's very good."

"Thank you, sir."

Crayley was just then prying off another rib. Gallant's plate rang like a bell when the meat dropped onto it.

Gallant looked pale.

"Some rum, Commander Gallant?"

"Yes!" Gallant said quickly. "Yes, please!"

But the food, though plain (and, to be honest, a trifle tough) was, as usual, good, and Gallant had no real cause for complaint. Nor, really, did Scruffy, for his "grub" with the English commander gave him the opportunity to acquire something that had, in the course of his voyage, been pitifully lacking, something far more desirable to him than rum was to Gallant: news.

"Fan*tas*tic ship you have here, Captain Scruffy," Gallant

was running on. "Simply marvelous. I've been looking forward ever so much to visiting an American frigate"—

"Double-frigate," Scruffy corrected affably.

"Heard so much about them. And there was that race in the Barbados. A cask of Madeira, wasn't it?"

"Rum," Scruffy corrected patiently, refilling Gallant's tumbler.

"Indeed? Thought it was Madeira," Gallant went on enthusiastically, "but you Roundheads don't like the elegant stuff, do you? Didn't think so. Plain people, plain clothes, plain tastes. But that's what's made you all what you are, isn't it?"

And on and on, Gallant sailing large before a freshening wind of garrulousness while Scruffy supplied rum and vainly attempted to steer the conversation through to the war between France and England.

"But about this *double*-frigate, you'll have to tell me the difference. We're all so unimaginative in England. Build 'em right the first time, and then you don't have to start experimenting with anything else. One ship of the line much like another. Man on the quarter-deck is what makes the difference *I've* always said. I suppose you build 'em stronger?"

" 'Em?" said Scruffy, trying to take a bearing in the gale, and wondering bemusedly about the construction of men on quarter-decks.

"Double-frigates, to be sure. Scantlings are *pret*-ty sturdy from what I can see, and I suppose you can pile on the canvas when you want to, though I'd think you'd perhaps pile on a little too much? But, then, that's where the scantlings come in, ain't it? And there was that race for the cask of Madeira"—(This time, Scruffy's correction was blown away by the storm.)—"wasn't there? Damme"—(This time, Scruffy's admonishment that *Seaflower* was a Puritan ship was also blown away by the storm.)—"if your ship didn't scorch the foaming billers.

One of the officers who was on board our ship told me that. A*ma*zing! Simply a*ma*zing! Hull down by afternoon!"

But at the end of this gust, Gallant, involved in downing some of what he obviously (and enthusiastically, to be sure) considered to be a tumblerful of excellent rum (And who would have expected something like that from a bunch of Roundheads?), was silent long enough for Scruffy to get athwart his hawse.

"What about Bonaparte?" he said in his bluff, affable way. "Did our degenerate idolater brothers across the Atlantic manage to track him down?"

Commander Gallant smiled at Scruffy's use of the affectionate term. "Oh!" he laughed (enthusiastically). "Oh! Yes! It was wonderful. Took Malta, but they're a bunch of effeminate louts there anyway, so who cares about them? Damme"—(The reader will kindly infer Elijah Scruffy's efforts to weather the storm in this and all subsequent occasions of ungodly profanity.)—"if they didn't wind up in Egypt!"

"You don't say," said Scruffy, who, already knowing, was caught somewhere between admiration for and dismay at the effectiveness of American intelligence.

"Oh, Lord, but I do!" Gallant stormed on. "Frogs didn't have the nerve to take on John Bull man to man, so they turned on the heathens of Egypt. God bless me, but they landed and took Alexandria!"

"The library," nodded Scruffy. "Tragic loss, that."

"Well," Gallant went on, "they must have knocked over a thing or two, mind you, but I can't say for sure if it was the library."

Scruffy sighed, and with his own hands he plied the commander with a little more rum.

But Commander Gallant already had a good wind behind him, and, with the administration of the rum, he shook out another reef in his sails and plunged onward while Scruffy manned the helm. Abukir. Anchorage. The French fleet swinging at its anchors. Enough channel for the English fleet to slip in. Fleet destroyed. Bonaparte trapped in Egypt.

"Brilliant man, your Nelson," said Scruffy when the storm had blown itself out. His eyes were closed as he imagined what it must have looked like—and sounded like—when the *Orient* had blown up, but a *thump* opened them, and he discovered that Gallant was face down on the table, unconscious, the surface of his oceans glassy and the moon and stars shining brightly upon the smooth water . . . or, perhaps, rum. "Quite brilliant," he continued on his previous tack, unable, on such short notice, to come about. "Oh, I should warn you about Puritan rum, Commander Gallant. It's strong stuff. Much stronger than that Madeira stuff."

Essentially comatose as he was, Commander Gallant could not but agree with him.

Scruffy considered, a little vexed at the sudden calm: he had hoped to hear more. But he could only chasten himself. He was a scientist, after all, and a scientist knew all about cause and effect.

Turning slowly philosophical, he went to the door of his cabin. "Pass the word for the crew of Commander Gallant's boat," he said to the Marines on guard duty. "Tell them to come collect their man. And send them back with a cask of rum . . . with Commander Gallant's name on it." The name, he reflected, *might* ensure that the barrel actually made it all the way back to *Witch of Endor* before it was drained.

Later on, when the little clockwork cutter was hull down on the horizon, Scruffy was still philosophical . . . and perhaps a little melancholy. Bonaparte stranded in Egypt. And Jenkins in Nuhr. And Mather with those mountains.

And American troops coming.

—Hmmm . . .

"What is it?"

—Nothing that you would understand.

"I would understand better than you think!"

Even under circumstances involving the possibility of sudden discovery and equally sudden death, Sari, Beshur, and Potatoes managed, over the course of the next two weeks, to fall into the kind of stable routine that human beings seek under all circumstances ... even those involving unpleasant possibilities.

Come morning, Beshur, lighting the way with an occasional priceless manuscript—or sometimes with an oil-filled lamp left behind by one of the nocturnal visitants to the library (about whom more later)—would set off into the pitch-black collections of (until now) unvisited and unread books, searching through dusty volumes on equally dusty shelves, looking for information (though he was not really sure of what sort). And, come morning, Potatoes and Sari would go with him; Potatoes because he was also searching for information (though he was not really sure of what sort, either), Sari because each of the men had independently determined that it would be much safer for her to be with *him,* and she was thoroughly tired of fighting about it.

"Here. Look: a book of diagrams."

—Idiot. It is merely a book about shipbuilding.

"Well, idiot that I am, I see that *this* diagram looks very much like the pavilion boat."

—What? Let me see!

"Oh, I surely do not wish to trouble you with a book that is merely about shipbuilding and of interest only to an idiot."

In truth, Sari did not mind overmuch. Having resolved to continue to go forward (as, it appeared, the Goddess wished her to), she did just that, and while Beshur and Potatoes examined (and, frequently, fought over) scrolls and charts, she, ignorant of all languages save her own, passed the time with whatever books she could find that possessed illustrations of one kind or another, looking at representations of things that she had never seen before and puzzling over their use and identity while Potatoes and Beshur continued their . . . discussions.

"Oh . . . it *is* just a boat."

—I *told* you so.

"Well, you never know. It certainly *looks* like the pavilion boat."

—It looks nothing at all like the pavilion boat.

And so they continued through the days, new passages and new turnings (winding deep into the mountain, opening up into vaulted rooms, occasionally confusing all three of them to the extent that they spent half the night finding their way back to the secret rooms behind the mirror . . . after which they would all fall onto the fine examples of overstuffed furniture that they had dragged out of the pile of (until now) unvisited and unseen museum objects and drop off into supperless repose) taking them here and there while Beshur and Potatoes darted up and down the shelves, intently scanning the volumes, manuscripts, and boxes, looking for . . .

. . . something.

—Where *are* they?

"Where *is* it?"

—What?

"What?"

—Nothing.

"Nothing."

—What do you mean *nothing*?

"What do *you* mean *nothing*?"

—I said *nothing*.

"I said *nothing,* too."

But though, as aforesaid, they would occasionally become lost, such disorientation became an unusual occurrence after Sari, with the aid of slate and a piece of chalk she had found among the museum objects, took to creating a crude map as they wandered, by means of which they would find their way back to the secret rooms with plenty of time left for Potatoes to make an excursion to the kitchen, where . . .

"Panas (blessed be He!) is good!"

"His mutton chops are broiled to perfection!"

. . . whatever staff member, apprentice, servant, slave, or chef who happened to stumble upon him would assume that, since the Isle of Kanez was forbidden to all save those who were approved by the priesthood, anyone who might appear on it, be they known or unknown, must be, *de facto,* approved; and would therefore allow Potatoes to depart without interference or alarm.

Nor did either of Potatoes' companions question him about his abilities in this matter, for Beshur was too caught up in his researches (whatever they were) to pay much attention to anything save himself, and Sari, though she indeed wondered about them (and about such things as how thieves, whatever their skill, came to know English, French, German, Arabic, and any number of the other languages in which the books in the library were written, as well as a great many other things that would normally have been beyond the ken of any standard-issue inhabitant of the Three Kingdoms . . . *including* the members of the priesthood), had, in the course of her wanderings, learned to keep her mouth shut and not ask questions to which she did not really want to know the answers.

"Thank you, Potatoes. These mutton chops are very good."

"Some wine? The marionette recommended it."

"Marionette?"

"A French word. Does it not have a delightful sound?"

"Yes. Yes it does. Thank you for the wine."

"It is my pleasure, lovely lady! The marionette—"

—Just give her the wine, will you? I don't want to hear about the marionette.

"Hah! You are jealous of my marionette! And I did not see *you* offering her any wine!"

—I was just *about* to offer her wine!

But as their wanderings, researches (whatever they were), and meals became a matter of routine, so, too, did the nocturnal visitants referred to above, though it should be clearly understood that, whoever the visitants were, they were apparently unconcerned with the contents of the library. No, with the exception of Obadiah Jenkins, whose (gray and noncommittal) shoes would frequently betray his presence by their (soft and noncommittal) *tap-tap-tap*— assuring the three companions that the Americans were still on the island and that, far below, the pavilion boat was still tied up and waiting to return to Nuhr—the visitants appeared to notice the books not at all. In fact, given the alarming screams, clanks, and thuds that broke the dark, brooding silence of the nighttime library, the visitants' attentions were obviously directed solely at one another.

And yet, come morning, when Potatoes, a sword in his hand, opened the door into the book collections, there was, invariably, no sign of any kind of intrusion at all . . .

"But I heard it."

"We all heard it, lovely lady."

. . . save for an occasional oil lamp that had been left behind . . .

"I am beginning to think that it is time for us to return to Nuhr."

"Lovely lady, nothing would give me greater pleasure, except . . ."

—Give me that lamp. I have work to do. Except what?

"Nothing."

—What do you mean *nothing*?

"Just what I said. Nothing. And what are *you* looking for?"

—Nothing.

. . . until, one day, as Beshur was leading the way into yet another section of the library (and it should be noted that although he insisted upon leading the way, he obviously had no better idea of where he was going than did

Potatoes or Sari), he stumbled over something and went sprawling (conveniently, as will be seen) into a wall.

The crash he produced, though infinitely satisfying to Potatoes, masked the sound of a *snick* from a nearby section of wall, which, as we saw in a previous chapter, indicated that there was something of importance concealed somewhere.

More on this later.

"A body!"

"And it is all dried up. The poor man!"

—Mummified (ouch!) by the dry air, obviously.

It was, indeed, the shriveled corpse of what once must have been a reasonably burly man. Potatoes noted the tattoo on the leathery skin of one arm (a design greatly favored by the priestly guards of a hundred years before), observed that the skull had been caved in on one side by something heavy . . . and:

"He is wearing a face cloth."

—Women's clothes!

"You forgot *just as I expected.*"

—Pumice to your *just as I expected*! It was you who began that, anyway!

"The poor man! But what was he doing in women's clothes?"

Indeed, the corpse was dressed entirely in the costume of a woman. Sari could think of nothing that would explain it.

"I do not know," said Potatoes. "What do the Sacred Texts say about it, Beshur?"

—Do not ask about the Sacred Texts, heathen!

"Heathen!"

"Please . . . both of you . . ."

But Beshur and Potatoes were obviously no longer thinking about either the corpse or its clothing.

"He . . . he . . . he called me a *heathen*!"

—If the sandal fits . . .

"A heathen!"

Perhaps, Sari considered, they had *never* been thinking about the corpse or its clothing . . . or about anything else, in fact, save . . .

. . . Oh. Oh, yes. That.

"I am sure that he did not mean it," she said.

—What? I certainly *did* mean it!

"Be*shur!*"

—If he is going to ridicule the Sacred Texts, then he is a heathen.

"I certainly was not ridiculing the Sacred Texts!"

—You certainly were! I could tell!

"Oh, to be sure! And did the Sacred Texts tell you that?"

—See? Ridicule. Humph! Unlike you, I *know* what the Sacred Texts say!

"Humph and more humph! Which version of the Sacred Texts are you referring to?"

—What do you mean?

"I have seen at least two."

—Two? Two what?

"Two versions of the Sacred Texts."

—What? Two?

"And one was easily *twice* the size of the other. So much for consistency."

—Two versions? Of the Sacred Text? *Where?*

And so it was that the routine came to an abrupt and decisive end.

Chapter Nine

At times, it seemed to Mr. Jenkins that Abnel was bent on showing him every last inch of the Isle of Kanez. More frequently, it seemed to him that Abnel was very much interested in not leaving him alone for any appreciable length of time. This in itself would have proved to have been an insurmountable obstacle with regards to Jenkins' clandestine researches among the collections of books ... were the escorts assigned to him by the Gharat not obviously convinced that, after sixteen hours of visits to sheep pens, parchment fabricators, carpenters' shops, book binderies, farms (well irrigated, Jenkins noticed), orchards, reading rooms (in which no readers were in evidence: Panasian law was very clear about things like that), and scriptoriums (in which, to be sure that no one was actually reading what he was copying, the originals were kept turned upside down and copied (Bodoni!) from back to front ... and, yes, Panasian law was very clear about things like that, too), their escortee would collapse into bed and sleep soundly for the next eight hours, at which time he would be awakened for yet *another* round of visits.

Which convincement left Jenkins very much alone (discounting, for the moment, Mr. Wool, who could be discounted, and ignoring Mr. Mather, who was not there at all) for those eight hours, but though the American ambassador was indeed greatly fatigued by the daily tours, the godly objectives of the Righteous States of America ensured that if the spirit was willing (and it was), the flesh was going to be (had *better* be) willing, too; and so, no sooner had the bowing and smiling priestly guards departed from his room with a *good night and Panas (blessed be He!) bless* than Jenkins was on his feet and at the door, waiting for the sound of their footsteps to fade away so that he might slip out into the corridor, down the hall, down a flight of stairs, and through the small, brass door that (he had found) led directly into the book collections. There he would spend an hour or two before the weakness of his flesh (advancing its own very convincing argument that the spirit had better look sharp and get its priorities straight . . . or *else*) took him back to his room and to bed.

But though day after day of futile searching for a clue as to the object of the Gharat's obsession made him realize that he would never find anything at all worthwhile among the scrambled volumes of the Library, still he could not drop his ambassadorial facade and simply *ask* Abnel what it was that he wanted. That would have been going much too far, in Jenkins' opinion, threatening (even shattering!) the tenuous relationship that existed between himself and the Gharat—and therefore between the Righteous States of America and the Three Kingdoms—the relationship (ripe though the word was with connotations of un-Puritan mechanics) that was all that Jenkins had to show for weeks of strenuous effort.

"I trust the honored ambassador has been enjoying himself?" Abnel said at dinner one night.

Jenkins noticed with distaste that the dish before him contained yet another variant on the lamb-and-grape curry of which the Gharat appeared to be particularly fond.

"Oh, yes," he responded properly. "Immensely."

"And I trust that the honored ambassador has been edified by the achievements of the Three Kingdoms?"

This statement, making as it did no reference at all to whether the achievements in question were current or long (very long) past allowed Jenkins to admit quite candidly that he was very much impressed.

"And so you find us worthy!"

"Very worthy."

It was coming. Jenkins knew that it was coming.

"Tell me about the minister."

Jenkins stared at Abnel. The Gharat's lips were smeared with grape juice, curry, and sugar. "The . . . minister."

"In their heads."

They were eating in the great refectory of the Library. Below the high platform occupied by their table, the staff members of the Library were also eating. Wool was down there somewhere, too. Jenkins had no idea whether Mather was there or not. Aside from the universal sounds of mastication, though, the room was silent.

"And I stood upon the sand of the sea," a voice drifted up morosely, "and saw a beast rise up out of the sea, having seven heads and ten horns, and upon his horns ten crowns, and upon his heads the name of blasphemy."

Well, almost silent.

What (Jenkins wondered, stifling an impatient word at Wool's hideously inappropriate gloss) did a minister in their heads have to do with it? He barely remembered the interchange at that first dinner. Something about grace before meals? Was that it?

Grace?

"Well," he said, attempting to keep his smile on straight, but feeling it sagging somewhere off to the left, "it has to do with . . . ah . . . truth."

"Truth!" Abnel was nodding vigorously. His gold fillet slipped down on one side, and so furiously did he shove it back up that he nearly poked himself in the eye.

"Yes," said Jenkins. "Godly truth."

"Ah!" said Abnel, as though in perfect understanding.

"That is the minister in their . . . ah . . . heads." And

Jenkins wished again that Abnel would simply *tell* him what he wanted, instead of beating about the bush by asking inane questions about figures of speech that he did not even remember having used.

"Ah!" Again: perfect understanding.

"I hope that is clear," said Jenkins.

"Ah! Very clear!"

But what did he *want*? The throne of the Three Kingdoms could even now be slipping away—and with it, the plans of the Righteous States—and this silly, heathen priest could only ask about ministers in people's heads!

"Ah!" said Abnel. "Yes! I understand now!"

"Tonight?" said Yourgi, blinking his blind eyes at Abnel.

"Tonight."

Yourgi put down the list of books (that, by long devotional habit, he had been running his lack of sight over just prior to going to bed) and cast himself at full length upon the marble floor, his hands clasped in supplication. "Ah, Holy Gharat! May Panas (blessed be He!) save you, but I cannot do that!"

Abnel was not one to be kept waiting with regards to lamb and grape curries, relationships with American engineers, or the consultation of early copies of the Sacred Texts in which resided, he had come to believe, the essence of the godly truth to which the American ambassador had been referring. "You . . . *cannot*?"

"It would be most dangerous for me or for anyone else to enter the library at this time."

"Dangerous?"

"Because of the drugs."

"Drugs? What drugs?"

The fading light that fell from the high windows of the secret museum rooms pooled around Beshur, who, sitting on the polished granite floor, was surrounded by several dozen scrolls that—judging from their color, texture, and wholeness (or otherwise)—appeared to group themselves into sets of widely different ages.

At present, he had an aged, crumbling specimen on his lap. Having succeeded in prying it open without destroying it, he was reading aloud:

—*Inscriptions are carved in stone for many uses: for Foundation Stones and Public Inscriptions, for Tombstones and Memorial Inscriptions, for Mottos and Texts, for Names and Advertisements, and each subject suggests its own treatment. Colour and Gold may be used both for the beauty of them and, in places where there is little light, to increase legibility.*

Arrangement: There are two methods of arranging Inscriptions: the "Massed" and the "Symmetrical." In the former the lines are very close together, and approximately equal in length, and form a mass. Absolute equality is quite unnecessary. Where the lines are very long it is easy to make them equal; but with lines of few words it is very difficult, besides being derogatory to the appearance of the inscription. In the "Symmetrical" inscription, the length of the lines may vary considerably, and each line (often comprising a distinct phrase or statement) is placed in the centre of the Inscription space.

Short Inscriptions, such as those usually on tombstones or foundation stones, may well be arranged in the "Symmetrical" way, but long Inscriptions are better arranged in the "Massed" way, though, sometimes, the two methods may be combined in the same inscription.

THE THREE ALPHABETS

The Roman Alphabet, the alphabet chiefly in use today, reached its highest development in Inscriptions incised in stone.

Besides ROMAN CAPITALS, it is necessary that the letter-cutter should know how to carve Roman small-letters (or "lower case") and italics, either of which may be more suitable than Capitals for some Inscriptions.

Where great magnificence combined with great legibility is desired, use Large Roman Capitals, Incised or in Relief, with plenty of space between the letters and the lines.

Where great legibility but less magnificence is desired, use "Roman Small-Letters" or "Italics."

All three Alphabets may be used together, as, for instance, on a Tombstone, where one might carve the Name in Capitals and the rest of the Inscription in Small-Letters, using Italics for difference.

Beauty of Form may safely be left to a right use of the chisel, combined with a well-advised study of the best examples of Inscriptions: such as that on the Trajan Column and other Roman Inscriptions . . .

His voice trailed off.

"But where is the commentary?" said Potatoes.

—There is no commentary, Beshur said.

"Impossible!"

His lips pressed tightly together, his face drawn, Beshur shook his head.

—It is not impossible. This is the earliest copy of the Sacred Texts of Panas in existence. You can see how old the scroll is. It also says *Sacred Texts I* on the tag, and given what I am seeing here, I am not inclined to doubt it. I think it dates to the foundation of the Three Kingdoms.

Potatoes also looked shaken. "But the commentary! The commentary written by the God himself!"

—It is not here.

Beshur picked up another scroll.

—Here. Listen. This is where it begins. In *Sacred Texts III*.

He read:

—*Listen to these, the words of Panas, the Sculptor God, who knows all things about the shaping of stone.*

Potatoes was almost angry. "Then this is . . . this is . . ."

—A treatise on stone carving, Beshur said. It is all here. Stripped of its commentaries, the Sacred Texts are nothing more than a set of instructions to the would-be carver of inscriptions.

He seemed to become aware of the words he was uttering and of the thoughts behind them. He stared straight ahead in the failing light.

—Sacrilege. They have ... have ...

His voice trailed off for a moment. Then:

—It is blasphemy!

Potatoes knelt beside him and picked up a scroll with a tag that said *Sacred Texts VI*. "*Thus it is seen,*" he read, "*that the carver, in emulating the God, does the God's work, and his carving is a model for the world.*"

—And so it began, Beshur said. And so now I know.

It was obvious that the knowledge gave him no satisfaction.

"Know?" said Potatoes, still staring at the scroll. "Know what?"

—The Texts. I thought that they had changed. No ... I *knew* they had changed. We had to memorize them in the ... ah ... the ... ah ... er ...

"Never mind, Beshur," said Sari from the shadows. "Go on. We are your friends."

Beshur struggled on.

— ... ah ... priests' house, and I ... ah ... I was *sure* that they had changed, despite the insistence of the priests that they had not. That is why I wanted to come here. To find out. To be sure.

Potatoes sat down heavily on the floor, picked up a scroll from a newer set, and examined it idly. The tag said *Sacred Texts CXLVIII*. "I wonder how many versions there are?"

—Hundreds. This is only a small sample. I saw many more.

Sari spoke up. "I saw a group of scrolls that said *Sacred Texts MMCMIV*. Is that a large number? The set was very new and very large. There must have been two or three hundred scrolls in it."

Beshur lifted his head.

—It is indeed a very large number, he said. Are you sure of it?

"I wrote it down on my slate. Here, see?" She held it up. "The scrolls were near where we found the body."

—They are scattered all over the library, then, Beshur said. Who *knows* how many there are?

Potatoes, his face in his hands, was shaking his head slowly. "A forgotten dust-hole of a kingdom, with stone-carving instructions as the basis of its religion. Unbelievable. And what could I do with it, even supposing . . . ?"

Sari looked at him with an odd expression. "Potatoes?"

"Nothing," he said quickly. "A figure of speech. No more."

"O Great Gharat, do you not remember the custom?"

"*What* custom?"

"It is written in the Sacred Texts!"

"Oh . . . yes . . . of course . . . *that* custom."

Yourgi picked a scroll from a rack behind him, unrolled it on his lap, and recited:

" . . . *let it also be guarded day and night, that its holiness may be magnified by its isolation, and that its sacredness never be profaned by a touch of a mundane foot or its contents sullied by the glance of an eye that can see but not comprehend.*"

Abnel examined Yourgi with a strange look. Yourgi considered, then fumbled through the rack and came up with another scroll.

" . . . *unless the priesthood, and, in particular, the High Priest himself, sees fit—*"

"Thank you, Librarian," Abnel said to the blind man. "Your memory of the Sacred Texts is magnificent."

"Panas (blessed be He!) is good!"

"His wisdom extends to all things!" responded Abnel. "But what about the drugs?"

Yourgi replaced the scrolls on the rack. "Since the Li-

brary is, by nature of the safeguards set up about it, isolated from all intrusion, the priestly guards assigned to
watching it at night took to intruding into it themselves.
Therefore, in accordance with the Sacred Texts, I took
steps to keep them out by burning a particular mixture of
drugs in different parts of the library every night."

"And do the drugs, in fact, keep them out?"

"Well . . . they frequently do not remember going in,
which is much the same thing, I suppose. And, in fact,
some do not come out at all, for they fall into a delirium
and attack one another, sometimes with fatal results. This
is unfortunate, but unavoidable. Most of the time we drag
them out in the morning. Some we never find, and I do not
know for certain what becomes of them."

Abnel nodded. "Panas (blessed be He!) is good!"

"His books are safe and unused!"

"But did you not think," said Abnel, "in accordance
with the Sacred Texts that you just read . . ."

Yourgi blinked blind eyes at him.

" . . . I mean, that you just quoted from memory . . ."

Yourgi smiled with self-deprecation.

" . . . to grant a dispensation to the priestly guards to enter the Library at night so as to better guard it?"

Yourgi cast himself at full length upon the marble floor.
"O, Great Gharat, my knowledge of the Sacred Texts has
proved deficient, and I must beg forgiveness!"

It was late, and the darkness of the dark library seemed
even darker now that night was falling outside its walls,
but Beshur had wanted to look at the copy of the Sacred
Texts that Sari had seen in the vicinity of the dried-up
corpse, and so, following the map on her slate, the Naian
had led her companions back to that section of the library.

"It was over there," she said, pointing.

Potatoes was peering at a shelf, but he abruptly lifted
his head and sniffed. "What is that odor?"

—Never mind about odors, Beshur said. We are here for the scrolls. I must find the latest version I can and see how it compares with what I memorized when I was in the . . . ah . . .

Even in the ruddy light of a burning page from another priceless book (a first-edition Gutenberg Bible this time), Beshur had gone quite pale.

"Never mind, Beshur," said Sari.

—I was . . . ah . . . just . . . ah *visiting*! That is it. I was visiting!

"Of course," said Potatoes reassuringly (which seemed to reassure Beshur not at all). "But that odor . . ."

But now Sari, too, was sniffing. Since she had first arrived in the library, she had frequently smelled something of the sort, and the odor had become so habitual as to be ignored. Tonight, however, and in this particular place, it was stronger . . . so much stronger that her herbalist training arose of its own accord and immediately identified it.

"Hemp," she said. "Burning hemp. The female flowers. And . . . and . . ." She frowned.

—A little hemp never hurt anyone, Beshur said. Where are those scrolls?

"There is something else, too . . ."

—It is not important.

Sari caught her breath. "Henbane!"

—Oh, well, a little henbane never hurt—

"And opium!"

—Oh, well, a little—

"Be*shur*!"

Potatoes was frowning in the light of a page from Isaiah. "We had best gather the scrolls and depart from this place. It is late, too, and I must get something from the kitchen for supper. Where are the scrolls you saw, Sari?"

Sari pointed again. "Right over there. By that hole in the wall."

"Hole?"

—Hole?

It was (I *told* you there would be more on this.) indeed a hole. But, in contrast to the small hatch that Bakbuk had found in the chambers of the Crown Prince, this was quite large ... actually a full-sized doorway. Forgetting, therefore, about both the scrolls (inconvenient) and the odor (very unwise), the three examined it, noting with some wonder how the granite blocks had been carefully hinged so that they would, with the tripping of the catch, swing open on their own, but would, when closed, remain completely undetectable.

"Magnificent," said Potatoes. "And it would not even sound hollow, owing to the thickness of the ..." He glanced appraisingly at Beshur's head for a moment. ". . . blocks."

Beshur was nodding.

—Just as I ... ah ...

He looked at Potatoes and Sari, who were both staring at him.

—Ah ... never mind.

"Give me another page of Isaiah," said Potatoes. "This one is almost gone."

With a fresh flame to guide them (and accompanied by the increasing odor of the burning herbs), the three entered the room beyond the secret door.

"You are certainly forgiven, Librarian," said Abnel, motioning for Yourgi to get up off the floor. "But it is still imperative that we enter the Library immediately."

Yourgi rose. "But, O honored Gharat, will not the morning be early enough to enter the Library? By then the drugs will have dissipated."

"This cannot wait for morning. It must be tonight."

Yourgi looked about as though seeking an escape. But there was no escape from the will of the Gharat, and so he had no choice but to cast himself once more on the floor. "O great Gharat, I beg you—"

"Tonight! Now!"

* * *

For all the magnificence of the secret door itself, the room that lay beyond it was not much to speak of. Plain, unadorned, and empty save for a few cases of scrolls, it was only just big enough for the three companions to squeeze into it.

"These are very old," said Potatoes as, by the light of yet another page of the Gutenberg, he bent to examine one case of scrolls.

—These over here look older.

"True."

Lighting another page (Isaiah was finished: it was Jeremiah who faced combustion now.) and handing it to Sari, Potatoes extracted the first scroll from the case at hand and unrolled the first section.

He frowned.

"What?"

—What?

"Nothing," said the thief, rerolling the scroll and thrusting it back into its place.

Beshur was angry.

—Enough of this *nothing* foolishness, he said. I will look.

And before Potatoes could stop him, he had withdrawn the same scroll and had unrolled it on the dusty top of the low case.

Holding the flaming page of Jeremiah aloft, Sari leaned closer and could not help but read over Beshur's shoulder:

Truly, it is no light or simple thing to create a religion, but the extension of knowledge demands that certain efforts and sacrifices be made. Thus was it deemed necessary that the wise among us formulate the religion called Naianism, which, as might be expected, revolves around the cultic worship of a deity named Naia. While this might be thought of as foolish or redundant or even heretical, as there was already a well-established religion of the god Panas (about which much has been written elsewhere), it

*will be noticed in the ensuing study that the deity in ques-
tion is female. The possibilities inherent in the development and evolution of this religion, observed with priestly
rigor, were thought to be of sufficient merit and curiosity
that the project was approved unanimously, and, in fact,
much entertainment has been afforded the priestly council
by the religion's independent growth, first as the supposed
"discovery" of the itinerant half-wit Loomar, then as the
devotional superstitions of a small group of his disciples,
then as a widespread spiritual practice of the poor and the
ignorant, and finally . . .*

"But what about the rats?"

Abnel started visibly (though this was lost on Yourgi,
who, as has often been pointed out, was blind). "Rats?"

Yourgi's (sightless) eyes were bright behind his spectacles. "Yes. Rats. There are a number in the Library."

"Rats?"

"They only come out at night. They are really no trouble at all."

"Rats?"

"Now that I am thinking of it, perhaps *that* is how some
of the bodies of the guards came to be missing . . ."

"Rats?"

"Oh, yes. Did the honored Gharat know that they must
gnaw in order to survive? Why, their teeth will actually—"

Abnel turned away. "Morning will be fine."

"They are holy rats, of course," Yourgi continued.
"They should pose no threat. I am sure they will find
something to—"

"Morning."

"My dear Gharat, there is nothing to fear! They are very
devout rats!"

"Morning!"

Sari turned away quickly, feeling cold and sick. Naia? A
creation? Then . . .

Then what? If Naia were an illusion, then this body that she wore, transformed utterly . . .

No, that did not make any sense, either. Her body was real. If she had had any doubt of that, she had only to look at the faces of Potatoes and Beshur (Oh. Oh, yes. That.) in order to receive independent confirmation. But how did one get a new body save by divine act? And if she had gotten her body by divine act, then what deity had given it to her? Panas?

An unfortunate thought. Now she felt even worse.

Potatoes caught the burning page that fell from her suddenly nerveless fingers. "There, there, Sari."

"I . . ."

Potatoes glared at Beshur. "Fool!"

Beshur was offended.

—I am a—

"Scholar," snapped Potatoes. "And a very stupid one at that!"

Sari was shaking her head. "I do not understand. This is . . . this is . . ."

Misunderstanding completely (or perhaps seeing an opportunity: it was a little hard to tell) Beshur rushed to her and took her into his arms.

—Oh, Sari, he said, I am so sorry. Allow me to comfort you in this hour of your need!

She was already feeling his lips on her forehead, and she pushed him back and turned away. She needed time to think: she saw no profit in being nibbled as though she were a ripe peach.

Standing in the doorway of the secret room, blearing at the darkness filled with unread and unused books, she noticed, by the light of Jeremiah, that there seemed now to be a palpable haze floating among the silent shelves.

Herbs . . .

Behind her, Beshur was arguing with Potatoes.

—I was just trying to help, he said. What else could I do?

"You can keep your mouth shut, that is what you can do. And you can keep your hands to yourself!"

—I was giving her what she needed!

"You were grabbing a handful of womanflesh, you scholastic lecher!"

Beshur was incensed.

—Lecher! he said. Can I help it if Sari has discovered the falsity of her religion? It is unfortunate that she has learned this, but it is probably good that she knows the truth. One should have no illusions. I wanted none regarding the Sacred Texts, and now I, too, know the truth. This is a good thing. Fortunately, you and I have the true religion, and though the Sacred Texts have proven to be deceptive, there is still Panas (blessed be He!) Himself.

A rustle as Potatoes looked over the scroll. "Incredible."

—It is certainly not incredible at all. Why the priesthood is capable of doing anything. It is—

"Pumice and sandstone to you! Shut up!"

Beshur fell silent.

"I wonder how many know this about Naianism?" Potatoes mused, as, her back to the men, Sari watched the flickering light of Jeremiah play on the growing haze.

Naia. A created deity? But . . . her body . . .

She could not explain it.

The sound of yet another scroll being withdrawn from a case.

"With the increasing hold that the heresy of Naianism has upon the hearts of the young and fruitful of these kingdoms," Potatoes read, *"it stands to reason that a concerted effort must be made to eradicate it. And since woman is water and water is woman, the rule of Panas can only be made universal by the banishment of water from these lands. Thus will the glory of Panas (blessed be He!) be made manifest . . ."*

—Banishing water? Beshur said.

Potatoes sounded grave. "Pumps," he said. "Water. That explains it."

—Explains what?

"The drought is artificial."

—But that is impossible! Beshur cried.

"A minute ago you were smugly telling me that nothing is impossible for the priesthood."

—But a drought! One might as well try to . . . try to . . . ah . . .

"To make up a religion?"

—Well . . . ah . . .

The smoke was thickening even more quickly now, the odor of the narcotic herbs growing stronger.

"Give me another page, Beshur."

A fresh flare of light. Sari heard another scroll scrape out of its resting place. It sounded dry, crumbling. It must have been terribly old.

—Artificial, Beshur said. This is terrible. While I am sorry to hear that all Sari's devotions have been proven to be for nothing, still, the fact that we . . . ah . . . I mean . . . the *priests* have been destroying the land for so long . . . well . . . now that I think of it, since Naianism was a sham in any case, perhaps it is best that it be . . . well . . .

Potatoes was reading:

"*. . . so we thought that it would be entertaining to make up a religion, and we decided to call our deity "Panas" . . .*"

—What? Let me see that!

Chapter Ten

(*An unknown region of the Great Library of Kanez. Mazed convolutions of intestinal, tomestupated gutshelves stretch forward, side to side, smoky with the exhalation of illicit drugs. In the background stretches a monolithic wall pierced by a single vulvic aperture from which fly, at periodic intervals, flashes of light, Biblical combustion, infantile castings of unprovoked blood.*)

THE BLOOD
Gaagaaagaaaagump! Splash! Dedededead!

THE FLASHES
Sppppitititit!

(*A dove circles slowly, brooding with bright wings over the ocean of pyrosublimed henbanopiatedcannibiKNO$_3$hydroberyl. The waves rise to fling spray at its feathered belly, fall away and dissipate, rise again, renewed.*)

THE DOVE
Where? Oh, where?

THE WAVES
Secret. Hidden. Let us in and we will tell you.

(The dove ascends and fades into the coldstone ceilingtomb. The waves hover amid the volumechoked shelves, dust of ages. Parchment flakes clump, arrange themselves into scrolls, books, letters in unknown languages.
Saridove, dovemaiden, naiamedallion askew, wandering, bumps into a bookshelf and smudges her tooperfect nose with dust. Rhinorubbing, she falls back, examines the erection with dopedulled eye.)

SARI

Always bumping my nose. Then I fall ill, and someone wants something from me.

A VOICE

Oh. Oh, yes. That.

(Echoes of the voice flutter with childsparrow wings among the beams of the dimshadowed ceiling. Sari pushes ahead and runs into the bookshelf again.)

SARI

Lost my way. Wish I had light.

(Potatoes appears, dashing and disreputable. He is garbed in cloth-of-gold, rubies flash from his ears, and his unskillfully shaven face is bright with gilt and polish.)

POTATOES

Allow me, lovely lady! The way up and the way down are one and the same. Nothing is more simple. I can provide anything you want. Harpies banished? I can do that. Libraries penetrated? *(He winks roguishly.)* I can do that, too. Penetration is my speciality. My chisel is strong and sharp!

SARI

I am a . . . a . . . a . . .

POTATOES

(*His rubies and polishedface flattering, flashing.*) Go ahead! I dwell upon your every word!

SARI

(*Paying no attention.*) . . . a . . . a . . . Na— (*She turns away from him, distracted.*) What is the use? Created. Just like my own body. (*She touches the fruitround of her girlish breast.*) Made, not begotten. Breakfast cakes. Brown and perfect. Whose hand? Cannot argue with facts. Mother said that.

(*The dark haze rolls, laps at the shelfshores. A freehaired Naian matron appears, her shoulder cloth embroidered with flowers, ferns, emblems of wet times, green times.*)

MESTHIA

Sari!

SARI

(*Gripping her medallion, blood welling from between her fingers.*)
Mamma!

MESTHIA

You cannot argue with facts.

SARI

(*Wearing blue, her youngirl features free of the blemish of old age and disappointment. She sits at Mesthia's feet, her head on her mother's lap.*) I cannot argue. I love him. I have tried to tell myself that I do not, but I do.

MESTHIA

Oh, we all love our men, Sari. I love your father. And he loves me. And Abnel loves Mather. And Bakbuk loves the Blue Avenger. You cannot argue with facts.

SARI

They will—

MESTHIA

(*Interrupting, stroking her maiden head.*) Yes.

SARI

And they will—

MESTHIA

Yes. That, too.

SARI

But . . . Naia—

MESTHIA

(*Reassuringly.*) Naia understands.

SARI

(*Grief-stricken.*) But Naia is a myth! (*A boulder rises up beneath her, bearing her aloft. At her feet is a lizard. About her stretches a dry riverbed. Behind her are the Mountains of Ern, dry and parched, and beyond the mountains, the glitter of lakes and seas and cataracts. The rubble of an avalanche lies scattered below.*) She brought me to the Caves for nothing! For a lie! And she did not even bring me! The lie brought me! There is no Naia! There are no Children of Naia! There is nothing. Only a myth and a community of superstitious idolaters! They deserve whatever the priesthood gives them! And I . . . ! I deceived myself, and I deceived them, too!

CHARNA

How grotesque!

JEDDIAH

I am sure that you will be a valuable person for my school!

SARI

(*Her tone turning earnest.*) You do not understand. I have nothing to teach. There *is* nothing to teach. Even if Naia were real, you cannot teach something that is different for every person. (*She puts her hand to her face.*) But what of it? Useless. Naia is a myth. And Panas—

(*A sudden knocking at the door. The lizard sprouts dovewings, flies away. A group of lusty Panasian youths barge in. In their dozen or so hands are sharp knives, pitchforks, hoes, scythes, awls, razors, and fleshhungry implements of every kind. They surround Sari, seize her, tear her medallion from her neck and throw it at Mesthia.*)

THE YOUTHS

We have come for the girl!

MESTHIA

(*Rising, putting the medallion in spreadthighed Sari's hand.*)
This I return to you. It is customary.

SARI

(*Her eyes on the blades.*) Many things were customary.

(*An earthquake. The walls of the library crumble. Floods of blood rush in, sweeping away the books and the shelves.*)

CHARNA

Do you want to hear the story about Naia's farting? It is wonderfully grotesque. (*She climbs into a crateful of insignificant brassware, closes the lid behind her. After a mo-*

ment, the lid pops up again, and her head appears.) After all, I am a professional, am I not? (*The lid slams to.*)

(*Sari, transfixed upon an upright blade, is lifted above the rippling ocean of blood. Her brow is weighted with face and head cloth, her streaming thighs wrapped in impure wool. She extends her arms over the troubled flow.*)

SARI
Behold! I am conceived without stain!

THE YOUTHS
(*Bowing down.*) His chisel is strong and sharp!

(*Instantly pregnant by the virtue resident in the sword, Sari immediately delivers children. The boys are given weapons. The girls are excised and passed about to the excited onlookers on plates, their vulvas oozing crimson and worms, their flesh poked and prodded by inquisitive, imprinting, impatient fingers.*)

A VOICE
How much for that one?

ANOTHER VOICE
I want this one!

YET ANOTHER VOICE
I saw her first!

ANOTHER VOICE
Pumice and sandstone to you!

YET ANOTHER VOICE
And to all your forebears!

MAUMUD
(*Swinging down from above, jerked into antic postures by*

godpulled hempen strings tied to his wrists and ankles.)
Do not shout! Do not shove! Plenty more where these
came from! (*He prods Sari, and her womb immediately responds with fifteen more whelps.*) Now then! Who is next?
Gold! I want to see gold! No plain silver for *my* daughters!

(*Sari's daughters are weighed, wrapped, bundled into
sacks, and shipped off. Three go north. Two west. Seven
southwest. The rest die of suffocation.*)

THE YOUTHS AND THE BYSTANDERS
Huzzah!

SARI
I love you, Maumud.

MAUMUD
Is she not tolerant? Is she not adaptable? Is she not understanding? A prize wife. And she left her religion for *me*!
Not one of you, I think, can offer any comparison between
your wife and mine. She came to *me*. *I* am the object of
her devotion. For *me* she gave up her family, her home,
her ways, her friends, her customs. And as for the taint of
Naianism that still clings to her, why a man can get used
to a little putrefaction in his life, particularly when it
comes in such a comely package! (*He thumps Sari on the
back. Another child drops and is borne off. Gold coins
clink into Maumud's purse.*) Meat is best hung for a few
days after slaughter. Tang of carrion. Flesh eaters!

SARI
(*Exhausted, her voice a papery whisper.*) I thirst.

MAUMUD
If the rug is stained, one simply sets a chest on the blot.
Is that not the way of the world? And when the rug is old,
one buys another. Is that not the way of the world?

SARI

(*Her voice even fainter.*) I thirst.

MAUMUD

Silence! How dare you use that word! I will not speak to you!

SARI

(*Almost inaudible.*) I thirst. Some water. Please.

(*Rising into the air on a whale-spout of dust, the Gharat Abnel writhes in delirium.*)

THE GHARAT ABNEL

Water! Pumps! Oh, pump me up!

(*Maumud lifts a hand to strike Sari, but suddenly, with a gulp, he staggers. Blood spews from his mouth as he collapses, his eyes bottleglazed and staring, his face green. Priestly guards, who might as well be played by the same actor, examine him, count his fingers, his toes, pull out his tongue and note that it is black.*)

THE GUARDS

(*Variously.*) Murder! She killed him! She must be found! Sound the alarms! Send out the magistrates! Send out the bailiffs!

(*Alarm bells ring. Horns sound. Soldiers set out from the gates of Nuhr. Naian homes are burned. Naian babies are sliced into roasts, ribs, steaks. From the tallest tower of the king's palace, a crier denounces the murder of Panas' beloved son. Testimonials are given as to the worthiness and benevolence of Maumud. Collections are taken up in his name, the moneys distributed to the city's foremost*) *beggars and cripples. Several Naian women are impaled in joyous celebration of Maumud's generosity, and a graven image of him is set up in the market square of Nuhr, there to receive daily libations of wine, clarified butter, and breakfast cakes.*)

SARI

(*Covered with flour.*) I do not ask for passage without work like a pampered priest.

YALLIAH

(*Bending low over Sari's work.*) Where did you learn to make breakfast cakes like a Panasian wife, O woman of Naia?

SARI

(*Starting away in fear, dropping a dozen perfectly-formed, Panasian breakfast cakes.*) I can explain everything. Really. I was an old woman, you see, and then I killed my husband. Well, I did not so much kill him as make him angry enough that he killed himself. But that is not really the way it happened, either. He would not speak to me, and then he fell over and died. And then I went to the Caves of Naia. But that is not it either. Not really. I tried to go to the Caves of Naia, you see, but they had been blocked by a landslide.

VOICES OF THE NAIANS

If she had only done it right! Naia in her male aspect!

SARI

(*Growing more and more agitated.*) And since the Caves were blocked, I cursed Naia, and so She made me young. Only that, too, is not quite right, since Naia was made up by the priesthood of Panas. As a curiosity. But that is not it either, because the priesthood made up Panas, too.

VOICES OF THE NAIANS
The old ways! The true old ways!

(*With a thunderroar, a drum rolls in from out of the labially opening wreaths of opiated haze. It rises into the sky, a full moon.*)

THE DRUM
DUM-DUM-DUM-DUM-DUM-DUM-DUM-DUM!

(*The round face of Golfah the Drummer appears in the rounderthanroundfloatinggoldendumdumdum moon.*)

GOLFAH THE DRUMMER
Starting together is good, but ending together is the most important.

ZARIFAH
(*From a distance.*) My child is dead! And you ... you curse my husband!

SARI
(*Confused.*) I ... I ... I can explain!

(*From all directions, the guards close in. Sari is discovered, stripped, raped, clitoridectomized, impaled, quartered, broken. Her body, dissolved in a solution produced by soaking topaz and emerald in water for 24 hours, is thereafter distilled and subjected to evaporation, the resultant salts ground to powder and scattered to the four winds.*
A bolt of lightning. A shower of rain. Naia appears, her face veiled. Her garments are of the skyblue, earthbrown, verdantvegetational green. About her head cloth is set a garland of springbright flowers.)

NAIA

You do not know me.

THE GENERAL ONLOOKERS

(*In consternated confusion.*) That is true. We do not. Never seen you before. Have not met. Do not believe we have had the pleasure.

A VOICE

(*Rising from the background.*) But I am a professional, am I not?

NAIA

I am the mother of all things.

THE GENERAL ONLOOKERS

(*In a chorus of enlightened inspiration.*) Ah!

(*Naia stretches forth a hand. Sari is made whole.*)

THE GENERAL ONLOOKERS

(*Applauding.*) Oh! Oh, yes! That!

SARI

(*Falling on her knees before Naia.*) Mother! You saved me! I was wrong! I will always believe in you. Indeed, how can I not believe in you? For You made me!

NAIA

(*In triumph.*) And you made *Me*!

(*Naia's veil falls away, revealing a crooked mouth set with rotting teeth. A skull! The image of the goddess crumbles into dust, powdering into sandy microstone.*)

THE GENERAL ONLOOKERS

Oh! Oh, yes! That! Knew it all along. Obvious to anyone. Just as we expected.

(*Sari flees from the hideous revelation. Bookcases rise up about her, bruising her perfect nose with their* lingam vitae *hardness. She careens down the long, dustyknowledge corridors until she comes to the secret door.*)

THE DOOR

Knock three times, pause, knock once, pause, and knock once again!

(*The door is suddenly jerked open.*)

ZARIFAH

(*Sticking her flushcheeked face out of the doorway.*) Now you have ruined everything!

SARI

But it is all made up!

ZARIFAH

(*The mark of plague plain on her forehead, crystals rattling within her brain.*) My child is dead!

(*Despite Zarifah's efforts to keep her back, the dead girl slips out of the door and begins running around Sari, circling her hummingbirdlike, her feverslack mouth black with sordes and dribbling with spittle, her forehead beaded with clammysweat.*)

THE CHILD

It was you! You!

SARI

But I never saw you while I could help! It was too late!

THE CHILD

(*Chirping.*) You made my mother believe! Pilgrim! You killed me!

(*Sari turns to run. She trips and falls into the arms of Beshur.*)

BESHUR

As I expected. All a lie. Fortunately I do not believe in any of this. I have never believed. Really. There is no quintessential atheist like a priest. (*He reaches into his breast and extracts a bloody heart. Long thorns transfix it in threespace, quivering x,y,z.*) Well, this *does* hurt a little. But I will get used to it.

(*The heart rises up on thorny legs and bounces back and forth on the limited expanse of his palm, jigging.*)

A WOMAN OF NUHR

And then we exchange gifts. It is a wonderful celebration. I never feel more like a woman than when I am exchanging gifts.

SARI

(*With desperation.*) But Naia is *real*. I am living testimony to her reality. I *know*.

BESHUR

(*Tossing away his antic heart.*) Nonsense. I am a scholar, you see, and I understand these things. I was taught these things in the ... ah ... (*He falls silent, flustered.*)

A VOICE

Say it!

BESHUR

... ah ...

ANOTHER VOICE
Admit it!

BESHUR
I was only visiting! That was all! Yes! Visiting!

THE VOICES TOGETHER
Strip him! Search him! Find him out!

(*From among the dimshadowed, smokewreathed aisles of books appear members of the religious police. There are several hundred of them, and they converge with great masculinity upon Beshur. The apostate is whirled around, stripped, and upended. Bright red letters glow from his buttocks, spelling out in unmistakable, heirophantic script:* FORMER PRIEST.)

THE VOICES
That is all the proof we need!

BESHUR
But . . . I was never ordained!

THE VOICES
A technicality. It says plainly in the Sacred Texts—

BESHUR
(*With defiance.*) You *made up* the Sacred Texts! They can say anything you want them to!

THE VOICES
(*Turning abruptly congratulatory.*) Absolutely correct! What magnificent insight! Reward that man!

(*The uneducated rabble converge upon Beshur, waving. The religious police hoist him upon their shoulders, and he is paraded through the length and breadth of the Three Kingdoms. In some villages, he is pelted with priceless, droughtreared flowers. In others, bowls of succulent fruit are placed before him. Women hold up their children to receive the touch of his hand. Priests, realizing the errors of their beliefs, come to the counseled. Benevolent Beshur grants to all what they desire.)*

THE WHISPERS

(Variously.) Is he not amazing? Such a model of intelligence. There is no deceiving one like him! Best scholar in his class! Beshur knows all! A natural font of wisdom.

THE (FORMER) GHARAT ABNEL

(Wearing sackcloth and scourging himself.) I was wrong! Forgive me! It was all a mistake!

BESHUR

(Lifting a hand in priestly benediction.) You are forgiven.

KING INWA KABIR

(Kneeling before Beshur.) I was an instrument of deception! Pardon me!

BESHUR

(Anointing him with oil and balm.) You are pardoned.

(By acclamation, Beshur is set up upon a throne whose twin pillars are wisdom and knowledge. He writes a book, founds a school, produces, out of thin air, a number of ancient documents which prove to the satisfaction of all that his pronouncements are not only accurate, but are also part of a well-established and sacred tradition whose origins predate recorded history. By royal decree, eleven hundred scholars and researchers are assigned to him to continue the great work, and a sprawling complex of buildings is constructed to house them all. Under Beshur's

rule, the kingdom prospers, the land grows green and fer-
tile, and everything multiplies. But a serpent rears its
head.)

THE SERPENT

I cannot multiply. I am an adder.

BESHUR

(*Looking nervous.*) You are pardoned also.

THE SERPENT

(*Craftily.*) I do not want pardon. I want explanations.

BESHUR

(*Distinctly ill at ease.*) Name your desire.

THE SERPENT

Where are you getting all that water?

BESHUR

(*Attempting, without much success, to conceal the canals,*
lakes, rivers, streams, and reservoirs that irrigate the
Three Kingdoms.) What water?

SARI

(*Old, withered, and concussed by the collapse of an earth-*
quaked house.) Some water! Oh! Please.

BESHUR

(*Staring into her face.*) I . . . I will give you water. But you
are not—

CHORUS

(*All together.*) Oh! Oh, yes! That!

THE SERPENT

(*Writing forward.*) You know very well what water.

(Beshur holds the old woman's head while she sips water from a cup. Water is dripping on him, rising about his feet. Flowers are blooming between his toes, upsoaring trees taking root behind him and growing twenty feet high in the space of a quickdrawn breath. A boat floats by on which musicians are playing love songs, and a doveshaped ship drops anchor behind him.)

THE ANCHOR

(Sinking rapidly.) Kersplosh!

BESHUR

Ah . . . er . . . water?

THE SERPENT

Water.

BESHUR

(Increasingly frantic, attempting to stretch his waist cloth wider and wider to conceal the spreading evidence of oxide of hydrogen.) Water? You must have misunderstood. There is a drought in the Three Kingdoms. It has been going on for three centuries. I could not possibly have had anything to do with it, since it began before I was born.

VOICES

(Excited. Doubtful. Confused.) Before he was born!

BESHUR

(Now clad in the costume of a street entertainer: brightly colored cottons, bells on his feet, cymbals in his hands. To his own jingleclanging accompaniment, he begins a sprightly dance.) Oh, yes. Absolutely true. Which is not to say that my researchers— *(His voice drops to an insinuating whisper as he puts his lips to the serpent's ear.)* —will not uncover some evidence of unethical behavior of one

kind or another on the part of my predecessors . . . as I am sure that you understand. (*Resuming his springleringle dance.*) But I myself am blameless. It all began before I was born. Ineluctable modality of temporal existence.

VOICES

(*Babelrising.*) But truth is eternal!

BESHUR

Absolutely true! But all things are relative, and since Panas is a created deity in any case, then all things become even more relative, since no clear moral precedent has been pre-established by an external cause. (*He grows old, gray, wise. A long beard unfurls from his chin, and his hunched shoulders exude knowledge and deliberation. He speaks in a dry, knowledgeable rasp.*) Therefore, it must be seen that any relative evaluation of the priestly interference with normal hydrological processes can only be truly judged within the context of the enfolding order. That is, externals such as the actual presence or non-presence of vivifying fluid cannot be offered as any evidence, pro or con, of any kind of foreordained or prescient knowledge of the presence or non-presence of the aforementioned vivifying fluid *as such,* but can be upheld only as a qualified and potential guideline, wholly unsuitable for all but the most impulsive and irrational action.

VOICES

(*Accompanied by gasps, shouts, whistles.*) Amazing! Astounding!

BESHUR

(*Warming to his subject.*) Furthermore, any admissions or denials on the part of the power ordained by the will and acclamation of the population as a whole to be installed in a position of leadership regarding these manifestations of a liquiscent nature can only really be evaluated . . .

(The roar and acclamations of the crowd widen, grow louder. Whistles and shouts of "What a man!" and "More! More!" rise up from all sides as Beshur's performance raises his audience's enthusiasm to giddy heights.)

BESHUR

. . . in the light of the actualized plenum. That is, the entirety of universal manifestation, in which case such minor inconsistencies as might, from time to time, arise in the narrative chronicle devised by various representatives of the aforementioned power installed by public will and acclamation must, by nature, be discounted, since proportion, taken in its most general sense, renders such inconsistencies inconsequential and, for the most part, trivial.

(Beshur is now standing knee deep in water.)

BESHUR

Is that clear?

(The roar of the crowd has become such that his last words are drowned out. More calls of "Astounding!" arise, and now Beshur is being hailed as a new prophet, one who will give the true interpretation of the words of Panas.)

BESHUR

(Turning abruptly into the weedy figure of an untried youth, his voice an adolescent squeak.) But that was what I told you in the beginning. Panas is a created deity. You can make him say anything you want.

(Stunned silence from all sides. A pigeon flutters over him, and a dropping splats on his freshly shaven head, runs down his forehead, drips from his nose.)

A VOICE

(*Angry.*) Heretic!

ANOTHER VOICE

(*Even more angry.*) Apostate!

BESHUR

But . . . but that is why you gave me control of your religion!

THE SERPENT

(*Rising from the depths of the water.*) What *about* the water?

BESHUR

(*In some confusion.*) Well . . . it is up in the mountains.

THE SERPENT

How do you know?

BESHUR

It is my duty to know! I read it in a book! I am a scholar! I was the first in my class at the . . . the . . . ah . . .

THE CROWD

(*Insinuatingly.*) Yeeeeees?

BESHUR

. . . ah . . . er . . . uh . . . priests' house.

THE CROWD

(*With one voice.*) Apostate! Seize him!

(*Beshur turns, flees. Moving staircases rise beneath his feet carrying him back as he strides in swift, splayfooted stasis. The crowd pursues. Beshur redoubles his efforts, gains on the moving stairs, reaches the landing where Po-*

tatoes and Sari are waiting in the room of the secret scrolls.)

SARI

Beshur?

POTATOES

(*Wearing the garb of a Panasian priest.*) He has come at last! (*He places Sari's hand in the patriarchal palm of Beshur, blesses them with the sign of the chisel.*) You are husband and wife!

SARI

(*Drawing back.*) I am here because the Goddess sent me! I *am* because the Goddess—

BESHUR

(*Ejaculating in whitehot lustpassion.*) Exactly!

(*Gripping her hand, he drags her into their Panasian home. Fine stone walls, jasper floors, amethyst windows. Fourteen children play on the floor, a ready-made family provided for Sari with the good wishes of the Sculptor God.*)

THE SCULPTOR GOD

(*Appearing at the window, his nose paneflattened and pocked.*) SO BE IT ARDANE!

(*The two lovebirds settle down to a blissful existence. Beshur carries for a living. Sari occupies his bed and cooks his meals and rears his children and washes his clothing and provides constant emotional support and comfort for him while expecting none for herself. Kindly magistrates come to their door to view them with satisfaction. Panasian prelates ask them questions so as to be able to better advise other young marrieds. A scroll dictated by*

King Inwa Kabir himself hangs on the wall, a treasured possession that will be passed down to and fought over by the many descendants of Beshur and Sari, who will constitute one of the great and enduring family lines of the Three Kingdoms for centuries to come, the men filling, almost exclusively, the high ranking positions of power and influence in the government as a result of their competence and unswerving loyalty to all things Panasian.)

SARI

We must leave this place.

BESHUR

(*Looking up from a contented couch.*) Leave? Why?

SARI

It is the drugs.

(*The couch folds, metamorphosing into a chute that unceremoniously drops Beshur down a reeking sewerhole. He falls into a silken chamber of pink and mauve, into the arms of a strange, androgynous boy-girl.*)

BAKBUK

(*Rapturously.*) Ah! My love!

BESHUR

I do not know you.

BAKBUK

Ah, but you do. You and I. Do you not remember the priests' house. Under the sheets?

(*Beshur and Bakbuk appear robed in the garments of Panasian novices. A sheet drapes over them. Head to groin and groin to head they lie, their lips seeking one another.*)

BESHUR

I do not remember.

BAKBUK

(*Face buried in Beshurgroin, cockmuffled voice.*) It was before they shaved my head and the razor slipped . . .

(*From above, a razor, giantswollen, bisects the scene with glintingedge, trailing a bloody cut behind it. It tumbles, falling openfaced, seeking the female ground into which to bury its gleaming, penetrating presence, disappears.*)

BAKBUK

. . . and made me a woman. And so I am. (*Excitedly.*) And so are you! How long is your hair?

BESHUR

(*Rising, throwing off the sheet, plainly disturbed.*) My hair?

(*With horror, he discovers that it falls below his suddenslender waist, curling in womanringlets like the tendrils of a grasping vine.*)

BAKBUK

Yes, your hair. It looks fine now. You will find fulfillment in your niche in life. For what do you want to keep that ugly mind of yours? To read scrolls? What a silly thing!

BESHUR

(*Fluffing her hair, feeling her breasts.*) Why, you are right. Absolutely right. I should have known when I saw the expression on your face at the time the razor slipped that you had come to terms with a revelation.

BAKBUK

(*With delight.*) You remember then! Yes! And I, a woman at last! Truly it is a delightful thing to be, with nothing to do but to follow the command and rule of others. Gone are the clumsy attempts at logic. Gone are the struggles with ethics and plans. I have . . . (*Glances appraisingly at Beshur, who is, by now, entranced with her own shapeliness.*) . . . that is, *we* have pretty faces, nice clothes, and bodies built only for pleasure. What more do we need than that?

BESHUR

(*With glowing revelation, and some sexual heat.*) Yes, just as I expected.

(*Faceless men stream in. Naked and erect, they press up against Beshur and Bakbuk, stripping the clothes from their silken frames, prodding at them with dirty fingers, manstiffness probing inquisitively for womancunt.*)

BESHUR

(*In rising panic.*) What . . . what . . . is this?

BAKBUK

(*All innocence.*) Oh . . . did I not tell you about this part?

(*Beshur, panic overwhelming her, turns to flee, pushing her way through a forest of upstanding pricks, her lithe body slipping through the throbbing interstices which climax whitespurtingly at the bulb and release of her tightwedged breasts. Ahead, Sari comes into view. Light falls on her from above. She is clad in white—untouched, virginal—her hair unbound, free.*)

BESHUR

(*Clasping her hem.*) Save me! I don't want to be a woman!

SARI

(*Puzzled, but compassionate.*) Then you are fortunate.

THE VOICE OF BAKBUK

(*Distantly.*) You are mine!

BESHUR

(*Imploringly.*) Save me!

SARI

From what?

BESHUR

(*Feeling the stubble of his still outgrowing hair.*) What am
I?

SARI

(*Puzzled, but thoughtfully.*) What am *I*?

VOICES

(*Rising in a cacophonous rabble of sound.*) We will fix
that! We have knives! Here, walk like this!

BESHUR

(*Clinging to Sari's hem.*) Do not let them have me!

SARI

Of course I will not let them have you.

POTATOES

(*Appearing at her side in a flash of light and smoke.*)
What is the matter with him?

SARI

It is the drugs.

POTATOES

(*Smugly.*) Tell him to lie back and enjoy it. We have to leave this place. If nothing else, we have to find some purer air. But we will need supper, too.

SARI

My head is not clear, Potatoes. I am not good for much of anything. But you are right. We must leave.

(*She glances over her shoulder, into the secret room. The skull face of Naia leers out. From farther in, a hand reaches out, covers the skull, pulls it back.*)

THE SKULL

Urk! Urk!

(*A clatter of bone. Naia's face, perfect and womanly and calm, appears.*)

NAIA

It is I! Daughter!

THE SKULL

(*From behind. Muttering.*) Do not listen to her!

SARI

(*Turning away from the vision.*) I wish I had not come here.

POTATOES

Believe me, lovely lady, I am of much the same opinion. Do you have your slate? We can find our way back.

SARI

(*Distracted. Showing the slate. On it is depicted the face of Inwa Kabir.*) Where ... where is my father?

BESHUR

(Angry.) We must leave. Now. These drugs have turned us all into gibbering idiots. Why in Panas' name do they burn such things in here?

(The chalklined image of the king turns its bushyeyebrowed gaze on Potatoes, who now wears the gleaming silk and gold of a Crown Prince. In one hand he carries a climbing rope, in the other, a book listing the attributes, preferences, descriptions, and names of his mistresses. On the spine is lettered, quite plainly, Volume 12: Aaaayatabah to Aaabathatha.*)*

AEID

(His gaze flicking back and forth between the book in his hand and the face of his father.) It has to do with security, I believe.

BESHUR

Security!

(Lowered from the ceiling on wooden clouds, Sari's mother, Mesthia, appears.)

MESTHIA

(Holding out her arm.) Why did you leave me?

SARI

(Shielding her face.) I had to leave. I loved him.

(The cat stalks through, butting its soft, felinefurred head against Beshur's calves.)

THE CAT

Mrkgnao!

BESHUR

And they did not catch me. I outwitted them. Climbed out through the aperture afforded not by chance but by design, the inside of the erection of men rendered at once contiguous and yet non-contiguous with its outside by nature of the orifice and its stricture, escape mandated by the very existence of containment.

INWA KABIR

Prop of my old age!

AEID

Prop? What kind of prop could I be, father?

INWA KABIR

Hard and erect! I have thought about it often. You were always there. I needed no more security than that. The ways of our fathers and grandfathers—

(*A troop of barefoot boys with powdered faces wanders through, prettypattering along, stuffing their faces with pomegranate seeds. Bloodred juice drips, falls from prepubescent chins, trickles down sunken, titillating chests, seeks nether regions.*)

INWA KABIR

—would continue without interruption, simply because you were there. And yet you filled your mind with foreign influences. You read forbidden books and forgot the sacred nature of the kingship!

AEID

(*Standing his ground.*) Father, Panas is a lie.

INWA KABIR

(*Aging noticeably.*) Lies are necessary. Did your wonderful books not tell you that? Then they cannot be quite so wonderful as all that, can they? Panas is a lie, and the Three Kingdoms are a lie, and I am a lie, and you are a lie.

AEID
And the drought!

INWA KABIR
The drought? Oh, no: the drought is the only real thing in the Three Kingdoms.

AEID
I tell you, Father, the drought itself is a lie, fabricated by the lying priesthood in order to destroy the lie of Naianism which they themselves set up against their lie of Panas!

A BAREFOOT BOY WITH POWDERED FACE
(*Sticking his shrillpipingsoprano head back in.*) Blessed be He!

(*In the distance, musicians bray on brass horns.*)

AEID
Three hundred years' water is up in the mountains. The scrolls we have found say it all. Dams, aqueducts, pumps operated by slave and criminal labor. A network of pipes and tunnels and catch basins, all designed to divert the rains and melting snows of the Mountains of Ern and send them over the passes and into the Airless Places, the interior valleys that by now must resemble something between an ocean and a swamp!

INWA KABIR
Where are you getting these ideas, my son?

AEID
From the scrolls of the priesthood itself, Father!

(*A Brobdingnagian scroll rises from out of the ground and opens up to display a screamer headline as though from the* Révolutions de Paris: *WE MADE IT ALL UP! After which, sudden and abruptly, the scroll rolls up as though spring-loaded.*)

THE SCROLL

Pflap-p-p-p-p!

(*From the spiralwound end of the scroll, Elysée Loustalot pokes out his conical head. A magnifying glass is screwed into his eye. His nose is a sharpened pen.*)

ELYSÉE LOUSTALOT

It makes excellent copy! Excellent!

AEID

(*Dressed in the garments of Robespierre: brown and severe. His hair is impeccably powdered. Steel-rimmed spectacles glitter on his nose.*) Let there be no doubt: everywhere I turn, I perceive enemies of the state! Scoundrels and traitors who would gladly see the grandeur of the Three Kingdoms prostrate before the interests of falsehood and superstition, who, not content with tacit disloyalty, are determined to sabotage the workings of truth and justice, and to substitute for them a craven, apologetic deference to deceit!

THE JACOBINS

Yes! Here is a man who *understands*!

THE MOUNTAIN

(*Re-echoing.*) Understands! *Yes!* Here is a *man*!

LA CHAPELIER

(*Wearing the robes, sash, and gold fillet of the priesthood.*) The time of progress is over! It is time for stagnation!

Down with spontaneous institutions! They must give way to the uncontested sovereignty of the people, manifested, of course, in representatives.

THE MOUNTAIN

(*Shuddering, quaking, releasing a fartstench of noxious fumes from beyond its peaks as it pisses noisily into the dry riverbeds of the Three Kingdoms.*) A royalist! A saboteur! A monstrosity!

(*From below, the head of Louis XVI is thrust up on the head of a pike.*)

THE HEAD

(*Bewildered by the cheers that erupt from the Mountain.*) What? Nothing.

AEID

(*Striding over and stamping the head into jelly with seven-league boots.*) Out! Traitor! You would betray us all into servitude.

THE HEAD

(*Slimemurmurbubbling.*) What is my crime?

AEID

I will decide that later! For now, you must perish!

THE MOUNTAIN

Hear, hear!

AEID

(*Pointing at La Chapelier.*) And there is another one!

THE MOUNTAIN

Seize him! Imprison him! The republican razor for him!

(*La Chapelier is seized, bound, dragged off to prison.*)

LA CHAPELIER
You do not know what you are doing!

THÉROIGNE DE MÉRICOURT
(*Distantly, as though from underground, an earthquake rumble.*) *Comité de salut public . . . liberté . . . coquins . . .*

AEID
(*From a tall podium, speaking with great deliberation.*) Tell me what you will, but if you demand that I no longer speak against the designs of the enemies of the *patrie,* if I must rejoice in the ruin of my country, then you may order me to do what you will, but let me perish before the death of liberty!

THE MOUNTAIN
A fine speech. A splendid speech. Oh, wonderful!

THE HEAD OF LA CHAPELIER
(*Falling into a basket supersaturated with seeping blood.*) Oh! Oh! Oh!

AEID
(*Pointing into the Mountain.*) And there is *another!*

(*All eyes turn to a man who is found to be reading a copy of the* Journal de Genève. *He is seized and dismembered on the spot, his heart torn out and held high, his head battered into a featureless stump.*
A storm. Lightning from above. Thunderclaps and roiling clouds.)

A VOICE FROM ABOVE
Desaelp llew ma i mohw htiw, nos devoleb ym si siht!

AEID

And there is yet *another!*

(*All eyes turn . . . etc.*)

THE GUILLOTINE

Ka-*thwack!*

AEID

And another!

THE GUILLOTINE

Ka-*thwack!*

AEID

(*With admirable restraint.*) I know that my words have something harsh about them, but the only consolation that can remain to me in the danger in which these . . . these . . . men have placed my beloved country is to denounce them with such severity. Anyone who objects to this must have something to hide.

(*And so the cycle begins. Priests, priestly guards, religious police, magistrates, bailiffs—all members of the established spiritual order, in fact, and even some who are not members at all, are rounded up and imprisoned. Day by day, the jailers pick cells at random, extract the inmates, load them into the tumbrels, and carry them to the guillotine. Heads fall. Blood spouts from severed arteries.*)

AEID

It is very scientific, very humane. It partakes of the essence of the revolution in which all stand equal before the law. No more of this public spectacle that inflames the hearts and souls of good and earnest citizens. No public penitential processions. No jump of the body upon the gibbet. No remains hanging on the gateways of our fair cities.

No! None of this! In its place, I present ease, efficiency, and compassion: the blade drops, the head falls off, the man is no more. It is quickly—even painlessly—over, and dignity is thereby preserved for even the most hardened criminal. I recommend, for this process, a bucolic, peaceful setting, far from the teeming cities. A garden, perhaps, set up in some lonely place, where the accused might derive some comfort from his surroundings at the time of his last breath. You see, I am no monster. I am the embodiment of humanity, the true representative of the revolution.

(*A statue of Hercules rises up, bearing Aeid upon its upturned hand. Below, individual pools of blood rise and commingle into lakes, the lakes into seas, the seas into oceans. Hercules stands with his feet immersed in crimson.*)

AEID
C'est affreux mais necéssaire. A minor inconvenience. We will have it cleaned up in no time, just as soon as the state is safe from the superstitions of Panasism and is, instead, firmly grounded in . . . in . . . ah . . . (*He falls silent, deliberating.*) In something else.

THE MOUNTAIN
(*Taking off their shoes, rolling up their trousers.*) In what?

AEID
I will think of something.

SARI
(*Holding her slate. The face of Inwa Kabir glares out in chalkdelineated grandeur.*) I wish I had never come here.

THE FACE
Are you not the idiot that climbed over the wall?

AEID

No.

THE FACE

Are those crystals? *Really?*

AEID

They are but rocks.

THE FACE

Have you been excised?

AEID

A barbaric custom. Arrest that woman and put her to
death.

THE FACE

It would be so much better if they only did it right!

AEID

(*Examining a scroll.*) But what is right?

THE FACE

You tell me!

THE MOUNTAIN

Kill them all!

AEID

(*Holding up a hand, appearing to come to his senses.*) No!
Stop! This is not the way! Reason is the way!

THE MOUNTAIN

It is reasonable to kill the enemies of the state!

AEID

No!

THE MOUNTAIN
(*Pointing in unison at Aeid.*) There is *another*! Seize him!

(*Aeid is caught. His hair is seized, his head pulled back, his throat cut. He is laid face up on a table while braybrass horns play. From above, harpies descend to tear out his liver. Galen and Hippocrates, hovering above on goldfleece wings, point with ivory wands and direct the removal with surgical detachment.*)

SARI
Come, Potatoes. We must go. I think the way out is over there.

GALEN
A little more to the left. You can see the circulation of the humor, which, inflamed by the gastric heat, infuses the bile with incandescence, and thereby drives the air through the system. This I have seen with my own eyes.

POTATOES
Just as I expected!

HIPPOCRATES
(*Prying at Aeid's liver with the end of his wand.*) I am only doing this to help you. It is a matter of undigested residues. (*He pokes a little harder.*) What have you been eating?

INWA KABIR
You have betrayed me, my son.

BESHUR
Just as you expected? That is your answer to everything?

AEID
Me, Father? I have not betrayed you. The priesthood and

the history of our isolated land have betrayed you. The drought is a lie foisted upon us by the priesthood, and the history is a monstrous joke formulated by the catastrophic forces that have shaped the geology of the earth upon which we walk.

INWA KABIR

I am dying, and you attempt to deceive me!

AEID

(*Growing desperate.*) Father, I am not lying. This is the truth!

POTATOES

(*Confidently.*) But you are absolutely right, Sari. Our brains have become thoroughly muddled with this foul air. We must leave.

BESHUR

(*Staring into space.*) But I cannot walk like that!

SARI

(*Wavering, taking him by the hand.*) Come.

INWA KABIR

I am dying, and you leave me!

AEID

It was not intentional, believe me, Father. I found myself in a position in which ...

SARI

(*Leading.*) Come, Potatoes.

INWA KABIR

You are not my son.

POTATOES

Yes. That is best. Stay low. Smoke rises. We will leave, and we will eat. That is surely the best plan. I will show you the kitchens. There is no cause for alarm.

BESHUR

(*Sourly.*) Just as you expected!

(*The image of Inwa Kabir fades into ashdust old age, its eyes poisonclouded and yellow. From his fingers rises smoke. From his mouth darts a scorpion. His body is stripped by nameless slaves, and the sere robes are presented to Aeid.*)

AEID

(*Struggling against the robes.*) Father! I love you! Listen to me! Do not deny me!

POTATOES

This way. The kitchen. Follow me. I know the way. We will . . . eat . . .

BESHUR

(*In the famishedvoice of a cannibisinhaler.*) I am hungry.

(*A dull sound, as of thunder.*)

SARI

(*Peering, searching, her eyes filled with tears.*) Naia?

Chapter Eleven

Yet more wondrous I,
Whose heart with fear doth freeze,
With love doth fry!

The Andalusian merchant of the madrigal persuasion had nothing on Bakbuk, who was, in addition to freezing and frying, also being brutally pulled in several diverse directions by a number of other forces, including loyalty, lust, hate, submission, and a by-now-unchecked femininity that threatened to rise up at any moment and put her on her back in the marketplace, her thighs spread (uselessly) to whomever or whatever was available, regardless of purpose, species, or even intent (sexual or murderous), if only to establish, once and for all, that her true status would allow the physical juxtaposition that had come to occupy all of her dreams and most of her waking thoughts . . . which, of course, put her right back in the middle of the above referenced loyalty, lust, hate, and submission (not to mention the freezing and frying with which the Andalusian merchant would have been infinitely more comfortable).

Her suspicions were correct, her hopes fulfilled, her nightmares made real: the Blue Avenger (enemy of the established order and firm, upright opponent of the laws of the priesthood) and Crown Prince Aeid (toothsome object of lust for the female and (in the case of Bakbuk) quasi-female half of the established order and firm ... ah ... firm ... uh ... upright ... well, perhaps it would be best not to carry this parallel too far, eh?) were one and the same, and Bakbuk, not only sworn by holy oath and ingrained personal devotion to obey the commands of her king to hunt down the former without mercy, but also impelled by the last vestiges of her independence and irony to destroy the object of a rising eroticism that threatened both, was, simultaneously, by that same criticism and by (Would you not know it?) those same commands, required, without fail, to safeguard the latter even unto the sacrifice of her own life.

Which was, indeed, exactly why she had ridden away from Nuhr, clad—for the sake of duty—as a boy.

Make no mistake: Bakbuk *knew* why she had fled. And, indeed, fled was very much the proper word, for faced with her newfound and unbearable knowledge, she had, once again, taken refuge in the enigma of the woman named Sari, thereby putting the question (which was by now no question at all) of Prince Aeid and the Blue Avenger to the side while she made an outward show of determining, in accordance with her king's stated wishes, what had happened to the prince ... not to mention Abnel, the Americans, and, in fact, Sari herself.

And so it was not *too* much of a deception that Bakbuk continued to perpetrate as she rode into yet another tiny village in the central wastes of Kaprisha, made for the Naian Quarter, and began to ask casual questions of those individuals who looked (even vaguely) as though they might be able to offer something more by way of information than magical correspondences, astrological signs, comments on the virtues (or, more frequently, vices) of their fellow Naians, health problems based on assumed magical attacks by unknown (but definitely hostile) individuals, or recountings of horrific experiences that had resulted from the faulty religious techniques of their (unnamed) associates.

Since she had left Nuhr, she had visited nearly a dozen of these small collections of decrepit (Panasian) stone and even more decrepit (Naian) mud: villages that were prisoners of their arid isolation, yet, at the same time, unwarranted beneficiaries of willful and random caprice on the part of whatever force or forces (Bakbuk no more believed in Panas than she believed in justice.) dictated the location of springs and viable wells. Here, as usual, was a single deep aperture in the ground that could be called moist without any undue stretch of the imagination. Here, too, was the squalor engendered by too many inhabitants who knew altogether too much about one another and who loved one another with the passionate hatred of provincials who were sure that all outsiders, even those upon whose existence and trade their survival depended, constituted a deadly and implacable threat.

As before, Bakbuk was noticed and immediately snubbed. As before, the appearance of a few gold coins caused her to be instantly accepted. Decidedly *not* as before, though, her inquiries met with success.

She had noticed a house that was rundown and dilapidated even by Naian standards, a definite oddity in an otherwise uniform (at least, in terms of neglect) neighborhood, and, sitting in the shade of an awning outside an eatery, she plied the leader of the Naian community with wine that, bad to begin with, was so expensive that it flowed from its jar rank with the taint of years that had not improved it in the slightest.

"Earthquake?" she said, nodding at the house.

The leader of the Naian community glanced at the ruin. "Oh, no," he said. "Not an earthquake at all. Did I mention that this was most excellent wine?"

"Yes, you did," said Bakbuk, half wondering when she was going to hear about astrological correspondences and the vices of the man's fellow Naians.

"Most excellent wine. The most excellent that I have ever tasted. Now, to answer your question, I must inform you that we do not have earthquakes here in Ouzal, since members of our secret order—I have not met them myself, but they include some of our most illustrious citizens who are well versed in the intricacies of the necessary operations, and I should explain that I am not among them solely for reasons of security, which requires that their identities be kept secret—meet every month to perform ceremonies that keep the earthquakes at bay."

The leader of the Naian community drank again.

"Most excellent wine," he said. "Did I tell you that?"

"Yes," said Bakbuk.

"Most excellent, indeed." The leader called for another cup of the rancid stuff while Bakbuk, simultaneously fighting down the steel edge of objective irony and the urge to thrust her breasts into the face of even this smelly, half-inebriated specimen of male Naianism, sought to regain control of the conversation.

"I am intrigued by your story about the earthquakes," she said.

"It is no story. Ours is an ancient order, a Great Brotherhood that traces its roots back to the beginning of the world. Naia has chosen us for important work." He drank again. "I am sure you notice that I say *us* and *ours*. This is because I have the honor of numbering myself among its members. It is only because I am the leader of the Naian community that I am barred from knowledge of the identity of my fellow initiates. Reasons of security, you know." Another drink. "Did I mention that—?"

"The house, though," said Bakbuk quickly. "What caused it to become so strangely decrepit?"

"Oh, they do that sometimes. The Panasian dogs say that it is from faulty building technique, but they are so superstitious about stones and such ... oh ... dear ..."

In some agitation, the leader of the Naian community had risen from his stool. Bakbuk blinked as he raised his cup of wine over his head and proceeded to walk three times around the low table, his eyes fixed glassily ahead.

No one else in the eatery appeared to take any notice.

"You must pardon the interruption," explained the man when he had taken his seat again. "I am required to bless all my food and drink in this way. It is part of the devotions of the Great Brotherhood."

"I see."

"Did I mention that this wine—?"

"The house?" said Bakbuk, rapidly losing hope.

"Oh, it just fell down. As I said, the Panasians say that it is faulty technique. Hmph! They speak as those who should not, what with all their little sordid scandals." The leader of the Naian community chortled smugly and tossed off another cup of rancid wine. "Like the one about Sari and Maumud. Now *that* was an example of divine justice if ever there was one."

"Sari?" (What? *Another* one?) "A . . . a Panasian . . . ?"

"An apostate, if you ask me, and I am an initiate of the Great Brotherhood, and we know about such things, even though I am not allowed—"

"Tell me about Sari," Bakbuk said, managing to keep the simper out of her voice with great success . . . much to her distress.

In truth, there was not much to tell. Sari, according to the leader of the Naian community, was an old Naian woman who, fifty years before, had converted to Panasism in order to marry the man she had loved, accepting the loss of her people, her religion, and a small portion of her anatomy in order to become a proper receptacle for a wad of patriarchal sperm. From that moment, she had dropped out of knowledge as far as the Naians were concerned, but she had recently resurfaced, indirectly, when rumors from the Panasian community had filtered into the Quarter. Maumud was dead. Sari was . . . gone. No one knew what had happened to her.

"If you ask me," said the leader of the Naian community (who was an initiate of the Great Brotherhood, about which he knew nothing . . . for security reasons), "it was the curse of the Goddess upon her. Most excellent wine!"

"How was that?" inquired Bakbuk.

"The wine? Why—"

"No . . . I mean the curse. How was that?"

"It is obvious. She became a Panasian. Naia struck her dead. Most—"

"How did the man—Maumud—die?"

"—excellent wine, I *must* say. As I heard it, the magistrates suspected some kind of foul play at first. Man dead, woman abducted. The Great Brotherhood, of which I am the leader, I should add, though this is no more than an honorary title because of my position in the Naian community, cannot concern itself with such things, our time being taken up with matters of cosmic import, and . . . my, this wine . . ."

The odor of the wine was making Bakbuk queasy, but she persevered, allowing herself no more than a exquisitely feminine wrinkle of her nose. "But the man? Maumud?"

"Some kind of brain hemorrhage, they say. Terrible accident, though no more than what should happen to the husband of an apostate. But Sari . . ." The leader of the Naian community shrugged and drank some more wine. "If you ask me, she got exactly what she deserved. Struck dead." He slammed his fist on the table, causing the cup to leap a hand's breadth into the air. "Dead!" But then he shook his head. "In any case, the Great Brotherhood, of which I am the undisputed leader, cannot concern itself with such small matters."

. . . rats and drugs and if he were not a blind man and such an intelligent one very much like Rosebud I do hope they can bring him around would hate to lose him but I did not like the way he stopped screaming in the middle of things and just when I was ready but no matter they will bring him around soon enough and then I can try again my it is hard but it was a particularly good one coming and if he had not stopped screaming like *that* well I would have but I did not so it is inevitable that it would come back like this always makes me hungry when that happens I would have him put to death immediately but he manages the library so well but this senseless delay a minister in their heads and the oldest versions of the Texts must have the truth that I am looking for it is true that we have altered a few things here and there it is the duty of a Gharat to make the will of God clear to the people and therefore there is no problem but inaccuracies creep in and my predecessors were not attentive to all the details of the texts those effeminate so-called scholars of Katha had a hand in it I *know* they did and them serving rich men whose women go about without their headwraps *in the HOUSE* and what will become of us it will go to sandstone that is what will happen but I can do something about that it is still hard that is a bad sign and Rosebud was so silent even when I took off the gag well that is no problem some attention from the slaves and he will be ready to play again I do wish I were not so hungry but that is probably because I stopped before I could come that always makes me hungry and actually I wonder if there is any of that grape and lamb curry left from dinner and the guards would get me some but I am so excited about the minister in their heads who would have thought that Jenkins would have just blurted it out like that and it within my reach all this time what was he thinking of giving away all his power like that but then he does not have to worry about people cheating him and disobeying him as I must worry since I am the spiritual leader of a bunch of thieves and *whores* who go about without their headwraps *in the HOUSE* and I am sure that he is on my side even though he is a godless heathen I am unwilling to just sit here and wait for morning I cannot sleep and Rosebud will not be ready for me for some time even with the slaves restoring him would be a pity but he did so well with the snake and the thread and he asked for the gag he said *please* and I said *yes* and *yes* again and he was still going *please* when I put it over his head with his heart going like mad and his mouth full of that cake I put it there myself saying *sweet sweet* and he laughing and the gag going in but then he screamed just when I was about to come and oh but it is stiff and I am hungry must walk yes I will walk and wait for morning and Yourgi and his drugs and his rats devout ones indeed I would show him about devout but he is necessary and besides he is blind and probably sees things in a different light and oh that was funny sees things in a different light yes ha-ha and what about the king well no matter I can return to Nuhr before anything can happen and perhaps the king will be dead and the prince too I hope they have not succumbed already for then some idiot will be claiming the throne and I will have to do something plenty of handles on the pump wheels they can always use a few more women just a distraction though if we cut them they would not think of the women but then we could not do the breeding and the women have those dirty things happen to them and are always splashing blood about and dribbling they might as well be infants cannot control their bowels and the devil smiles when the men see them though if the men are cut that is probably not a consideration and I wonder whether Rosebud was breathing yet it is so hard I will walk yes I will walk until morning and then Yourgi will lead me to the earliest copies of the Texts so that I can determine what to do about the minister in their heads bunch of effeminate *whores* up there in Katha and what do they know about anything save drinking coffee and I was trying to talk about the temple tax the unmitigated gall of those *whores* up there I am agitated now and oh it is hard and I will walk yes I will walk down to the kitchen and they will set up a table for me and give me food at my command that is what they will do because I am the Gharat and a minister in their heads soon it will all be mine even if the king is not dead though the prince will have to die that is essential he thinks he knows everything like those effeminate *whores* up in Katha but that will not be much to worry about and here is the kitchen but there is no one here I will have someone punished for this Yourgi will let me know who I should have punished this is absurd there should be someone here blind he is but he keeps everything in order sees things in a different light ha-ha and there is no one but I can find something for myself and that will keep me occupied until morning so hard and I hope that Rosebud is not badly damaged here is the pantry I am sure that there is something here that I . . .

"His roast beef is tasty even when cold!"

. . . can eat oh yes roast beef is indeed tasty cold and how convenient that there should be three servants standing in the pantry with a roast beef waiting for—

. . . ?

—!?

"Ah . . ."

"GUAAAAAAAARDS!"

If the thief called Potatoes had ever wanted to smack the Gharat Abnel in the face (not that anyone save an individual with the most depraved of criminal tendencies would ever want to do such a thing), his desire could not have been better fulfilled, for, after uttering a strangled and surprised cry, the Gharat went down under a gang rush that would have done credit to the burlier members of one of the football teams of a future age.

Leaving Abnel flat on his back with a roast beef sitting on his chest, the three companions plunged along one corridor, then another, and wound up at the top of a flight of stairs, down which they did not so much run as tumble.

—Where are we going? Beshur said amid the clatter of sandals on stone.

This time, his question was neither rhetorical nor unhelpful, for not only was Sari asking precisely the same question (silently), but Potatoes himself was caught up in its ramifications.

But only for a moment. Reaching a quick decision, "Down!" he shouted, and he gestured with the torch he had seized from the kitchen . . . just as the stairs gave out upon a lower floor that (unfortunately) was occupied by a number of guards. With swords.

Oddly enough, several of them appeared to be wearing women's clothing.

Sari felt ready to faint, but the guards (apparently operating under the same assumptions that had been guiding the members of the kitchen staff for the last several weeks) only waved them on past, thereafter racing up the stairs that the three had just vacated, their swords unsheathed and ready to do the will of the Gharat (who was still calling them, his voice faint with distance).

"Quickly," said Potatoes. "This cannot last."

"No . . ." Sari murmured blearily. "It cannot."

The hallucinations had left them as soon as they had quit the narcotic-laden air in the library, and so their steps were reasonably steady as they pelted down another flight of stairs, and then another, descending deeper and deeper into the depths of the library.

"Are these not the stairs we came up when we first left the boat?" Sari managed to gasp.

"I think so."

Beshur was gasping as much as Sari, as much, in fact, as Potatoes, but:

—Just as I expected.

"Shut up!" Potatoes snapped.

—Shut up? You tell *me* to shut up? After doing such an

intelligent thing as handing a roast beef to the Gharat of the Three Kingdoms?

"It was a very good roast beef."

—It was a *roast beef*! What in the name of Panas were you thinking of?

"Force of habit. That was all. Just force of habit. Like . . . like shaving one's head."

Beshur's hand flew to his scalp, causing him to lose his balance and miss the last five steps of a flight, his momentum immediately taking a hand in the affair and sending him directly into a wall.

Suddenly, distant but clear:

Snick!

Potatoes and Sari stopped short beside the fallen scholar. "That has done it," said the thief. "He has opened another panel somewhere. A very talented head."

Beshur was rubbing the brilliant article, which had been abruptly augmented by a large lump.

—Oh . . . my . . .

With Sari on one side and Potatoes on the other, he managed to stand up and descend most of another flight of stairs before he came to himself enough to begin complaining that he could not manage another step, that his head was splitting, that he had surely lost his wits as the result of yet another (the third, if you happen to be keeping count) violent encounter between his skull and a stone wall; but, as it happened (Would I lie to you?), when they reached the bottom of that particular flight, the light from Potatoes' torch revealed that a portion of the wall had swung inward on hidden hinges.

"This is doubtless the panel that Beshur activated," said Potatoes, pushing it fully open.

Much to their puzzlement, though, the room behind the door was no more than a closet, a cul-de-sac, a nook. And in it was only one object: a curiously ornate thing that, standing up from the floor, looked like nothing so much as a lever.

Potatoes examined it. "Gold," he said. "Solid gold."

Beshur left off rubbing the lump on his head.

—Gold?

"Yes."

The scholar crowded in behind the thief while Sari, breathing hard and listening to the distant sounds of pursuit, stood outside.

—Oh, *that,* Beshur said.

"Oh, *what*?"

—It is the lever that controls the pavilion boat. Odd, the diagram indicated that it was in another part of the library. I suppose there are two.

The sounds of pursuit were growing louder. "Potatoes," said Sari. "Beshur. They are coming." She wondered whether she was really all that afraid of capture. Naia was a fabrication, the drought a manufactured disaster: she was not at all sure she would mind the oblivion of death.

But no: there was the fact of her body. What did it mean?

Potatoes was shouting at Beshur. "Do you mean to tell me that you knew of this all along?"

—Only for the last week or so, Beshur said, wincing. Please, not quite so loud. My head . . .

Potatoes was reaching for the front of Beshur's shoulder cloth. "You . . . you . . ."

"Friends," said Sari. "Please."

Stopped from dismembering Beshur on the spot only by (Oh. Oh, yes. That.) Sari's voice, Potatoes seized the lever and pulled it from one extreme to the other. Instantly, there was a grinding, and then a dull, rushing sound followed by a gurgle.

"Down!" he cried. "Quickly!"

With the sound of many footsteps now clearly audible behind them, the three plunged down the stairs. They had come farther than they had thought: this flight opened up into an immense, black room in which burned a half dozen red lamps.

And in a channel cut in the living rock of the floor floated the pavilion boat, gleaming with gold and gems, straining against the gilt ropes that held it fast against the rushing current.

To cross the floor was the work of a moment. To swarm up the gangway took the space of a breath. Casting off required the flick of a hand ... though Potatoes was ready with a ship's axe had the knot proved reluctant in the slightest. The current took them instantly, moving them along, cradling and rocking them, and they passed into the tunnel just as, with a clatter of weapons and a chorus of shouts (and a few articles of women's clothing), the priestly guards burst into the room, upsetting the red lamps, falling over one another in confusion.

Chapter Twelve

If Bakbuk has been thinking that, by running off on an overland chase after the elusive Sari, she is going to shatter her king's belief in her and thereby show herself to be anything less than competent, she is utterly wrong.

For one thing, Sari, though remaining elusive—despite there being at least *two* of her—appears to be much more intriguing than was at first apparent, for as Bakbuk proceeds eastward, stopping in at one little village after another, buying (frequently wretched) wine, and listening to (variously) stories about fevers inconvenient to children; demons lethal to children; drummers' guilds; predestination as a necessary consequence of incarnation; the ancient, sophisticated, utopian, and decidedly beneficent culture of the Naians (thoroughly and deplorably obliterated by the nouveau, primitive, dysfunctional, and decidedly unbeneficent culture of the Panasians); and the effectiveness of clitoridectomy as a vermicide, she is discovering that the old Sari (Sari #1) has more than a little in common with the young Sari (Sari #2), whom she (Bakbuk) accompanied on a caravan trip from Katha to Nuhr. There is the matter of the Caves, to be sure. But now it also appears that they also share the trait of uncommonly skillful herbalism, and Bakbuk is unable to decide what to make of two women—one old, one young—both herbalists, both named Sari, both journeying to or from the Caves of Naia.

Surely, she considers, this is straining coincidence a bit too far; but, unfortunately for her attempt to prove herself incompetent, it demonstrates more than adequately that her hunch (Dare she call it *intuition*?) regarding Sari, much as she wanted it to be wrong, was, nonetheless, completely right.

But Bakbuk has failed on another front, too, for King Inwa Kabir (who, what with Bakbuk's departure, Abnel's continued absence, and the threat of immediate insurrection posed by any demonstration of authority whatsoever on the part of Kuz Aswani, is now, for the sake of the kingdom, carefully engineering a slow but steady return to health), though wondering what has become of his sworder, remains nonetheless unshaken in his faith in Bakbuk . . . and, in fact, would remain unshaken under any circumstances. Indeed, were Bakbuk to be discovered playing the role of harlot, accepting money from . . . say . . . even *Christians* in exchange for allowing them the free use of her body for anything from hours to days (which is not to say that Bakbuk, in the extremities of her current distress, has not considered doing exactly that), the king would only nod sagely, understanding without the need of any explanation at all that Bakbuk was simply being extraordinarily clever in the pursuit of some goal that, doubtless, had something to do with the security of the kingdom, and more than likely even more to do with the security of the king.

So as Bakbuk continues in her efforts to destroy herself, she is not succeeding at all . . . which is either utter failure for her (since she wants to be incompetent) or blindingly splendid triumph (because she is failing to be a failure, thus proving herself to be even more incompetent than she ever dreamed).

This, of course, does not bother Inwa Kabir in the

slightest. Resting comfortably now on a pile of cushions in his audience room, and quite able to handle the affairs of his kingdom (Thank you, Kuz Aswani.), the king, pleased with his success, is enjoying the solicitude showered upon one who has recently recovered from a grave illness ... and, in fact, is privately considering arranging to have himself poisoned more often, if only for the respite from hard, gem-encrusted thrones and tedious councils of state afforded by the condition (providing, of course, that said condition does not go too far). Indeed, he wants only a definitive report from Bakbuk, Kuz Aswani, or Haddar (Well ... no, not Haddar. Haddar has been acting too strangely for Inwa Kabir to want anything thought about or reported by him, and, besides, no one can *find* Haddar half the time.) regarding the attempted poisoning, preferably a report that will coincide with his own version of the matter (which has been devolving, with amazing tenacity and convenience, onto the person of the overly tax-conscious Abnel) to make him perfectly happy.

Well, perhaps not *perfectly* happy. There is still the matter of Sari, the Naian woman who saved his life. He would very much like to reward her, and it disturbs him that she has vanished so completely.

But that is not quite it, either. Sari, he is confident, will turn up sooner or later. Her work is, in any case, done. If she wishes to avoid the rewards of her labors, then so be it. No, the real question (now that he is thinking (all by himself) about the matter of disappearances) is Aeid.

He can avoid it no longer. Having dealt with the poisoning—both its cure (Sari) and its blame (Abnel)—Inwa Kabir is, once again, faced with the initial problem. And, by Panas, it is *still* insoluble. Poisoned or not, vanished or not, the Crown Prince has been reading forbidden books. And, worse, he has been harboring forbidden opinions, opinions that bring him into uncomfortable political proximity to the Freedom Fighters of Khyr (at least, as seen from a reactionary point of view). Then, too, he has already fled once—or maybe even twice—for reasons that, owing to the effects of the sweetmeat, he could not explain. But perhaps there was no explanation to begin with. Or perhaps the explanation was so damning as to be intolerable.

It is this last possibility that Inwa Kabir finds the most worrisome.

"I must have it thought about," he murmurs to himself, causing Kuz Aswani, his chief minister (and a very proud chief minister at that, holding as he does an office that only a *man* can hold), to straighten up abruptly and exclaim:

"Panas (blessed be He!) is good!"

And Inwa Kabir, who has heard Kuz Aswani exclaim that very thing several dozen times in the course of the morning, nods wearily and does not reply.

"Let me hear you—" But Kuz Aswani, perhaps realizing that such an adjuration is, perhaps, not quite appropriate (or safe) under the circumstances, breaks off in mid-sentence.

But Aeid is *still* the Crown Prince, and is, therefore, the continuity of the kingdom. He cannot be replaced. And so Inwa Kabir resolves, all by himself, without the assistance of ministers, counselors, slaves, or even trusty Bakbuk, that he will change the temperament of his son. What he will do, he does not know at present. But he will—all by himself, without the assistance of ministers, counselors, slaves, or even trusty Bakbuk—think of something. He *must*.

But while he is considering all this, a messenger arrives. It appears that Sari has been located. She is alive and well . . . in the Naian Quarter.

"Bring her here immediately," says King Inwa Kabir, wondering, as he does so, why he should be thinking of perfumed loins and concubines at a moment like this.

Though Inwa Kabir's command is addressed to the messenger, Kuz Aswani is quick to fall on his face before the (soft, cushioned, non-gem-encrusted) throne, and, kissing the ground between his palms (there are no steps involved, and therefore we may omit any concern about his teeth; and if you do not understand this reference, go back to Book I, page 42), exclaims: "May it be as though it has already been done, All Highest."

King Inwa Kabir nods wearily, for he has also heard *this* several dozen times in the course of the morning. "Go and do it, then."

"Let me hear you say—"

And once again, Kuz Aswani, coming to a realization about what is safe and what is not safe, falls silent in mid-sentence and goes and does it.

Potatoes had vanished.

He had guided them to the pavilion boat, managed their escape from the Isle of Kanez, orchestrated their departure from the shell of the Great Library and their essentially unnoticed arrival back at the room over the fish shop in the Naian Quarter, and then, after saying that he would be back after a while, he had left . . .

. . . and had not returned.

It had been days now, but Sari was, in some ways, not at all surprised, for so much of what she had believed and counted on throughout her life had, in the past few months (Dear Naia! Had only a few months been sufficient for such demolition?), been shown to be illusory that she could not help but wonder whether Potatoes, who had appeared, without explanation, from out of a teeming market square and who had, again without explanation, vanished in the teeming Naian Quarter (or beyond), was not an illusion also. Perhaps his existence had been no more real than the hallucinations brought on by the drugs in the Library . . . or her memories of the Naian religion that she had cherished throughout her life. Perhaps it had been no more real than . . .

But, leaning as she was with her elbows on the window-sill, she put her hands to her face, and that was the end of *that* particular line of thought. An illusion? Everything? Including her smooth skin, perfect face (a little *too* perfect where her nose was concerned), and youthful body?

Noise from the street. Vendors. Dust. The sound of wind chimes, and the ever-present *Hunna-hunna-hunna-HIN!* that would have worked ever so much better had they only done it *right*.

She turned back into the room. Beshur was sitting cross-legged on his pallet, his head in his hands. Through the spaces between his fingers, he was staring morosely at the floor. Sari recalled that he had been faced with just as great a shock as she.

"I am sorry, Beshur," she said.

—What? he said, lifting his head. About what?

"About Panas."

He seemed to consider, then:

—Oh, *that*. It is nothing, really. I never believed in Panas anyway. It was . . .

Just as I expected, Sari thought.

— . . . just as I expected. An attempt on the part of those in power to manipulate those who are not in power. How clever! And the Sacred Texts are reinterpreted or even entirely rewritten to suit the needs of the moment! No wonder quoting them is forbidden!

Sari watched him.

—Fascinating, he said. Utterly fascinating.

He dropped his head back into his hands and resumed staring at the floor.

Could that have been it? Could Potatoes, faced with the same disillusionment that was possessing Beshur (despite his denials), have . . . ?

"I am worried about Potatoes," she said. "It has been several days."

—Oh, him, Beshur said after a moment. He ran off.

Just as I expected, Sari thought.

—Just as I expected. He is a thief, after all, and thieves are basically dishonest and undependable. Unlike working men, you understand.

He looked at her meaningfully.

Oh. Oh, yes. That.

"I am going to go up into the mountains," she said. She was not looking for approval or argument. She was only telling him of a decision that she had already made.

But Beshur was shaking his head.

—Why do you want to go up into the mountains? he said. There is nothing in the mountains.

Just as she expected. "There is water in the mountains."

—Well, yes . . . that. If you believe the scrolls. But—

She whirled, her temper giving way at last. "I have told you that I am going up into the mountains. I will do that. I am tired of untruths and illusions. I am tired of religions that someone has made up. I am tired of people who speak one way and behave another. I am tired of superstition. I am going into the mountains to see if there is water there. Perhaps that will tell me if *anything* is true in this land of . . ."

He was looking at her, and she read the refusal in his face. He would not help. He would press her to stay in Nuhr, or, more likely, to go away with him to some little village somewhere where he could live out his fantasies of married life. Having lost the basis of both his faith and his intellect, he now appeared to be trying for a more material satisfaction.

He was still looking at her.

Oh. Oh, yes. That.

". . . of lies," she finished.

Beshur sat for some time. Then:

—You are a very attractive woman, Sari, and as you well know . . .

Wanting very much to scream, wanting almost as much to throw something at him, Sari attempted to cling to some modicum of courtesy by simply leaving. She had crossed the deserts as an old woman: she would cross them as a young one. Beshur or no Beshur, Potatoes or no Potatoes, she would go to the Mountains of Ern and discover, at last, the truth about the Three Kingdoms.

Behind her, she heard Beshur rising.

—Wait!

"I have no time for you," she said. "Come to the mountains if you want. Otherwise, get out of my way. The Goddess—"

—The Goddess is a myth!

She turned on him. "What do you know of Gods or Goddesses, apostate priest?"

He was stricken, and his hand, as of itself, flew to his head. Sari turned away in disgust, but when she reached the door and opened it, she found that her way was blocked by men. Large men. Men in the livery of the palace guards of King Inwa Kabir.

OK, so admit it. I got you hooked now, don't I? Told ya! You see, I'm a *writer,* and it's my job to get people like you hooked. Not that there's anything wrong with people like you. I just mean that . . . well, there's, like, *writers,* and then there's other people. You know: ordinary people. The ones who watch the tube and get their ya-ya's off on what people like me do.

So now you're wondering about the Library. About how Sari and her gang got out of it what with the king being in better shape—at least he's not faking that he's not in better shape, if you know what I mean—and the guards starting to watch their asses again. Well, you know, that's just what I was figuring you'd be wondering, and you know I did that real deliberately, on account of I've been reading this guy named Trollope (Weird name, huh?) who

was one of those old geezers who did their thing in the
Victorian era. Yeah, repression city. But he was kind of a
cool guy in any case. Anyway, what I got from this cat is
that you don't always have to show everything in a
straight line. I mean, he goes and backtracks with shit like,
"Doubtless the reader will have judged from the actions of
our heroine that she received the letter," when it's obvious
that that's what happened. And then he goes back and tells
you about the letter. So you see, I'm doing the same thing.
Isn't that hot? I can play this game better than he can!
That's why I'm a writer. I know the tricks. And I hooked
you with 'em, didn't I?

OK, OK, so now you want to know what happened
when the pavilion boat showed up at the dock in the Nuhr
basement. (You can't guess, can you? Isn't that *great*?)
Well, what the guards see coming up the stairs are three
people. Two of them are dressed like guards, and the third
is done up like a high priest. You see, it's a long trip from
Nuhr to Kanez and from Kanez to Nuhr, and the guys who
usually go back and forth, when they're not butt-fucking
each another, want food and a change of underwear and
stuff like that. So there's clothes and shit on the boat. So
here comes these people up the stairs, and . . . oh, yeah, I
gotta mention that the one in the high priest's robes looks
like a beach ball, on account of he's so fat, and he's wearing a veil and not talking much. So this is real fun stuff
right here, 'cause the guards want to look under the veil,
but if they do, and it *is* the high priest . . . the wadda-
yacallim . . . the Gharat . . . then their ass is grass because
no one gives the Gharat any shit about anything. And the
beach ball scene is a riot, too, 'cause this guy is *so* round
that he's having trouble getting through doorways and
stuff like that. I mean, this is thigh-slapping time, and people like you will be rolling in the aisles, on account of
people like me know what we're doing.

So the guards who are with the fat boy give the guards

in the fake Library the fisheye like they're saying "You
dickheads gonna hassle the HP?", and the guards in the
fake Library do this "Nosuh, nosuh!" routine and help
them on their way, and all the time the round dude isn't
saying much, but that's OK because the high priest doesn't
say much to anyone. At least not to guards.

So what you finally find out when they get away from
the Library . . . and this is funny, too, because it's hard for
them to just plain *get* away from the Library, 'cause the
Library guards are out for Brownie points and want to es-
cort the Gharat to the palace and all that, and the Gharat's
guards (I'll have 'em dressed different or something, so
people like you can tell who's who, 'cause I know you're
not gonna be paying that much attention in any case, on
account of you're going after your girlfriend's tit or something, but that's OK. I sure as hell won't mind if you're
going after her tit, 'cause I'm getting my cut of the moola
regardless.) . . .

Where was I? Oh, yeah. The Gharat's guards have to do
some fast talking to keep the Library guards from tagging
along like a bunch of kid sisters, and it all has to be real
polite so they don't tip off the Library guards that something isn't kosher. After all, the Library guards aren't dum-
mies or anything like that, even if they're *not* writers. (Get
it? That's a joke. Hey you gotta admit that I can turn out
good stuff.) So they do the "your humble servant" stuff,
with enough raghead shit mixed in so that it has the right
flavor, on account of flavor is real important when you're
doing fantasy stuff, not that the dweebs who usually watch
it know anything about flavor. Throw in a couple of turbans and they're satisfied, if you know what I mean. I
mean, like, *sure* Princess Jasmine runs around in her
skimpies and makes goo-goo eyes at cute young guys.
Man, you try getting away with that kind of crap in that
part of the world and you see just how far it gets you. Not
that I think that what they do over there is a bad idea,

really, on account of all these skanky libbers have given our gals all kindsa weird ideas and have really been cramping the style of guys like you and me. Hey, that's right, brother! Like my old lady ... I mean, my ex-old-lady. The *bitch*. Got all these ideas in her head about going it alone, and she tossed me out of my own apartment. Can you believe that? Stupid cunt. But that's just what I mean. Now, those towelheads have got a few good ideas, only Princess Jasmine wouldn't like them at all, but getting back to the point, she's good business, 'cause she's cute, and she's showing some skin, and she looks exotic, which is all the idiots who watch the thing care about. "Oh, yeah: turbans and skimpies. Yeah, we're in *that* part of the world, and we don't have to think about nukes and Uzis, just look at the pretty girl." So I throw in some turbans, and a few other things, and the groundlings get the idea. Now I'm not talking about *you*. *You* know what I'm talking about, 'cause you're one savvy guy. I'm talking about the people who don't know *anything*. And I can call the shots here, 'cause I'm cagey, and I'm a writer, and real soon now, this thing that I've been telling you about is going to hit big, and then I won't have to worry about this crappy bus with the Crips there in back smoking joints and the fucking DRIVER WHO WON'T TURN ON THE FUCKING AIR CONDITIONING EVEN THOUGH IT'S ONE HUNDRED AND TEN FUCKING DEGREES IN HERE! (He-he ... give *him* something to think about, won't I?) Nah, I'll be able to afford gas for my car again ... hell, I'll be able to afford a chauffeur and even a *limousine*! You know, go in *style,* and all that. Which is what I sure as hell deserve, on account of I'm a writer and I know this shit, and creative people like me ought to be rewarded for what they do.

You know, when I was in college, someone showed me one of these artsy-fartsy-jacksy-offsy papers that some students up in Santa Cruz were printing. And it had, like, this manifesto at the beginning. Now, doncha know, most of it was crap, because they were all full of themselves, but there was one line in there that I still remember. It went something like "Society owes the artist a living because the artist is a messenger of God." That's what *I* think. I think I'm a messenger from God, and these dweebs in front of their tubes better start coughing up their shekels pretty damn quick, 'cause I'm worth it!

Yeah, me and you, brother. But you want to know what happens *after* they get out of the Library? I mean, after they get hauled in front of the king?

Oh ... yeah, yeah. The guards and the high priest guy are trying to get away from the Library guards. Well, they *do* get away from the Library guards, but they have to do some fast talking, and then, when they get out of sight, they duck into, like, an alleyway or something like that, and they pull off their clothes, and wouldn't you know it, it's Potatoes and Beshur and Sari. Sari was the one all done up in the high priest outfit, which is why she was wearing a veil and not talking much, and she's been all padded out with cushions and stuff, 'cause she's a little skinny thing, but, I'll tell you, she's a real looker. I'll have to get some really gorgeous actress to play her, and I just know they'll be lining up for a chance to get in on this movie, 'cause it's gonna be a hot one.

So you can see what a riot this is gonna be, what with Sari so muffled up in the cushions that she's half choked, and Potatoes and Beshur peeling away the cushions and she's half naked under there. God, all the guys'll be getting hard-ons watching this, on account of, like I said, Sari's one good-looking chick.

So, anyway, that brings me to where they're in front of the king. Now, I've put this scene together real careful, on account of this is one of those things they call pivotal points in the story. Like, I've been leading up to this for a long time, and everything that comes after this is gonna kind of like come *because* of this ... if you see what I mean. But you might not see, I guess, because, after all, I'm a writer and you're not, and some of these things are too subtle for your average, run-of-the-mill Joe. Which is not to say that you're average or run-of-the-mill. Or even that it would be a bad thing if you were. You're just different than me, and you're not gonna understand the same kind of things that I understand. You see what I mean?

Anyway, Potatoes is gone, so it's just Sari and this Beshur feep who are dragged in. Now the king isn't a bad sort of dude, and mostly he just wants to find out what's going on with the poison and all, and what happened to Sari and the rest when they disappeared for so long. Problem is, if Sari says anything about where she's been, it's curtains for her and Beshur. So the king is grilling Sari, and Sari's scared shitless, which is pretty much what you can expect from a girl who's gonna get herself stuck up on a stake in the market square if she says anything wrong, and it doesn't matter diddly squat if her name means "dove" or some kind of Indian sportswear. (That's a joke. Get it? "Sari?" Isn't that *great*?)

But Sari is a spunky sort of gal, and she's willing to brass the whole thing out if she has to. She hasn't got much choice, you know, but what I mean to say is that she's not one of these girls who takes one look at a cockroach and keels over ... like my girlfriend—my *ex*-girlfriend—did once. You know: the *bitch*. She's got some balls. Not my ex-girlfriend. I mean Sari. But she's not like these libbers, either, 'cause they *really* want balls, and Sari doesn't. If you know what I mean. You dig Rush? Waddaya mean, Rush who? Oh, never mind.

So Sari is going on and telling the king as much of the truth as she can without getting turned into a shish kebab. Like she saw someone leaving the prince's rooms that night, but she doesn't know who. (And she *still* doesn't know, on account of I'm a pretty clever guy, and I know how to handle this suspense stuff.) 'Course, she doesn't say where *she* went that night, on account of it's curtains for her if she does. You see, she's spunky, and she's a girl, but she's not stupid like that *bitch* that tossed me out of my own apartment so that I have to live in my car, and I can't afford gas to get anywhere and so I gotta take this FUCKING HOT BUS.

Now, the king actually kinda likes Sari, on account of she saved his life. He actually wants to, like, throw a big bash for her, and he's willing to buy into everything that Sari and Beshur (Remember Beshur? The feep?) are telling him, including their story about having no idea where his son is, which is just about the only accurate thing that anyone's saying about anything in the whole goddam story. 'Cause they don't.

So you can see that this is real intricate stuff, what with Sari playing Russian roulette without knowing how many bullets are in the gun, and Beshur piping up every now and then and tossing in some really *stupid* thing that nearly queers the whole deal for both of them, and then Sari giving the old gun another spin and trying again. But you gotta admit that this is *funny* stuff, too, 'specially since I've stuck in Kuz Aswani, who used to think he was turning into a ferret until he got religion, and Haddar, who thinks that his dick has gotten loose and is crawling around without him. Isn't that a riot? Where was I? Oh, yeah. These two guys are in there, too, and the fundie is always going on with his praise-the-Lord crap like it was the 700 Club or something, and the other guy is always looking out the window for his dick. You'll see what I mean when it gets into the theaters, and it will, too, because this is absolutely *great* stuff, and it'll beat the O.J. trial any day, hands down, which isn't to say that the O.J. trial isn't funny as hell. Just that this stuff is even funnier.

Anyway, the capper comes when Sari is just about ready to believe that she's actually gotten out of the jam, and

Beshur has actually kept his mouth shut long enough for
the king to decide that they're both all right, and he's just
about to give orders so that they'll get a bunch of awards
and money and stuff, and be given, like, this big banquet,
when—

Chapter Thirteen

The golden door to the audience chamber slammed open with an echoing clang, and, without so much as a "The soldiers of the All Highest wish . . ." (for which omission the guards were severely punished: Panasian law was very clear about things like that) or even a "The Gharat of the Three Kingdoms wishes . . ." (for which omission no one in or near the audience chamber even so much as *thought* of punishing anyone: Panasian law was very clear about things like *that,* too), Abnel, his white robes (Were they? They *were*!) dripping, torn, and grimy, entered the room, followed closely by Jenkins and Wool. (What happened to Mather? Best not to ask.)

The High Priest was flushed and angry, and the first sight of him that Sari got was when she, turning around from her place before the (cushioned) throne of the (supposedly recovering) king, wound up almost face to face with him; and though she saw his eyes flick up as though (No, it could not be. Could it?) he were thinking (Yes!) "How *does* she do that with her hair?" (She could not for the life of her understand why a thought like that had crossed her mind.), his expression turned instantly severe, even (Was it? Yes, *definitely*.) vengeful, while, behind him, Jenkins maintained a studious "Oh, how *in*teresting!" look and Wool goggled through his spectacles as his right hand, empty of any writing instrument, dutifully (and invisibly) took down everything that was said ... on the leg of his breeches.

Abnel, though, unconcerned about pens or appearances (though his eyes flicked once more to Sari, as though to ask "How *does* she do that with her hair?" (It should be noted that Sari wore her hair in the old Naian fashion—long and unbound and free of any ornament—so there was nothing particularly remarkable about her hair.)), lost no time: while the guards at the door of the audience room were being hauled away despite their protests (Panasian law, as aforesaid, being very clear about things like that), he pointed first at Sari, then at Beshur, and declaimed in a loud voice:

"Arrest them in the name of Panas!"

And then, after a moment of confused indecision:

"(Blessed be He!)" he added.

Which words Wool took down in invisible, vermicular shorthand on the leg of his breeches, being somewhat inconvenienced by the lack of table, paper, pen, or ink (though his knees and ears—arranged appropriately—were very much in evidence).

"Let me hear you say—" began Kuz Aswani, who then, with an astuteness that could be attributed only to a real *man* and not to anything as silly as a ferret, closed his mouth abruptly and fell silent.

"Seize them!" cried Abnel.

Now, as will be obvious to the reader, this command on the part of the supreme religious authority of the land put the guards who were supposed to be doing the seizing and arresting (as opposed to those who were now incapable of seizing or arresting anyone, having been themselves seized and arrested and hauled away to a fate that Panasian law was very clear about (and it would not do to speak of it, monsieur)) in something of a quandary, for the individuals whose arrest and seizure was being called for by the supreme religious authority of the land were precisely the same individuals who were, at that very moment, on the verge of being proclaimed worthy of gifts and honor by the supreme *secular* authority of the land, and as Panasian law was excruciatingly clear about things like *that,* the guards wisely stayed right where they were.

Inwa Kabir looked at Abnel. "Why do you wish to have them arrested?"

"Let them be driven backward, and put to shame, that wish me evil," came a morose voice.

"Quiet, Wool."

Abnel (though it might be remarked that he was still, every now and then, examining Sari with that how-*does*-she-do-that-with-her-hair look) was still pointing at Sari and Beshur as though to make very clear to the guards who were present not only that the identity of those whom they were supposed to seize and arrest was very clear, but that the finger indicating the necessity of seizure and arrest could just as easily be pointed at *them*; and, Panasian law being very clear about things like that, the finger in question could well be so pointed at any moment. "They have trespassed in the Holy Library."

"Sanctify yourselves, therefore, and be ye holy: for I *am* the Lord your God."

"Quiet, Wool."

King Inwa Kabir was obviously unprepared for Abnel's response, and the words popped out of his mouth as though he had not thought about them (or had them thought about) even for an instant: "*What* library?"

For a moment, Abnel was dumbstruck, and Sari could well understand why, for with the addition of a certain amount of stress and a small amount of guilty conscience on the part of the Gharat, the king's question could easily be interpreted as a veiled comment upon the clandestine location of the Great Library. Regardless of the Gharat's discomfiture, though, neither Sari nor Beshur could say anything about the Library, for whether the Library was in Nuhr or on the Isle of Kanez, it was still forbidden ground for them. Nonetheless, Sari, thinking quickly, could add, with a double meaning that (she was sure) would be instantly perceived by the Gharat:

"Yes, honored Gharat." Big eyes. All innocence. And that slightly-too-perfect nose! Sari had remembered a thing or two over the last few months. "*What* Library?"

Which put Abnel in a position that could possibly be fully appreciated only by a guard who had been ordered by the supreme religious authority of the land to arrest someone who was on the verge of being feted by the supreme secular authority of the land and faced him with the question of how much Sari knew and how much she was willing to tell. Still, though, he was, after all, the Gharat, and despite his wet, torn, and soiled robes, he possessed a certain power that stemmed from several hundred (well, all right: several *thousand*) years of unquestioning obedience and submission on the part of the Panasian population of the Three Kingdoms, and so he could avoid much of the problem simply by reiterating his statement.

Which is what he did.

"They have trespassed upon the Holy Library!"

And, without the necessity of having it thought about by anyone but himself, Inwa Kabir appeared just then to realize what library it was that the Gharat was talking about.

"Oh, *that* Library!"

"Yes! *That* Library!"

Barefoot boys and temple taxes aside, this put matters in an entirely different light, as everyone, including King Inwa Kabir, had to admit; and though Inwa Kabir could not but consider (without the assistance of anyone else) that Sari had saved his life, and though he was also of the opinion that, regardless of what had happened to Aeid, it would be infinitely more convenient if the Gharat turned out to be the individual guilty of the attempted poisoning, the immediate present did not appear to be a particularly auspicious time to act on such considerations or opinions, for with the Gharat wielding, overtly and consciously, the full weight of the supreme religious authority of the land, the word of the supreme secular authority of the land (though puissant enough when it came to nocturnal knocks at doors, bags over heads, daggers inserted between ribs, and bodies disposed of without any comments or questions by anyone . . . and, in case you were wondering, Panasian law was very clear about things like *that,* too) was not going to count for much. At least not for the immediate present.

Still, Sari *had* saved his life, and as Inwa Kabir was, indeed, not entirely sure that the convenience of Abnel being the source of the poisoned sweetmeats was nothing more than a convenience:

"Are you sure?" he said.

"He draweth also the mighty with his power: he riseth up, and no *man* is sure of life."

"Be quiet, Wool."

And Abnel glared at the king. "Of course I am sure!"

Which left Sari looking at Beshur as she wondered how much fight it was worth putting up against so many who were so well armed. She assumed that Beshur was thinking exactly the same—

—He has a point, I suppose, said Beshur.

Sari blinked. "Be*shur*!"

—Well, that *is* what is written in the Sacred Texts, Beshur said petulantly. For what it is worth.

"The tongue of the just *is as* choice silver: the heart of the wicked *is* little worth."

"Be quiet, Wool!"

—I *am* a scholar, after all, Beshur said.

"Did you actually *see* them?" asked Inwa Kabir.

Abnel was distracted by Wool's words, Jenkins' response, and Beshur's unfathomable comments. "See? Who?"

"I do not care *what* is written in the Sacred Texts," Sari was saying to Beshur. "They have no reason to—"

—But they do, Beshur said. It is *their* Sacred Texts, after all. For what it is worth.

Inwa Kabir stared at Abnel. *"Them."*

And Abnel appeared to understand at last. "Them? Yes! I saw them. In the . . . ah . . ."

And here, Abnel paused because he was attempting to decide whether mentioning the kitchen would be a fatal error or not. Should a library in the middle of a teeming city have a kitchen? There were arguments both for and against such a provision. For one thing, scholars who might be working late among the books would certainly appreciate having a source of refreshment close at hand. But then, the Sacred Texts made it very clear (Did they still make it clear? He would have to go and look. And the truth! The minister in their heads! Pumice and sandstone to Yourgi's miserable, devout rats!) that there should be no scholars in the Great Library, for what was the use of having scholars in a library in which it was forbidden to read the books? So, there being no scholars, there was no reason for there to be a kitchen. Still, though, any library worthy of the appellation "great" should certainly be worthy of possessing something as elementary and basic as a kitchen, even if there were no scholars to make use of it. But then again, perhaps it would be considered unseemly if the High Priest of Panas were revealed to have identified intruders in the Great Library (and never mind for the moment where that Great Library happened to be) in, of all places, the *kitchen*. Of course, that the High Priest himself had been the one to discover the intruders by having been in a place to which his duties did not normally call him was an excellent indication of just how dedicated, selfless, and determined a High Priest he was, and so, having already committed himself to having *seen* the intruders, Abnel decided to commit himself still further:

". . . in the kitchen! All three of them!"

"Three?" said Sari, recognizing an opportunity, however small, when she saw it.

"Three?" said Inwa Kabir, doing much the same.

"And now abideth faith, hope, charity, these three; but the greatest of these *is* charity," said Wool.

"Be quiet, Wool."

"Let me hear you say—" began Kuz Aswani, but again he decided, regardless of whether Panasian law was clear about it or not, that silence was very much the best policy.

Again, though, confronted with a difficulty, Abnel fell back on authority. "Well, there were three when *I* saw them!"

—I do not think that, technically, the number really matters, Beshur said. Does it?

"Be*shur*!"

—Well, it is true, is it not? After all, nothing really matters now that the Sacred Texts have been shown to be a complete—

And here Beshur broke off not because of any influx of common sense, but rather because Sari, in an instinctive scramble for self-preservation, had launched herself at him and clapped a hand over his mouth.

"I beg your pardon, All Highest," she explained. "My companion has been . . . ah . . . ill. He is not himself. Please forgive anything unfortunate that he has said."

"And be ye kind one to another, tenderhearted, forgiving one another, even as God for Christ's sake hath forgiven you."

"Wool, *quiet*!"

But Abnel, though distracted for a moment by Wool (and with just a quick how-*does*-she-do-that-with-her-hair glance at Sari), had seen his chance. "And the All Highest has been ill himself," he declared with great magnanimity. "It is a terrible thing, and I am sure that the All Highest will wish to retire in order to continue with his convalescence while I . . . attend . . . to these unfortunate and fatiguing matters."

—Dath ith pr'bl'g uh guhd udulgh, Beshur mumbled beneath Sari's hand.

"Be*shur*!"

Inwa Kabir rested his gaze on the figure of the Gharat.

"I assure you, honored Gharat, that I am in the best of health."

Abnel, obviously sensing that matters regarding the king's health had to be handled with great caution, bowed low. "Panas (blessed be He!) be praised—"

"Let me hear you—ah . . ."

"Let us hear you say *what*?"

"Ah . . . never mind."

Was that a hiss?

"—for the All Highest's miraculous recovery after being not only in danger of losing the All Highest's life but . . ." (With a sidelong glance at Sari, who still had her hand clamped over Beshur's mouth. (And how *did* she do that with her hair?)) ". . . of being . . . *bewitched* . . . by this . . . this *Naian*."

"Thou shalt not suffer a witch to live."

"Wool, for the love of God, be *quiet*."

Abnel, distracted once again, finally turned to Jenkins. "What is he saying?"

"Any number of things," Jenkins explained. "Scriptural quotations. I am terribly sorry." He glared at Wool, who was still goggling at the empty air, taking down the exchange in invisible, vermicular shorthand on the leg of his breeches. "It will not happen again."

But Abnel was looking at Jenkins hungrily. "Scriptural quotations?" he said. "You mean, the . . . the *truth*?"

Jenkins squirmed.

"For *your* people, that is?"

"Well . . ." And then, with righteousness: "Yes!"

"What did he say? That last time."

"He said: *Thou shalt not suffer a witch to live.*"

Jenkins was speaking in French, and, as quite a number of the individuals in the room understood that language, including Inwa Kabir himself, the effect was electric. Suddenly, most eyes were on Sari, who was, yes, *still* holding her hand over Beshur's mouth.

—Ught duh e suth?

"I do not know," said Sari, who, having no scholastic pretensions, understood neither French nor English.

"Is that . . . what is done in your land?" Abnel was saying to Jenkins.

And Jenkins, suddenly confronted with an opportunity, said, with great enthusiasm: "Yes!"

"What is a *witch*?" asked Kuz Aswani, whose French was not particularly good.

Abnel turned to him. "A sorceress, Chief Minister."

Kuz Aswani abruptly joined in the overall electrified effect. "A . . . a . . . a . . . sorceress?"

His eyes glazed and frightened, he was suddenly backing away from Sari, bumping into guards, running into inconveniently placed pillars, missing the door entirely (because he was not looking where he was going). "A—" *Thump!* "—sorceress!"

And then, turning only briefly so as to determine the exact location of the door, he bolted through it, the guards calling frantically after him, "The soldiers of the All Highest . . ." but, too late: they, also, were hauled away (Panasian law being very clear about things like that) as, back from the corridor down which Kuz Aswani had bolted, there drifted an uneasy *chuckle-chuckle-chuckle*.

Inwa Kabir had plainly lost the initiative. Worse, Sari saw that he was himself beginning to have doubts about the herbalist who had saved his life. Though it was obvious that the king trusted Abnel not at all, it was also obvious that the Gharat was not one with whom to trifle.

And Abnel, seeing that Inwa Kabir had turned hesitant, seized the moment for himself:

"Arrest them!" he said, pointing once again at Sari and Beshur. "They have been practicing magic!"

And as the guards advanced on Sari, she, still gamely trying to beat a game she knew she was destined to lose, was about to say "*What* magic?", when . . .

"ADIPOSE ALBINO APTERYXES UP THE ANAL APERTURES OF THE ARROGANT—!"

[Caps Lock *off.*]

But the alliterative cry of the gloriously blue figure who is just now swinging in through the window by means of a conveniently placed rope (Don't ask.) is cut short by the inconvenient presence of the same pillar that so incommoded Kuz Aswani during his retreat, and though the collision produces—

Thump!

—much the same sound, the Blue Avenger, owing to his greater velocity, is not simply incommoded but, rather, sent sprawling, and the guards, breathing a sigh of relief that this is not any sort of individual who requires any sort of royal protocol whatsoever, do not even wait for a pointed finger of the Gharat or a word from Inwa Kabir: they are already running to seize and arrest him.

But it takes more than a collision with a pillar to stop the Blue Avenger, and the Superlative Solitaire is on his feet in a moment . . . and it is about then that the guards realize that they are in trouble, not because the Blue Avenger has a sword (after all, the guards have swords, too) or because he looks, beneath that mask (Do not forget the mask!) as though he is quite willing to use his sword (after all, the guards would not be guards if they were not willing to use their swords, too). No: the guards realize that they are in trouble because the fighting skills of the Blue Avenger are well-known, and, owing to the fact that so many guards have been dragged off (by other guards) to a fate that it would not do to speak of (monsieur), there are only two guards left in the audience chamber. (Someone will definitely be punished for this: Panasian law is *very* clear about things like that.)

The Blue Avenger is apparently quite cognizant of the martial depopulation of the audience chamber, for with a murmured "Allow me, pretty lady," he steps between the guards and Sari (He appears to have the uncanny ability to completely ignore Beshur, even though Sari's small hand is, yes, still over Beshur's mouth.), and proceeds first to knock the guards senseless with a couple of small, numbing blows, then to herd Sari and Beshur (while still taking no notice whatsoever of the latter) toward the door while Abnel, Inwa Kabir, assorted counselors, servants with brass horns, and boys with powdered faces look on, stunned into helpless inaction by this azure apparition (save for Haddar, who is looking out the window so intently that he does not appear to notice anything).

But . . .

"Seize them!" Abnel cries in an attempt to repeat his former success, but his voice is a little too high, a little too strained, and a little too frantic to have the proper effect.

The Blue Avenger pauses only long enough to face the High Priest. "Seize yourself, you miserable, fraudulent sodomite!" he says, punching him full in the face and sending him staggering back directly into the lap of the king . . . which is a serious breach of protocol, and Panasian law is very clear about things like that, but as there are no guards readily available, no one can do much about it.

However, this last condition—the lack of guards—does not persist, for just as the Blue Avenger and his companions reach the door, they meet with the first group of guards who hauled to the prison of the palace the first group of guards who had been found (by Panasian law) to be derelict in their duty, the first group (the haulers, not the haulees), having finished their task, choosing that very moment to return to the audience chamber.

For a moment, the two groups stare at one another, then:

"Seize them!" Abnel cries, his voice (again) a little too high, a little too strained, and a little too frantic.

This time, the Blue Avenger is too far away from the High Priest to make any remarks about his sexual practices or to offer a well-placed fist. Besides, the Blue Avenger has other things on his mind. Such as the guards.

There are a fair number of them. Still, the Blue Avenger is a skilled combatant, and the majority of the guards go

down before one of them lunges forward, butts the Blue
Avenger square in the stomach, and knocks him back into
the audience chamber as his mask (Do not forget the
mask!) goes flying across the room.

Thoughts momentarily current among those present:

My mask!

The Crown Prince!

My son!

Potatoes!

Ooooooh! Him!

("*Ooooooh! Him!*"? But Bakbuk is ... is ...

... no ... wait ...

... *Haddar?*)

At this revelation, the guards hesitate, but a nod from
Inwa Kabir sends them forward to surround their demoral-
ized (and unmasked) quarry. Sari and Beshur, still in the corridor, see the companion they know only as Potatoes seized
and dragged before the throne. But they, too, have more
pressing concerns, for, just then, they meet with the second
group of guards who hauled to the prison of the palace the
second group of guards who had been found (by Panasian
law) to be derelict in their duty, the second group (the haulers, not the haulees), having finished their task, choosing that
very moment to return to the audience chamber.

For a moment, the two groups stare at one another, but
an instant before Abnel can complete the cycle with yet
another cry of "Seize them!" that is excessive in several
ways, the Blue Avenger (or Potatoes, or the Crown Prince,
or whatever you wish to call him), turns about, and in his
very best princely voice, calls out:

"Just in time! Guards! In here! There is work to be
done!"

And as the guards, in mute, instant obedience to their
Crown Prince, bustle past Sari and Beshur and into the audience chamber, the Blue Avenger looks directly at Sari,
and in a voice that is not at all princely, but rather a mix-

ture of the concerned, the yearning, and the passionate, shouts:

"Fly!"

... of the greatest importance that repairs to retaining structures (RTRS) be made in a timely manner. Practically speaking, though, RTRS should be made as soon as possible after the structural disturbance (D_s) that necessitated them in the first place, as repairs left undone (RLU), owing to the minimum erosion rate (MER) of the retaining structure composition material (RSCM) subjected to a fluid flow of even moderate volume (FF_{mv}), can rapidly lead to a potential structural failure (SF_p) of monumental proportions.

Therefore, it should be noted that although RTRS were made in this referred-to incident in a relatively timely manner, this, in light of SFp, is clearly outside the tolerances demanded by the project, for the original model mandates the effective containment of water (EC_w) without any accidental discharges (D_a) save of non-trivial size for a period of at least four hundred years, else the coefficient of random error (CRE) becomes too large for any worthwhile conclusions to be drawn from the project.

It should also be noted that the volume of contained water (V_{cw}) has, over the course of the project, grown to a sizable amount, depletions owing to evaporation, redirection, and accidental (but trivial) discharge notwithstanding, and calculations based on the gross weight of the contained water (GW_{cw}) indicate possible geologic disturbances of a greater or lesser degree should the FF_{mv} create an MER of such an extent that a non-trivial proportion of V_{cw} be discharged in a non-trivial amount of time. This possibility should be uppermost in the minds of the repair crews (RC), even though its likelihood is considered to be relatively small, especially if RTRS are made in a timely fashion.

Furthermore ...

Chapter Fourteen

Pudda-pudda-pudda.

It was back. Terribly, terribly back. Panas had forsaken him, his manhood had deserted him, all his beliefs were shattered. Once again, Umi Botzu leered knowingly from distant doorways and windows, watched from out of cupboards and cabinets and mirrors and knotholes and cracks . . . and laughed at the poor creature who was slowly succumbing to his spell.

Chuckle-chuckle-chuckle.

And Kuz Aswani could blame no one but himself. After narrowly escaping the clutches of the sorcerer, Umi Botzu, he had entered into the presence of the witch, Sari, and had thereby exposed himself, by his own doing, to yet another casting of the awful spell. There was no hope for him now.

Whiffle-whiffle-whiffle.

All his devotions, all his praises, all his determined clutchings at the trappings of humanity had been in vain. He had fallen again, and now there was no escape. The spell, cast now by two determined and skillful sorcerers (And who but the most skillful of sorcerers could have so successfully counteracted the workings of such a terrible poison?) could be resisted by no human power, and he had, through his own inadequacy and foolishness, shown himself to be unworthy of any divine intervention.

Bounce-bounce-bounce.

And now he was alone, trapped in an isolation that was all the more painful for its imperceptibility to those about him. Imprisoned in a body that was slowly but inexorably resuming its course toward complete ferretization, he was still prevented from explaining to others what was happening to him. Which was not to say that others would not eventually be able to *guess* what was happening to him.

Sniff-sniff-sniff.

After all, chief ministers to the monarch of the Three Kingdoms did not, under ordinary circumstances, grow fur all over their bodies and alternately writhe in sinuous grace and careen with thoughtless ecstasy along the corridors of the palace. Which was what he would eventually be doing, whether he wanted to or not. After all, that was what ferrets did.

Wiggle-wiggle-wiggle.

For now, though, his plight was invisible, unnoticed; and though he could attend the king, oversee the courts, and perform all the duties and functions of a man (and a chief minister at that), Kuz Aswani knew that he would not be able to do much of anything that had anything to do with manhood (or ministry) for very much longer, for the changes were gnawing at him again, and soon his thoughts would be occupied by raisins and corners and rearranging: the perfect ferret.

Hissssssssssss.

Even Sabihah had not noticed, and (Panas (blessed be He!) willing) Kuz Aswani was determined that she would never notice. Poor Sabihah! She had suffered so patiently for so long! Draggings-about by the scruff of her neck, sound thrashings prior to intercourse, corners filled with feces, bedclothes tucked in all around until she must have been near-suffocated . . . she had endured all these, and she had endured them without complaint.

Unk-unk-unk.

But Kuz Aswani would torment her no longer. So long

as it remained within his power, he would be a man for her, and he would treat her with no more abuse or violence than any (unferretized) Panasian man would treat his wife. There was no sense in causing her to suffer for what was, in the end, his own fault, and therefore he intended to make very sure that his plight remained unknown, unnoticed, unsolaced, and secret ... until the very end.

Pudda-pudda-pudda.

"In the name of God. Amen."

President Winthrop finished his sermon (it had gone on long past the limitations of what could be considered mere prayer) and sat down, gesturing Elijah Scruffy to a chair in front of his desk. Scruffy remained standing only long enough to allow Winthrop's buttocks to hit the wooden seat first, and then he lowered himself rapidly, for the president's sermon had gone on quite long enough for his legs, unused to the immobility of the land, to become quite insistent in their protests.

Winthrop was a big, ponderous man who, in distinct contrast to Jenkins' thin gray reluctance to commit himself to anything, was very definite. About everything. His hat was black. His jacket was black. His breeches were black. His shoes and stockings were black. Even his buckles and buttons were, as far as Scruffy could tell, black, and all of it, every stitch and thread, spoke without reservation or deference of the monolithic godliness that infused every action of the President of the Righteous States of America.

And it was with that definite, uncompromising godliness that Winthrop broke the seal of Jenkins' report and read the pages silently. Then, after some moments of silent contemplation, and with the same godliness, he read them again.

Scruffy fidgeted. The big clock in the hallway seemed to be ticking just a little too loudly, the women confined to the stocks in the snowy, windswept town square outside and below the window were moaning just a little too urgently, and the good captain found himself imagining all sorts of things that might have been included in the report. Perhaps Jenkins had mentioned his games of chess with Turtletrout. Or the books he kept hidden in his chest. It did not matter that it would have been difficult, if not impossible, for Jenkins to have known about either, because it was difficult, if not impossible, for Scruffy to know whether or not Jenkins knew. About either. And when Winthrop reached the end of a page and frowned for the better part of a minute before he turned it over and continued reading—with the frown still in place—Scruffy's apprehension expanded into excruciating torment.

But at last Winthrop set the report aside.

"A godly man," he said in a godly tone of voice.

"Yes, sir," said Scruffy, hoping that the lack of armed soldiers taking him into custody was an accurate indication that the report had contained nothing by way of chess or books.

Winthrop picked up the report from his desk, and for a moment Scruffy was dreadfully afraid that the president was going to read it once again, leaving Scruffy to listen to ticks and moans and wonder about games of chess and certain books hidden in the chest in his cabin; but after examining the title page in silent (and godly) contemplation, Winthrop set the report down once more and repeated, with changed emphasis:

"A *godly* man."

"Yes, sir," Scruffy ventured, seeing as how the identical response a minute before had not gotten him locked up.

His relief, though, was short-lived, for Winthrop said (in a godly way):

"You understand you're going to have to say good-bye to *Seaflower,* don't you, Captain Scruffy?"

Good-bye? To *Seaflower*? Stripped of his command? Had everything been revealed? *Everything?* But before Scruffy could follow this line of thought to the inevitable (and disastrous) conclusions, before he could confess all

and throw himself on the mercy of God (probable) and of
the Righteous States of America (improbable), Winthrop
continued:

"*Fist of God* is waiting for you to take command at this
very moment."

"*Fist of God*?"

Winthrop eyed him. "You're a godly man, Elijah
Scruffy, and, in the Righteous States of America, while un-
godliness is punished, as witness the fate of those sacrilegious Quakers . . ."

A long pause. Some reply was obviously expected.
"Yes, sir," said Scruffy, not at all reassured by Winthrop's
pronouncements about his godliness.

". . . godliness is rewarded—I say *rewarded*—greatly."

Scruffy, not knowing what to say, and having exhausted
replies that experiment had established as safe, decided to
say nothing.

"You're perhaps unfamiliar with *Fist of God*."

"Yes, sir," said Scruffy, attempting the tried and true
once more, but getting caught up in the question of nega-
tives and positives and immediately contradicting himself:
"I mean . . . no, sir."

Winthrop did not appear to hear him. Rising from his
desk, the president strode manfully (and in a godly manner) to the window and pushed open the shutters. "Rise,
Commodore Scruffy, look upon your new command, and
give thanks to God!"

Commodore! Scruffy was stunned. Nonetheless, he got
up from his chair, stumped to the window . . . and gasped
involuntarily, for, following the president's pointing finger,
he saw, floating at ease deep in a corner of Boston harbor
that was hidden from the sea, the largest ship he had ever
seen flying the Cross and Stripes. No frigate this, nor even
double-frigate: this was a full-sized ship of the line, rivaling in size even the largest of the English fleet. Though
somber in coloring like a proper Puritan ship, *Fist of God*,
bristling as it was with cannon, needed nothing by way of

the gutter finery of the lands across the Atlantic to proclaim power, might, truth, and . . .

. . . well . . . godliness.

"May I be the first to wish you joy, Commodore," Winthrop was saying . . . in his godly way.

"Yes, sir," Scruffy said blankly. The fresh, light snow that had fallen the night before made *Fist of God* seem to float among clouds. A touch of ice in the rigging sparkled. "I mean, thank you, sir."

"You will, by God's mercy and grace, be in command of the fleet that will be sailing for the Three Kingdoms within a week."

"A week!"

President Winthrop turned slowly and examined Scruffy with the air of a saint taking the measure of a recalcitrant sinner. "Do you find anything amiss with your orders, Commodore?"

Scruffy realized that he had made the capital error of actually calling attention to himself. Even under the best of circumstances, this would not do, but when the matter of his books and his frequent games of chess with Turtletrout were added into the equation and multiplied by his new command, it put him in an exceedingly dangerous position. "Why, no, sir. I warn't finding anything . . . ah . . . amiss."

The silence grew. Winthrop loomed over the stout captain like a thundercloud over a rotunda.

"I was just . . . ah . . . surprised."

"Surprise is a godly quality," Winthrop admitted. "Moses was surprised by the burning bush, and his surprise led to curiosity, which allowed him to perceive the godliness of God."

Scruffy, encouraged, ventured further: "I warn't expecting that we'd be setting sail so quick, is all."

Winthrop was nodding. "And doubtless you have missed your wife and wish to spend some time with her."

Which brought Scruffy to a dead stop. Wife. He did indeed vaguely recall a wife . . .

"You are married, are you not?"

. . . somewhere.

"Commodore?"

"Oh! Yes, sir! Very!"

"A godly thing, marriage."

Still fighting with his memory. Yes, Scruffy recalled at last that he was married. Now . . . there was the problem of her name. And of where she lived. He assumed Boston. Maybe Bookshave. Still . . .

Winthrop, he realized, was waiting for a reply.

"Yes, sir!"

"Well, you may give my regards to your wife, but you will have to console her with the knowledge that it is God's work that calls you away from her godly, Puritan-siring bed so quickly."

Scruffy allowed himself the recklessness of being honest. "I was surprised that so many men could be ready so quickly, sir."

Winthrop obviously had his (godly) mind on women and Puritan-siring beds. "Men?" he said with a strange tone in his voice.

Scruffy hastily explained. "The . . . the soldiers, sir."

Winthrop looked relieved. "Oh, yes. You're a godly man, Commodore, to be thinking of duty when your thoughts are doubtless with your wife . . ."

Doubt racked Scruffy again. *Was* he married?

". . . which is why the Synod and I hold you in such high esteem."

"Ah . . . yes, sir. But . . . the men . . ."

"All the men, Commodore, are ready and willing to serve their God and their country," Winthrop said in a tone that indicated that only one God and one country were available for serving. "They are prepared to go on board the transports immediately." Once again he examined Scruffy. "Just as soon as the commodore of the fleet takes up his command and the last of the provisions and green-stuffs are loaded."

Scruffy knew when to quit. "Yes, sir."

"I'll leave you to see after your new ship, then, Commodore, and I will remind you again that you and your command represent the strong, godly arm of the Righteous States of America, and that the mission upon which we are sending you is—"

A knocking at the door interrupted him.

Winthrop turned toward the door. "Enter in the name of God!" he shouted.

In Scruffy's estimation, it was well that the door had been closed at the time of Winthrop's invitatory blast, for it opened to admit a pale, blond stripling of a man—a clergyman, judging from the ministerial band he wore—who might well have been dismembered had the president's voice been unmuffled by two inches of oak.

And the thought of the pale clergyman's limbs flying in sundry directions was a fresh reminder to Scruffy of his new command. *Fist of God.* Why, he would wager that those guns on board were at least 36-pounders! What an immense amount of metal a ship like that could throw! The thought of the power he now commanded made him dizzy enough even without any considerations as to the inevitable fleet that went with the coveted title of *commodore*.

He was brought out of his disoriented reverie by the pale minister's voice:

"Dearest brothers, we are gathered here in the presence of God in order to greet one another. Is this not a Christ-like thing? I mean . . . to greet one another, not to gather. Though *gathering* itself is a Christ-like thing, too. I mean . . . that is . . ."

He fell into a sort of confused silence. Winthrop took him by the hand and drew him to Scruffy. "Commodore Scruffy," he said, "this is Mr. Dimmesdale."

Scruffy was painfully aware that Winthrop's introduction had accorded him the greater prestige, which was something highly unusual in a land in which ministers (of the proper, godly sort) were held not only in spiritual esteem, but in high social regard as well. Again, Scruffy thought of Jenkins. And of Mather. But any upsurge of suspicion he felt in his (save for the matter of chess and of books) bluff, openhearted breast now was overshadowed by a cold edge of fear. How important had he become? How many eyes were now going to be looking at Elijah Scruffy . . . and at Turtletrout, games of chess, and chests of books?

"Mr. Dimmesdale will be your chaplain, Commodore."

Scruffy blinked. "A chaplain?"

"While a godly captain may suffice for a frigate," said Winthrop, "or even a double-frigate, a ship of the line, particularly an *American* ship of the line, needs a godly chaplain in order to care properly for the souls of the godly seamen on board."

"But—" Scruffy began without thinking.

Fortunately for Scruffy, Winthrop was ignoring him in favor of the minister. "Mr. Dimmesdale will also be functioning as your official historian."

"H-historian?" And again, thoughts of chess and of books came tumbling through Scruffy's mind. It was one thing to be a captain of a double-frigate, to fight independently, and to answer to his superiors with results that spoke for themselves; it was quite another to have a historian on board, a historian who would be taking notes, looking over shoulders, making unwarranted (or, perhaps, warranted) speculations . . .

Oh, God! *Speculations!* And one did not even need hard evidence in order to speculate! Only suspicions! And unwarranted (or warranted) suspicions at that!

Mr. Dimmesdale began again: "Dear brothers in Christ," he said, "is not history a wonderful thing? Yes it is! For history demonstrates to us—poor, benighted, unbelieving sinners that we are—the veracity of God's holy word—"

"Amen!" rumbled Winthrop.

"—and shows us that God's holy will is always done. In time. I mean, is done immediately, of course, but sometimes there is—"

"Thank you, Mr. Dimmesdale," said Winthrop. "I have informed Commodore Scruffy of his command and of your position on board his ship, and I trust that you will accompany him when he goes to look at *Fist of God* so that the godly sight of a commander coming to his command with his godly chaplain at his side may be presented to our godly American seamen."

And Mr. Dimmesdale bowed to President Winthrop. "It would be my greatest pleasure, sir. And why would it be my greatest pleasure? Why, it would be my greatest pleasure because to do the work of God is always the greatest pleasure that—"

"But first," Winthrop went on, "it would be a godly thing indeed to offer appropriate thanksgiving to the Source of All Legitimate Command."

He folded his hands and raised his eyes heavenward.

Scruffy's legs were already aching.

Ineluctable modality of the law. Gone. Captured. Mask, then face. Potatoes. Why? Impelled by the pre-extant fact of the God's will (even though the existence of the God is now hypothetical only, seeing as how the intellectual aspect of His creation has been demonstrated by the hyperlogical plenum of the imagination)? Present and past actions one and the same. Water, she said. Before. Time and space. Future mandated by past realities. Potatoes as a male aspect of Sari. Sari as female aspect of—

No!

With me now. Mine.

They had food and blankets and water, and they were traveling east. For Sari, this was a returning that would bring her first to her home village—if any village could be called the home of one who had, in essence, been born out of the rubble of the buried Caves of Naia—and then, step by step, village by revisited village, back to Katha. Only then would her course diverge from its returning, for the Caves (if, indeed, there had ever been any Caves in the first place) were no longer her goal. Rather, her goal was the water that had originally nourished the Caves, the water that lay higher up, the water pent up for three hundred years by the priesthood of Panas.

"It will be night soon," she said to Beshur.

—And then?

"And then we will travel," she said. "It is safer. We have far to go, and I do not wish to be discovered."

—We need travel no farther than the first village, Beshur said.

She looked at him.

She wants me. I know she wants me. See it in her eyes. Repressed femininity, now unleashed by the revelation of the uselessness of her faith. Will come to me soon enough. Masculine striving against circumstance. Feminine yielding.

Hairbellyfingers . . .

. . . moistopening . . .

Here, walk like—

No!

—Well, maybe a little farther than the first village, he admitted. No one will know us.

Dreams. Delusion. No basis in truth. Truth. Can speak nothing else. Scholar. Almost priest. Though chisel of intellect is feminine secret penetrated and made to bear fruit. Potatoes an obstruction. Imprisoned now. Bother me no more. Handed her over in any case. Here, my man, take her. Mine now. Right of possession. She knows. I know. Foreordained. Happened before. Brought together by will of the God in whom I no longer believe. Useful construct. Priestly reasoning. Know what I am doing. Face the reality while she labors under delusion.

Dominate.

"I am going to the mountains," she said. "I am going to find the truth."

—There is no truth. It is all made up.

They had managed to get out the city. They had even managed to tarry long enough to gather supplies from the room above the fish shop, Beshur obstinately maintaining that they would need little (intending to travel, as he still maintained, no farther than the first or the second village), Sari determined to take enough to see them through until they were far enough away from Nuhr to enter a village without fear of recognition and capture, at which time they would replenish their stores and continue toward the mountains.

But, regardless of details, arguments, or their journey's ultimate destination, they had escaped. And was this therefore yet another example of Naia's providence? Was Naia providing? Still? Even though She had been revealed to be no more than the work of a priest's fantasy?

Sari, prepared to rise and walk across the darkening sands, sat for another minute, peering at the distant mountains whose lower slopes faded into evening shadows even as their peaks burned like torches in the last of the sunlight. Yes. Still. Naia was still providing. Even Potatoes' last word to her—*Fly!*—had been, in essence, a provision, for, despite her reluctance, that word had carried her out of the audience chamber, through the corridors, past the confused guards, and into the shelter of the teeming city.

Providing. Still.

Who was Naia?

She touched her breast. Reassurance? Confirmation? "We must go."

—I am hungry!

"We will eat when we rest."

—But . . .

She looked at Beshur. "I am going. I am going *now*. You may remain behind if you wish."

—No. No.

"Then come."

They moved into the darkness. Sari found that she was thinking about Potatoes.

Chapter Fifteen

May 26th:

Gotta do something with this prince guy and his dad. Father and son bullshit. Old fart telling his kid what the hell is going on and the kid telling the old fart that he's an old fart. Funny. Classic. Eggenschwieler. Million laughs. Playboy of the Western World. No competition. Already set up, but have to do something. Show comedy. Present tense. Done before. Cue for slapstick. Good. No slapstick. Keep it light. Prince comes in with chip on shoulder. Dignity. King is there with "Gee-whiz, son" bullshit. ~~Dad talking to me about Gloria. What a feep. Like that. Didn't un.~~ Doesn't understand.

————>DIFFERENT!!! Keep twinks off balance! Make 'em think!

Aeid ever gotten anyone pregnant? Add in later? Kid? Where? What did they do with it? Check notes. ~~Wonder what Gloria~~ ...

Put in something about the revolution. Old dad won't hear it. Revolution taboo. "No go there, bwana! Taboo! Taboo!" Heh. Old jungle bunny cartoons? With the bugler? Alligator coming out of the swamp. Big belly. Anyone get it? Prob not. Bugle in background. No bugle: Scruffy/marines in America. Not set up, anyway. Alligator ... crocodile? Which? Won't work. (Later?) Do something else.

OK. Aeid comes in looking for fight. "You've sent for me, father." Something like that. Inwa Kabir wants to avoid fight. "Hello, son."

Father, I want to kill you. Good stuff. Work in "face from the ancient gallery"? Shaved off beard. Good enough? (Do they have galleries? Check notes: images.) Killing father. ~~Dad said~~ Dad says "I'm concerned about you." Lovey-dovey. Does he mean it? Yes.

(Will Scruffy recognize without beard? Grow back? Sari and Beshur recognize prince?)

Mother, I want to . . . Freudian. YES!

~~What about Aeid's mother? Never see her. Empress Elisabeth. (Nervous Splendor.) Feeps couldn't hold her. Wanders away. Tattoos. Wandering on beach in France reading poetry. Bring in Scruffy? Storm. Has to touch on coast. Meets her. "How d'ye do, ma'am," and who the fuck are you? Ties it all in. Storm later though. Two storms? Why not?~~

Both wondering what the other wants. Inwa holds cards. Aeid? Isn't thinking. Probably Sari. Never got her in bed. Mad. Abnel finally got him. Abnel = fruitcake. Wanted to get Abnel. Did: hit him in last scene. Inwa Kabir mad? No. Wanted to get Abnel arrested. Poisoning. Frustrated. Abnel holds cards? Not quite. Better shift power. Getting on toward end. Make things HAPPEN.

————————>Father and son in same boat: Abnel against them both.

"I'm concerned about you, father."

What's IK's angle? He's against Abnel . . . taxes. Suspicious. Same side as Aeid. Even more than Aeid. Poison. What's Aeid done that's got him pissed? Not pissed. Worried. Nothing about library. Doesn't know. Abnel hasn't told. Doesn't want to buck prince yet.

Abnel wants to off prince. Biding time? Get him later? "I saw him in the library." Gharat's word is law?<—— Problem.

So IK is touched. "Concerned about me?" Then: "I

don't need anyone to be—" No. ~~Dad like that. Old bastard.~~
~~(Sari as Gloria? Nah . . . too much. Don't tell them every-~~
~~thing.)~~ IK trying to be good guy. Touched. "Thanks, son.
I'm feeling much better."

"I'm glad to hear that."

Don't know what to say. Staring at each other. Probably
first thing they've said to each other that hasn't been official. Could get too drippy if they really care. (Parody of
Thanksgiving dinner? Might work.) Keep it in background. Aeid too hung up on the political thing to be a
softy.

Anyone else in the room? No. Private. (Where's Abnel?
Jenkins? Doesn't matter. Avoid mention.)

Aeid keeps trying to talk about politics. Revolution.
Stagnation. (Play up stagnation stuff.) Blame it on Abnel?
No: doesn't know where he stands. Thinks dad ~~was~~ is in
cahoots with Abnel. "I'm also concerned about the future
of our country." YES! . . . IK is concerned about future of
the country, too. But he's concerned because <u>Aeid</u> is the
future. (Be sure to bring up before.) So they start going
around in circles, thinking that the other is talking about
something else. (Fits in with main theme.)

"Our land is in great danger."

"You can feel confident that the danger is past."

"I feel it's more pressing than ever."

"Nonsense. The immediate danger is over. I'm now
concerned about the future."

"Well, so am I."

"Indeed? You show it in an odd way."

"How else can I show it?"

===>NO CONTRACTIONS! FORMAL SPEECH!
Make sure old guy sounds old, young guy sounds young.
(Must have it thought about thing? Probably.)

What's Kuz Aswani doing?

IK thinks Aeid is talking about him and his illness and
how Aeid keeps bucking the system. (Make sure you get
his Blue Avenger stuff in here, since that's the main beef

right now.) Aeid is talking about Abnel and the backwards country and how they all have to get off the stick and start to do something.

Make sure that IK's suspicions about Abnel come out. Barefoot boys and stuff. He's an old guy, but he's not ~~dad~~ stupid. Remembers Texts. Language limits thought? Something like that. (This could be real deep: they don't think about the changes in the Sacred Texts because they can't think about stuff like that. Orwell.<—— Bring out!) Torques IK's lugnuts that everyone listened to Abnel in the audience chamber and wrote IK off as a sick old man. Poisoning, too. Get that in. Aeid under suspicion, but the old man doesn't want him to be the one. Pretty much made up his mind about it, too. Problem: how to get the blame onto Abnel? (Abnel is the poison guy, so IK is actually making the right choice for once. For all the wrong reasons.)<—— Theme. GOOD STUFF!

Got to get Aeid out of the throne room (Throne room? Bedroom? Setting? Interior? Exterior? and the city at the end of the scene. Link up with Sari and Beshur. Search? Probably. No, he knows where they're going. More Blue Avenger stuff? Ropes out of nowhere. (Check Crimson Pirate for ideas.) ~~People collaborating with him?~~

Re ~~dad's~~ IK's suspicions. Aeid sees as potential weakness. Counts too much on them. ——>Blows it. (Set up for this in previous scene. Blew first encounter when he came back from Katha.) Puts dad on Abnel's side? Prob not. Doesn't work in any case, but IK's sympathetic because he's thinking of Abnel and the poison. (POV? Aeid? IK? ~~Soldier at door?~~)

Climax: Aeid tells ~~dad~~ old guy off. (Tells him about water and made-up religion? No. Get too confusing. Not sure himself.) Really opens up and lays into him, then walks out. ~~Dad~~ IK shocked shitless. Ooooo . . . maybe he has a stroke or something!<—— !!!!! YEAH. Solves "word is law" problem. And Aeid leaves without knowing. Abnel in charge. Whole cause is hopeless now, so ending won't get anyone hacked. Confusion when Aeid leaves. The guards notice IK, Aeid doesn't. Aeid gets out of palace and city. Goes off to find Sari and Beshur.

~~Can't work in C.P. Rudolf with mother scene. Too bad. Would be nice. Suicide.~~

Cut to chase.

Abnel trying to hunt down Sari, Beshur, and Aeid. Tension!!!

Creep. Lunge.
Thwap!
Missed!
"Come back here!"

Bakbuk, not old, not weary, not frightened of anything (save herself), and not (save in her fantasies) female (and having the convenient presence of a horse), has made considerably better progress toward the mountains than did a certain old, weary, frightened (of everything) woman (definitely) named Sari (who traveled on foot). In fact, Bakbuk's journey has brought her, with a quickness that would be surprising were it not for the parenthetically aforementioned presence of a horse, first to the city of Katha, and then, turning north along the narrow path that is dignified in local parlance by the term "road" (though no one, including the Naians, uses it), to the dry stream bed through which once gushed the waters of the Caves of Naia.

She had little difficulty finding it, for, even though the heat and continuing drought have conspired, over the last few months, to turn this recently-dry stream bed into an all-but-exact double of the long-dry stream beds common throughout the Three Kingdoms, once she identified herself to the priests of Katha as the (suitably male) sworder of King Inwa Kabir and stated her destination and the urgency of her errand, the priests (smirking a little, for reasons which we now understand very well) made haste to provide her with all the information she needed to reach her destination. The Small Library of Katha, it seems, though not so great as the Great Library (and never mind for now which Great Library or where), nonetheless contains a great deal of information ... including copies of the Hymns of Loomar (complete directions to the Caves of Naia included).

But if the information given her by the priesthood was helpful, her visit to this place—a place visited by *both* women named Sari in the course of the last few months—proves to be even more helpful ... albeit in a disturbing sort of way.

Over the course of her life, Bakbuk has striven, in all ways, to make herself serviceable to King Inwa Kabir, and to this end, she has learned many things. Weapons and lethality are two of her most obvious skills, but she has in no wise neglected tracking and observation, and her sharp eyes (undimmed, for the moment, by any conflicting thoughts regarding the Blue Avenger and Prince Aeid) have picked out two sets of tracks whose presence is still obvious despite the efforts of sun and wind (which have been in cahoots as much as have the heat and continuing drought mentioned in the last paragraph but one).

One set, splayfooted and uncertain, leads up to the stream bed. Another set, delicate, yet sure, and displaying the directness of youth, leads down. Indeed, Bakbuk's thoughts, though not confused at present by questions of divided loyalty, are nonetheless spinning a little as the result of what she is seeing, for the youthful tracks coming down have no counterpart going up, and the case is just the reverse with the aged tracks.

Very strange. She checks again, getting off her horse and mincing (she is still trying) to a particularly undisturbed area. It is obvious: youthful out, aged ...

Well, you get the idea.

Bakbuk, though, having never believed in anything save her sword (and she has now even stopped believing very much in *that*), is almost afraid to get the idea. And yet, here at the mouth of the stream bed, it seems that it is almost impossible *not* to see the idea, for though there was, up until now, always a possibility that one or the other of the two Saris might have taken a different route to this point, the surrounding cliffs would have forced both of them to tread the same path once they reached the stream bed.

And yet here, even farther up the stream bed, is the same anomaly: old feet in, young feet out.

Bakbuk looks toward the high, cloud-wreathed mountains. As enigmatic as the vermiform writing on the paper she snatched away from the Americans, these tracks yet offer a strange sort of impelling meaning, and her lips silently and unconsciously murmur the phrase that she heard Sari utter many times in the course of the caravan journey from Katha to Nuhr: *Naia provides*.

But what, in this case, did She provide?

Dawn finds her red-eyed and white-minded. The setting of the sun disallowed any further searching on her part, but though darkness came to the land, she did not sleep, and with the return of the light she is back at the trail, making her way slowly, up the stream bed, finding still the anomalous juxtaposition of age and youth, with still no sign of any additional passage into or out of that might bring concord to the discord.

And now Bakbuk moves much slower than did Sari, for while fear lent the panicked old woman a fleeting strength, Bakbuk is forced by the dictates of thoroughness and even reason (though what such a little empty-headed slip of a thing would want with *reason* is anyone's guess) to move forward with excruciating care, so as not to miss a single clue.

Still, the old feet (in) and the young feet (out). Here the wind has erased the trail for a short distance, and Bakbuk searches feverishly for continuity. Here she finds tracks again, tracks that point still in the same anomalous directions. Here there is evidence of coming and going, of a wandering uncertainty in the youthful steps. And over *here* . . .

Bakbuk bends over the imprint of a body. Someone fell. Judging from the tracks leading away, the young Sari fell. But leading up to the top of the boulder from which the girl's youthful body had been, by whatever means, precipitated—

Bakbuk sees. She knows. And then she, too, is at the top of the boulder, crying out, pleading, imploring a strange, female deity for one favor, one simple, elemental boon that has already been demonstrated to be possible, that has already been granted to another.

Oh, by Panas (blessed be He!)! I did it *again*.
Did Sabihah notice?

"But supposing he comes back and wants him?"
"Wants him? Like *this*? Did you look at him?"
"Of course I looked. It is my duty to look."
"Yes. I believe I have noticed you looking a great deal."
"I am only following orders. I am a proper guard, and when I am given orders to look, I look."
"Well, you did not look at *him*. Not very well, at least."
"At him? I certainly did."
"And you still want to keep him?"
"Yes."
"Like that?"
"Yes."
"But . . . *where*?"
"Right here."
"Ridiculous. We are right above the refectory."
"Well, what if he comes back and wants him?"
"We could always put him back."
"Oho! So you do not wish to keep him here because it is too close to the refectory, but you are willing to pick

him up and move him. And then you are willing to move him again in a few weeks."

"He will probably not want him in any case."

"His ways are very different from ours."

"I have noticed that."

"We are but guards. Our duty is to *obey*."

"But he . . . he is *dripping*!"

"All the more reason not to move him."

"Of course. He can drip to his heart's content, and it can run down out the door, down the hall, down the stairs, and straight to the door of the refectory."

"We can keep the door shut. And besides, he is not dripping *too* much."

"He will get worse."

"He might dry out."

"Well, yes. He might."

"And then our difficulty will be solved."

"Suppose . . ."

"Yes?"

"Suppose that he does not *want* him to dry out?"

"He left no orders to that effect."

"Hmph. A good guard can anticipate the orders of his superior."

"I knew that."

"And so suppose . . ."

"We could . . ."

"We could what?"

"Well, I do not know."

"Put him in a sack?"

"That is possible, but it would be rather disrespectful."

"What *would* be respectful under the circumstances?"

"I do not know. Where would we put the sack in any case?"

"A good question. I suppose we could leave it here."

"So near the refectory?"

"There you go on about the refectory again! He would be in a sack!"

"That might confine things for a time, but he might give off some kind of ... well ... gas. The sack might explode."

"Explode!"

"It could happen!"

"Yes, and *he* could come back."

"He *will* come back."

"Not for some time. And by then he will have someone else."

"You cannot be sure of that."

"I have seen it a hundred times before."

"But what about the ... you know. The rats."

"Have you been listening to Yourgi again?"

"What do you mean?"

"There are no rats. That is just a tale he makes up."

"Well, there may be no rats, but there are certainly bugs."

"Bugs?"

"Bugs."

"Are you sure?"

"I *looked*."

"Bugs ..."

"Lots of them."

"What about ... ah ... maggots?"

"A few."

"Well, that puts things in a different light."

"It certainly does."

"Bugs."

"All sorts."

"You ... looked ..."

"I ... well ... I peeked. I did not look under the mask, if that is what you mean."

"And maggots ..."

"Yes."

"And you did not look under the mask."

"Of course not. Why?"

"Well ... to see if ... his eyes ..."

"I did *not* look under the mask."

"I could not bear the thought if there were bugs . . . well, you know in his—"

"I *did not look*."

"Bugs."

"Yes."

"It is warmer in there than I thought."

"The sugar attracted them."

"Sugar?"

"And the honey. I am sure of it."

"Did you find the snake?"

"The rats ate it."

"Rats? I thought I told you that there were no rats!"

"Well, *something* ate the snake."

"Bugs."

"Bugs? Eat a big snake like that? Nonsense."

"Since there are no rats, it must have been bugs."

"Whatever. I have no intention of arguing the point."

"An *entirely* different light. And so close to the refectory . . ."

. . . out of the way now and I will have my own way at last not one of them shall escape three hundred years will not be wasted I will have them a minister in their heads and the tax too oh this is really very good indeed and as soon as I can I will take the pavilion boat back to the library and find out for certain what the truth is but there are some things to do here will not take long I have Jenkins in any case and he is a bit scrawny but he might do after a while once I bring him around to my way of thinking I do not like the one he calls Wool would have to dispose of him but that is all right some money and a house and maybe some women and some boys he would like that after all he helped in the audience chamber and I will not forget that not that Jenkins helped at all what would I call him now that Rosebud is gone I do not know will have to think but that will come later and I will call for the tax im-

mediately good thing Aeid is out of the way too saves me
the trouble of having him killed it will be much more effective to bring him in after a few weeks or months once
I have everything nicely settled call him a parricide and I
must find the girl and her man most important since they
know about the Library and they might have seen things in
there would be better to have them silenced as soon as
possible will call for guards they cannot have gotten very
far are probably still in the city this will be very good I
can demonstrate that I am not one to trifle with unlike my
predecessor stupid fool let things get out of hand child-
ishly simple to take it away from him and where is the device I must have it still on Rosebud he *did* like it a great
deal will get it back when I return will have to go soon so
easy to take it away he did not know what I was doing and
then he removed himself very convenient Panas is with me
but of course He cannot be other than with me because I
am the Gharat and now I am the king too the first since
Abramelin's time and Jenkins is looking at me I would
wager that he finds me attractive he would be willing and
in any case I have drugs that will make him cooperate until he is used to it and then he will tell me all including the
truth too bad about Rosebud but at least I will still have
the device and what good is a device if one cannot use it
no more since Valdemar is gone tightened me into it the
first time I believe I came right there in his shop most
wonderful no more will take care of the device I am almost healed and call for the guards to find the girl and her
man immediately up to no good I am sure and those effeminate so-called scholars in Katha can eat pumice for all
the good they are laughing at me well I will settle with
them after a time they can keep on with the pumps and the
water but I have something better and they will find that
I am in charge and that I have my own plans and they will
do what I tell them to do and they will too once they see
just how much money will come to them from the tax if
they cooperate with me and how the plan will succeed in

only a year or two and then there will be no more sneaking and no more laughing and a minister in their heads it will be so wonderful oh I am hard it is inevitable and Jenkins standing over there he will do what I want also when he finds out that the king's word is the king's word and none dare argue against it and now the king is also the Gharat will send out the guards immediately and I wonder what the prince would be like an interesting idea I have drugs . . .

Chapter Sixteen

She was going to the mountains. She was going to *know*.

Amazingly, that one surety in a world that had, with the reading of a single scroll, turned utterly vague and deceitful provided Sari with a sense of detachment that allowed her (three weeks on the road now, and still looking over her shoulder every minute) to sit before this smoky fire and listen—yes, once again—to the dried-up meanderings of an equally dried-up young woman.

"Mucus," said the woman from the other side of the fire.

Sari and Beshur had arrived in Sayam, the last village through which they would pass before they reached Katha. But Sari and Beshur were strangers; Sari and Beshur were, to outward appearances, Naians (and Sari had decided that the term was as good as anything else); and, therefore, in the opinion of the Naian inhabitants of Sayam, Sari and Beshur had to pay their respects to their elder.

"Mucus," the woman said again.

"Just so," said Sari, patiently enduring the reminders of what had happened in the course of her first visit here.

Beshur was intrigued.

—Tell me more, he said.

"It all comes down to mucus," said the woman, young and thin and desiccated beyond her years. "Mucus in you, mucus in me. Though there is much less mucus in me than there is in you."

—Yes, Beshur said. I can see that.

Sari endured the interchange patiently. Arguing with the woman was as senseless as arguing with the Gharat Abnel; and, in any case, she supposed that a firm belief in the evils of mucus was as good a foundation for one's life as the conviction that the Sculptor God had Himself hewn the building blocks of the cities from the Sacred Quarries ... or even the certain knowledge that one had been touched—touched directly—by a Goddess who had never revealed Her face.

"She might as well be Naia Herself," she murmured.

"Mucus is at the root of everything," the woman was saying. "It affects everything we do. Now, you might wonder how I know that there is more mucus in you than there is in me."

—I would indeed, Beshur said. This is quite fascinating. I am a scholar, you see, and—

"I can tell, believe me. You look hideous."

Beshur blinked and sat back.

"Ah," the desiccated woman went on, "you do not believe me, but that is the result of the distorting effect that the mucus has on your perceptions. If you have dust in your eye, you cannot see clearly, can you?"

—That is very true, Beshur admitted.

"If you have mucus in your body, you cannot perceive your body clearly."

—Hmmm ... yes. I see your point.

Sari listened mutely, numbly, and perhaps the greatest part of her growing horror was at the fact that she *was* numb, that she no longer cared.

"And *you* ..." said the dried-up young woman, turning to Sari.

"Of course," Sari said softly. "And me."

"You are full of mucus, too."

Sari nodded. "Yes. Liquid. Slime. Any number of unpleasant things. A great tragedy."

Biting as her words might have been, she uttered them with such matter-of-fact acceptance that the woman did not even notice. But, Sari reflected, perhaps she would not have noticed in any case.

"It slows the circulation of your vital fluids."

"Yes."

—Sari! Beshur said. You understand! I had no idea! You must tell me all about this!

"You will be wanting babies soon," said the woman. "The mucus will interfere."

"I am certain that it will."

"You eat unwisely. You have too much mucus."

And then the woman looked at her carefully. Sari knew what was coming.

"Have you been excised?"

"More often than you could believe," said Sari.

Still, the woman could not be diverted. "That thing you have breeds worms, and they will kill your children unless you are excised."

"Thank you." Numb. Still numb.

—You know, Beshur said, she may have a point.

"Several, I think," said Sari.

"Do not interfere with my calling!" the woman admonished . . . though, from the flat, unmoved tone of her voice, more urgency might well have been expected from a sack of flour. "I must speak the truth! My calling has come from Naia herself, and I have taken the name Truth Teller in order to bear witness to that!"

—I have never examined any tabulations of such things, Beshur was saying, but do you not think that some correspondence between sizes of families and excisions of the mother might be established?

"Probably," said Sari. She was going to the mountains. She tried to keep her mind on that.

—Have you—?

Sari rose, looked at Beshur. "Shut up," she said. And then she turned and left the house. Once before she had left. Then, she had been running. Now, she walked. Slowly. Deliberately. Her steps—youthful, determined— were toward the east, toward water.

Enumerate the reactions of the inhabitants of the Naian Quarter of the village of Halim to the appearance not only of priestly guards but also of royal palace guards within the municipal boundaries of their enclave.

Acceptance. Tolerance. Apprehension.

Why acceptance?

Broadly speaking, the primary response—to anything— of the Naian inhabitants of any city, town, or village within the boundaries of the Three Kingdoms could not be other than acceptance.

Why was this?

Because of the legal restrictions inherent in the social and economic status of the Naian inhabitants. These restrictions, being not only impossible to escape, but also so enculturated into the basic psyche of said Naian inhabitants that their (the restrictions') influence, though overwhelmingly powerful, was essentially unperceived by those so enculturated—though the inescapability of those restrictions was, inevitably, the predominant factor in that unperceived influence—limited the Naian inhabitants to two possible responses, the more palatable of which was the above-mentioned acceptance.

What was the less palatable of the two responses?

Madness and death.

And therefore the acceptance of the presence of the priestly and the palace guards resulted from . . . ?

The unequivocal fact that there was nothing that the Naian inhabitants could do about it.

Why tolerance?

Given that the inhabitants of the Naian community, by virtue of the inescapability of their condition, could not but be impelled to compensate for that condition, the development of some compensatory psychological reaction—characteristically, one that involved some element of perceived choice—was inevitable.

Elucidate the incremental development of that compensatory reaction.

The need for autonomy. The need for the illusion of autonomy in non-autonomous situations wherein autonomy is impossible. The compensation for the illusory nature of the required autonomy by the concomitant development of an illusory sense of superiority. The gradual devolvement of that sense of superiority upon the very characteristics from which the non-autonomy initially arose. The unconscious establishment of that sense of (illusory) superiority as an unquestioned and axiomatic *sine qua non*. The avoidance, rejection, and even violent severing of any association with individuals who do not share in the general illusion (of superiority).

What alternative to this multi-staged, compensatory reaction existed for the members of the Naian community?

Madness and death.

Why apprehension?

Discounting for the moment certain nameless and universal fears that demonstrate a remarkable persistence and similarity even among representative inhabitants of widely disparate cultures and historical periods, the causes of apprehension were primarily twofold. In the first place, a tacitly, generally, and intrinsically assumed illusion of autonomy and even superiority on the part of a non-autonomous and non-superior community is, by nature, a fragile construct, incapable of withstanding, even partially, a non-illusory show of force on the part of the enfolding culture. Since the disturbance of such illusions is, even under the best of circumstances, extremely traumatic for those harboring them, even so much as a threat of a (non-illusory) show of force on the part of the enfolding culture invariably gives rise to a certain apprehension on the part of the non-autonomous community. Thus, as the appearance of priestly and palace guards could not otherwise but implicitly threaten exactly this show of force, apprehension on the part of the inhabitants of the Naian Quarter was a direct and unavoidable consequence. In the second place, a more real, immediate, and experientially confirmed possibility inherent in the appearance of priestly and/or palace guards was that of the actual demonstration of the non-illusory power of the enfolding culture in such a manner as to directly affect the health or (possibly) ill-health of specific but randomly chosen representatives of the non-autonomous community.

Did, in fact, any such overt demonstration of power take place?
Yes.

Did, in fact, that display of power bear directly on the health or ill-health of any specific individual or individuals of the non-autonomous community in question?
Yes.

Describe the manner in which said specific individuals came into contact with that display of power.
The instruments of that display of power (that is, the priestly and palace guards who had appeared in the Naian Quarter) first announced publicly that they had come to ask questions regarding certain travelers who might or

might not have visited the enclave within a given period of time that might or might not have extended from that moment to some indefinite temporal point lying approximately three weeks in the past. Upon ascertaining that there was good reason to believe that such travelers had indeed made such a visit, the priestly and palace guards began to question, at random, selected inhabitants of the enclave.

Did this questioning meet with success?
Yes and no.

Why yes?
By their nature, The inhabitants of the enclave were perfectly willing to discuss to the point of violent argument almost any subject, including, but not limited to, the practice of magic, proper symbolism when applied to abstract conceptions of deity, techniques designed to inculcate children in the particular version of the Naian cultus practiced in the locale, the skillfulness with which local teachers of the Naian spiritual tradition utilized said techniques in order to inculcate their students with Naian cultus, the weather, the effectiveness of crystalline stones for the prevention of disease, the necessity for aggregate groups of practicing drummers to begin and end with relative simultaneity, the reality of sickness and death as realizations of inter-incarnatory choices made on the part of those afflicted (with particular emphasis on such choices as having been made by recently deceased children), male and female aspects of Naia, appreciation of the toil of others from the perspective of indolence, and cats. And thus, the priestly and palace guards found themselves given a great many answers to a great many questions.

Why no?
None of the answers had anything to do with the matter

considered by the guards to be both at hand and of primary importance.

Describe the manner in which the health or ill-health of certain specific individuals was affected by this contract.

It is a well-known but regrettable fact that, although vested with an authority that necessarily denies to them the convenience of immediate self-expression and gratification so readily available to the general population, priestly and palace guards are, nonetheless, prone to the weaknesses afflicting all human beings in that even the most extreme vigilance on their part cannot guard them completely against lapses into said self-expression and gratification, particularly when such lapses are impelled by severe, external provocation. This being said, the provocation furnished by Golfah and Zarifah (a husband and wife known to have recently lost a child to what some unkind individuals would term a very preventable fever) was of such severity that it could not but surpass the vigilance of the guards against such lapses.

Provocation?

As the result of certain hints, then indirectly related tales, and then, finally, under more intense questioning, outright exposition, said Golfah and Zarifah indicated not only that their child had died of what some unkind individuals might term a very preventable fever, but that they had themselves allowed the child to die in order not to interfere with what they considered to be her inviolable free will.

With what emotion were these confessions offered?
Pride.

Explain the above answer.
Sufficient space having been devoted to the above ques-

tion of illusory superiority and compensation for non-autonomy, further explanations along the same vein would be superfl—

Explain it, dammit!

Very well. As per (ahem) the above discussion, communal non-autonomy in a socio-economic situation leads, by nature, to a compensatory denial of that non-autonomy through the assumption of an illusory sense of autonomy, itself amplified, under certain extreme situations, into a sometimes tacit, often active, illusion of innate superiority. In the same way, the development of a compensatory (but nonetheless illusory) sense of superiority in the psychologically non-autonomous individual—the individual's psychological self-determination having been surrendered to a given belief system, which is thereafter caused to be the determining factor in any qualitative evaluation of ethical or behavioral questions, to the detriment of any reasonable or rational thought—is equally well documented, and the repeated, effusive, and proud (even righteous) declamations by Golfah and Zarifah regarding the death of their child and their quasi-active participation in its realization is but one example of this among many.

What was the reaction of their Panasian interlocutors to these repeated declamations?

Incomprehension. Disbelief. Outrage.

Incomprehension?

The thing said was not the thing said that they understood could be said under any circumstances.

Disbelief?

The thing said said the action that they understood could not be because it would not.

Outrage?

The thing said said an action so monstrous that they themselves acted because they could not not.

What could be said to have been the general outcome of the outrage on the part of the priestly and palace guards that stemmed from the various and repeated declamations on the part of Golfah and Zarifah regarding their deceased child?

Madness and death.

"It is indeed tragic, but we must understand that Golfah and Zarifah decided to have this encounter, and, in fact, they decided upon exactly what sort of outcome they desired to have as the result of it. Certainly they can have no complaint themselves, since they made this decision before they were born. It would, of course, have been foolhardy to have meddled in their decision, since to do so would have seriously compromised their free will, which is a dangerous thing to do."

Compared to getting out of the city of Nuhr, which had been, indeed, a surprisingly easy thing to do (even for a renegade (and well-known) Crown Prince), finding Sari and Beshur was proving to be otherwise. Had it not been obvious that the two had paid a visit to the room above the fish shop and had taken supplies and belongings appropriate for a trip across the desert, Pot—, uh, that is, Aeid would have had no idea even where to *begin* to look.

But the single clue was sufficient. They were going into the desert. Doubtless Sari intended to journey to the mountains in order to determine for herself the existence or nonexistence of the vast quantities of water that, according to the priestly records in the library, were pent up in what by now were enormous, high-altitude seas.

The desert, though, was large, and Sari and Beshur were

but two people. There was plenty of room for them to lose themselves in the wastes, which, as the Blue Av—, uh, that is, as Aeid reflected, was exactly what they wanted, considering that detachments of palace and priestly guards had been riding into the east, detachments that had obviously been sent out to search for them. To be sure, he had followed those detachments, but only at a respectful distance, for he was sure that they were searching not only for Sari and Beshur, but also for *him,* and with the innate wiliness of a thief (for he was indeed a thief, as well as a prince ... and a good many other things, too), he knew that if a group of men were searching for someone, the safest place for that someone to be was in a place they had already searched.

And so, when the guards swept through Ouzal, interrogated a number of Naians, and then departed, leaving behind a number of broken arms and skulls, Aeid was there the next day, *tsk-tsk*ing sympathetically, absolutely and unequivocally deploring the actions of the tyrannical guards (who were no more than the pawns of a discredited and dying religion in any case), helping out with the broken arms and the broken skulls alike, and gathering what information he could ... which was (owing to the abovementioned innate wiliness) considerably more than what the priestly and palace guards had been able to come up with, regardless of the broken arms and skulls.

And when the inhabitants of the Naian Quarter of Halim patched themselves up, buried their dead, and tried to get on with life, Aeid helped them to patch themselves up, assisted the gravediggers, agreed wholeheartedly with the general pronouncements upon the wisdom (or, rather, lack of same) involved in interfering with another's free will (even if it killed them) ... and, again, found out all sorts of information.

And when he got to Sayam ...

"Who *are* you?" said the priestly guard, peering at Aeid

with eyes that did not appear to gleam half so brightly as the sword in his hand.

. . . it appeared that he was a bit early.

"I am . . . ah . . ."

And here (Would you not know it?), the lack of planning caught up with him again. He could not be Aeid, of course (since the guards were looking for Aeid), nor could he be the Blue Avenger (for the same reason). So, after dithering for some three centuries (so it seemed to him), he came up with:

". . . Potatoes!"

Another guard came over, also peering at him with eyes that did not appear to gleam . . . etc. "Are you not the idiot who climbed over the wall?" he said.

Fortunately, Ae—, uh, Potatoes was a thief of rare talents. "Not at all. You must be mistaken."

"You are a stranger here, are you not?"

"Of course not!"

Leaving the negative, to be sure, hanging in a delightful state of uncertainty. Was he not a stranger? Or was he not *not* a stranger?

It was a little hard to tell, and the guards puzzled over it for the better part of a minute until one said:

"This must be the prince."

The second squinted at Potatoes. "You are the prince, are you not?"

"Of course not!"

(As above.)

Both guards peered at him for a time before the second spoke. "He *must* be the prince."

"How can you say that?" said the first. "He has told us that he is not the prince. Surely the prince would not lie."

"*Did* he tell us that?"

"You know," said the first, "now that you mention it, I am not exactly sure." Thereupon, turning back to Potatoes: "You *did* tell us that, did you not?"

"Of course not!"

(As above.)

"See?" said the first.

"See what?" said the second.

"I told you. And as the prince would tell only the truth, then he cannot be the prince."

The second was not so easily convinced. "But what if he is the Blue Avenger? Then he would lie, would he not?"

"Of course not!" said Potatoes. The first guard glared at him. "Oh. Sorry."

"Of course not!" said the first guard. "Because the Blue Avenger *is* the Prince."

"Is he?" said Potatoes.

"Yes!"

"Oh."

"I am confused," said the second guard. "This man looks like the prince."

"He has no beard," said the first. "The prince has a beard."

"That is true. But the Blue Avenger does not have a beard. Does that mean that the Blue Avenger is not the prince?"

Potatoes spoke up. "I think that is what it means, indeed."

"So we are looking for *two*, then?"

"No, just one," said the first. "The prince has a beard, but he shaved it off to become the Blue Avenger."

"He shaved it off later," said the second. "The Blue Avenger had a beard to begin with."

"Hmmm . . ."

"Perhaps," Potatoes offered, "there are two Blue Avengers."

"And one Prince Aeid," mused the first.

"You are sure of that," said Potatoes, "are you not?"

"Of course not!" both guards said at once.

"Oh."

The first guard was carefully putting the pieces together.

"So, if he has no beard, then he cannot be the prince, who has a beard. But the prince shaved off his beard at some point, and therefore the Blue Avenger has no beard."

"That sounds right," Potatoes put in.

"So he cannot be the prince, because the prince has a beard, and he cannot be the Blue Avenger, because the Blue Avenger, who has no beard, but who had one once, is the prince, who has a beard."

The second guard was nodding. "That sounds like it."

"And therefore this man here, who has no beard, cannot be either the prince *or* the Blue Avenger."

The second guard paused in his enthusiastic nodding, frowned, and peered at Potatoes once more. "Are you *sure* you are not the idiot who climbed over the wall?"

Chapter Seventeen

Six weeks to reach Boston. But who knew how long it would take to ship the equipment and the men? Not long, please God! Then six weeks back.

How long had it been? Four, five ... maybe even six weeks already? It was hard to tell. He had left his notebook on the Isle of Kanez, and the barbarous calendar of the Three Kingdoms did not appear to bear any relation to anything that he had ever seen before. Without his notebook, he could only flounder in uncertainty.

Jenkins lay awake in bed, his eyes open to the darkness, his ears filled, much against his will, with Wool's muffled snoring and murmured Biblical quotes. The ambassador's mind, though, was taken up with numbers. One week, then two. Two was (maybe) when Abnel had started sending him off on tours of the island. Then another several (Maddening inaccuracy!) weeks. By his best count they had been on the Isle of Kanez for four or five weeks. Give or take a week. Or (Drat!) more.

And how long had it been since they had returned to Nuhr? Two weeks? A month? Maybe. The days were beginning to run together for Jenkins. Barefoot boys, servants with brass horns, Abnel's ... well ... *looks* at him from beneath half-closed eyelids, constant interminable meals with too much food, too much sugar, too much unintelligible music ...

It was all turning his days into a featureless blur, and, worse, he suspected that it was deadening his mind, taking the edge off his determination to control Abnel, to make sure that the Gharat was ready and willing to receive the ten thousand American troops when they arrived in . . .

. . . in what? Drat! There it was again! Three weeks? Five?

"And being turned, I saw seven golden candlesticks . . ." mumbled Wool.

"It cannot be seven," Jenkins snapped. "Seven would be completely—"

He caught himself. Snapping at a sleeping man! Did he need any better proof that the heat and the syrupy diet of the Three Kingdoms were affecting his mind?

"And the twelve gates *were* twelve pearls . . ."

Jenkins held his tongue. It was just Wool, and Wool was asleep. He recalled that everyone in Wool's family was much enamored of quoting the Holy Book and that Wool took very much after his late grandfather, Cotton (after whom he was named), in his devotion to finding what he considered to be pertinent verses for every occasion.

But the time . . .

He tried counting on his fingers. He tried retracing the events that had occurred since he had given Scruffy his sealed orders and had sent him off to Boston. But he could not shake the nagging suspicion that days and even entire weeks were escaping him when it was critical that he know as exactly as possible when Scruffy would return, so as to better prepare the ground for the American troops.

But then it occurred to Jenkins that, really, he had not been doing much of anything at all to prepare the ground for the troops. Since Inwa Kabir had died, in fact, the ambassador had not seen any more of the government of the Three Kingdoms than what had been represented by the interminable meals and the barefoot boys and the servants with the brass horns. Abnel, in fact, seemed bent on excluding him from all official business (not that there appeared to be much official business going on in any case), and there was a general sense of ... well ... fuzziness about the place, of things slipping willy-nilly from day to day without much direction at all.

Well, that went right along with what Jenkins had been feeling for the last ... how long had it been? Drat! Weeks, maybe. How many? He did not know. It was imperative that he know, and yet he did not know at all.

Sleep tugged at him, but he fought to stay awake. Scruffy ...

He awoke the next morning with his body seemingly on fire. Fever? Just what he needed! Scruffy returning in ... well ... whatever, and the only liaison between the Righteous States of America and the Three Kingdoms laid up with a fever!

But it was not a fever. No, not at all. Aside from the vague memories of disturbing dreams, Jenkins' mind was clear. He was a little tired, certainly, but he had no sense of the delirium of a fever. In fact, the pain he felt, intense though it was, appeared to be localized in his joints, and, puzzled (and wincing a great deal), he managed to rise from his bed and stagger to the window where, in the growing sunlight, he pulled back the sleeves of his nightgown to discover ...

Merciful God! Were those *bruises* on his wrists?

—I really do not see what you are so upset about. After all, it was only a question.

"It is not something that you would understand. And, in any case, it is not really important. Thank you, sir. Yes, two of those. No ... better make it three."

The Goddess had not spoken. The Goddess had not acted. Perhaps She reserved her favors only for those born Naian, no matter how tainted or mutilated they might have been by their flirtations with Panas. Perhaps She had elected to act only once, leaving future suppliants to cry

out in vain. It did not matter. Naia had been silent. Naia
had done nothing.

Three days had Bakbuk remained atop the boulder near
the buried mouth of the Caves of Naia. Three days had she
implored the strange and exotic female deity for a release
from the chains of sexlessness that bound her. Three days
had she deluded herself with illusory feelings of imminent
transformation. Three days had she been left unchanged.

—Not important? How do you think it makes me feel
when you do not speak to me? We are traveling together,
and therefore it is natural for you to speak to me. But you
do not.

"I have things on my mind that concern me very
much. The blue one: I might as well have a color that I
like. Thank you!"

—The least you can do is to have a care for my feelings.

"Wrapping them up is not necessary. I will take them as
they are. I am caring for them as best I can."

Unchanged. Entirely. She was as she had always been.
Naia would not speak. Naia would not act. And so, her
supplies running low, Bakbuk descended from the top of
the boulder, found her horse, and turned south: back to
Katha, her torments, her divided loyalties, and her
unfulfilled yearnings.

And what would she do if she found *him* now? Before,
she had been safe in her ignorance. Certainly the Blue
Avenger had been one to be apprehended and brought to
justice. But just as certainly, the Blue Avenger had not *yet*
been apprehended, and therefore Bakbuk had been free to
indulge herself in fantasies from whose effects she had
been entirely shielded. But then she had discovered that
the Blue Avenger had been considerably more accessible
than she had ever thought.

Yet, once again, fate (Or Naia? Did the Goddess so

mock one who was neither one thing nor another, who remained barred from ever being either?) had promptly put both the Blue Avenger and Prince Aeid beyond her reach, and she had no idea where he had gone, or whether her current journey had everything (No! Yes!) or nothing (Yes! No!) to do with him.

A tightening in her blank groin. She seized her breasts, shook her hair loose until it fell from her head cloth and cascaded over her willing shoulders like a river of night.

"Please," she whispered. "Please."

—All I can say is that you have an odd way of caring for them. One would think that you do not care at all.

"I have things to do. As you well know. How much are those, please?"

—You are still intent on going up to the mountains? Have you not tormented me with that enough? I have told you over and over again that it does not matter whether the reservoirs up in the mountains are real or not.

"It matters a great deal. Dear Naia, that seems like a low price for something like that! Are you sure your father wishes you to sell so cheaply? You are sure?"

—Actually, I am inclined to believe that they are not real at all. Naia is a fiction. Panas is a fiction. The diversion of the water is a fiction, too. This is consistency. I am a scholar, and I understand such things.

And now here is Bakbuk in Katha, and here she (yes, it appears, in spite of her clothing and her hair, that she is very definitely *she* these days) is looking strangely haunted as she makes her way through the streets, but she is obviously not quite so haunted that she fails to notice Sari and Beshur in the Panasian market. In truth, it would be hard to miss them: Beshur, his hands unencumbered, is gesticulating wildly (and occasionally running into things) as he makes his points, and Sari is carrying a large bundle of purchases, everything from (Bakbuk looks more care-

fully, possibilities and theories floating through her delicate little featherbrained head despite her best efforts)
waterskins to traveling provisions to ropes.

Ropes?

"I am sure that you do. Very well, then. Two of them.
Please tie them up securely so that they do not break. And
that basket over there? You have frequently reminded me
of that."

—As well I should. You frequently slight my knowledge, or at least you make no use of it, which is the same
thing as far as I am concerned. Now, if you ask me—

"I am *not* asking you, Beshur. I am *telling* you. I am going where I am going. You may come or you may stay.
Yes, thank you. That is lovely. Naia bless you. And Panas,
too. They . . . they both look after us all, I am sure! Thank
you. But I am going. I want to know the truth."

Regardless of ropes or possibilities or theories, though,
Bakbuk unconsciously shrinks away from Sari, putting her
horse between herself and the Naian. But it is not so much
a horror of revealing herself that prompts this action as it
is the thought that there, right there in the marketplace,
carrying her skins and her ropes and her dried fruit and
bread and grain mix and dates, is one who *has been
touched* by powers beyond the human, powers to whom
such gross and clumsy alterations as were performed on
Bakbuk are as nothing.

Sari . . . once old, now young. And Naia . . .

Abruptly, Bakbuk pulls on her horse's halter and all but
drags it into an alley so narrow that the noon sun sends but
a sliver of light down into it. There, trembling, she leans
her head against the beast's side and shakes, able, for the
moment, neither to move nor to think.

Yet the thoughts rush through her head, tormenting her.
Sari, whole. Bakbuk . . . nothing. Nothing. No sex. No
function. No goal.

But perhaps she does have a goal after all. The only goal left to her. Physical wholeness has been denied her, first by the surgeon's knife, then by the refusal of the Goddess. Function has been stripped away by her own inability to see herself as having any. But she has a goal: the goal given to her by her king. She has not found Aeid, and she devoutly hopes that she never will. But she has found Sari. And she will therefore carry out her orders. And after that . . .

But . . . ropes. Could it be? She must find out. She *must*. Maybe . . . maybe . . .

"What do you make of that barometer, Turtletrout?"

Outside, the sky was a blue so brilliant that there seemed to be a touch of polished metal about it, and the wind . . . well, the wind had died away to a whisper, and the air had acquired all the pertinent characteristics of a furnace. Scruffy had been on the verge of ordering the fleet to start the pumps and douse the sails in order to make as much headway as possible before they were entirely becalmed, but then he had noticed the barometer.

Turtletrout, now technically a captain, but in reality entirely guided—and willingly so—by Scruffy's commodorian orders, stooped and examined the barometer. "Very low, sir."

"Low? It's so low that I warn't sure it warn't broken. I had to take the shield off to see the quicksilver."

"Very low indeed, sir."

The deference in Turtletrout's voice was unmistakable, and Scruffy sighed inwardly. Turtletrout was not stupid—no man could rise to the rank of first lieutenant by being stupid (at least not in the American Navy)—but he lacked what some would call a *spark*: that blend of ambition and imagination so necessary to one who would command. The changed circumstances of this voyage had reproached Scruffy over and over for that lack of spark in his first lieutenant, and he had become determined not only to find that spark in Turtletrout but to fan it into a respectable blaze.

"We're going to have a blow, it seems," he said.

"Yes, sir."

It was no different a response than would have been given by any American sailor to a man of superior rank (for the English *aye-aye* had, long ago, been purged from the vocabulary of Puritan seamen, along with gutter finery and the feminization of ships). And yet there was that deference again, too much deference for Scruffy to be entirely comfortable, and he chastised himself silently for its existence.

A clatter of feet on the steps down to Scruffy's large cabin. A midshipman poked his head in through the open door. "Signal from *Seaflower,* sir. *Barometer falling. Request orders.*"

Scruffy examined the barometer once more. It was, if anything, even lower than when he had asked Turtletrout to step into his cabin. "Message to fleet," he said, *"Take storm positions. Prepare for heavy weather."*

"It is so grotesque!"

Even with her arms full of supplies for what she expected to be a difficult journey into the mountains, Sari cringed, and, after sidestepping carefully into the shadow of a potter's booth, she peered over the rim of a tall urn. But no, she did not see Charna: only a properly veiled Panasian wife who was now in the process of being cuffed by her enormous husband.

"I will teach you to speak without being spoken to!" he was shouting.

The woman endured several blows, then crumpled into the moistureless dust of the marketplace, after which her husband paid for his cheese and left, dragging her unconscious form behind him.

—What is it? Beshur was pressing.

"Nothing," said Sari. "Nothing at all."

* * *

"I am looking for a Naian woman."

"Ah! A Naian woman. Well, as you can see, there are not very many Naian women here in the Naian market, as their husbands have all learned that the heat of their vulvas makes them quite irrational and not at all fit for judging prices and quality effectively, and there is no better indication of this lack of judgment than the fact, the very fact, that not one of them who has come to the Naian market—that is, what few there have been, and I can only suppose that those few must be unmarried, and therefore, being without the guidance of a man, cause themselves to be taken advantage of by unscrupulous merchants who will use the confusion produced by the heat of their vulvas against them—not one, mind you, has ever fully appreciated the quality of these magnificent blocks of wood, which, I can tell you without hesitation, are suitable for the making of the most incredible objects, if only they would fall into the hands of one such as yourself, who, unencumbered by a vulva and its corresponding heat, necessarily perceives them in all their true usefulness."

Aeid glanced over his shoulder. Since he had been surprised by guards in Sayam as he was leaving the house of a Naian woman who had a particularly curious notion about mucus (And how was it that Sari appeared to be so incredibly different from all of her superstitious, ignorant, and obsessive co-religionists? Why, the girl had a brain in that pretty little head of hers. True, it was a bit of an obsessive brain at times, as witness the fixations she had about the work of the Goddess, clearing the Caves (he trusted that the hidden scrolls had settled the matter of the Caves for her), and now, doubtless, the water that was theoretically trapped in the high, interior valleys of the Mountains of Ern (and, yes, he himself half believed that the water was indeed up there, but he would never tell his father about it), but it was a brain nonetheless, and at times he fancied that if he read a few things to her out of the

Encyclopédie, or perhaps from Tully, she would not only comprehend them, but might well profit thereby.) he had been looking over his shoulder a great deal. And not without results. There seemed to be priestly and palace guards *everywhere* these days, and Aeid did not doubt that there were more than a few religious police lurking about, too, carefully disguised as common (and, in the case of the Naians, decidedly uncommon) citizens. But despite the speeches of the vendor of uncarved blocks, no one in the vicinity appeared to be paying much attention.

He pulled his head cloth down a little more, deciding that being conspicuous among the Naians by the presence of a head cloth was better than being conspicuous among *everyone* by his appearance. "That is fine," he said, having lost complete track of the vendor's statement after the fourth virtual parenthesis. "But this Naian woman would have been ... well ..." There was no elegant way of putting it, though his *philosophe*'s sense of proportion recoiled at the clumsiness of the expression. "... *here.* Regardless. You would remember her." And what, he wondered, if this apparently idiotic vendor was himself a priestly agent? Too late now! "Dark hair, flashing eyes, a nose ..." He fumbled for words, and noticed that, to his chagrin, he was getting a ...

Did anyone *notice*?

"... a nose ... that ..."

"Ah, a nose! And I can tell you that the fragrance of these—"

But the vendor of uncarved blocks was suddenly brought to a halt in mid-eloquence.

"Oh ... *her,*" he said.

All of Aeid's attention was suddenly focused on the vendor. Which meant, in this case, that he not only took notice of the lustful expression in the vendor's eyes (and even if the vendor noticed that Aeid was, he would have nothing to say, for the vendor himself was, too, and there was a manly code of ethics about such things that prohibited calling any attention whatsoever to them . . . a code that the writer, a mere woman, cannot hope to understand or to explain), but also that he took no notice at all of the appearance, on the other side of the market square, of Bakbuk, who, distressed and distracted and looking not at all like the sardonic Bakbuk who would have taken the greatest of pleasures in calling attention to the fact that they *both* were (because Bakbuk did not participate in any code of ethics besides Bakbuk's own), took, in turn, no notice at all of the presence of Aeid at the stall of the vendor of uncarved blocks.

"Yes," said Aeid. "*Her*. You have seen her?"

"Ah, who could forget her?"

"So she is in Katha! When did you see her?"

And here, Bakbuk, on the other side of the market square, was passing out of sight. Aeid had not noticed Bakbuk. Bakbuk had not noticed Aeid.

"Let me see," said the vendor. "It was several days after the individual with the bushy eyebrows insulted my magnificent blocks of wood; and, though I can see disbelief in your eyes, I must tell you that in absolute point of fact, that individual saw fit to calumniate my wonderful blocks, yes, standing before me and before the magnificence of my blocks of wood, standing, in fact, exactly where you, who are so discerning that you can perceive immediately how truly perfect and worthy of any worthy use are my blocks of wood, are standing at this very moment, he said the most outrageous things, while I, having taken my lesson from the quiet glory of my blocks, remained silent, knowing full well that the individual with the bushy eyebrows who was standing exactly where you are now standing showed by his slanderous comments not only that he himself had no discernment, but also that he was himself—"

"*When did you see her?*" Aeid, in his desire for knowledge of Sari's whereabouts, was almost shouting, and was

thereby attracting the attention of some bystanders who
had, up until then, been paying no attention at all.

"—worthy only of dwelling in mud, as have the—urk!"

This last expression, though not a word, was produced
by the vendor of uncarved blocks as a direct result of Aeid
taking hold of the front of his shoulder cloth and, by the
application of a combination of vector forces, dragging
him forward and lifting him at least one inch off the
ground.

"I beg you, brother," said Aeid, smiling, "tell me when
you last saw ... uh ..."

Did anyone? Notice?

"... her."

"I ... I ... I ..."

"When?"

"I ... I believe it was two days ago."

"Have you seen her since?"

The position (exactly 1.32876 inches off the ground) appeared to have had the effect of focusing the vendor's attention ... with the unfortunate (and, unfortunately,
unnoticed by Aeid) side effect of also focusing the attention of the bystanders, who began looking very hard at
Aeid. "N-no."

"Very good," said Aeid. "Thank you, brother."

Whereupon Aeid lowered the vendor to the ground and
departed. Whereupon one of the bystanders followed Aeid.
Whereupon another bystander approached the vendor of
uncarved blocks.

"Was that not the idiot who climbed over the wall?" he
asked.

"Ah," said the vendor, "a most discerning individual
who immediately perceived the worth of these magnificent
blocks of wood, which, I can assure you, can be made into
a great many useful objects of all sorts, providing that the
object desired is worthy of being made of such magnificent blocks of wood as these. Why, I can tell you ..."

Chapter Eighteen

As steep as were the slopes that led up from the caravan trails and the central wastes of the Three Kingdoms to the garnet-and-onyx-encrusted walls of the city of Katha, those to the east—those leading into the mountains themselves—were steeper. Jenkins and his companions had found the trek difficult even with the assistance of riding asses and priestly guards who knew the way and were familiar with the problems of such travel, but Sari and Beshur were journeying on foot, and they had no one, human or animal, to aid them.

Still, they pressed on. Or, rather, Sari pressed on. Beshur merely followed. He protested, true, but he followed; and whether he followed because, despite his denials and his surety that the inland seas of water reported by the priestly documents were entirely of a piece with the fabricated deities that had, for centuries, alternately nurtured and tormented the Three Kingdoms, he wanted to see either final confirmation or absolute denial, or because he simply could not bring himself to leave the object of his fantasies and his (sometimes overtly frugivorous) desires, Sari was not sure. Beshur was, doubtless, not sure either.

—Are you—?

"Be quiet and climb."

And climb they did. By the end of the first day, the path had turned into a faint scratch in a thin film of dust on otherwise bare rock, and by the end of the second day, even that had vanished, leaving Sari and Beshur to make their own way through a landscape of tortured, upthrust ranges crisscrossed by scarps, ledges, cracks, fissures, and even an occasional vent from which drifted the odor of brimstone.

At the crest of a knife-edged ridge, Beshur looked out across the landscape, bewildered.

—And Panas carried the rocks from the Quarries out of *this,* he said.

His words were all but swept away by the dry wind.

"I thought that you did not believe in that anymore."

—I do not, Beshur said . . . a little too quickly.

But his reference to the Sacred Quarries reminded Sari of a disturbing fact: the Quarries, which were also (theoretically) in the mountains, were a holy place of the Panasian religion. That being the case, she and Beshur would be likely to encounter others while on this journey, be they pilgrims (highly unlikely, since, if the documents were correct, the Quarries—if they indeed existed at all— were probably flooded . . . along with everything else), priests (possibly, since the Quarries were a holy place (but, then again, see *flooded* and *if they indeed existed at all* immediately above)), or guards (almost surely, since the Panasian religion appeared to utilize a well-nigh infinite number of guards).

They would have to be wary. But being wary was not an easy thing to do when, half the time, they were struggling up slopes that threatened to pitch them into what seemed bottomless gorges, and, the other half, they were sitting with their backs against a stone, gasping for breath in the thinning air.

But Sari could only shrug inwardly. Naia—if there was a Naia—would provide. Judging from what had happened so far, in fact, Naia would provide even if there was *not* a Naia.

On the fourth day, they came across the first earthwork.

A simple affair, almost rude in its execution, it lay deep in a high valley, and it was in ruins. But it was quite definitely a kind of dam that had been cast across a ravine to block the flow of water. There was, however, no water behind it, and no indication that there had been any for a long time.

"Well?" said Sari.

—It could be for any of a thousand things, Beshur said as he got to his feet. And you will notice that there is no water.

"I notice that," said Sari. "But I see that it is old, too. It could well be that this was a first attempt, and that later efforts have diverted the water up higher."

Beshur shrugged. It was obvious that he did not want to believe in either the dams or the water, that he still desired only that Sari accompany him to the nearest village and settle down to an improbable long life of equally improbable material bliss. But:

—Speaking of water . . .

"What about water?"

—Our skins are almost empty.

It was true. The high-altitude air was pulling the water out of their bodies at an alarming rate, and Sari was reluctant to cut back on their rations and thereby add thirst to their difficulties.

"Naia will provide," she said.

—I am a scholar, Beshur said. I understand these things. It would be much better for us to—

Sari cut him off. "I understand, too."

—No, said Beshur. You do *not* understand. The diversion of the water is a *fiction*. This must be clearly understood.

She pointed at the dam. "Is *that* a fiction?"

—It might be anything, Beshur said firmly. It might even be a hallucination brought on by the thin air. You must know that the interior plateaux are called *The Airless Places*.

"I know that," said Sari, just as firmly. "But I know also that one does not trip over hallucinations."

Beshur was indignant.

—I did not trip. I *stumbled*.

"As you wish," said Sari. "I am going on."

And that night, the clouds gathered, and there was rain.

At first, they reveled in the downpour, Sari, heedless of Beshur's presence, stripping off her clothes and letting the unaccustomed shower take the dust and grime of a waterless land from her skin. But soon, too soon, Sari realized that the cold night air made twice cold by the altitude was now made three times cold by the rain, and, transitioning abruptly from reveling to shivering, she lost no time in dragging Beshur and the supplies into the shelter of a cave.

"We will need a fire," she said as she wrung out her hair. Yes, she was cold. Very cold. She could hardly get her words out for the chattering of her teeth.

Beshur was fully clad, dripping, and just as cold. He, too, was shivering. Nevertheless:

—But someone will see the smoke!

"Not in this rain, I would think. In any case, it does not matter. We build a fire or we perish of cold."

Grumbling (but, yes, shivering, too), Beshur gathered what bits of ancient, dry brush and old, drought-withered wood he could find, and, in a few minutes, Sari had made a tiny blaze that she tended as carefully as the one she had nursed during another lifetime in the house of her husband.

Beshur kept his back to Sari while he warmed and his clothes dried. Sari, still naked (and hugging the fire so closely that she all but burned herself) hardly noticed. The rain poured down outside, and she wondered whether there would be a corresponding flood in the River Forshen, or whether the widely scattered earthworks and pits and traps would catch the water, divert it, carry it back into the—

—This cave goes back a long way, Beshur said, his voice drifting to her as though from a distance.

Sari lifted her head. His voice was indeed coming from a distance: she had dozed off, and Beshur was no longer on the other side of the fire. "It does?" she called.

—Yes, and—*oof!*

The *oof!* was accompanied by a *thud!,* and Sari was on her feet in an instant. Seizing a small oil lamp that she had filled when her hands had stopped shaking enough to allow it, she followed the sounds into the depths of the cave. "Beshur!"

Faintly:

—Mmph . . .

"Beshur!"

It was very dark, and there were rocky overhangs and stalactities on which she nearly brained herself more than once. Still, when she found Beshur, he was essentially unharmed except for a bruise on his forehead and a barked shin, but, since he was again lying full length on the ground, she automatically looked up and around to see what secret door he might have opened.

There was no secret door. There was, however, farther up the passageway, a flash of something grayish white in the darkness.

Bones.

"Did you trip?" Sari asked, her eyes still on the bones.

—I *stumbled,* Beshur said with some heat.

"Oh. All right." But after relighting Beshur's lamp, she left him rubbing his shin, picked her way up the passage, and bent over the bones. Her eyes widened when she saw that it was a complete skeleton, and that it was human.

No: not human. At least, not *completely* human. Something else.

Unaccountably, she shivered. "An ape?" she asked Beshur, who had come up beside her.

—Ape? he said distantly.

She recalled that she was still naked, and that he was

looking at her shoulder (which was glowing softly in the soft light of the two lamps) as though it were, yes, a ripe peach. "The *bones*."

—Bones?

She kicked him, and he finally looked. The sight of the skull regarding him gleefully out of empty sockets jarred him away from thoughts of fruit enough for his face to lose its vacuous expression. "Bones," she said. "An ape, perhaps?"

—No, he said. It is not an ape.

She shivered again. "Surely they cannot be the bones of a man! Look at those arms!"

Beshur knelt and ran a hand over the bones. Dry, picked quite clean by whatever insects or scavengers eked out a life here in the high ranges, they were laid out as though for an anatomy lesson.

—I think it *was* a man, he said. Or, at least, a *kind* of a man. I am a scho—

"A kind of a man?"

—Degenerate, Beshur said. Very degenerate. Perhaps inbreeding? Who knows? But it was not an ape. The skull is not right. I know these things, you see. I am a scholar.

Sari shivered yet again, feeling a chill that had nothing to do with her nakedness or the cold. What hands, she wondered, had built the dams and dug the tunnels? What hands now moved the pump handles? What thousands of beings diverted the waters of the two great rivers of the Three Kingdoms, turned them back into the mountains, had been turning them back now for over three hundred years? "But it ... it had to have walked on four feet!"

—Not all the time, Beshur said with distressing objectivity. It still could grasp with its hands. See? Look at how the thumb—

Sari turned away. "Thank you, Beshur. I understand."

—No, you do not. Look at that hammer and chisel next to it! And ... and ... and look at those ... those arms!

Sari knew that he was not referring to the bones any-more. Fruit. "H-hammer and chisel?"

Beshur was suddenly silent.

... oh yes and he looked very nice with the snake and he did not protest at the thread either but then he could not protest and I wonder if he remembers now perhaps not but he did smile in that knowing way when I showed him the thread and very soon I am sure I will not need the drugs and he will be very willing in fact I am sure he is willing already because he must know what I am doing and yet he goes along with it and a minister in his head he will do whatever I say very soon and I will know the truth though I cannot take the chance of leaving everything unattended with that impostor prince on the loose he might come back oh that honeyed tongue he has yes that was very nice too with the honey and he did not object to that either and his tongue going in and out just as I wanted and perhaps it is not too late to retrieve the device from the island he would look fine even though it would not fit quite so well be-cause it was not made for him but I am sure something could be done and Wool I do not know what to do with but he seems content to leave us alone but I wonder if anything could be done in any case there will be time to retrieve the device later on once we dispose of the impos-tor prince I will have the leisure to do anything yet a min-ister in their heads he will do what I want and I will find the truth and those *whores* who go about without their headwraps *in the HOUSE* will find that they will not go about that way any longer and what would he look like in a face cloth oh very well I think perhaps I will give him a little more tonight but I have not heard anything from the search parties I cannot believe that they would fail and what will happen if they do not find any of them but that is impossible I have given orders and I am king now and high priest too and they must succeed or they will find out what it means to disobey just as he found out and he did

look fine yes that felt very good and now that I think of
it where is Bakbuk I have not seen him or her or it I do
not know what to think at this point but I will dispose of
him that is good enough when he turns up it would not do
to have him lurking about was loyal to the king too and if
he suspected that the poisoning but the king did not die of
poison fell over from shock when the impostor prince left
just as he intended I am sure a parricide then I will soon
control everything and those so-called scholars in Katha
will no longer laugh at me but not Bakbuk would be no
minister in *his* head I know that and he is no good for any
kind of recreation sterile as a sheepskin not even good for
breeding up in the tunnels time for another shipment I
think but that is not necessary anymore now that there will
be a minister in their heads and therefore I will dispose of
him as soon as he shows up yes I will do that yes . . .

Chuckle-chuckle-chuckle!

Beshur's silence continued even after the cold and the
dwindling oil in their lamps forced them to retreat to the
fire. In fact, it continued even well into the next day,
when, in a chill, misty fog that had replaced the rain, the
two scrambled over rocks and picked their switchback way
up the cliffs, making slow progress toward what they
hoped (given the lack of direct sunlight by which to orient
themselves) was the east.

But, midway up yet another slope, Sari grabbed
Beshur's sleeve. "Listen."

Both of them stood still. In the mist, sounds seemed
strangely loud, strangely close . . . and yet distant. Sari
heard her heart beating with her exertions, heard Beshur's
breathless gasps in the thin air. But there had been something else, too.

—What? Beshur whispered.

"It sounded like a footstep."

Beshur's wide eyes glanced fearfully back along the way they had come.

—Do not joke like that, he said.

"I am not joking. I heard something."

—The skeleton frightened you, Beshur said quickly. It is a common thing for women to be frightened of such things. Intimately tied as they are to the flesh, it is . . .

"Be*shur!*"

—. . . natural for them to be disturbed by unequivocal signs of death.

He was still speaking quickly.

—I understand these things, you see. I am a—

The unmistakable sound of a footstep brought him up short. His eyes, already wide, grew even wider.

—a . . . a . . . a . . .

"Scholar," said Sari as she strained her eyes into the mist. "Yes. Thank you."

She could see nothing. The cold mist (They were, doubtless, actually *inside* the clouds that so often hid the summits of the mountains.) turned into an opaque wall three feet from her eyes. All her planning, all her careful foresight regarding supplies and water had not prepared her for either this numbing cold or the thin air that at times turned the slightest exertion into a studied effort of will, and this virtual blindness made it all worse.

"We cannot stay here," she said. "Let us go forward."

—But . . . but . . . but . . .

"Move!" she whispered fiercely. "Whoever is out there can see us no better than we can see him."

Another step. Closer.

—B-b-b-b—

"Or them."

—B-b-b-b—

"*Move!*"

Beshur moved, and they continued climbing.

But the slopes only increased. Roped together, holding on by fingers and toes, Sari and Beshur inched their way up yet another rock wall. A scrambling below, though, told them that they were still being followed.

And then Sari's foot slipped. Flailing and falling, she wound up dangling at the end of the rope while a rattle of pebbles cascaded down the cliff, bounced off her head, and vanished into the misty depths. Her vision swam, and for an instant she thought that surely the rope must give way at any moment and send her plunging after the pebbles. Miraculously, though, it held, even though she knew that it was attached to nothing more solid or dependable than Beshur, whose climbing abilities were, it appeared, solely dependent upon his sexual obsessions.

It seemed to her, in those moments or hours of dangling, that this journey, this search for truth, was no more sensible or sane than had been her pilgrimage to the Caves. Then, she had been confronted first with a confused, superstitious, and possibly illusory heritage, and, then, finally, with the complete destruction of the shrine. Now she was faced with the absurdity of this second search, the utter irrationality of any belief that placed either water or waterworks—dams, conduits, aqueducts, pumps . . . whatever—in a tortured, impassable landscape such as this. Water? There was no water. Pumps? How could pumps exist in such a place? How would they be carried in? How would they be operated? Surely an endeavor the size of what was hinted at by scrolls in the Great Library would have left more clues to its existence than a single, ruined dam and one skeleton of . . . something.

She swung ($T=2\pi\sqrt{\frac{l}{g}}$) freely, but then, after a brief, initial tug, felt herself being drawn up. "Just let me fall, Beshur," she said, her forehead pressed against the rope. "It is useless. You are right: it was all a fiction."

But she continued to ascend, and Beshur's voice drifted down to her, interspersed with gasps:

—No, he said. It is true. There were stairs in the darkness beyond the skeleton. I looked after you had turned away.

A passage led up into the mountain. The mountains are probably riddled with tunnels.

Startled, swinging, she stared into the mist. "You are sure?"

—I am, he said unhappily. I was not going to say anything, but I must. I am a scholar, and I must cleave to the truth. It is true. It is all true. It is not a fiction.

"Then why are we still struggling up here when . . . ?"

Beshur continued to haul her up with muscles made hard by carrying.

—If we had explored the passage, we would have become lost, he said. At the very least we would have been discovered immediately. And, besides, I did not . . . that is, I . . . ah . . .

He fell into a confused silence broken only by occasional gasps as he continued to draw on the rope.

"I understand," said Sari. "You are right." She closed her eyes. He had not wanted to tell her because he had hoped that she would give up, return to civilization, and settle down with him. Yet, despite his confirmation of her beliefs, she still felt the impelling desire to trust neither inferences nor hints, but to seek out the reservoirs of water, to see for herself, to *know*.

To know . . . and perhaps (the thought coming to her unbidden, provided, maybe, by a Goddess in whom she no longer knew whether to believe or not, a Goddess who was willing to provide all sorts of things, looked-for or not, regardless of that belief or lack of it) to *do* something about it?

Do something about it? But what?

"Oh . . . Naia . . ." She had learned to recognize these moments and these realizations. Yes . . . yes . . . she was supposed to do something about it. It did not matter that she did not know what. That would come. It had come at the Caves. It would come now.

—Of course I am right, came the reply from just above her head. I am a—

"Yes," she said. "Of course."

—Besides, Beshur said as he swung her up to a small plateau, I would surely not let you fall. After all, I . . . I . . . I . . .

His voice trailed off.

Sari peered at him through the mist, sighed. He was seeing ripe fruit again.

A rattle of pebbles from below.

Sari looked about quickly, inwardly cursing the blinding presence of the mist. Water was what she had been searching for all this time, and yet here was water all about her: too much water, though, and in decidedly the wrong form! "We must escape."

Beshur shook his head. Or, at least, she *thought* that he shook his head. As it was, his gesture was no more than an indefinite movement in the clouds.

—We will have to descend, he said. There is no other way.

"But . . ." Sari glanced down into the white depths. More gravel. Closer. "But . . ."

A soft scrape of flesh on stone indicated that a hand had reached over the edge of the cliff, and as Sari bent to watch, she saw (murkily) its fingers feel out and then tighten in a crack.

Self-preservation told Sari to strike, to stamp on the hand, to kick it loose, to send its owner plunging into the chasm below, but her own recent rescue had made her too acutely aware of the murderous fall for her to wish to inflict that fate on another, and so she stood, at first staring at the blurry movement at the edge of the cliff, then shrinking back from it until she found her way blocked by yet another chasm.

Beshur was right. The only escape was back the way they had come. They were trapped.

Another soft scrape: a second hand had joined the first. Doubtless it, too, was finding its hold, gripping . . .

"Beshur . . ."

—As I expected, he said with an edge of hysteria in his voice. Two hands. No more, no less. It would be utterly absurd to expect that an individual with one hand could negotiate the slopes, and even in the priestly archives there are no reliable records of three-handed individuals, so, therefore, four hands being completely out of the question, two hands were precisely what I expected. And you see that I am right, for I . . . I . . . I . . .

A shadowy form now. Someone was coming up.

—. . . am a . . . a . . .

Steeling herself, Sari came forward and knelt between the hands. "Who are you and what do you want?" she said.

—. . . a s-s-scholar!

A girlish face examined her ironically through two feet of thick fog. "May Naia bless you, sister," said Bakbuk.

Chapter Nineteen

(Having had it pointed out to her that her writing is several grade levels beyond the average comprehension of literate Americans, the author hastens to correct the balance by supplying the following section in a more suitable and intelligible form.)

Mongo say, "Hard rocks."

Basho say, "Rock hard."

Mongo hit rock. Mongo hurt Mongo. Mongo shake fist and say bad words.

Basho laugh at Mongo.

Mongo hit Basho. Basho get mad, hit Mongo. Sherpo grab Mongo and Bongo grab Basho. Sherpo and Bongo pull Mongo and Basho apart.

Mongo shout at Basho.

Basho shout at Mongo.

Sherpo and Bongo hit Mongo and Basho. Sherpo tell Mongo and Basho they bad. No fight. King's guards not fight. King's guards good guys. No fight each other. Only fight bad guys. Bad guys talk funny. Bad guys wear funny clothes. Bad guys bad. Good guys fight bad guys.

Now Mongo and Basho sorry. They hang heads and say they sorry they bad.

Mongo say, "Long climb. It hard to climb. It cold. Me get mad. Me sorry me hurt Basho."

Basho say, "Me sorry me hurt Mongo."

Sherpo say, "We find girl, take her back. We go home. We warm then. Get money."

Mongo happy. Mongo say, "We find girl and go home!"

Sherpo happy. Bongo happy. Basho happy.

All say: "We find girl and go home!"

Mongo hit rock again. Not hit hard. Mongo not hurt. "Rock cold."

Sherpo say, "Rock cold."

Mongo say, "We find girl and go home."

Sherpo say, "Yes."

Mongo say, "What we do with girl?"

Sherpo say, "We take girl home!"

Mongo say, "We kill girl?"

Sherpo say, "No, we not kill girl."

Mongo say, "Gharat kill girl?"

Sherpo say, "Gharat kill girl."

Mongo say, "Why we not kill girl?"

Sherpo say, "Gharat say no kill girl."

Mongo say, "Gharat say no do *anything* to girl?"

Sherpo say, "Gharat say no kill girl."

Mongo hit rock again. Not hard. Mongo not hurt.

Mongo think. Mongo say, "Girl warm."

Sherpo say, "Girl warm."

Mongo think some more. Mongo say, "Girl feel good."

Sherpo say, "Girl feel very good."

Basho say, "Girl feel very, very good."

Bongo say, "Girl feel very, very, very good!"

Mongo say, "We not kill girl."

All say together, "No!"

Mongo say, "We take girl to Gharat."

All say together, "Yes!"

Mongo say, "Girl feel good!"

All say together, "Yes!"

Aeid— ... uh ... no ...

Ahem. Try again.

The Blue Av— ...

No.

Once more then.

Baroz—

NO!

(The author expresses her heartfelt regret for the occurrence of the above errors, knowing as she does how trying they must be to the reader's patience. She offers as her only excuse the fact that, owing to her examination of the page proofs for *The Dove Looked In,* she has been unable to work on the present book for over a week, and has consequently lost (temporarily) the thread of the narrative.)

One last try then . . . (ahem) . . .

Potatoes (like Aeid and the Blue Avenger (So there!)) knew (but not Baroz) ropes (at least, *probably* not Baroz), and he knew climbing. But descending the outer walls of the palace of Nuhr or even swinging like a madman from the facade of the Temple of Panas with the tables of the tax gatherers square in his cognitive gunsights was one thing (or, rather, two things . . . but leave it at one for the sake of the example); climbing up the cold, windswept cliffs of the Mountains of Ern was entirely another. Then, too, the palace and the temple had, at least, been familiar to him. (Does that make three now? The author is not sure. Please bear with her: the page proofs were hard work and she is still a little dizzy.) These mountains, though, were a complete unknown. There were no instructions, no legends, no stories, no scraps of lore or even ill-drawn maps to guide him. Everything was unknown, strange, and . . .

He saw the palace and priestly guards on the second day.

. . . very dangerous.

(More than likely not Baroz. But one never knows.)

Mongo say, "We take good care of girl!"

All say together, "Yes!"

* * *

There were at least four of them, with more, doubtless, concealed by the tumbled rocks and convoluted ridges. Somewhere beyond them, he knew, were Sari and Beshur; and yet, *getting* beyond them, even if he had wanted to, was more than likely impossible, since there seemed to be, at most, only one way of getting from anywhere to anywhere, and the guards were most inconveniently positioned along that one way.

But they were moving, and so Potatoes moved too. Keeping out of their sight, he followed them deeper into the mountains, the air thinning rapidly and the cold increasing until, Panas (or Naia, or random chance, or the Pentium™ chip with the floating-point error that is, doubtless, what is *really* in charge of the universe) seeing fit to show the intruders into the holy mountains what *real* cold was like, clouds gathered, rain fell, and, come morning, a chill mist hung over everything.

Still, the guards pressed on into the mountains, and so Potatoes pressed on, too, groping blindly for handholds and toeholds on insanely steep cliffs, scaling ridges and following trails by feel more than by sight. And then, out of the mist, quite distant, but nonetheless quite clear, he heard:

"Bakbuk!" Sari was already taking the sworder's hand and helping her (She thought she was helping *him*, of course, but we know better.) up to the tiny plateau. "What are you doing here?"

"I am here for you," said the sworder, and there was a curious tone in her voice that might have told someone who was not frightened, not cold, and not disoriented by the all-pervasive mist and moisture that her words meant a little more than what they appeared to mean to someone who was. (Frightened, cold, and disoriented, that is.)

Sari, though, who was indeed frightened, cold, and disoriented, was characteristically grateful for what she perceived as an offer of aid (and hoped, at the same time, that Bakbuk would leave it at that). "Bakbuk! Thank you!"

Bakbuk bowed. "It is my pleasure."

Still with that curious tone in her voice. (See above: *not frightened, not cold, and not disoriented* . . . etc.)

"I must inform you, though, that we are fugitives."

"I am aware of that."

"You—?"

In reply, Bakbuk put a finger to her lips and gestured off into the mist-shrouded depths that surrounded the plateau.

—What is he—? Beshur started, not being able to see Bakbuk, her gesture, or, in fact, much of anything.

"Shhh!"

Beshur fell silent. From out of the mist came the sound of leather scraping on stone. Actually, many leathers scraping on many stones.

"Guards?" whispered Sari.

"Guards," said Bakbuk. "They have come to capture you and take you to the Gharat, who intends to kill you, as far as I have been able to ascertain from their conversation. Actually, they appear to have some plans of their own for you, as well."

"Plans?"

"Recreational plans."

Whether because of the mist or her chill agitation, Sari did not notice the look that passed over Bakbuk's girlish face.

"But . . . we are trapped here!"

Beshur stepped forward.

—You forget, he said, that *I* am here!

Bakbuk examined Beshur, who suddenly appeared to recall something and subsequently shrank back a step or two, stopping, to be sure, at the edge of the plateau . . . which was, to be sure, not all that far away. "Well," she said, "trapped is certainly one word for it."

—But . . . we must escape!

"As you have already observed to Sari," said Bakbuk, "there is no escape save *down,* and *down* is where . . ."

Again there came the sound of many scrapes of leather on many stones.

". . . the guards are."

—Perhaps—

"No," said the sworder. "They have heard you. They know you are here."

—Maybe—

"No chance of that," said the sworder.

—What about—?

"Not likely."

—If—?

"Never."

The fear on Beshur's face was obvious even through several feet of thick mist. Sari, terrified herself, found herself irrationally worrying that he was going to start blubbering again.

—Is it . . . is it hard to learn to walk like that? he said at last.

Bakbuk stared at him for a moment, then shrugged as though determined to ignore a mouse that had fallen into a dish of curry. "As I said, I came for you," she said, turning back to Sari.

It was Sari's turn to stare. At Bakbuk. Even through fright, cold, and disorientation, the tone in the sworder's voice was by now making it obvious that *I came for you* could mean many things, several of which were potentially unpleasant.

But there was little time for her to consider the matter in any depth, for, through the swirling mist, she was now seeing dark shapes on all sides of the plateau. Two . . . four . . . eight . . . maybe ten men were approaching, crawling up the sheer slopes on all sides.

"Oh . . . Naia . . ."

This invocation on the part of Sari caused Bakbuk to . . . to . . .

To what? Did the ever-competent and incessantly-ironic Bakbuk actually *tremble* at the name of the Goddess? Perhaps. It was hard to tell. But Sari felt uncertainty in Bakbuk's hand as the sworder took hold of her arm and guided her to the center of the plateau.

"Stand here, if you please."

Yes: uncertainty. A tangible uncertainty.

—What about me?

Bakbuk eyed Beshur as though considering several creative answers. Then, with a sigh: "Stand beside her."

Beshur appeared to be about to ask something else, but as Bakbuk drew her sword, he appeared to lose all interest in the subject and hastened to join Sari.

It was over very quickly, for, in the course of their climbing and their freezing and their hitting rocks and their quarreling, Mongo and all his friends had forgotten that an individual who stands at the top of a slope has a natural advantage over those who are below, and that this advantage is magnified greatly if those who are below are encumbered with handholds and footholds and concerns about pitching headlong into the rocky depths beneath their feet. Nor did Mongo and his friends have any idea that among those above them was the king's personal sworder ... though it should be noted that there was no particular reason for them to have known this, and therefore this failing should not weigh heavily in any evaluation of their success, failure, or subsequent behavior.

As it was, though, their subsequent behavior included a great deal of flailing about (in several cases with handless arms or fingerless hands), a great deal of screaming, and (bearing out their concerns in a most palpable manner) a universal pitching headlong into the rocky depths.

Through the mist, Sari watched as Bakbuk examined her bloody sword, wiped it, and sheathed it. But then the sworder turned to her.

"We must go," she said.

"Go?" said Sari. "Go where?"

"To Nuhr."

"What—?" The strange tone in Bakbuk's voice was becoming uncomfortably clear, its potentially unpleasant meanings crowding very much to the fore.

"I was sent by the king to bring you back to Nuhr," said Bakbuk, "and I will do as I have been told. You will come with me. Now."

—He has a point, Beshur said (unhelpfully).

Sari shook her head. "Bakbuk has no point whatsoever . . ."

An inexplicable look of pain crossed Bakbuk's face, visible in all its depth even through the swirling mist, and yet Sari could not spare any sympathy for it. Her task—her *duty,* as she had come to believe—lay farther up, farther into the mountain ranges. Naia (whatever She was) had provided. Naia (whatever She was) would continue to provide. But Sari could no more go back now than she could have gone back when she had been in the Great Library.

". . . for I have business in The Airless Places that will not wait."

Bakbuk was obviously struggling with several mixed emotions. "I suppose," she said, attempting irony (but failing miserably), "that you will now tell me that you have been sent by the Goddess."

"As a matter of fact: yes, I *have* been sent by the Goddess."

Fear and pain were in the sworder's eyes. But: "You will come with me," she said. "I have orders, and I will obey them."

The mist swirled. Sari shook her head.

"I have orders, too," she said.

Bakbuk reached for her sword.

Sari backed away.

—He indeed has a point, Beshur said quickly (and unhelpfully).

But before Bakbuk could advance to seize Sari, there was a scramble at the edge of the miniature plateau, and before the sworder could react, another dark form arose in the mist.

"Leave her alone," said Potatoes.

Noise. Noise. Noise. Vegetation blown from who-knew-where driven horizontally for who-knew-how-far to cram itself into the shrouds of *Fist of God* right alongside seaweed and even a jellyfish or two whipped up from the creaming surface of the ocean. Dull, ochre light. Wind. Thunder. Broken ropes cracking like whips. Lightning blasting down and shivering the fore and main topmasts into splinters. Canvas blown to lint in a twinkling.

. . . he does look fine and he will look finer and if I could do without the drugs he would be finer still like a corpse nodding back and forth not even stiff but have to put up with that for now until he sees that I will have what I want for I am king and priest too and a minister in their heads but I wish his hands did not clench so squeeze me right off will have to do something about that . . .

As near as Bakbuk could tell, she and the prince (for she knew who he was) were as near-perfectly matched in combat skills as was humanly possible. And there was an uncanniness in the manifestation of that equality, a strange blending of psyches on the cramped, mist-shrouded plateau, a blurring of the distinction between one sword and another, the inspired strategy of one combatant countered in a moment by the instinct of the other seized upon (seemingly) simultaneously with the initial formulation.

Stupid girl!

Was that *him*? Still watching? Still gloating? And was that *her* now, returned (under cover of darkness, perhaps, for everyone knew that magic and darkness were as inseparable from one another as both were from the mystery of womanly wiles and female musk) to help *him*, to watch as the victim she had claimed spun helpless in the fast-growing shroud of silk she wrapped about him?

An explosion. A 36-pounder gone off somewhere, triggered by lightning, blowing out its portlid. Spray flung horizontal across the decks. *Fist of God* plunging through a turbulent atmosphere of water and wind with no up, no down, no direction at all save ahead. Salvation alone in keeping the ship running with the wind. Death in the smallest failure of rigging, and no more certainty than that. The boats on their booms straining against their frappings, the bowsed-up guns seemingly ready to break loose at any moment and run thundering across the deck, churning men into paste with their immense weight.

. . . but must not use drugs had not thought of that Rosebud never did that perhaps they are different all different well that is true stone is stone different grades imposed by men had not thought of that but minister in their heads when can I return to Kanez for truth Lady Ivory (oh he will like that name after a while) will tell me no more but he does not have to tell me he has already told me all and when the guards find the prince and that Naian whore who does not wear her headwrap in the HOUSE *then I will do what I want and Lady Ivory already does what I want but it will be better without the drugs and that does feel fine . . .*

Sari and Beshur clung desperately to a small tongue of relatively level surface that projected out from the main body of the plateau while, only a few feet away, a lethal dance of thrust, parry, cut, and strike went on. Bakbuk, his face gray in the clammy fog, stood his ground, and neither did Potatoes yield an inch. Both faced a deadly opponent not only in the flesh-and-blood human being held little more than an arm's length away by the minuscule size of the plateau, but also in the sheer drops to all sides, drops set about with and climaxed by scores of jagged rocks.

Stupid, stupid girl!

Scampering from one side of the room to the other, wiggling as only a ferret (or one who will soon *be* a ferret) can wiggle, *chuckle-chuckle-chuckl*ing with a voice that, reduced to the boinks and squeaks and hisses and (yes) chuckles that were all the expressions a ferret could command (discounting, for the moment, the wiggles and capers and bounces and rollings that, for ferrets, at least, provided a wealth of nuance to the above-mentioned vocalizations), would soon lose all trace of human speech, could he not feel the spell growing on him? Would it happen when he was conscious? Would it happen as he slept? Would he have any memory of . . . before?

Girl!

Sailors straining, shuddering with the fatigue of days of storm, their near-comatose sleep snatched in dribs and drabs during what could not ever be called lulls but only moments of lesser tumult and horror, sailors hauling, pulling, forcing *Fist of God* up into the wind to lie to. Leeway matching headway, holding fast, immense bows shouldering titan seas aside, the ship's stumpy masts pitching through a full quarter circle and the storm blowing on and on, a meager mizzen staysail all the canvas spread to the torrent of air and spray threatening to sweep even an inch more into tatters and turn the American ship to broach to and receive the next wall of water on the beam and so be swallowed up by the churning sea and a thousand men dead in moments.

. . . and hold still pumice to you wretch I want it there and I wish he would stop clutching like that where is that slave I want that snake NOW I am sure that he will like it only have to wean him away from the drugs little by little and maybe that would be the way to do it wean him little by little and he would come to like it then would take a few weeks but I will have to go to Kanez and will not have time and he would recover and then I would be forced to start over again and what about those ships they have been gone for some time now I wonder . . .

And still Bakbuk, her spirit racked by her growing doubts, strove against Aeid. She loved him. She hated him. She wanted to kill him. She wanted to die herself. Blades clashed, shearing off sparks of bright metal. Her feet fought for balance and brought her forward as she drove him back. Here was her disgrace made real and given a face: Aeid . . . Prince Aeid. Handsome to the point of ravishment, whole as she had never been—*would* never be—whole, sure of himself as she would never be sure again. His very presence threatened to bring her to her knees before his unalloyed masculinity. And yet her spirit would rebel, would send her curved sword flickering into Aeid's defenses, batting them expertly aside and cutting at his throat.

Pudda-pudda-pudda? How long had he been bouncing? Did he recall? No? And was the corner now so full of excrement that he must seek another? Where were his rags? Was that Sabihah running away? And was there no king now to give her permission to live apart from him, to pension her, to care for her while her husband (Husband? Could a ferret be *anyone's* husband?) snuffled and rolled and slept in rags? And were his memories slipping away from him even now, leaving him adrift in a weasel wonderland of curiosity and recreation, with no worries save how to best rearrange a room that had already been rearranged?

Girl! Girl! Useless girl!

And then a massive sea rising above *Fist of God,* tipping the American ship crazily on its side. A groan, tight lashings straining, spray flying from them in a hovering mist blasted away in an instant, blasted away just as they break, a three-ton cannon careening away from the side, its wheeled carriage adding its own thunder to the flash and the concussion as of a million of its brethren roaring above, its mass parting lifelines, breaking rigging, sending a shock up the topmastless mainmast as though to split it

to its base. The ship in peril instantly, *Fist of God* tipping
crazily back to the beginning of yet another turbulent os-
cillation, the sheets trimming the mizzen staysail directly
in the path of the gun and the seamen tending the sail just
beyond that.

*. . . what did they have in mind and what did Lady Ivory
say to them before they departed and are they coming back
but of course they are coming back and there was that
matter of trade agreements but Lady Ivory has not said
anything about that look at that his lips pursed oh my yes
he does train well even better than Rosebud and I wonder
what happened to Rosebud oh I will find out when I return
to Kanez but then what would I do with Lady Ivory suppose I could drug him and take him with me yes that
would be a good idea just a little more time and this is
fine . . .*

And at the sight of the blade leaping for his throat, Aeid
instinctively stepped back and to the side, his own blade
ready for the deadly riposte. But the plateau had deceived
him, and his foot came down with nothing beneath it save
air and a thousand foot drop. Teetering for a moment,
wondering in the back of his mind why Bakbuk did not
drive in and finish the job while his arms whirled like useless wings, Aeid toppled, but he seized the edge of the plateau just at the last moment and dangled with death
beneath him as the mist swirled all about. And then Sari
was screaming at Bakbuk to spare him, crying out that she
would return to Nuhr, there to meet whatever fate the
king—or Abnel—decided was fitting for her.

And was he happy now? Did he look into the faces of
Umi Botzu and the Naian witch and roll ecstatically as
they scratched his belly and played with his tail and rolled
a wooden ball toward him, their voices loud with peals of
laughter as he scampered and played? Was there no
thought of his old life? Was everything gone? Was nothing
missed?

The cannon bearing down on the sheets and the men,

and Turtletrout leaping forward straight for the berserk gun, a line in his hand, his own life forfeit (a change in the sea or a random wave sending the careening arcs of the ship's masts doubling back upon themselves, the cannon retracing its path and smearing the first lieutenant across the wet decks) with the smallest particle of bad luck. His luck holding though, and Scruffy watching his quick hand darting a loop around the gun carriage and then Turtletrout flinging himself across the deck to a cleat and making the line fast, bawling for help, for other hands, for other lines to trip and secure the gun, bawling in the stern, uncompromising tone of one born to command.

. . . oh yes I will take him but not now this is too good truth can wait until he is ready I wonder what he would look like in silks and fetters oh quite fetching I am sure and the slaves will make them quickly enough and in any case I should remain here until the guards return with the impostor prince and the Naian woman it would not do to be gone when they arrive and oh yes that is what I will do yes . . .

Sari stood, her hands clenched, screaming. Potatoes, despite his obsessions, was her friend, and he was perhaps *more* than her friend, for she was suspecting now that there were other parts to his life, parts that she did not know so much as sense. Regardless, Potatoes (as Potatoes) had saved her a hundred times, and now Potatoes was hanging only by the strength of his fingers, totally at the mercy of the strange, girlish sworder who had, through a protracted fight, already shown his willingness to kill him. And yet her shouted promises of acquiescence seemed to make no impression upon Bakbuk, for, visibly shaking, he stood above Potatoes for a long minute, oblivious, so it seemed, to everything save some inner turmoil. Nor did Sari's entreaties appear to have anything to do with the sworder's sudden decision to bend, to drag Potatoes to the top of the plateau, and then, with a glance at Sari that staggered her with its bleakness, to turn and depart, the sound of his careful descent down the precipitous and rocky sides of the plateau fading slowly ... much more slowly than the indistinct and turgid darkness of his lithe form.

Were there any raisins?

Chapter Twenty

Dearly beloved brothers in Christ, it is nothing more . . .

Dearly beloved brothers in Christ, it is no more . . .

Dearly beloved brothers in Christ, it is . . .

Dearly beloved brothers in Christ, I cannot but be honored by my position, for it is my responsibility to write these poor words which will eventually comprise the true history of the relations of the Righteous States of America with the pagan kingdoms of the western coast of Africa. And yet, this is most Christian, even Christ-like. The responsibility, I mean. To write. I mean, to write the history.

And—

The history of the relations.

And it should be borne in mind by all God-fearing Christians (and you are all God-fearing, I am sure, for the words of the Gospels make God's truth so eminently clear that only benighted heathens like those of the western coast of Africa (along with many others, to be sure) cannot understand it or comprehend it (God's truth, I mean.)) that history itself is a showing forth of God's righteous plan for the world, and that, therefore, the task of writing this history, even with the willing and helpful cooperation of those participating, directly or indirectly, in the great events through which God's glory is revealed and endlessly magnified, is too weighty a responsibility for any mortal being, particularly when that mortal being is a mere, humble

*minister like myself, to bear up under save by that same
infinite grace. Of God. That is, God's infinite grace.*

Fist of God looked like an entirely different ship. Where
the American ship of the line had come out of Boston Harbor gleaming like a newly printed Bible (and proud of it,
thank you), now there was a battered, thoroughly abused
look about it. Seaweed and even palm fronds still hung
from parts of the hastily knotted and spliced rigging,
which presented a dreadfully chopped up appearance. All
three topmasts were gone, and with them the sleekness of
a well-made, well-rigged ship. In fact, words like *stumpy*
and *disconsolate* would not have been out of place in de-
scribing *Fist of God,* and the overall impression was, perhaps, something like that offered by those women of
Boston whose indiscretions, duly discovered and judged in
the sight of God and man alike, forced them to wander
about the town, bareheaded and shaved to the scalp, in the
dead of winter.

Elijah Scruffy, also presenting an overall impression of
stumpiness (though this was his usual appearance: it had
nothing to do with the storm), inspected the damage with
a look that itself had much of the disconsolate about it.
Sails gone. Masts gone. Jury-rigged yards that would have
made a lubber laugh. Halyards that might as well have
been put through a pair of shears, their ends still flapping
free in a most un-American and unseamanlike manner,
flapping free because there were so many more pressing
things to which to attend . . . such as eight feet of water in
the well and a hull that looked as though it had been battered by forty-two-pound balls.

And the decks. Decks covered with the stains of seaweed and pulverized fish. Decks scarred with the dents
and gouges left by a three-ton cannon that had first gotten
loose and rolled free and then, tripped, had scraped across
the smooth oak with every pitch of the ship until
Turtletrout and the braver members of the crew had se-

cured it. Decks so wrenched and strained by the violence
of the storm that their oakum-filled seams had spurted tar
and fiber to the extent that daylight could be seen from the
upper gun deck.

And if the decks were so, then what of the hull? Eight
feet of water in the well. And that mainmast . . .

"Well," he said to Turtletrout, who was bobbing his
head at everything in his usual, slope-headed way, "we
had to have a blooding, but I warn't expecting *this*."

"No, sir."

Scruffy eyed his first lieutenant. Turtletrout looked
much the same. He acted much the same. He even played
his game of chess much the same. And yet . . .

No, a man did not rise to the rank of lieutenant—or of
captain—in the American Navy by pure chance or by the
whim of his superiors. And after that incident with the
cannon in the storm, perhaps Scruffy had to remind himself a little less incessantly about Turtletrout's technical
rank . . . in spite of the head bobbing and the slope-
headedness.

"Mr. Carlyle to see you, sir," said one of the midshipmen.

Leaving Turtletrout to bob his head at the damage,
Scruffy turned to hear the carpenter's report just as a cry
arose from the lookouts who had been posted to the tops
of the broken-off masts.

"Land ho! Deck there!"

*And as history can only show forth the word and great-
ness of God, as all true believers and true Christians—
though actually the two are one and the same, all others
being pagans and heathens and destined for the fires of
hell—know, it is with joy that I write of the great storm
that afflicted the ship and tried sorely the faith of those on
board. It came upon us, as the Holy Scriptures say, like a
thief in the night, just as God's judgment will come upon*

us without any warning, catching even the most vigilant unawares . . .

. . . catching even the most vigilant unaware . . .

. . . without any warning, and no one will have looked for it, but will have lain . . . laid . . .

. . . but will have remained in comfort until the time of the archangel's trump. At which time they will be very surprised. The most vigilant, I mean. Not the archangel, who will know all about it, of course. If God intends him to. To know. But even the vigilant will be caught unaw—

It came without warning, as I said, and it drove us on for many days, scattering the fleet (and, indeed, the other ships lie . . . lay . . .

. . . and, indeed, the other ships are scattered still), our mighty and righteous ship wounded as Christ was wounded by the heathen Roman pagans. But by the grace of God all will be made well.

The ship, I mean.

And—

The ship. Not the pagans. They are all dead, anyway.

And so is demonstrated—

The pagan Romans.

And so is demonstrated the power of Almighty God, who can thus take the works of men and drive them before Him like so much chaff, and so the ship was drave . . .

. . . drove . . .

. . . was driven for many days, and only yesterday came there a great calm, yes, a great calm that brought to the minds of those pious American souls on board the great calm that preceded the making of the word, at which time the Spirit of God moved upon the face of the waters.

Drave . . . driven . . . droven???

Hmmm . . . ha . . . PIGS! Tracked me down and brought me back to this island, and all for the glory of Panas. You know the guns, they said. And you will serve the guns. PIGS! I serve only Panas, but they say that Panas and the guns are the same. So now I must introduce others to the guns, and to the slow-match, and they, too, can lose their legs when we run the guns out! PIGS!

But here is the lookout, and he—PIG!—is telling me that there is a ship on the horizon! A ship! Brimstone! Full of PIGS! And how he should know a ship when he sees one, I do not know, for I am the only one who is intelligent, and I can ram the ball home smartly, and they left me my stones and took my leg, and now they tell me I must serve the guns!

PIGS!

And so, dearest brothers in Christ, we lie . . .

. . . we sail upon calm waters, alone, like Noah's dove, searching for some friendly port in which to rest. And surely there can be no more friendly port than the loving hands of almighty God, into whose care we commend our souls on a daily basis, lest the powers of hell find dominion over us and drag us into the fiery pit at the hour of our death, which could be at any moment. Our death, I mean, which, as this recent tempest, as sudden as that which broke over the boat that carried Jonah, has well demonstrated, could be at any moment.

And yet, putting his trust in those Hands, our brave captain (God's hands, I mean.) and his virtuous first lieutenant, having that implicit faith in the goodness of the Lord which so characterizes the pious men of the sea, now turn their attention to the material welfare of the ship and those who sail in it, for even Jesus gave thought to providing food and drink for his disciples; and among the Lord's last words were instructions to the saintly John for the material welfare of his mother. I mean, Our Lord's mother.

"Noon, gentlemen."

Noon on board *Fist of God*. The bell rang, the glass turned, and the sextants on the quarterdeck—midshipmen's and master's alike—lifted. The observation was made, and in a few minutes, the position of the ship was calculated. The master came to Scruffy with the information and a chart that was not too dampened with seawater.

Scruffy, his attention torn between the ship, the observation, and the land that was now visible as a dark thickening on the horizon, at last managed to correlate the three.

"It's that island you saw before, sir," said Turtletrout, looking at the chart.

"Yes." Scruffy was calculating. Speed. Wind. Probable shifts in the weather. "The storm drove us well southeast of where we're supposed to be. The fleet will be regrouping north of that Runzen peninsula, and here we are down well past Nuhr."

Turtletrout was bobbing his head again, completely neutralizing any impression of competence that Scruffy was trying to keep in mind. "Fleet's probably past Nuhr, too."

"Yes, Turtletrout. But *where*?"

Scruffy calculated some more. The island—uncharted—was a temptation for several reasons, not all of which were frivolous. A quiet bay with clear, tropical water would give him a chance to inspect the bottom of the ship, and a sandy shore would be a good place for unloading everything and drying it out. Then, too, a gallows built on an opportune cliff would be invaluable in replacing the mainmast if Mr. Carlyle decided that the repairs he had made to it (If asked directly about the mainmast, Mr. Carlyle would reply that he was perfectly satisfied and confident . . . all the while anxiously looking at it as though it would fall on his head at any moment.) would not do.

"Mr. Carlyle!"

"Sir!"

"Fish me some topmasts and let's get some sail on this ship. I want to look in on that island."

"Yes, sir!"

And so, in just such a way did our beloved and saintly captain (for all true men of the sea, provided they be

*American men, are saintly in their own various ways,
which is another indication not only of the goodness of
God, but also of the many ways in which that saintliness . . . I mean that goodness is shown forth. The goodness of God, I mean. By the saintliness of the captains. I
mean, the saintliness of all true men of the sea. Provided
they be American. Men. Ah . . .)*

*And so, seeing that Divine Providence has seen fit to
provide us with an island—previously unknown, but a haven for all that—our saintly captain has elected to steer
our mighty but wounded ship straight for it, in order to
better renew its strength. Of the ship, I mean. Not the island. The ship's strength. And—*

So now I go and look, and I see a ship, too. Hah! A
ship! And for the glory of Panas, whom I serve—and I
serve only Panas and not these PIGS who tell me to serve
the guns—we will put the penises of the cartridges into the
cunts of the guns, and we will ram the balls home smartly,
and we will take wads from cheeses. And we will introduce the slow-match to the pow—!

PIGS!

—what was that?

"Inhabited, sir," said Turtletrout.

"And shooting," said Mr. Carlyle.

"Thank you, Mr. Carlyle," said Scruffy. "It had come to
my attention." Then, lifting his voice into a seaman's roar:
"Hard a-weather!"

"Forty-two pounders, sir," said Turtletrout. "I'd guess."
"But not very accurate, sir," added Mr. Carlyle, who, despite his words, had just had his hat removed by forty-two
pounds of moving metal that thereafter thudded onto the
deck (adding yet another dent), rolled, and plunged
through a scupper.

"Thank you, Mr. Carlyle," said Scruffy. But then, shifting back to a roar: "Beat to quarters!"

Drums sounded. Gunports opened. Tompions slid out, and the 36-pound cannon of *Fist of God* probed out of their gunports like fingers, searching for an enemy to maul.

More puffs of smoke from the battery on shore, and now Scruffy could see the faint outlines of a building. It was made of the same rock as the cliff upon which it stood. Irregularly shaped as it was, and the light lying behind the cliff as it was, its presence was so obscured that Scruffy did not wonder that no eyes on board *Fist of God* had seen it until it had opened fire. Still ...

"Any colors showing?" he called to the lookouts as *Fist of God,* with fished topmasts and five feet of water in the well, slewed around clumsily, at once increasing the distance between itself and the battery and presenting a moving target to foil the island gunners' aim.

"No colors, sir."

"Damnably odd," said Scruffy, forgetting his piety for the moment. Another ball blasted overhead. "Foxed!" he muttered. "Simply foxed! And me without even a tompion out! I ought to be sold for scrap!"

But despite Scruffy's self-deprecation, the distance between *Fist of God* and the island was increasing only slowly, and though Mr. Carlyle had judged the accuracy of the battery well, randomness proved a reliable shot now and again, and another ball found its mark, hulling the ship just above the waterline.

"Mr. Preeble!" he shouted. "Lay those guns yourself. Fire at the embrasures. Keep it slow and steady, like a good Puritan, and we'll have the starboard guns next."

Preeble was a master of gunnery. He knew cannon as he knew Scripture, and he demonstrated both now: the larboard guns, set for maximum elevation, went off, one at a time, slowly and surely, each one accompanied by an appropriate verse from Jeremiah.

At the battery, stone chips flew, and one embrasure was now noticeably larger.

Cheers from the Fists!

And so it came to pass, my dear brothers in Christ, that an enemy arose out of the sea . . . or, rather, out of an island in the sea. Well, not out of an island, but up on an island . . .

And so it came to pass, my dear brothers in Christ, that, speaking figuratively, an enemy arose out of the sea, and he attempted to smite us greatly. But the spirit of God was upon us, and in a mighty voice did the guns of our ship defy the devil and all his works—

Oh . . . my!

Ha . . . PIGS! They shoot back. Well, I do not know who they are or why they shoot back, but they shoot back and so they defy Panas, whom I serve (and I do not serve these guns that those PIGS told me to serve), and if they tell me to put sheepskin into the God's gun, then the guilt is on them. But if that ship shoots at me, then I will shoot at it, sheepskin or no sheepskin, and I will point these guns carefully, even though I do not know what they mean when they say to *run the guns out* for, truly, I would not want to catch one if it began to run!

And now one gun has been destroyed by those PIGS who fire at us from the ship. The God's gun! Brimstone and pumice! Sacrilege! Very well, we will shoot back, and we will shoot better!

Thrust! Thrust! Um . . . ma, ma, ma!

—So that the devil must be confounded, for it is written in Holy Scripture that the devil will be confounded, and it is the proof of God's glory that such confounding will be within the sight of all. And—OH!

* * *

"Come about! Larboard guns again! Mr. Preeble, fire as they bear!"

And *Fist of God,* having just discharged a starboard broadside, swung ponderously around to present its freshly loaded larboard guns to the battery. The turn was slow, much too slow for Scruffy's taste, but he was unwilling to strain the ship: a piece of rigging carrying away and leaving the ship wallowing within range of the battery would spell death for every man on board.

Once again, the guns began to speak, pounding out great, thumping syllables in their deliberate and impelling voices. The rock about several of the battery's embrasures had by now been reduced to rubble, and several of its great guns had been silenced. Had Scruffy known what sort of force was ashore, he might have sent out a couple of boats full of stout, Puritan soldiers to take the battery and destroy the guns (Let those troops he had been carrying for the last six weeks show what sort of godly things they could do!); but, as it was, he had no idea even of the nationality of the battery that was attacking him, and the battery, for its part, seemed disinclined to tell him.

But from the sound of the guns, he would have sworn (had he not been a good ... well, mostly good ... Puritan) that they were *French.*

"Frog-eating bastards."

A sharp crack as a rope parted. At Scruffy's side, Turtletrout whirled, and Scruffy saw the lieutenant's eyes evaluate the damage. It was a dull, slope-headed evaluation, but it was quick and accurate.

"Mr. Phipps! Have that halyard spliced immed—"

Scruffy had turned back to the battery as Turtletrout had begun to speak, but the odd way in which the first lieutenant had stopped in mid-sentence made him swing around. For a moment, he thought that Turtletrout was looking at his feet, for the lieutenant must certainly have had his head bowed to a remarkable degree to present such a curious figure. And then, with a sick chill, Scruffy realized that

Turtletrout *had* no head, that one of the forty-two-pound cannon balls from the battery had sheared it off in an instant.

And as Turtletrout's body collapsed, crumpling up like a wad of wet paper, falling, seemingly, into itself and into the growing pool of crimson on the oak deck, Scruffy, his sickness growing, turned again to the battery, his sight veiled with red.

Another shot howled overhead. Another crack as rigging parted. Even randomness would tell, given time.

"Hit 'em lads! Again! And again! I want those frog-eaters *dead*! FIRE!"

The glory of the Lord is made manifest, and the work of God speaks through the voices of His children. And thus is the enemy confounded, for the nerveless strength of evil is no match for the might of the pious, and so our guns hammer at the abode of the wicked, demonstrating the righteousness of God. No ... the strength of God. In His righteousness. And so in his righteousness does the voice of our captain speak ...

And they say to me, shoot any ship that comes, and they do not say anything about ships shooting back. PIGS! And they say even less about ships shooting back and destroying my guns. Pumice! Er .... ah ... hmmm ...urg ... PIGS! And now my priests are killed, and they can no longer serve the guns. And so they can no longer serve Panas. And, in any case, there are only two guns left to serve, whether they be Panas or be guns. And the ship is still shooting at us!

And ... hah ... PIGS! They have given us powder, and they have given us shot, but there are no more wads in the cheeses. Well, here is a cat, and it does not come from a cheese, and it is not a wad, but it will *be* a wad, and—

"MRKGNAO!"

* * *

*And so in his righteousness does our captain speak in a
great voice, urging all who hear him to be valiant and not
to swerve in their service to the Almighty. And, to a man,
the pious sailors obey, each urging his great iron . . .*

Each urging his great brass . . .

*Each tending his gun as though not only his life but the
glory of God depends upon it, and each sending his balls
sure and true into the abode . . .*

Into the fortress of the enemy . . .

*Into the fortress of evil. And thus is it—
OH!*

"Come about! Fire as they bear!"

Fist of God, true to its name, had reduced most of the
battery to wreckage. Only one or two of the guns spoke
now, and those only intermittently. But Scruffy, having
watched two of his crewmen bear away the lifeless and
headless body of his first lieutenant, ordered that the bom-
bardment of the island continue.

And so it did, the ship's thirty-six-pounders growing
hotter and hotter, jumping clean off the deck now with every discharge, the danger of a premature explosion as the
flannel powder-cartridges slid through the nearly red-hot
muzzles growing staggeringly large. Smoke wound thick
about the clumsy *Fist of God,* but Scruffy could still see
the ruins of the battery silhouetted against the sky, and he
kept the gun crews at their work, determined to have the
battery—embrasures, guns, gunners, mountain, and all—
leveled to the ground.

A thump against his chest. He looked down to see the
head of a cat hanging from his coat by one of its fangs.
Almost unthinkingly, he detached it and tossed it into the
sea.

Where was Turtletrout?

Oh . . . yes . . .

"*Fire!*"

And then a plume of smoke curled from the battery.

Growing, expanding, it increased in the space of a minute (And still the guns of *Fist of God* roared.) from a thin ribbon to a puffy cloud.

"They're on fire, sir," said Mr. Preeble.

"We'll show 'em fire," said Scruffy.

"Sir?"

"Come about! Starboard guns! Fire as they bear! At 'em!"

And the mighty . . .

PIGS! PIGS! PI—!

. . . soldiers of God . . .

"Again! Come about! Larboard guns! At 'em, lads!"

And suddenly, with a crack that ballooned out from the island in a visible shock wave, the magazine of the battery blew up, leaving behind it fragments of rock, bent and broken guns, and a blaze that grew and grew, eating down into what appeared to be an abyss that had opened up in the mountain. Scruffy gave the order to cease fire, but the blaze on the island burned on. Hours passed. A night and another day passed, and still it burned, its smoke drifting across the sky, shrouding the sun, blotting out the stars.

Chapter Twenty-one

The moon, reduced to a thin, waning crescent, rose into a sky burdened with clouds. But, just above the horizon, a hand's-breadth was clear, and Sari, Beshur, and Potatoes, perched on the western rim of a great, shelving depth of shadow so black that it could well have been the fabled edge of the world beyond which everything material fell into silence, death, and loss, saw not only the moon, slipping into view like a half hoop of silver, but also a shimmering reflection, a trembling as though upon a liquid surface.

"Water," said Sari. "It is the water."

As they watched, the moon mounted into the clouds, and it and the reflection faded from their sight.

What has become of Bakbuk?

Why, here she is! And very fetching indeed she looks this bright, sunny morning (As though mornings could be anything *but* bright and sunny in the Three Kingdoms!) as she makes her way through the streets of Katha toward the Naian Quarter! But where is her face cloth? Where is her head cloth? Is she not a proper little Panasian girl, all womb and no pleasure save for her man who will, doubtless, come along some day, blood her properly, and use her as his father used his wife and *his* father used *his* wife and so on up the ancestral line to the first Panasian male who held a knife in one hand and his bound mate in the other, and, after a thorough examination of the external female sex organs, fell to considering?

Oh ... quite right. Bakbuk. How thoughtless of us to forget.

So she is, after all, not *quite* a proper little Panasian girl (for more reasons than her choice of dress), but has she, then, opted for Naianism? For rank and superstition and complacent ignorance? For a naïf innocence that is poles apart from her carefully cultivated irony and universally applied cynicism?

Bakbuk?

It seems to be so, for not only are her head and face bare, her black hair brushed and combed until it is a lustrous fall of silk from her head to her waist, but she has also (Do not ask how: I really have no idea.) managed to procure a bronze medallion that proclaims her a daughter of her mother. And, unlike the medallion that Sari encountered in a certain marketplace in the central wastes—a medallion, it might be well to repeat, that was being worn by an individual whose distinctly male characteristics made him just as ineligible (according to Naian tradition and Panasian law both) to wear it as Bakbuk's utter sexlessness makes *her*—this medallion, worked with exquisite precision, bears all the hallmarks of authenticity.

Why this place, though? Why these clothes? Why this medallion? Does Bakbuk really believe that one can become a Naian simply by an alteration in costume? Is she, perhaps, thinking that a change in her religious affiliation will somehow induce Naia to perform a miracle after three days of pleading, prayer, and entreaty proved ineffectual? Or is this but further evidence of her self-abasement, an outward sign, so to speak, instituted by herself, to give not grace, but rather further guilt, a sealing of her repeated failures (failures capped, a little over a week ago, by the largest of them all: a titanic, colossal failure against which there can be set no sufficiently redemptive act, no matter how extreme) with the final and irrevocable sin of apostasy?

One of these? Two of these? Three of these? All of these?

None of these?

Nevertheless, here she is. Such a pretty little thing. Her step is light, almost buoyant, and her eyes, bright and shining, have a hint of vacuousness about them that is so appropriate to a pretty girl. Not a thought in her head! Well, perhaps one or two: about nice clothes, and about a handsome man ... as is quite fitting for a maid, even if that maid is rather new-made (if you will forgive the expression).

Bright and shining. Very bright. Very shining. Perhaps ... perhaps a trace of madness?

Dear Bakbuk, where does thee go? Does thee seek to lose thyself in the Naian Quarter, among the scurrying inhabitants, the run-down houses, and the ill-made wares? Has thee, who has traveled with us all this time, looked at thy life and found it to be as dust? A parti-colored sham with no escape? Does baring thy head and face and wearing a medallion that is not thine to wear convince thee, even in the slightest (thee who has never allowed the slightest adulteration of a perfect and lifelong skepticism) that thee has found, in this place of incense, wind chimes, and chanting, a haven, a home, a place where thee will be accepted?

Go thy ways, Bakbuk. Go and do thy best. Find what fulfillment thee can. A little while and we shall see thee; and yet a little while and we shall see thee no more. Yet, regardless of where thy steps take thee, whether into horror or into glory, know that our thoughts and prayers go with thee. Lo, even unto the end of time.

It seemed to Sari that, somewhere along the twisted path that she had traced from Ouzal to Halim to Kestir to Sayam to Katha to the Caves of Naia to Katha to Nuhr to

Katha again and finally into the fastness of the mountains themselves—somewhere, she had lost herself. It was not that she had been bodily transformed and had, therefore, lost the familiar physical appearance so integral to one's perception of identity (though she had). It was not that she had lost her home, her family, and the very foundations of her fondly-remembered religion (though she had). No: somewhere along the above-mentioned path, the identity of Sari had evaporated, or had at least become secondary, its place taken by her function as a kind of instrument of the Goddess.

On the surface, this might have been seen by those who termed themselves her co-religionists as a desirable thing, a willing yielding of self to an egolessness that was an echo of pre-birth dreamtime, a returning to the golden age of thoughtless infancy that, though lost forever to the encroachments of sentience, still beckoned from the borders of consciousness. But Sari had lost her surface, too—perhaps she had lost herself *because* she had lost her surface—and so she could not be seduced by such deceptive yearnings. Or perhaps, having already lost herself to something that went beyond ego or consciousness, something that seemed to be, at times, all encompassing mind, transformation, and a kind of harrowing love so painful that it made absolute hate seem an almost attractive proposition, she had nothing and no time to give to a poor, pale, unsatisfying imitation.

Instead, she had what she had: a being, a self that had been transformed into something that went *forward,* step by step, toward a goal that had been at first clear and then nebulous, even impossible, a goal that had now refocused, her impelling duty narrowing and concentrating as though by means of one of Elijah Scruffy's burning glasses until it had become a white hot reification of sheer *drive.*

This luminous clarity had come to her on the day following her pre-dawn glimpse of the pent-up waters of three lands, when she and her companions had begun

searching for the workings that had created such a vast, inland sea. They had found them soon enough, for there
were many, clustering thicker and thicker the closer they
drew to the actual shore of the waters . . . a shore made up
of an ever-changing combination of dikes, dams, drowned
rock walls, mud flats, cliff faces, and a hundred other natural and artificial barriers that contained the vast waters.

Here, pumped up from cache basins and holding ponds
below the watersheds and snowpacks, transported by pipes
and aqueducts and tunnels to spill into a titan reservoir
(there to sit idle until evaporation turned the shallows to
crusts of minerals or redirection sent cataracts tumbling
eastward into the unknown and unexplored interior valleys) was water in abundance. Here were fertility and life
bottled up in the high, interior valleys of the Mountains of
Ern.

Here was the bounty of three centuries of rain and snow
. . . squandered.

And here were those who maintained the workings, who
operated the pumps, who dug new cache basins and holding ponds, who patched the pipes and repaired the aqueducts and the tunnels: the men—the criminals—who had
been sent into the mountains on the basis of even the
slightest infraction of Panasian law. And here, also, were
those who, with the aid—willing or not—of kidnapped
women, had been bred to their tasks for as long as the
workings had been in construction and operation: dull,
shambling things of huge stature, immense strength, and
little intelligence, one of whom had, long ago, wandered
away and died in an isolated cave, turning with time into
the unsettling skeleton found by Sari and Beshur.

And Sari and her companions continued, searching out,
examining, looking on with a kind of horrified fascination
as they realized the fantastic scope of what the priesthood
of Panas had accomplished in the Three Kingdoms.

A drought. A man-made, man-sustained drought. A
drought created for no other reason than curiosity, a tinker-

ing with religions and societies that were themselves man-made, man-sustained.

They had come at last upon a long, narrow rift valley that gashed through foothill and mountain alike as though the ranges to the west had been struck with an immense axe. Though originally extending straight into the heart of the giant reservoir, the valley had, over time, been slowly filled up and blocked with a thick, rammed earth dam that was something of a mountain itself. At its base, it looked to be several miles thick. At its top, though, it was no more than the distance one might walk in the space of a minute.

Hidden among boulders, gasping with the cold and the thin air, Sari and her companions could not but marvel at the sheer size of the pile. But then there came a rumbling, a swaying of the ground.

—Earthquake! Beshur yelped (unhelpfully) as he looked for a way to rush (instinctively) outdoors, forgetting for the moment that he *was* (obviously) outdoors.

"Shhh!" said Potatoes.

The ground continued to sway, and Beshur yelped again, but this time his yelp was muffled . . . owing, perhaps, to Potatoes' hand, which was firmly clamped over his mouth.

But Sari, momentarily distracted not only by her own instinctive fear of the earthquake but also by Beshur's outburst, turned back to the rammed-earth dam to find that a fissure had opened up in it. The gap was not wide, nor was it very deep, but water was spurting from it, cascading down the long, western slope, and pooling at the base of the dam. Given time, the water would eventually wind down the valley toward the dry stream beds and River Forshen, and, providing that evaporation did not entirely eliminate its existence, eventually reach the sea.

As she watched, accompanied now by Potatoes (who still had his hand over Beshur's mouth) and Beshur (who still had Potatoes' hand over his mouth), the fissure grew, the flow of water widening and deepening it . . . and increasing itself thereby with a rapidity that made her wonder whether the whole pile would soon come down.

But, no: within minutes, a swarm of workers—human, almost-human, and all gradations in between—came pelting along a narrow path that led down to the dam from the opposite direction. They were apparently used to such emergencies, for they set to work immediately, filling and bracing, rolling boulders, and setting up bulwarks of wood and stone to take the pressure of the water until the fissure was filled in. Soon, surprisingly soon, the flow stopped, the dam was repacked and rammed, and the workers went away.

It had taken less than an hour.

"What would happen," Sari said, "if no one came to repair the dam?"

Beshur had managed to extricate his mouth from Potatoes' hand.

—It is quite obvious, he said. The crack would become larger and larger, and at last would become too big to fill. A great deal of water would be released, and much if not all of the work would have to start over again.

Potatoes looked at him expectantly, waiting.

Beshur shifted uneasily.

Potatoes continued to wait.

—Ah . . . I am a scholar. And I know these things.

Sari nodded. "We will make it so, then."

Beshur stared at her.

"Tonight."

"Come back here!"

Raisins?

The moon had waned fully now, and, working mostly by feel, Sari and her companions crept up the steep paths and made their way to the top of the rammed-earth dam.

Just as Beshur had expected (and he told them so), there was but a single watchman at the dam: someone standing atop the enormous pile to monitor its integrity and to sound the alarm in case a rift was caused by earthquake or by chance.

Well, he would not sound any alarm tonight, for Potatoes, gliding through the darkness as silently and smoothly as oil, attended to him, afterward scouting out the top of the dam, looking for weak places (none, unfortunately) and for additional guards (none, fortunately—though Potatoes had devoutly wished for the presence of a second guard so as to embarrass Beshur, who had insisted (he was a scholar, after all, and he knew these things) that there would be only one).

Sari had watched from the shelter of an overhang as Potatoes had glided away to do his preliminary work. By tacit agreement, it seemed, Beshur and Potatoes were no longer urging her to return to the flatlands, nor had they raised even so much as a patient sigh against this current endeavor. No, it seemed that, with the confirmation of the existence of the pump works, the earthworks, and, most important of all, the immense volume of contained water that had for three hundred years been building up in the interior valleys of the Mountains of Ern, her companions' objections (if not their fantasies) had come to an end, and they were now willing partners in her plans.

Brutal plans, as it turned out, and for more reasons than the silencing of the watchman, for there was digging to be done—a long, shallow ditch to run straight across the top of the dam: just enough to let the water begin to flow, after which erosion would suffice to deepen and widen the excavation—and the rammed earth, pounded and tamped by thousands of hands, strong human and fantastically-strong almost-human alike, seemed almost the hardness of stone.

But they had their own hands and their own strength, and they had sticks, and, in truth, the ditch did not have to be very deep at all ... a comparative scratch would suffice, provided that it stayed undetected and unrepaired. Still, though, the distance of a minute's walk was a long distance indeed when it had to be excavated out of such rammed earth and stone; excavated, for that matter, in the dark, and in comparative silence.

They labored, scraping their tiny notch in the top of the dam, working on into the night. They spoke as little as they could, for words took strength and air, both of which were better utilized in extending the trench. And extend it they did, lengthening it gradually, a trickle of water following ...

"Beshur?"

—What?

"You are veering off to the side."

—Oh ... sorry ...

... behind, moistening the hard-packed earth and, to the extent that their digging could pause for an instant to allow it, softening what lay ahead so that their task was eased, albeit imperceptibly.

And Sari could not but see the trench as yet another instance of that Goddess-given providence whose every manifestation depended upon movement forward. Forward to Halim. Forward to Katha. Forward (There was never any going backward, was there?) to Nuhr, to Kanez, to the mountains. As she had first recognized in the Library ...

"Beshur!"

—It is hard to see in the dark!

"Keep to a straight line!"

—All right. All right.

... and again and again afterward, her way, malleable though it was, was nonetheless clearly marked. It was her way, it was Naia's way. Far from being locked into ritual, or drumming, or crystals, Naia (whoever or whatever She was) was a constantly evolving, constantly changing Presence that demonstrated its existence not in externals, but in a kind of belly-filling confidence that could be appreciated only from within; and, having been stripped of her external identity, having become no more than a moving forward that embodied that Presence, Sari—

"Be*shur!*"

—Why are you always singling me out?

"Why? Because you are the one who is always veering off!"

—I deserve to be treated better! I am a—

"Gobble!"

Beshur stopped in mid-sentence.

—No, he said at last. I am not a gobble. I am a scholar.

"Gobble?" said Potatoes.

"Gobble?" said Sari.

"Gobble!"

Sari and the men looked up, simultaneously realizing that, involved as they had been in their work, they had failed to notice that there were no longer three people atop the dam, but *four*. Which was somewhat unforgivable, really, as number four was in the vicinity of eight feet tall, almost as broad, and blotted out the stars as though a small moon had decided to go into eclipse not ten feet away.

"*Gobble!*"

It was one of the almost-human things that had been bred from the degenerate stock of twelve or more generations of Panasian convicts. Beetle-browed, with hands that bore an unsettling resemblance to shovels, it advanced on them, a dangerous light in what could be seen of its eyes.

Potatoes straightened, sizing it up, but Beshur, still stinging from having been singled out for inaccurate digging, ran forward, his stick held high. After halting before the shovel-handed thing for what seemed a full minute's worth of uncertainty, and apparently unable to think of anything more imaginative, he banged it on its head with his stick.

"Gobble!"

—Gobble, yourself, you idiot! Beshur shouted as he banged it again.

But, the next moment, the thing plucked Beshur's stick from his hands as though it were a twig, flexed it between its two hands . . .

. . . and broke it.

"Oh," said Potatoes. "Very nice, *indeed!*"

—Just as I—

"Gobble!"

The thing was shambling forward, reaching for Beshur, but Potatoes was already moving. Circling behind it with the stealth of a thief (which, Sari considered, was to be expected . . . though she continued to wonder about Potatoes, about his familiarity with things that he had no business being familiar with, about a certain indefinable . . . well . . . *air* about him that had nothing in common with the squalor of thievery and everything in common with what she had seen of the pomp of the court of Nuhr (And what about that figure she had seen leaving the prince's room on that night that had proved to be such a turning point for herself, for Naia, for, indeed, everyone?)), he sprang quickly, one arm going about the thing's neck (giving the impression that Potatoes was attempting to embrace a full-grown palm tree) while the other came up . . . accompanied by the glint of razor-sharp metal.

"Gob—!"

And then the thing was down, twitching.

"Guards! Ho!"

Sari whirled. Up on the narrow path that led down to the dam from what she assumed were priestly dwellings and barracks (And what about those . . . things? What did they sleep in? *Stalls?*) was the movement of dark figures—small, large, and very large—against the lighter color of the heavily-trodden earth and rock.

Potatoes had seen, too. Having leapt clear of the toppling thing, he grabbed Beshur's arm. "Come," he said, "we must hold the path."

—But I do not even have a pointed stick!

"Yes," said Potatoes, dragging him toward the base of

the path, toward the advancing figures. "You threw it away." But he was already pressing his own digging stick into Beshur's hands while, with practiced movements, he sheathed his knife and drew his sword.

There was a small hope that the two men would be able, at the very least, to delay the advance of the guards and their ... ah ... various assistants. The path down to the dam was narrow, allowing those who traveled upon it to thread their way only in single-file. If Potatoes and Beshur worked fast enough and skillfully enough, they would have to deal with only one or two enemies at a time (and Potatoes was privately planning to use Beshur as an obviously-inept decoy who would hold the attention of the guards and their ... ah ... various assistants while he himself, concealed by confusion and darkness both, attacked from the flank).

Sari, for her part, was digging furiously. There was nothing she could do against the invaders, even if there were room for another defender at the base of the path (and there was not). She could only continue to move forward, holding to her plan, to what she assumed was the Goddess' plan. And so she funneled her thoughts, her desires, even, now, her physical being into that single, brutal goal: the completion of the ditch.

Rising above the thump and scrape of her stick were thuds, an occasional scream, frequent gobbles. The path was narrow and treacherous, and Beshur, flailing about ineffectually, was an excellent decoy for Potatoes, even more so than might have been expected, since Beshur did not *know* he was a decoy.

Sari dug, the thread of water from the reservoir following her as she progressed slowly toward the western edge of the dam. Screams. Thuds. Gobbles. And Sari dug. Her stick blunted and splintered against hard earth and harder stone, but she continued, her concentration wholly filled by striking, prying, and that faint, quivering, almost subliminal sheen of water.

Her stick broke. She cast it aside and used her hands. Her nails shattered quickly. she paid no attention. Cuts in her fingers and palms bled freely, and patches of skin worked loose, crusted thickly with dust and mud. She did not notice.

More screams. More thuds. Frequent gobbles.

And then, suddenly, so suddenly that, concerned only with going forward, she was caught unawares, she came to the edge of the dam. Her thoughts spinning with fatigue and thin air, unable for the moment to comprehend that she had reached her goal and that a threadlike dribble of water was now spattering into the abyss over which she teetered, she was in danger of falling. And, in fact, she *did* fall, toppling over the man-made precipice as though in pursuit of the vitalizing moisture that she had so striven to release.

A strong arm caught her, dragged her back. She saw the figure of a man against the stars. Faintly, in the back of her mind, she sensed that the trickle of water had increased.

"Potatoes?"

He did not reply. Lifting her hands, he examined them, frowning. She knew that he was frowning. She could not see his face, but she knew. Somehow, it did not seem overly remarkable to her that she knew. Or that he frowned.

The water increased. More screams. More thuds. More gobbles. Beshur was doing his unwitting work well. But if—?

Before she could even begin to frame her question, the man bent and lifted her hands to his lips, placing a kiss directly in the middle of each of her mutilated palms.

Startled out of her fuzziness, Sari peered at his face. It was too dark. She could not see.

The flow of water increased.

"Who . . . ?"

"Hail, daughter of Naia," he said. And then he was gone.

"Sari!"

Stupidly, she sat down beside the widening rivulet, feeling warm, feeling cold, feeling, at the same time, numb. She heard moving water.

"Sari!"

And then Potatoes and Beshur were beside her, lifting her, carrying her away. Beshur was gobbling ... er ... gabbling about the glorious battle and the magnificence of his defense that had been helped out (just a little) by Potatoes' sword. All the guards, it seemed, were dead: pitched off the cliff at the side of the path or killed outright by Potatoes (well, maybe helped out just a little more than just a little), and the way was clear.

The water was flowing faster now, burbling, cutting through the hard-packed earth, undermining the stones. By dawn, it would be beyond the repair of even the most determined band of workers ... and there were now no workers.

"Did you see ..." Sari murmured. "Who was ... ?"

"See?"

—Who?

"That man ..."

"There was no man."

—What man?

"He ..."

—You must have been imagining it. You are very tired and cold. You must rest. I am a scholar, and I know—

"Shut up and carry her, Beshur."

Carry her they did. Dawn found them several miles away, and in the growing light, they could look across a wide gulf of air and see that Sari's shallow trench had grown into a large river. Water, bright water, was pouring over the lip of the fast-eroding dam in an ever-deepening, ever-widening cataract.

Sari watched, her hand pressed to her mouth. And then

she noticed that her hand did not hurt. Neither of her hands hurt, in fact. Despite the battering and abuse they had received, they gave her no discomfort at all.

She looked down at them. Her hands were whole, healed, perfect. Not a stain, not a blemish. And there, in the middle of her palms, where the strange, unlooked-for lips had lingered, was a mark like a flower.

"He . . . he called me daughter of Naia," she said.

"Who?"

—He?

But a deep rumbling made her look up. The earth was shaking, swaying, the distant cataract increasing. Lumps of earth and rock were falling away from the face of the dam, and the river had turned into a deep gash. The earthquake grew, the geologic forces unleashed by the sudden decrease in the weight of long-confined water now tumbling into one another, setting off others, piling into a catastrophic vibration so intense that the rock walls on either side of the dam actually blurred with the rapidity of their motion.

And then the dam crumbled, vanishing like a puff of smoke in a high wind, revealing, all at once, as though a curtain had been stripped away, a wall of water nearly a thousand feet high, the sunlight refracting through it in distinct layers, from clear emerald at its surface, through darker shades of algae and sediment, to the darkness of brackish, half-congealed mud at its base . . . but only for a moment; for in the next instant, the wall surged forward in a screaming, shouting, roaring chaos that filled the vast rift valley and shrieked its way down toward the lowlands, carrying away boulders, hills, and even entire mountains as the combined waters of three centuries were unleashed.

Chapter Twenty-two

Well, Hel-*lo!* Your name is Bakbuk, then? What a lovely name! But it is fitting, is it not? A lovely name for a lovely woman! Oh, Naia has blessed you exceedingly! She has made you an attractive and beautiful woman, and She has also given you a lovely name to go with your attractiveness and your beauty. I must tell you, though, that She has blessed me too, for She has allowed me to be a part of a religion that honors and respects attractive and beautiful women, for, truly, attractive and beautiful women are perfect incarnations of Naia, who cannot be anything but attractive and beautiful; and is it not wonderful that my religious duties require me not only to educate attractive and beautiful women in the performance of their duties to Naia (which I take very seriously, indeed) but also to *embrace* attractive and beautiful women, since they are perfect incarnations of the Goddess. And it is their *duty* to be embraced by me, as I am sure you understand.

Oh, you need not protest my need to fulfill my religious obligations! This is, after all, a part of your spiritual training, and, since you came to me in order to learn such things, I am doing no more than what you asked. After all, Naia is a woman, and She knows about and approves of things like this, just as I do, because I am a man who is in harmony with the feminine side of his nature. You really ought to take my guidance and not struggle quite so much, because our relationship is approved by the Goddess, who has given me both the ability to perceive and the duty to honor your lovely and attractive charms, since, as I said, I am in harmony with the feminine side of my nature.

But ... but I find that—*blasphemy!*—you are no woman at all! Only a crude imitation! Therefore you are not lovely or attractive, and, in fact, you are not an incarnation, perfect or otherwise, of Naia. Moreover, by deceiving me, you have caused me to neglect my duties to the Goddess!

You have come to me for lessons? Then I will teach you a lesson, indeed. I will teach you very well. No, do not try to escape. Your tricks and your sacrilege are over forever, for I will make very sure that you never, never practice such sacrilegious deceptions on anyone else. It is no good struggling, for I have you, and I can assure you that your screams will do you no good, particularly when I can choke them off just like this, and when you are unconscious, you cannot scream in any case, and then I will take this knife, and ...

What is that noise? It sounds like—

"And that is why you need to be excised. Because of the worms. And because of the mucus. There is mucus everywhere. Mucus in you. Mucus in me. But there is very little mucus in me, and a great deal of mucus in you, which is why—

"What is—?"

"Husband?"

It was still strange to see Yalliah without her head cloth, her gray hair unbound and blowing freely in the warm desert wind, but Ehar, determined to accept changes in his wife as he accepted such things as new caravan routes, the rising of the moon, and (He tapped his gold earring, but the genie within apparently found nothing of consequence to report.) sandstorms—accept them, that is, with the grace of a patriarch who knows that he is, after all, in charge, whether appearances indicate otherwise or not—firmly reminded himself to take no notice of it, nor of the bronze medallion, glinting in the afternoon sun, that she wore . . . the Naian medallion that she had found among her belongings shortly after they had left their curious passengers in Nuhr.

"Husband?"

"Hmmm? Yes, my dear?"

"Do you see that?"

And she pointed. And Ehar looked. And then he looked again. And then he turned around as though quite willing to break his neck if only he could thereby turn around a little faster, and he was shouting—screaming—at the rest of the caravan:

"To the south! Hurry! Hurry! Hurry! Run! Run for the Peaks of Adamant!"

"God! Freedom! Lib—!"

"Dugbah! Oh, what a wonderful name! Did you know that it means *dove* in the ancient language? Aruhn and I know that because we are experts in all the old ways. We have dedicated our lives to bringing back all of the arts that were lost when the Panasians—

"Wha—?"

"You see, we must always respect the complementary powers of man and woman. There is man's power, and there is woman's power, and each has its place. We have to respect that place and honor each equally. That way, we achieve *balance* in all things, and so we must acknowledge one another as individuals who are different, and who have different tasks and different abilities. Husband and wife. Do you—?"

* * *

"Deck there! Land ho!"

"Is it Nuhr?"

"Yes, sir. It's Nuhr. But I can see the mountains, too, sir, and they look . . . well . . ."

"Speak up, man!"

"They look . . . uh . . . funny, sir."

"Funny?"

He had raisins. He had a box of soft rags. He had corners. He had toys. He had everything that pleased and delighted a ferret.

Except for one thing. He did not quite . . . well . . . *look* like a ferret. Ferrets were not pale and naked. Ferrets had tails and fur. Ferrets had masks. Ferrets had beady eyes and a wonderful, positively delightful stare with an intensity that allowed no one, even for an instant, to think that they had anything on their minds except the suitable rearrangement and dismantling of whatever might come to hand. Or, rather, to paw.

But these lacks were well made up for by the raisins, rags, corners, and toys. And besides, Kuz Aswani was sure, very sure, that Umi Botzu and the Naian witch would not be satisfied with anything less than utter perfection, and so he was certain that he would not have to put up with nakedness, the lack of a tail and mask, and the absence of beady eyes for much longer. Soon enough, he would have everything that he needed.

And, that night, as he was wiggling and bouncing on the cool grass in one of the king's gardens (now the Gharat's gardens, but this was a technicality lost on a ferret), he paused for a drink in one of the many ponds, and there his attention was suddenly fixed not on the fleeting flashing of fishy tails and fins below the surface, but on the lamplit reflection that stared back at him from the surface itself. A brown reflection. A furry reflection. A reflection with a tail. A reflection with a mask. A reflection with wonderful, positively delightful beady eyes that looked as though they were intent upon the rearrangement and dismantling of entire *kingdoms,* and—

A woman stared back at Haddar from the mirror. A perfect complexion. Full, kissable lips. A faint look of dreamy idiocy in her eyes. Perfect breasts. A downy delta of—

What was—?

Groaning, half delirious, his muscles and joints burning with a fire that was but a faint echo of the pain that he felt in other, more personal regions of his body, Jenkins staggered up from . . .

. . . was that a bed? Pink silks? And . . . and *oil*?

(Bronze by gold . . .)

Something was wrong. Something was terribly wrong. Shambling, staggering, he fell against a wall because his ankles appeared to be bound, and there was some sort of curious belt or something else around his waist that was holding him—

Leather? Steel?

He could not tell, and he made his way painfully— taking the small, mincing steps that the fetters about his ankles forced him to take—toward what he thought was a . . .

. . . a window? Open? Yes?

And there he looked out. Out at the torchlit city that lay below, shimmering in the desert night. And then from the city he lowered his eyes to his hands, noticing, in the light of the sconces, that there were both bruises and bangles about his wrists, wrists that came away with a dark smudge of kohl when he wiped at his eyes with them.

(Bronze by gold . . .)

The pain was burning in his groin, up his back. He could hardly stand. Bound and bewigged, clad in silk and satin, he wavered, fainting, at the window; and, as he fell back, his eye caught the dark and titanic movement of a wall of froth and black water that, roughly following the course of the old, dry river, but spreading far beyond it, spreading miles beyond it, inundating the countryside as it smashed through the jasper walls of the city as though they were built of nothing more substantial than wooden blocks, was bearing directly down on the palace of . . .

. . . of Nuhr? Yes? Was—?

"Hard a-starboard! Topsails. Topgallants! Set the studdingsails! Double the backstays! Every stitch, boys! Every stitch we can carry! Good God!"

Now, you gotta understand that I'm being *real* clever with this flood stuff. I mean, I've been setting up for this since page *numero uno,* on account of I'm a real writer. Not one of these dork-headed hacks. Most people would just say *Oh, yeah, there's this big flood, and everyone cashes in their chips,* but that's not my style, 'cause I do things *right.* For instance, I went to the library and checked up on floods, and I found out all sorts of good shit that ordinary people just wouldn't bother with, on account of they're ordinary people. Which is not to say that ordinary people aren't worth anything. I mean, you two guys are ordinary people, sure, but you're obviously going somewhere. I could tell that right away. No point in arguing, is there? But I was telling you about the floods, and about how I looked up a whole bunch of stuff so I could get some . . . some . . . wadayacallit? Verisimilitude. Yeah, that's it. Verisimilitude. Hot stuff, I'll tell you, and even a couple of jigaboos like you guys can tell right off just how hot it is, on account of you're jigaboos that are going someplace. Not that I mean any harm when I call you jigaboos. I mean, there are all kinds of people in the world, and we can all joke around with each other, can't we? You'd call me a honky, wouldn't you? Sure you would! So

I'll call you jigaboos and you call me a honky and we can all yuck it up, right?

But, anyway, so I did a bunch of research, and then I started to play real cagey with this foreshadowing stuff. Like, I put in some stuff about earthquakes, and about how the glaciers in New England pushed the ground down, so that when they melted, the ground came back up and made earthquakes. Hey, you can't make this stuff up, can you? Let those *X-Files* dudes top that! But I just slid in that stuff so smooth that everyone makes these unconscious associations, and they understand just what I want them to understand without being able to figure out how I'm doing it. Now that's artistry, if you ask me. And then I did this thing where I was imitating Faulkner for a little bit. Well, you'd have to have read him before you'd understand him, but, anyway, I slipped in this little thing about river erosion and digging channels that I remembered from grade school. I mean, it was really hot, and it's stuff like that that sets real writers apart from hacks, and that's why this movie deal is going to go down *any day now*. Man, it's gonna be hot, and you guys are a couple of A-number-one good guys, aren't you? So that you'll, like, help me on my way, won't you? So I'll remember later on, right? And help *you* out? Right?

But anyway, the capper is the end, of course. It's real hot. I mean, *The Poseidon Adventure* ain't got nothing on this. The ultimate disaster movie. Yowza! Won't that make them sit up and take a better look at Yours Truly, who knows exactly what he's doing and who's gonna take everyone who ever did him dirt and rub their noses in it real damn good! See, I got this three hundred foot wall of water just steamrolling everything that gets in its way, which is most of the land, on account of it's really spreading out. See, that's what I was setting up for. The reservoir started to drain, and the weight let up, and then there was an earthquake because the weight let up, and the earthquake split what was left of the dam all the way open. So, you

see, that's why I put in all that crap about New England
and stuff. So the feeps out there in the audience can figure
out which end is up. Not that you two guys need any help
figuring out which end is up. I mean, you're really pushers
and movers, aren't you? Both of you, right? And, hey, us
pushers and movers gotta stick together, right? Yup, and
we're pushers and movers, all of us, which is why I got
some money together and got gas in this car so that I can
make this important appointment with a . . . like . . . a *producer,* see? And show him how I'm a pusher and mover,
on account of I got a nice car and gas to put in it, and a
script with a dy-no-mite punch in it in my backpocket, just
for them to try on! Whoopsa!

Boy-oh-boy! So this wall of water just sweeps everything away, like someone shook an Etch-A-Sketch. Cities
and towns go *boom!,* and that's it. No more cities and
towns. Some people escape to higher ground, and of
course I have Ehar and Yalliah and their bunch escape, on
account of they're good guys, and people like to see good
guys get out of a tight spot, just like I'm a good guy, and
you guys are, too, and good guys gotta stick together,
right? But most everyone near the rivers bites the big
green weenie, and so, you see, this prince guy never finds
out that he made his old dad drop dead, 'cause number one
he walked out before the old man fell over, and number
two the water takes out the palace and everyone in it, and
so it looks like the flood did everyone in. So I don't have
to worry about any guilt trips or anything. Subtle, eh? And
it's kinda like life, too, when you just don't know what's
coming around the corner. Just like I didn't know that I
was gonna find you two guys in my car this morning.

But, like you guys might have guessed, 'cause you guys
got brains, Sari and her guys come out of the mountains to
find that the whole place is all wet. (Hehe! That's a good
one, huh?) There's mud everywhere. It's real nice mud,
too, like they used to get from the floods in raghead land.

I mean, Egypt. With that Nile River thing. You know about the Nile, don't you? Sure you do. I mean, that's the Old Country for guys like you, isn't it? Well, Africa's a big place, and that's a little north of jungle-bunny land, but you get the idea. Right?

Anyway, like I said, it's nice mud, and everything is suddenly growing like nobody's business. Plants coming up all over the place, and the water's back, so it looks like smooth sailing for the whole country, once they clean up the mess and count noses to see who they've got left, which isn't very many, but they've got enough to keep everything going. Fortunately (and you can see just how clever I am), not only the king is dead, like I said before, but that Abnel dude and his current squeeze are dead also, which leaves the throne open for the prince with no hassles at all, except for finding a few new counselors. And with Sari and Beshur standing around twiddling their thumbs and looking for something to do, everybody, even guys like you, can guess who's gonna be the new counselors.

Oh, yeah. I need to mention that they get all the way down to the coast, even though that's obvious from what I said before, but (and this is even more clever) this hike down to the coast gives the prince guy a chance to do all this great prince-type shit with all the survivors that they find. I mean, it's charisma city, if you know what I mean. People just hanging all over him, and he's doing the BMOC routine, or whatever you want to call it. Sure, Sari and Beshur are shocked as hell when it turns out he's a prince, but, what the hell, they adjust pretty well. I mean, just about anybody can adjust to a prince when the prince happens to be a personal friend. Just like anyone can adjust to a rich screenwriter when the screenwriter turns out to be a personal friend. ¿Comprende?

Hey, you're really on the ball. But when I say total destruction, I mean, like, total destruction. They get to Nuhr, and there's nothing there. City's gone. Palace is gone. Total wipe-out. Slime wonderland. The library is gone, too, on account of Scruffy and his bunch shelled it until it caught fire. And, see? I slipped in some of that old Umberto Eco *burn up the library and get existential* shit, too, didn't I? 'Course, you guys don't know diddly about Umberto Eco, on account of you and the horses you rode in on were all probably stuck in remedial reading for the last six years of grade school. Which doesn't mean to say that there's anything wrong with remedial reading. No. Hey, if you need it, you need it. No shame in that, right? That's what America is all about, right? And that sure as shit hasn't stopped you guys from being a coupla dudes who are going places, because I can tell that you're going places. Just like me.

So you can see that everything's pretty much wrapped up in the final scene. The prince guy becomes king, and the water's come back to the land. And, sure, a buncha people got killed, but, hey, that's the movie business, right? Can't make an omelet without breaking a few eggs, right? (You guys know what an omelet is? OK. Good.) And Sari's a little messed up on account of she's the one who came up with the idea for releasing the water, but she kinda got a pat on the head from God at the end of it all, so she'll eventually get over it.

The only thing that's left is that thing with the American troops, which is kind of a no-brainer 'cause the whole thing was on account of Napoleon—you know, the short guy with the funny hat—and Napoleon isn't going to be in Egypt for longer than another few months anyway. So the plan isn't worth shit in any case. How's that for existential, huh? But Scruffy shows up without his fag boy, since the fag boy got balled and lost his head (Jesus! Aren't I hot!), and even with a couple of guys like you, I sure don't have to get into how Scruffy can't even, like, wear a black arm band or anything, on account of they'd string him up in a minute if they knew he was queer. Which isn't to say that he's not broken up about it, just that he can't *say* anything about it. Isn't that *great*? That'll get the twinkie market for sure!

So here's Scruffy coming into what's left of the harbor with his ship and a few of the troop transports he's managed to round up. They're all kinda banged around, what with the storm and then the flood coming out to sea, but there's still a bunch of troops there, and there's still this whole American plan hanging over everyone's head (even though, like I said, it won't come to shit historically). So there's gotta be some kind of wrap-up for all the dweebs who don't know about Napoleon (Jeez, where the hell have *they* been, anyway?), and, boy, I'll tell you those guys can get pissed if they've paid their shekels and you don't give them some kind of a wrap-up they can understand. But that's what sets me apart, on account of *I* deliver, 'cause I'm a real writer, and as soon as I get to this appointment I'm going to right now, this producer guy is gonna see just what I can do, and, man, we're gonna get all kinds of money out of this. Notice that I'm saying *we* now? That's because I'm gonna cut you guys in on this, on account of I'll need guys like you to help me out with a big project like this. And if you're willing to break a few arms here and there, that's OK with me, too. I've waited a good long time for this deal to hit, and you can bet it's gonna hit today, and you guys can get in on the *ground floor*. Yeah! And no one can give you any shit anymore! Right?

But, like I said, this ending is real subtle, even if I have to spoon-feed the masses. You see, I had Scruffy get a bit of a hard-on about the prince guy when he saw him in the city, and I made a point of mentioning that. Something about *dash*, remember? Yeah, yeah, you haven't read the screenplay, but take my word. It's in there, and it's hot. I mean, Scruffy's hot. (Wow! Looking down the barrel of a gun, and I can still churn them out! I'm one cool guy, can't you see?) So now that Scruffy is out one butt-fuck buddy, he's kind of looking for another, and when he recognizes the prince guy, he gets kinda won over, and he'll do anything for him. 'Course, the prince isn't into that kind of stuff, so that side of it doesn't come up (Oh, wow! There's another!), but since Scruffy's orders say that the troops are supposed to be bossed around by the local authorities (and if you saw the script, you'd see just how clever I was to put that in, 'cause it made *perfect* sense then), he just hands them over to the prince guy, and so now the prince has a bunch of troops he can use to unbury the city and get his country back in shape. So it all works out just in time for the fade-out with the big violins and stuff like that.

Cool, huh? A real modern epic. I mean, this could go for three hours, easy, and it's really the kind of shit that they'll eat up at Cannes, on account of they're all homos and politically correct and that sort of thing, but they're all a bunch of softies, really, and they give awards to shit like this and then go home and dress up like Judy Garland. But that's OK, because they can do what they want to, just so long as they appreciate my stuff for the kind of art that it really is, just like you guys can appreciate it. Can't you? I mean, you can see that once I make this appointment that I'm almost gonna be late for since you've kept me so long, I'm gonna make all kindsa money, and I'm gonna cut you in on it, you can bet on that, because I'm going places, and you're going places, so why the hell don't we all go places together? So that's why I'm not gonna give you my car keys, on account of I'm going places, and I've got things to do, and I'm gonna help *you* by doing them. You see, first, I'm gonna make a big entrance, since I slicked this car up real good so I could look like what I am. Someone important, you know. And then I'm gonna breeze into this producer guy's office and give him a pitch that'll knock not only *his* socks off, but *everyone else's* socks off, too, including a couple of ignorant spades like you guys. And then I'm gonna—

Trieste-Zurich-Englewood, 1995

[THE END]

FANTASTICAL LANDS

☐ **THE FOREST HOUSE by Marion Zimmer Bradley.** Fate had marked Eilan to become a priestess at the Forest House. But Eilan must hide the terrible secret of the different, forbidden path she chose—to love Gaius, a soldier of mixed blood. With powerful enemies poised to usurp the wealth of magic the Forest House sheltered, Eilan could only trust the great Goddess to find her destiny amidst the treacherous labyrinth in which fate had placed her. (454243—$14.95)

☐ **AN EXCHANGE OF GIFTS by Anne McCaffrey.** Meanne, known to others as Princess Anastasia de Saumur et Navareey Cordova, has a Gift which no lady, much less a princess royal, should exercise. For Meanne has the ability to make things grow, and to create the herbal mixtures that will soothe and heal. Promised to a man she can never love, Meanne flees, seeking shelter and a new life in a long-deserted cottage in the woods. (455207—$12.95)

☐ **THE JIGSAW WOMAN by Kim Antieau.** Keelie is created from the bodies of three different women to be a plaything for her doctor. Not satisfied with the life given to her, she sets out to find one of her own. From ancient battles and violent witch hunts, to Amazonian paradise and Sumerian hell our heroine spirals through epic distortions of history and magic, finding that her salvation lies not in the promise of the future, but in the lessons learned in the past. (455096—$10.95)

☐ **DELTA CITY by Felicity Savage.** Humility Garden must once again fight the god Pati, whose cold-blooded ruthlessness made even his followers bow to his whims. But Humility would not be cowed into submission and vowed to retake Salt from the Divinarch. "Humility is as bold as the author herself."—*New York Times Book Review* (453999—$5.99)

☐ **HUMILITY GARDEN by Felicity Savage.** Young Humility Garden's only dream is to escape her squalid homeland. She is about to embark on a journey that will teach her the secretive ways of the ghostiers, the language of the gods, and the power of eternal love. (453980—$4.99)

*Prices slightly higher in Canada

Buy them at your local bookstore or use this convenient coupon for ordering.

PENGUIN USA
P.O. Box 999 — Dept. #17109
Bergenfield, New Jersey 07621

Please send me the books I have checked above.
I am enclosing $_____ (please add $2.00 to cover postage and handling). Send check or money order (no cash or C.O.D.'s) or charge by Mastercard or VISA (with a $15.00 minimum). Prices and numbers are subject to change without notice.

Card #_____ Exp. Date _____
Signature_____
Name_____
Address_____
City _____ State _____ Zip Code _____

For faster service when ordering by credit card call **1-800-253-6476**

Allow a minimum of 4-6 weeks for delivery. This offer is subject to change without notice.

The Roc Frequent Readers Club
BUY TWO ROC BOOKS AND GET
ONE SF/FANTASY NOVEL FREE!

Check the free title you wish to receive (subject to availability):

☐ **DR. DIMENSION:**
Masters of Spacetime
**John DeChancie
and David Bischoff**
0-451-45354-9/$4.99 ($5.99 in Canada)

☐ **EARTHDAWN #2:**
Mother Speaks
Christopher Kubasik
0-451-45297-6/$4.99 ($5.99 in Canada)

☐ **EARTHDAWN #4:**
Prophecy
Greg Gorden
0-451-45347-6/$4.99 ($5.99 in Canada)

☐ **HUMILITY GARDEN**
Felicity Savage
0-451-45398-0/$4.99 ($5.99 in Canada)

☐ **THE DARK TIDE:**
**Book One of the *Iron Tower*
*Trilogy***
Dennis L. McKiernan
0-451-45102-3/$4.50 ($5.95 in Canada)

☐ **SHADOWS OF DOOM:**
**Book Two of the *Iron Tower*
*Trilogy***
Dennis L. McKiernan
0-451-45103-1/$4.50 ($5.95 in Canada)

☐ **THE DARKEST DAY:**
**Book Three of the *Iron Tower*
*Trilogy***
Dennis L. McKiernan
0-451-45083-3/$4.50 ($5.95 in Canada)

☐ **PRIMAVERA**
Francesca Lia Block
0-451-45323-9/$4.50 ($5.50 in Canada)

☐ **THE STALK**
Janet and Chris Morris
0-451-45307-7/$4.99 ($5.99 in Canada)

☐ **TRAITORS**
Kristine Kathryn Rusch
0-451-45415-4/$4.99 ($5.99 in Canada)

☐ **TRIUMPH OF THE DRAGON**
Robin Wayne Bailey
0-451-45437-5/$4.99 ($5.99 in Canada)

To get your FREE Roc book, send in this coupon (original or photocopy), proof of purchase (original sales receipt(s) for two Roc books & a copy of the books' UPC numbers) plus $2.00 for postage and handling to:

**ROC FREQUENT READERS CLUB
Penguin USA • Mass Market
375 Hudson Street, New York, NY 10014**

NAME_____

ADDRESS _____

CITY_____STATE_____ZIP_____

**If you want to receive a Roc newsletter,
please check box ☐**

Roc 🆁🅾🅲 Books

Offer expires December 31, 1996. This certificate or facsimile must accompany your request. Void where prohibited, taxed, or restricted. Allow 4-6 weeks for shipment of book(s). Offer good only in U.S., Canada, and its territories.